RAVE REVIEWS FOR [NAOMI NEALE!](barcode: D0560669)

I WENT TO VASSAR FOR THIS?

"An enjoyable, sa... the narrative voice that carries readers from confusion and despair…to a You-go-girl! finale that's sure to please."

—*Publishers Weekly*

"Witty and fun, Neale's highly original time-travel is delightful."

—*Booklist*

"Careful research and quirky characters…enhance this clever premise…a fun story, with page-to-page action, that follows Cathy's relationship with Hank and the quest to return home."

—*RT BOOKreviews*

"*I Went to Vassar for This?* is full of offbeat wit, glorious irony and delightful characters, combining the best of chick lit with the best of time-travel romance into an appealing combination you won't want to put down."

—*Affaire de Coeur* (Reviewer's Pick)

"Naomi Neale generously seasons her wonderfully creative chick lit novel…with a deliciously snappy sense of humor and exactly the right dash of sweet romance."

—*Chicago Tribune*

THE MILE-HIGH HAIR CLUB

"Surprisingly realistic characters and lots of saucy southern charm create a story of family, friendship, and love that is deliciously fun and simply irresistible."

—*Booklist*

"Neale writes a charming North meets South story, with a little *Miss Congeniality* thrown in."

—*RT BOOKreviews*

MORE HIGH PRAISE FOR NAOMI NEALE!

CALENDAR GIRL

"Hip, sassy, and filled with offbeat characters who will steal your heart."

—*USA Today* bestselling author Katie MacAlister

"Neale's addictively acerbic writing style and endearing heroine make for a deliciously humorous book that is a natural for Bridget Jones fans. Yet Nan's realistically complicated relationships with her family and friends add emotional depth, granting Neale's novel an appeal that reaches beyond the chick lit crowd."

—*Booklist*

"Beneath the laugh-out-loud antics of assorted characters lies a simple fairy tale with a happily-ever-after ending…. Get this one for the keeper shelf—to read scene after scene for a good laugh on a cold winter night."

—*RT BOOKclub*

"Chick lit and contemporary romance readers will laugh with Naomi Neale's naughty and nice tale."

—*The Midwest Book Review*

"Naomi Neale deftly combines chick lit with laugh-out-loud contemporary romance… If you enjoy romance sprinkled with chuckles, *Calendar Girl* is a delightful way to spend your reading time."

—Curled Up with a Good Book

THE MAN IN ACTION

"Becky!" The human anaconda otherwise known as Portia Daye came for me with arms outstretched. Since falling to my knees and crawling away wasn't a real option (honest, I checked), I found myself accepting one of her strangulating hugs. "What in the world are you doing here?"

"Well, you know." I laughed lightly, trying to make it sound as if the posh After Ten was my usual little hole-in-the-wall bar where everybody knew my name.

She laughed along with me until we'd run out of false hilarity. Then her face fell slack. "No, really."

I looked at A.J. He looked at me. Portia watched the two of us exchange complicit glances, her eyebrows ever-so-slightly knit, though not to a degree that actually might risk a future wrinkle. "Well…" I started to say.

"A.J.?" Portia placed her drink on the bar beside us and stood with her hands on her hips. "What's going on here?" She looked from him to me, and back again. "There's something you're not telling me."

"Okay, Portia, look. Here's the truth. The utter, un-varnished truth." Could she tell I was stalling? "Okay. The truth. I was feeling kind of…"

"We're dating." You know what? A.J.'s explanation was totally *nothing* like mine was going to be. My jaw actually dropped as I gaped at what he'd said. Portia's did as well; she regarded us both with shock and, my pride was hurt slightly to see, a little bit of apparent nausea. The big stupid lug to my right, in the meantime nodded solemnly. "Yep. We're an item." He grabbed me around the shoulders and pulled me close, rubbing my arm. "Aren't we, honey?" I literally couldn't an-swer, so shocked was I.

NAOMI NEALE

METHOD MAN

Making It

MAKING IT®

February 2007

Published by

Dorchester Publishing Co., Inc.
200 Madison Avenue
New York, NY 10016

ISBN 0-505-52697-2

The name "Making It" and its logo are trademarks of Dorchester Publishing Co., Inc.

Printed in the United States of America.

Visit us on the web at www.dorchesterpub.com.

ACKNOWLEDGMENTS

As always, I would like to thank my dear friend, Patty Woodwell, for leaping into the fray with her suggestions and gentle amendments during my writing process. This book is all about the cocktails, however, and so I must thank my regular Sunday night circle of friends for their companionship, their karaoke singing, the strawberry daiquiris, and the Jiffy-Pop. Mike, Brian, Craig, Lydia, Amy, and Charlie—the next round's on me!

ONE

There's a certain type of woman, resilient and tough as nails, who on the day her divorce is final, bids the whole relationship a hearty good riddance with a devil-may-care laugh and a toss of her hair. Then she goes about her business with a can-do attitude that inspires lesser mortals around her. The stinker probably even does some charity work on the side. And never has problems with her complexion.

Lord, how I wanted to be that woman.

Instead, on the day my papers came through declaring that I, Rebecca Egan, was free from the shackles that had bound me for five years, I turned out to be the type of woman who sits alone in a swanky venue named Club Venetian, one pathetic hour earlier than her sister and friends are due to arrive for carousing and commiseration, praying that in the interim no one would notice me. Or more precisely, hoping that only the *right* people would notice me.

1

"It's loud in here, huh?"

At first the fellow perching on the barstool next to mine smelled vaguely sweet, like one of the candy-colored cocktails people kept grabbing from the pony-tailed bartender at the room's other end. When I turned to answer, though, I caught a whiff of something acrid and musky that could have been a particularly foul cologne. Maybe a cat had sprayed his tie? I didn't care to think about it. He was at least fifteen years older than I, and sported a comb-over that made Donald Trump's coiffure look like a triumph of modern hairdressing. This guy was definitely *not* the right kind of person.

I pointed to the bank of video screens up above, then to the speakers thumping out dance music, and with a regretful smile mimed being unable to hear. Bad move. It only made him move in close so he could bellow, "I *said,* it's kind of *loud* in here!" Holy cats—was my eardrum ruptured? Sadly, it seemed to be intact enough to hear his follow-up: "How about I buy you a drink?" Musk wasn't the only aroma coming off the guy—with his alabaster pallor, his mouth breathing, and his expression of desperation, he was plainly bad news.

What would Alice have done? I wished she'd get there. My older sister was the authority on the no-nonsense turn-down. From puberty onward she'd been developing an entire vocabulary of *no* based on gestures as small as the twitch of a lip, the slightest spasm of an eyebrow, and a bland, uncomprehending smile. I had to have picked up something from her after all these years, right?

"I've got one. Thanks, though." Over the boisterous techno beat, I brandished the Cosmopolitan I'd been nursing for the entire twenty minutes I'd been sitting at the dark mahogany bar of Club Venetian, trying to cultivate the mysterious air of that certain type of woman I wanted to be—someone who hadn't popped into one of the most exclusive watering holes in the West Sixties by her lonesome but who was merely by herself for a few moments, waiting for her no doubt debonair and well-groomed escort.

Not escort in the rent-a-boy sense. That would just be icky.

"How about . . . hey. . . ." By now, my pasty would-be paramour was speaking to the back of my head. Alice's patented About-Face Dead Cut should do the trick. In high school and college, more men had seen close-ups of my sister's pert blond ponytail swinging in their noses than had actually glimpsed her face. Not many guys were willing to keep yelling at a girl's shoulders, and few of them had the nerve to work their way around to her front for a second rebuff. All I had to do was wait him out. I crossed my legs at the knee, just like my sister might have if she'd been around, took the tiniest sip from my Cosmo, and observed my surroundings.

During my marriage, Club Venetian might have been one of those spots I could have visited for an anniversary drink before a show, if I'd had a husband who had been at all sentimental about anniversaries. Or about anything at all. The upscale bar was decorated like a British gentleman's club, but its slabs of dark wood paneling and reproduction paintings of fox hunts and weedy country estates were in stark contrast to the decidedly modern neon-colored drinks and the flatscreens everywhere, displaying music videos and infotainment shows. It was famous for the most expensive cocktail in the city—the Sixty-seventh Street Martini, each of which sold for a shocking sixty-seven dollars. I worked in a bookstore for less than a subsistence wage. What the hell was I even doing here?

Mentally I slapped myself on the wrist for a bad attitude. I'd wanted a break in my routine, and that's exactly what I was getting, right? Right. My musky friend, by any calculation, should have taken the hint and given up the chase by now, anyway. Slowly I swiveled around, as if merely looking toward the rear of the bar for a friend. Sloo-oowly. Very, very . . .

"Hi again!" The mouth-breather was still lurking behind me, grinning like a hyena from ear to ear. He looked like he wanted to eat me. From the way he nervously licked his lips, he very probably did. Ew.

My sketchily bolstered confidence instantly vanished, along with my Alice-inspired smooth moves. What was the point of being single again and dressing up nicely, of making myself smell good, if I was doomed to a single life where this was the only kind of guy I'd attract? Heck, what was the point of getting up in the morning? Of bathing?

The only consolation I had was that at least I wasn't being beleaguered from both sides. Alas, that peace of mind lasted only a few seconds. "You know," said a new masculine voice in my other ear, "I heard a rumor that women are like parking spaces. All the good ones are taken." The nuances of his tones were so polished and flawless that they sounded almost actorly; I had a quick mental image of the voice's owner practicing the line in the mirror before leaving his urbane apartment for the evening, perhaps while adjusting a crisp silk tie over a freshly dry-cleaned shirt. My poor heart, light again, pitter-patted at the realization that I, Rebecca Egan, freshly minted divorcée, had just been on the receiving end of a smooth pickup line. Yes! "And the rest of them are handicapped," he finished. "So which are you?"

My temper, already frayed, snapped at the pickup line's cheesy conclusion. "You *ass!*" I snarled, whirling around. "Oh, not you." My anger evaporated into annoyance, as did all visions of crisp ties and urbane apartments, replaced by the realities of a too-tight, almost-see-through black shirt that showed off Nautilus-built pecs and a little too much chest hair. I *knew* the guy—he was the brother of one of Alice's friends. "A.J.!"

At the sight of my face, the dark-haired gym bunny recoiled. "Oh, crap, it's Egan. Don't be surprising a guy like that!" The one thing of which I could never accuse A. J. Daye was subtlety. He'd no doubt been one of the intrepid pioneers who'd laid the original route for the one-track mind. I'd never actually seen him during broad daylight, but whenever I'd gone out with Alice and the girls to some club or trendy restaurant, there he'd be at the bar, collecting phone numbers from interested females and glares from jealous guys. His lips slid back to reveal an expanse of white, sparkling, Hollywood teeth. "Kidding! Oh, come on, don't work yourself up. I knew it was you. Where's that estrogen posse of yours? My little sis said they were all going to be here."

A.J. had always reminded me of one of the little boys in grammar school who chased girls and pulled their pigtails—not to make them cry but because he didn't know how to tell them he liked them. Fortunately for the friends and family who had to look at me, I'd grown out of pigtails long ago. "They're on their way. You can leave now."

"And pass up the opportunity to hear you thank me?" When I stared at him blankly, he waved out both hands, "The Price Is Right" hostess–style, at the space behind me. Cautiously I turned, only to find an empty chair where Comb-over had been sitting. The relief on my face must have been obvious because he smirked and prompted, "Thank you, A.J.!"

"Thank you, A.J.," I dutifully mumbled, making a show of rolling my eyes.

"My job is done, then." He mimed wiping his hands. Already he was looking around the bar for better company. "Keep it cool."

"Hey." I don't know what impulse made me want him by my side. Maybe it was simply because the sheer bulk of all those muscles would drive off any would-be creeps. Maybe it was because I still had time to kill before the gang arrived, and he was a semi-familiar face in a crowd of strangers. "You meeting someone?"

"Portia, later," he said, referring to his sister. "What'd you do, show up early so you could pick up a guy? Good luck with that. And before you go off on me because you think I'm being rude," he added, holding up his hands as if he could tell that was exactly what I'd planned to do, "I didn't mean that you're not *pretty* or anything. You just strike me as a lost little lamb in a field of wolves, kid."

"I can take care of myself, thanks." A.J.'s condescension made me instantly reconsider having him around until my friends arrived. "Feel free to go annoy women with your awful pickup lines, or whatever it is you do."

He watched me flutter my hand in a dismissive wave with only the merest of raised eyebrows. "Your choice. But when you get bit, don't come running to me." He took a step as if to go, then pivoted back and pointed. "And that parking space thing wasn't a *real* line. I was just making a joke."

"Uh-huh." My turn to smirk. I didn't believe a word of it. A.J. appeared to be readying a retort, but at the last moment he thought better of it, shook his head, and walked away. Good: Now all I had to do to endure the next few minutes was look like I belonged.

Which I wasn't sure I did. Everyone in the Venetian was so pretty and exquisitely groomed. I was willing to bet none of them had borrowed their nice clothes from their sister. They moved languidly and easily around the room, chatting and laughing with each other as if they spent every Happy Hour there.

What did a worn-out twenty-nine-year-old divorcée have to add? I felt like Babar the Elephant lumbering into a convention of lithe and nimble gazelles, hoping nobody would notice the difference. What happened to old elephants? After their divorces, they lumbered to their sister's apartments to die, that's what. Not for the first time since Sean had announced he was leaving me, I had a sudden, depressing vision of a very single Rebecca working in her bookstore until she was one of those bowed and beaten Central Park old ladies who tosses stale breadcrumbs to the birds while she eats her boiled egg lunch on a bench, scarf tied around her head to protect it from a chill on even the warmest days.

Maudlin tears stung the corners of my eyes—and I so did not want to give in to my own stupid over-sentimental fantasies. I blindly grabbed for my purse and was about to ease myself down from the barstool and hide my drama queen self in the restroom when I felt the lightest of finger-touches on my back. "Excuse me," said a deep male voice.

"Sorry," I said, not even looking around.

"No harm, no foul, clumsy." I turned and let my eyes focus. Fantastic: I *was* Babar the Elephant, and now I was being pachydermically insulted by a Patrick Dempsey look-alike—broad forehead, dashing eyebrows, wavy hair, humorous eyes. A little smile played across his lips. "You kind of blink a lot, don't you?"

A wistful feeling washed over me, then swiftly disappeared. Under any other circumstances I might have enjoyed being called clumsy by a handsome guy in an expensive-looking jacket. Okay, it was pitiful to admit that might have been the highlight of any ordinary day, but there it was. "Sorry," I mumbled.

"Nothing to be sorry about. Just an observation. Hey." Again he rested his fingertips lightly on my shoulder blade, almost as if he was unwilling to touch me at all. "Can I ask a quick question?" I hesitated, bag over my shoulder, hand on my leather jacket. (Or to be more accurate, one of Alice's several leather jackets. My sister certainly did like her Marc Jacobs.) Finally, I nodded. "I'm just going to make a quick guess here. It looks like you need somebody to talk to. Am I right?"

By all that was good and holy, I knew I was feeling a little bit down, but did I look like some kind of suicidal maniac? Had someone in the management sent him over to calm me down because I was bringing down the bar's tone? "I'm fine. I'm just waiting for some friends."

"Well, let's wait together for a bit. I'm Mitch, by the way. Can I ask your name?"

"Sure," I said, leaning in a little so I could be heard over the music. "It's Becca. Rebecca."

"Becca. Nice name. I like that. Hey, can I ask another question?" I nodded again. The guy had a deep, rumbly voice that reminded me of one of my favorite uncles, teasing but kind at the same time. "It's kind of an assumption on my part. But I'm kind of hoping someone else finds these places as intimidating as I do."

I laughed again. "Oh my gosh, yes. I was just thinking that."

He looked around the bar, craning his neck over his shoulder at a throng of women laughing at a photo one of them had taken with her camera phone, but barely giving them a second glance before turning back to me. "It just kind of seems like everyone here is trying to be someone they aren't. Know what I mean?"

A.J. firmly in mind, I nodded. And here I'd thought I was the oddball.

"Okay, I'm going to confess something embarrassing about me. Ready?"

"What'd I do to deserve that?"

"You were here."

How could I help but smile? "Shoot."

He laughed in anticipation of a punch line I could only imagine. "I changed outfits four times before I came out tonight. Four times!" Mitch held up as many fingers to emphasize the point, before raking them through his short, tousled hair. "Just to freakin' come to the freakin' Club freakin' Venetian! I mean, everyone told me how upscale it is, and at heart it's not that different from your local T.G.I. Friday's."

"You seem pretty exasperated with yourself." I giggled.

"Four times! I'm the kind of guy who usually throws on the first thing he sees that's not in the dirty clothes basket. Tonight, apparently, I'm a girl! I bet you never worry about your appearance."

Okay, that was the second thing he'd said so far that didn't exactly sound complimentary. Did I really look un-put-together? But hey, a little companionship without reciprocated physical attraction was fine with me. "Yeah, I do. I mean, I did. These clothes aren't even mine!"

"Mind if I see?" So naturally did he take my hand to help me down from the barstool that it wasn't until I had both feet on the floor that I realized he was holding it; his head moved from side to side as he appraised what I wore. He helped me back up before saying anything. "Well, if they aren't yours, they surely ought to be."

I couldn't help but return the tiny squeeze he gave before letting go and reaching for his martini. "Thanks," I finally said, glowing a little. I settled more firmly on my stool. "That's the nicest thing anyone's said to me in a while."

That last confession had been honest enough. It seemed to make him think for a minute while he sipped. "You know, my mom always told me I was really good at reading people. Hey, want to see a picture of her?"

"Sure!" This was going swimmingly. I wasn't a total social nincompoop at all.

He kept talking as he reached into his pocket. "So anyway, what I pick up about you is that you're a pretty independent thinker. But at the same time you've got a soft spot you don't like showing to a lot of people. Right?"

Wow—hadn't I just been having such a sentimental side a few minutes before? "That's uncanny!"

"Another thing . . . wait a second. Here we go." I could see some pretty high-profile credit cards opposite the plastic photo insert in Mitch's wallet. He pointed at a snapshot of himself in an untucked, striped shirt of many colors, arm around a beaming older woman whose hair was as platinum as his American Express.

"I love that photo!"

"Isn't she a doll? She turned sixty last month. My sister and I threw her a party at Chuck E. Cheese, the one in Brooklyn? And oh, my God, was she ever embarrassed when she had to go up and get her birthday crown with a nine-year-old. Isn't that a hoot?"

"That's mean!" I said, but I was laughing when I said it.

"I know! That's the point!" he said, joining in. "Besides, greasy pizza, video games, all the kids and grandkids . . . you'd love it too, right?"

I grinned, tossing hair back from my face. "Maybe I would at that."

"You're artistic, right?" He leaned against the bar. Obviously he wasn't planning to go anywhere for a while, and I didn't mind a bit. "I can tell. There's something about your face. You have artistic ideas, or you do something, I don't know, maybe literary or . . ."

"I work in a bookstore!" He threw his hands up in the air, modestly conceding he'd been right all along. I was totally amazed. How had he known? "You *are* good!"

"My mom's never wrong." He folded up the wallet and replaced it in his jacket pocket, but not before pulling out a twenty and, with a quick gesture at the bartender and not a single word, indicated that the two of us would like another round. "You don't mind if I get us more drinks, right?"

"I'd love it." I was glowing, wasn't I? I was putting off more wattage than all the Venetian's little hanging lamps combined. "I'd really love it." My smile was now so wide that my face would probably ache in the morning.

"I'd love it too, Becca." Once again he reached out and, right as the bartender returned with another Cosmo for me and a martini for Mitch, placed his hand over mine, squeezing a little harder than the last time. My fingers wrapped around his thumb, returning the gesture. I couldn't ignore the tingling at the base of my spine when our eyes locked. "You're great to talk to. Hey . . ." He began to pat himself down, as if searching for something in one of his several pockets. "Would it be okay with you if I made a quick phone call?"

"Well, sure."

"Don't go anywhere. You'll stay here, right?" he asked, finally pulling a cell phone from his pocket. "You'll be here when I get back?"

"Sure!"

"No, not 'sure.' That sounds tentative. Say 'yes.'"

"Yes!"

"Say yes, you definitely will! Because if you *are* here when I get back, well, I'll do something rash and crazy."

I grinned. "Like what?"

"Hmmm. I'll kiss you if you let me. Oh man, I can't believe I said that." He slapped his forehead. "I shouldn't have. Unless you want me to."

He was so intimate and forward in a funny way that any remaining muscles that I might have had restraining my smile from full intensity weakened. "Yes, Mitch, I will be here when you get back." Something occurred to me, dampening the sunniness I felt at the prospect of a kiss from him, even if it was just of the fun-'n'-flirty variety. Wasn't that what I'd come out for? "Kissage of a minor variety not involving tongues is definitely up for negotiation," I said, tossing back my hair and feeling very, very worldly. If this was what Alice had felt like her entire life, I was grateful to be blessed with a single night of it. I felt *amazing*, just like the Ugly Duckling must have upon waking up and finding himself all snowy white and long-necked.

He didn't say anything to that. Mitch merely tossed me a quick salute, nodded sheepishly, and made his way in the direction of the quieter end of the Venetian where the restrooms lay, twice ostentatiously looking over his shoulder as if to make sure I wasn't sneaking off. What a goof.

"Boy. Like I said, you're an easy jackpot," I heard from behind me.

"A.J.," I growled, swinging around. His short-sleeved shirt had somehow come undone at his sternum and was stretched tightly enough that it revealed the center ridges of his pecs. "Why can't you leave me alone? And what's that on your head?"

Perched at a jaunty angle on his gel-crispy hair was a miniature trilby hat. Not miniature as in too small; miniature as in palm-of-the-hand, perhaps-made-for-a-chihuahua. "Like it?" he asked. "I always carry a conversation starter."

"Who in the world is going to start a conversation about that hat?" I all but shrieked.

"You did."

"I didn't—!" Oh, but I had. His tone of voice was so calm and reasonable that it provoked me even more. "Were you *listening* to me?" I wanted to strangle the guy.

"For one thing, I gotta keep an eye on you. I've got this protective nature," he said, not adjusting his sprawled posture. He nodded and let a broad smile fly in the direction of a hot young babe who happened to be walking by right then. "Second, by jackpot, I mean, *ka-ching!*" He imitated pulling the lever of a one-armed bandit.

My friend Sarah had always claimed the Daye siblings were unholy foreshadowings of the end times to come. I was beginning to agree. I wanted to stomp off, but what would Mitch think when he came back and found me gone after I'd promised to stay put? "You're not wanted here."

"Hey." He threw up his hands in defeat. "It's a big bar. I can find plenty of receptive chicks to talk to. If you want that greenhorn pickup artist—and believe me, he is, because I can sniff 'em out from forty yards or less—making you leap up the Yes Ladder like a trained dog at the Westminster Kennel Club, fine. I'll take a hike."

"Mitch is not a pickup artist." He knew I'd argue, the bastard. A.J. hadn't even tensed a muscle to move. "He's a nice, sincere guy."

"Oo-kay." His eyebrows shot up in an exaggerated way as he shook the ice in his drink and sipped the last of the liquid at the bottom of the glass. Then he set down the tumbler and reached for his back pocket. "Hey, have I ever shown you pictures of my mom?" he asked, flipping to a plastic photo insert. He brandished a snapshot of himself with a pleasant, perfectly ordinary-looking woman of sixty or so. That was the woman who'd produced A.J. and Portia? I guess I'd expected to see someone in an Emma Peel leather catsuit. Or the big monster from *Aliens* with the drippy fangs. "She says I'm really good at reading people. Know what I think? I think you're feisty and independent on the outside, but inside you're really soft and warm and love stuffed animals and bunnies and marshmallow Peeps."

"Shut up," I growled, hating him.

"I used to use the mom photo thing all the time when I started with The Method. Though what I usually do now is combine it with a touch of spirituality." He opened up the insert so that two photos showed at once—one of A.J. in a super-tight T-shirt that exposed roughly an acre of biceps, arms wrapped around the necks of both his diminutive parents, and below it a black-and-white shot of a serious A.J. in a sharp suit having a conversation with a handsome young priest. "Gets them every time."

"Method? A method for picking up girls?"

"Seven steps to git it, hit it, and forgit it," he said. I stared at him with loathing. "Don't be hating. It's fool-proof."

"What kind of girl falls for that crap?" He merely raised his eyebrows for an answer. "Shut up. I'm not. I didn't."

"I love that photo!" he gushed, plainly imitating me. I wanted to slap him. Before I could retort, he looked at his watch. "The way I time it, you've got one minute and thirty seconds before Loverboy comes back from his 'phone call.' " I hated the way he made air quotes with his fingers. Only people with above-average I.Q.s should be allowed to make air quotes. "So do you want to hear how it's going to play or not?"

"No."

He ignored me. "You've been climbing the schmuck's Yes Ladder, princess. You've answered yes to every single question he's asked, starting from the first and littlest, then bigger and bigger, and he's hoping that you'll have the habit by the time he pops the really big one. And you *will* say yes. You all do." He cut off my protest. "You've already imagined going back to his place, right? What's to stop you?"

"I—I . . ." I couldn't think of anything to say. Yeah, I'd thought about going back to Mitch's place. In my mood, he could easily have persuaded me to ditch my friends so we could indulge in a little physical affection on his sofa after a drink or two. I certainly didn't intend to *sleep* with him, but I could see myself being easily tempted. "I didn't say yes to all his questions." I had an uneasy feeling I actually had, but I didn't care to admit it. Not even to myself.

He shrugged. "You could be right. I've only been here for a minute or two. So how many 'sults did he give you?" At my blank stare, he looked at his watch and snapped his fingers. "How many 'sults? Insults. A real pickup artist always starts off his target with a 'sult. It lowers her guard. Makes her feel like he's not after her for her looks, so he can slip in under the radar. I always use something like, *Damn, your feet are big, aren't they?* or maybe, *Man, it's good to see a girl with a few extra pounds, with all these model types around*, or *Is that something hanging from your nose? Gross!*"

While he'd been speaking, all the ardor I'd felt for Mitch had begun to drain away. A. J. had personally pulled the plug on any hopes I might have had for the evening. "Two," I said in a low voice, though loud enough for him to hear. "He kind of insulted me twice. He called me clumsy, for starters."

"Oh, yeah, good one!" I still hated him a little. He must have been able to tell, because he said, "Oh come on, Becca. It's a game. The mating game. Everyone knows that. Don't take it to heart. You've been playing it too, giving him CFs. Checkered flags. What they wave at the start of a race?"

"I know what a checkered flag is."

"Every pickup artist looks for checkered flags. He'll wink at you, see if you wink back, squeeze your hand to see if you do the same. He'll watch if you cross your legs, or lean in, or touch your hair. All CFs." I had a sinking feeling he was describing me to a tee, and it made me grind my teeth. "Okay: Let's make a bet. I say your little playmate's going to come back from his 'phone call' in . . ." He checked his watch once more. "Forty-five seconds to a minute. It's called the trial separation, a two-minute test to see if you're willing to wait around for him. If you are, he knows he's got you, hook, line, and stinker." I was so indignant that I didn't even bother to correct him. "And he's going to say something like, *Oh, hey, I was meeting someone here, but I'd rather talk to you some more. How about we go back to my place?* It'll be another yes on the ladder, and Mitch's Mini-Me's one step closer to getting a piece."

"His what?"

"His Mini-Me." He pointed downstairs. "His—"

"Got it. Thanks. Lord, you are so crude." I looked around the room, fearful of having Mitch see me talking to this dolt.

"Hey, I'm stating facts. Are we on? If I'm right, you go out with me as my wingman this weekend. Not on a date," he assured me, since I'd already begun mouthing objections. "Be my wingman. I'll show you more tricks of the trade."

"We are *not* on. I don't even *know* you that well." I hesitated. If A.J. shrugged again, I was going to knock off that tiny little hat, and his tiny-brained head along with it. I set my jaw. "And if I win?"

"Name your prize."

"Fine. Then you'll leave me the heck alone and take yourself and that monkey cap to some other bar!"

Luckily for the hat, A.J. didn't shrug. Instead, he nodded. "Sure. Ain't gonna happen. But sure. If it makes you feel good." He turned his back to me and faced the bar. "Thirty seconds."

Thirty seconds. My whole body felt atremble with indignation. Not every guy was a pickup artist. They didn't all subscribe to this idiotic . . . what was it? Seven-step method? Twenty seconds. Mitch was a nice guy. An honest guy. The kind of guy I'd like to talk to. Ten seconds. Why was I even counting? A.J. wasn't the expert he thought he was. That chihuahua hat was weighing too heavily on his brain. Five, four, three, two . . .

It was at that point that Mitch shouldered his way through the nearest cluster of people, mumbling apologies while he kept his gaze firmly on me. I shivered a little at the coincidence of it. Automatically I opened my mouth to welcome him back, but then I noticed something that gave me pause. "You've got your coat with you," I said, nodding at the jacket over his arm. "You don't have to . . . go . . . do you?"

"You know, it's like this." His tongue darted out and moistened his lips. "I was supposed to be meeting my best friend here tonight. He's just getting over a bad relationship. She left him. Really ugly. He's been . . . well, he's kind of been going nuts with the womanizing since then, and I told him I'd meet him here tonight. What the heck: You understand how it goes with friends, right?" I nodded with reluctance, understanding considerably more than Mitch probably knew. "I called him and told him I was going to stay in tonight instead. So I was thinking if we were still here when he arrived . . ."

"Oh." It was the only syllable I could utter.

"You weren't, you know, wedded to staying here, were you? All these phony people." He made a face. "Wouldn't you rather go back to my place?"

You know, the closer I looked at Mitch, the less he looked like Patrick Dempsey and the more he resembled one of those weasely runts from the school playground who, by dint of whining and groveling and flattering, managed to relieve me of my pudding cups on a regular basis. The little ratfink! I knew it meant admitting to myself that for the last few minutes I'd imagined myself basking in the warm bath of mutual attraction when really I'd been soaking my sorry ass in Machiavelli's dirty dishwater, but there wasn't any way I'd be climbing his Yes Ladder any longer. Woe to the man who pisses off the recent divorcee! "Mmmm," I breathed, sounding breathy and receptive to the idea. I touched my hair and let my finger fall down to my lips, then my neck, which I brushed gently. "You know what?"

He responded to my checkered flags with another lick of the lips. Moving in closer, he murmured, "What?"

"I have to ask my boyfriend."

"Your . . . huh?" Mitch nearly performed a spit-take.

With great delight I turned around and tapped A.J. on the shoulder. "Yeah, babe?" he asked, standing up. He was a better actor than I thought, managing to look totally blank. Of course, that might have been his default expression.

"Honey, this nice guy wants me to go home with him." I bestowed my sunniest smile on both men.

"Does he, now?" A.J. stroked his jaw and considered his rival. Both men were no slouches in the working out department, but A.J. had a good four inches and eighty pounds on the smaller guy. "Well, I don't really know about that."

"Hey, now . . ." Mitch had gone from confident and swaggering to skittish; he actually seemed to think that A.J. might pound him into the Venetian's shiny wooden floor. "I didn't know . . . I wasn't looking for trouble . . . I'm not . . ."

"So that's a no, then?" I said, deferring to A.J. with a pout.

A.J. glowered. "Honey, call me old-fashioned, but I'm thinking that's a definite . . ."

He didn't even have to finish the sentence. Without warning, Mitch scampered away, darting between startled customers and barging through the crowd with his coat and dignity flapping behind him. I was so astonished at the cut-and-run that it took me a moment to catch my breath—but then my laughter came out, loud and long.

A.J. waited for me to stop and for the people in our immediate vicinity to cease staring before he spoke again. When he did, it was with crossed arms and a smile on his face. "I'm thinking I just won a bet there."

I grabbed my Cosmo, slugged down the remnants from the bottom of the glass, and set it back on the bar. "Shut up."

"You're gonna be my wingman," he said in a teasing sing-song voice.

"Shut up, I said."

"Eg-an's gon-na be my wing-man!"

"Shut up times three!"

The chances of A.J. ever closing his mouth were slim. Especially now that he had a hold over me. He was another little boy on the playground, dancing around me, happily teasing, while I tried to stalk away with my lunch box back to the cafeteria. "Admit you liked turning the tables on that schmoe. It was a great sting! Admit it!"

I grinned. It had been a dismal day, but the last bit . . . yeah, I'd enjoyed it. It was the closest I'd come to being playful in months, and it was utterly unlike anything else I'd ever done. "I admit nothing."

"Ooh," he said, biting his thumb. "Hottie with a body at three o'clock."

I watched him smooth out his shirt, then flex briefly to make his muscles pop in what I could only think he assumed would catch a woman's eye. "What're you going to do, use one of the stupid pickup lines from this Method of yours?"

"Don't mock something that works, chickadee." He adjusted his shirt's neck. "Gotta hit it. Have fun at Camp Feminista."

"For the love of God, take off that damned hat!" I called out after him before he disappeared.

Seven-step method, my aunt Fanny.

TWO

"Everyone says the first year of a marriage is the worst. But you know what?" I asked. On the silenced flat-screen overhead, two hosts on E! beamed over clips of two minor celebs holding hands. They'd just been wed, apparently. "The toughest year is the *last*." I considered the couple's smiling, happy faces, knowing they'd be pulling a Britney-and-Jason or a Renee-and-Kenny any hot second now.

"Folks, we're finally getting some bitterness!" Rani Chakraborty patted my hand.

"I'm not bitter! Cheering for celeb break-ups is fair game in my book," I announced stiffly.

"About time," muttered my friend Sarah, absorbed in some personal project.

"I'm not bitter!" I protested. I honestly wasn't. I was just having a little fun.

"You want the cure, Becca? Closure. Google it. No, wait—do you even know how to Google? She doesn't, does she?" After two Sixty-seventh Street Martinis, Rani's deep alto was a little too loud and her laughter a little too shrill, but none of the busy bar's well-dressed patrons seemed to notice. With what I hoped was affection, she mock-slapped me on the biceps. "Look it up in one of your antique dictionaries, then: closure. Every good divorce needs one."

"The first rule of Divorce Club is, you do not talk about Divorce Club." My sister Alice, one long and elegant leg crossed daintily over the other at the knee, didn't have to raise her voice to make herself heard. Her left eyebrow levitated in the direction of the paneled ceiling and the colorful blown-glass lampshades hanging from its lofty reaches.

"What do you mean? I've been good to myself today. I took off from work and went on a shopping blitz after signing the papers." My reflection, squashed and flat, danced along the edge of the martini glass I rotated slowly between my fingers. First of the evening, thank you very much, and Rani's treat. Actually, she'd already bought a couple of rounds of Manhattan's most expensive martini, and I worried she might have to sell a kidney on the black market when the final tab came around. "I'm drinking. I took myself out for *ice cream* earlier," I said, hoping I'd made that particular indulgence sound like a chore. "I almost—" I stopped, not wanting to admit I'd almost allowed myself to go home with a pickup artist. "What more can I do? I've spent weeks, *months*, making my peace. So my divorce is official as of three o'clock today. I'm no different from yesterday, right? What? What?"

Rani and Alice had exchanged skeptical glances during my assurances. Rani hoisted a fresh martini. Not her own, apparently, because Alice gently raised her hand, guided the drink back down to the table, then pushed a nearly empty glass in her direction. Rani accepted it without comment, though her expression at what little liquid remained seemed distinctly regretful. "Come on, Sarah. Tell her. You're always in analysis."

Alice sighed heavily and took another sip. "The second rule of Divorce Club is you *do not* talk about Divorce Club."

At the sound of her name, Sarah looked up from scribbling in her little Moleskine, peering at us through her cat's-eye glasses. "What's that supposed to mean?" Family dogs, from their front porches, made the same kind of suspicious growl at the approach of a strange postman.

"What did you do to celebrate your divorce?" I asked Sarah, trying to change the subject. "I mean, I remember what we did for yours," I said to Alice. "I mean, it was like ten hours of *Beaches* and *Sleepless in Seattle* and a pizza or three."

Sarah ticked off her fingers. "One: I cut up my wedding dress. Two: I cut up my wedding photo album. Three: I Frisbeed the wedding DVD into the Central Park Reservoir."

Ooch. And they called me bitter. "Portia?"

Our heads all turned to the last member of our fivesome, who had spent the last half hour interested more in the bar's other male patrons than in our conversation. "Sorry?"

"She wants to know what you did on the day your divorce was final," Alice said.

"I can't wait to hear this." The tips of Sarah's dark bob swung forward as she peered over her glasses.

"Oh, when I divorced Ken?" If you liked your girls pouty and pretty, Portia fit the bill admirably. Her big, wide eyes studied the ceiling as she thought for a moment. "I told his best friend that Ken had a little bitty penis."

The answer was so unexpected that I couldn't help but laugh. "That's kind of funny!"

"After I slept with him."

There really was no good way to respond, was there? I moved on. "How about you, Rani?" She shrugged, looking evasive. "You don't remember?"

"She drank," Alice said, shaking her head. "And drank."

"I did not."

"And threw up."

"Maybe you'd better lay off on those martinis." I was glad this little celebration was on someone else's dime. Even the bottled water in the Venetian ran a cool nine-fifty. "What is *in* a sixty-seven-dollar drink, anyway? What makes it worth a dollar for every street?" I didn't care if I sounded like the world's biggest cheapass; I couldn't keep my mouth shut any longer on the matter. "It doesn't come with a gold nugget at the bottom. It's not erasing my crow's feet."

Alice patted my hand. "Sit up straight. You don't have crow's feet."

"Aw, thank you!" Older sisters are known the world wide for being hypercritical, so the compliment genuinely touched me. "But I had a point in here, some-where. Oh, yeah. What's so special about the Sixty-seventh Street Martini? Did James Bond himself shake and not stir the damned thing?" As if on cue, all five of us at our corner of the bar let our eyes wander to Franco, the lanky bartender in the shiny red-and-gold vest, he of the sleepy bedroom eyes, the Satan-goatee sculpted into a point that touched his second shirt but-ton, the slick ponytail, and the neck tattoo only half-obscured by his collar. Bond he definitely was not. Not even the George Lazenby version.

"Hi!" Portia raised her hand and wiggled her fingers at the bartender when he gave us the once-over, then ran the self-same fingers through her long, dark mane. Oh, lord. She was touching her hair. Her eyes were sparkling. Worst of all, her breasts were doing that to-tally Portia thing they always did in the presence of anything with XY chromosomes who was old enough to shave, inflating to life and seeming to strain against her Banana Republic dress. Talk about checkered flags. We all noticed. Sarah looked pained. Alice pre-tended not to see. Rani stopped talking altogether, to gape. "Sorry?" said Portia, her fingertips automatically flying to her sternum.

"Ew," Alice repeated with emphasis.

"He looks like he's been dipped in salad oil!" Rani hissed, not doing too fantastic a job of keeping her eyes off Franco while pretending not to talk about him. "No."

"No what? You don't think . . ." If she'd been starring in a conditioner commercial, Portia's hair couldn't have spilled any more prettily around her shoulders as she turned again to study the bartender. Portia and I both had hair of a similar length and dark brown color. Hers, however, always managed to spill, or fall, or tumble beautifully, or any of the more extravagant and complimentary adjectives applied to hair. Mine merely hung. Her reappraisal must have convinced Franco that he'd be getting lucky after his shift that night, because his big, heavy eyes seemed to grow even larger and droopier as he gave her what appeared to be some kind of patented sex stare. Portia's shoulders rose as she giggled. "No, don't be silly! I don't want to *sleep* with him! He reminds me of a collie I once had. Well, a collie-beagle mix, really. All shaggy up top and pitifully small down below." She beamed once more with tenderness at Franco, whose face had fallen when obviously he'd overheard. "Poor old thing. Hi!" she added, breasts hovering again as a broad-shouldered Wall Street–type sporting curly hair and good Armani sauntered by with a grin on his face.

"To answer your question." Sarah had spent the better part of the last forty minutes furiously scribbling . . . well, I didn't know what, since with Sarah it could have been anything from one of her ever-changing life plans to furious letters to U.S. congressmen to an IKEA shopping list. But now she read to us from the narrow, leather-encased menu that had been sitting nearby. "Club Venetian's famous Sixty-seventh Street Martini is blended with only the choicest of blah-blah-blah, the rarest of cognacs, made with the juice of the champagne grape blah-blah-blah, a second precious cognac made with extract of Basque apples, blah, twenty-year-old port, and the juice of the Fiji pear, for the most discerning of blah-blah." She set the menu down and went back to her writing.

"Essentially, we're paying a premium price for the illusion of being pandered to, then." Alice, as always, had commandeered a corner barstool and pointed her knees to the room's center, though she somehow managed still to lean back and remain part of the group. Nine-point-seven points for grace. A whopping ten for the way that every man entering the dark and cozy confines of Club Venetian couldn't help but notice those shapely and elegant legs as he edged by. I'd spent a protracted, invisible adolescence in the long shadow of those gams and knew all of my sister's tricks, so I had to give the pose a mere six-point-four for practicality. She re-crossed her legs at the knee, hooked her heel on the chair's brass rail, and adjusted her skirt somewhat primly while still managing to show a maximum amount of skin. "Not that we begrudge you, of course."

"Good, because my Visa's maxed out." Rani scooped a handful of pistachios from a bowl on the bar, cracked one open while awkwardly cradling the rest, and flashed her teeth. "You're paying. Joke," she added hastily when Alice began to blink almost as rapidly, nostrils flaring.

"Hi there!" Despite creating a one-woman sirocco with her eyelashes, Portia didn't get more than a double-take from the pair of young executives passing her chair. When they kept walking, however, she pouted a little and muttered, "Rude!"

"You know," I told her, trying not to grit my teeth, "there are a lot of women, me included, who would take the memory of that blatant a double-double-take and cherish it for years, kind of like a little old lady cooing over old flower petals pressed between the pages of a family Bible."

"Oh, Rebecca!" Portia's expression was all compassion: wide-open eyes, cocked head, arms held together at the elbow as she reached out for my hands over the bar, which simultaneously had the effect of deepening her already considerable cleavage. "I know things seem grim with everything being official today. The utter and complete failure of your marriage, I mean. It's got to be a slap in the face, doesn't it?" While I blinked several times at that, she breezed smoothly on. "But your life's not over. You're not *that* old. You won't die alone. Probably."

"I'm not even thirty!" All the confidence I'd been feigning all day rapidly began to erode. "And what do you mean, *probably?*"

"Darling." Portia tossed her hair over her shoulders and squeezed my hands. The wedding band Sean had given me hadn't seen an airing for months, but somehow today my ring finger felt especially naked. "Don't you *ever* listen to my radio show? I had a segment yesterday called Middle-Aged Sex: Fact or Fiction? It was a very provocative topic. Statistically, you're as likely to win the Mega Millions as you are to find a lasting relationship at this point in your life. Or be hit by a comet. Basically, once a woman reaches a certain age, she becomes more or less . . ." Her shrug knocked my confidence a bit, but the word that came after was certain to leave a nasty bruise. "Invisible."

"That is a lie," said Sarah, roused again from her notebook. She stabbed her pen in Portia's direction. "Statistics lie. In this case, those statistics have been altered in order to discriminate against a particular demographic. Our demographic. Yes, you too." So vigorous were her thrusts that the pen's inky plastic insert shot out and onto the bar. Her fingers scrabbled after it. On their way back, they rested on my hand for a moment. "Don't listen to that liar's lying lies. You'll be fine. Absolutely fine."

"I can't believe you called me a lying liar." Portia didn't really sound outraged; she probably merely liked the way arching her brows made her face look. "If you listened to my program, you'd have heard the segment recently in which a statisticarian . . ."

"Statistician," murmured Alice. Like the rest of us, she played quiet little Switzerland whenever Sarah and Portia indulged in one of their senseless face-offs.

"That's what I said, Alice. There was a statistician on my show, and he said that ninety percent of statistics were absolutely truthful, which I think you'll agree is something to think about. I'm a responsible member of the media, Sarah. We're not allowed to *lie*. It's in our Hippocratic Oath."

"Guys."

Everyone ignored Rani.

"Oh my sacred aunt." Sarah looked close to banging her head on the mahogany bar. "Having a chat show on the radio hardly makes you a responsible member of the media."

"I don't know how it wouldn't."

"Guys?" Rani tried again, abandoning her empty martini glass in front of me and trying to insert herself between the two foes.

"AM radio?" Sarah sneered, delivering the death blow.

"Sarah, you are such a snob. Yes, you are. You should hear yourself on this topic. Soooo defensive! Psychologists have a name for what you're doing, you know."

Sarah sat back in her stool and crossed her arms. Whatever project she'd been working on before had been completely forgotten. The conversation had ventured into her favorite territory now. "Oh? Do they? What's the name for it?"

"Yes, they do. It's a fact." Rather than answer the question, Portia let her eyes dance over a trio of broad-chested men with Mediterranean complexions as they walked past. One of them looked over his shoulder, unconsciously ran the tip of his tongue over his lips, and promptly slammed a shoulder into the corner of one of the booths. With a smug, catlike smile, Portia returned her attention to the rest of us. "And anyway, Sarah, why does it always have to be you, you, you? If you listened to my radio show . . ."

Sarah's canines dug into her number-two pencil. "You mean the one you wanted to call 'Me, Me, Me'?" she said with a hint of menace.

"Don't be silly. It's 'Portia Daye's Radio Show with Portia Daye,' which you would know if you'd only switch it on once or twice!" It was really a pity that one could only be so facetious with Portia; subtlety flew over her head like a space shuttle over Cape Canaveral. "Anyway, I thought we were all here to support poor, sad Rebecca. And look at her, sad as can be." When I felt everyone turn their heads, I wanted to cringe. Couldn't this conversation simply *end?* If helping me out was what my gal pals intended, they were doing a piss-poor job of it. If anything, I'd walked into the club feeling relieved, though not completely lighthearted. The previous year had been practically the worst of my life. Months of self-doubt capped by the discovery of Sean's cheating hadn't done wonders for my ego, let's just say. That afternoon, though, I'd signed the papers without reservation, lawyer at my side nodding with approval, and walked out a free woman. I didn't feel like mourning. I'd done enough of that. I wanted fun, and a break from the usual. Not reproach and my buttinsky friends insisting over and over again that I was miserable. "She's sad and lonely and worried that no one is going to want a middle-aged alcoholic." Portia opened her doe eyes as widely as possible while she took a deep swig of her drink.

"I've only had . . . !" Suddenly, I caught a glimpse of the glasses collecting in front of me on the bar. All my friends had pushed the dregs of their 67th Street concoctions in my direction. Any casual passer-by would have gotten the impression that I was one Jell-O shot away from requiring an emergency liver transplant. "Oh, for heaven's sake." While the others tried reasoning with Portia, I tried gesturing to Franco to get him to clear the counter. His ponytail whipped in my direction the minute he saw me wave my hand. "Hey! Barkeep!" I called out. "I know you can hear me!" Nothing.

Oh, by all that was sacred, I *was* invisible. Or ignored. The tonnage of my heavy heart pulled me back down into my chair as I tried to decide which was less desirable. I'd just worked out that ignoring required intent and more effort, and therefore had to be worse when I heard that unmistakable voice again, this time doing the Joey line from *Friends*. "Ladies . . . how *you* doin'?"

He'd lost the hat, I noticed. "A.J.!" Portia hopped off her chair and skittered with baby steps over to the guy, arms outstretched. "How's my favorite big brother? I'm so glad you came!"

"He's fine. And how's the smartest little sister a guy could have?"

Portia glowed at the praise—partly, I suspect, because A.J. was the only person who might ever pay her that particular compliment. "Did you listen to my show today?"

"Of course I did!" Even as he spoke, A.J.'s attention was elsewhere. His eyes glittered as they scanned the room, occasionally halting to scan one of the more attractive babes present. He reminded me of a snake on the prowl for small, helpless prey. "The one about the, you know. I really liked the way you handled that guest."

Portia's face lit up. "Which?"

"The one . . . you know. The one with the thing."

When Portia pouted, she looked like a nine-year-old denied a stuffed animal. "Not the second one!"

A.J. said hastily, "No, the first. Great work on that. I laughed. I cried."

"Oh!" Portia hugged him again, moved by impulse. "You say the sweetest things!"

"Yeah, he's a specialist in sweet things, all right. You know what line he used on me earlier tonight?" I looked over to Sarah and told her. Alice gasped and shook her short blond hair; Rani made a small cry of outrage into her glass.

Sarah sighed. "Why in the world, whenever we have a girls' night out, does A.J. have to tag along? He's inevitable and unwelcome, like death, taxes, or a really nasty hangover after a night of heavy drinking."

"What kind of woman falls for that kind of line, anyway?" I wanted to know, still antagonized at the memory.

Alice had dealt with A.J.'s type all her life and she wasn't about to waste her time on another big lug with only one thing on his mind. Instead of looking at him, she scanned the room and murmured at large, "It wasn't the shrewdest of lines, that's for certain."

Sarah stared at the brother and sister as if she'd been handed a charter membership in the Society to Eliminate Society of All Things Daye and had an assignment to bring in their severed heads for the group's first show-and-tell night. "The good ones are broken. And the rest of them are *handicapped?*"

"That's so insulting!" said Rani, pulling back her hair and putting her latest empty glass among the others in front of me. "It's men who are emotionally handicapped, not women."

"That's not insulting. It's *beyond* insulting."

Like Alice had with him, A.J. didn't even bother to look at Sarah as he wiped imaginary lint from the broad planes of his chest. "Only to the handicapped ones."

"Oh my God." Sarah shut her notebook, crossed her legs, and flung back her shoulders, ready for a fight. I put my fingers to my temple, trying to will away the headache that was brewing. Sarah had occupied the best friend slot of my life for a good couple of years, but all the purging she did on the leather sofa every session with her therapist inevitably left her spoiling for a fight. Either that, or she'd been memorizing Julia Sugarbaker's tirades from "Designing Women" reruns again. "I've got to say, A. J. Daye . . ."

Portia made an amazing discovery. "That rhymes."

". . . that I shouldn't be shocked when you appear and prove, for the hundredth time, that you're adrift in the gene pool without benefit of a flotation device. I don't mind when you show us how you can toss beer nuts in the air and catch them in your mouth. When you're doing your celebrity so-called imitations, you're marginally amusing, though probably not for the reasons you think. When you're buying drinks you're tolerable for a few seconds." My poor brain was frazzled at the barrage of words, but Sarah didn't pause for so much as a perceptible breath. "But when you're being your usual sexist, misogynistic self, of all the people I've ever encountered, you are without doubt the most condescending."

"No, I'm not, little missy." Club Venetian was too posh an establishment to stock beer nuts. A.J. grabbed a fistful of pistachios from a nearby hand-blown glass bowl and tossed one into the air. It plummeted down into the gaping cavern his dentist called a mouth; he chomped on it happily, tossed another few down the hatch, nodded at the bartender, and called out, "Hey, bro. How about clearing up for the ladies?"

Never mind that I'd all but screamed at the gin-monkey moments before to do the same thing; a couple of words from Portia's overgrown pet chimp was all it took to get a reaction from Franco. "Sure thing, A.J." Pair by pair, the dirty glasses began to disappear.

"You know everyone, don't you?" Portia always seemed a little in awe of her big brother. Hero worship, pure and simple.

Beneath her breath, Alice muttered, "Bartenders, strippers, all the doctors at the V.D. clinic," eliciting more than a few giggles from Rani, who'd slung back most of someone else's martini.

"All part of my Method, girlio." With one hand, A.J. accepted a foaming pilsner from Franco, while with the other he reached for the front of his pants and hitched them up. They were nearly as tight as his shirt. Definitely there were more buns on display than in the window of your typical baker. "All part of my Method."

"Becca, I'm sorry. I thought this was a nice place," said Sarah, still in it for the battle. "Obviously it's not, if certain people have been here often enough to have a regular drink."

"Hold up." A.J.'s voice was loud under normal circumstances, but pushed, it sounded sharp enough to cut through the bar's ruckus. With happy hour in full swing, space was increasingly at a premium, and a number of newcomers were covetously eyeing our stools. "Just hold up. You're lucky I hang around with you chicks at all."

"Oh, gee, what did I do when I was younger to deserve that kind of luck?"

"Sarah," I said, warning in my voice. All the noise and alcohol, not to mention the disappointment I'd had earlier with Mitch, had already revved up the circular saw that was my headache. Every little jolt of dissension only helped it slice another cross-section from my skull.

"Something really good?" A.J. ventured.

"Hmmm." Sarah pretended to consider. "I was thinking more along the lines of kicked a puppy, pulled the wings off butterflies . . . maybe I ran over a nun, then backed over her forty-seven times, to deserve the kind of luck that makes *you* appear every time we . . ."

"Sarah," I begged.

"Is this still about that pickup line?" an angry A.J. wanted to know. Not angry enough to forego a swig of his ale, I noticed. "Because if you're gonna fault me for treating Rebecca here like a real girl . . ."

"Yes, it's about . . ."

"Hey!" My unexpected protest was so loud that for a moment, I silenced our immediate vicinity. Once everyone had ascertained that I still had my purse, my glass, and my virtue intact, they went back to their business. "That's enough."

A.J.'s jaw was the only slack thing on him. "You didn't let me finish."

"Now see what you've done?" Sarah demanded. "You've pushed her over the edge."

Rani attempted to hop up from her stool, but her feet were so unsteady that she nearly fell down. "Are you okay?"

"I think it's time someone went home for an early evening," said Alice in her best big sister tones.

"Stop it!" I snapped. If Rani couldn't get out of her seat, I surely could. I waited until I had my feet on the floor before I added, voice firm but low, "All of you just stop it! I wanted to have fun tonight, not a pity party! All this arguing isn't fun! If I got pushed over the edge, you're the ones who wheeled me there and tipped the barrow." My friends all managed to summon abashed expressions, while to my right, A.J. smirked. "And you," I said, directing my attention to him. "You're an idiot. I *am* a real girl. Always have been, always will be, no matter what my marital status is or isn't or . . ." Everyone stared at me as if I'd committed some unspeakable act for sticking up for myself. "What I'm trying to say is that just because I signed some papers today doesn't make me any different from . . . all I wanted was a fun night out to break the routine and you're all . . . you treat me like I'm some kind of . . . pitiful . . ." Hundreds of words careened in my throbbing head, though only a few managed to make their way out. None were the right ones. I felt my lower lip trembling for a second time that night. "And now I'm going to . . . I hate that you've made me . . . I need to . . ." To my horror, tears were welling in my eyes. I *hated* crying in front of anyone. I clapped my hand to my mouth, grabbed for my purse, and started the miles-long dash to the women's room before anyone could witness the unspeakable happen. "Bathroom!" I finally blurted.

Sarah looked as miserable as I felt, but it was Rani who spoke. "I'll go with you."

What they say about misery loving company isn't true at all. I shunned it, waving my hands in my wake. "Just leave her be." That was Alice, ever superior, knowing me better than I knew myself. "She's always been . . ."

What? What had I always been? I was too far away to hear the rest of the sentence. I wasn't rival enough to Alice that she'd actually stoop to anything unkind. There were a lot of things I'd always been. Tall, for one thing—taller than anyone else in fifth through seventh grade, when finally the boys had started to catch up to me. Stubborn, for another. Stubborn enough not even to consider a reconciliation with Sean when everyone had tried to talk me into it. Red-eyed? No, I hadn't always been that, I realized in front of the mahogany-framed mirror in the women's room. I grabbed a fistful of hand towels and dabbed them carefully against my eyes. My straight dark brown hair fell around my face, the tips tickling my jawline. It was a mess. Two glamazons slithered past me wearing twin expressions of mingled disgust and pity, as if Club Venetian had taken to employing lepers as bathroom attendants. I didn't care how I looked, personally. Those skinny wenches could just . . . well, there was that stubbornness again.

I'll take Things I'd Always Been for a hundred, Alex. I'd always been married. No, it had only seemed that way. That particular state of being had lasted only for five years, the first four a luxurious dip into domestic bliss. We'd giggled and held hands through the engagement and the wedding, sipped icy drinks throughout the honeymoon until our brains had frozen, and then spent that first year lining our love nest with all the necessities a loving newlywed couple might want—the pots and pans and place settings and tablecloths and rice cookers and chenille throws for the new furniture. Then there'd been the years when I'd catch Sean's eye from across a crowded room and warm when he'd wink at me, certain that we'd be one of those couples that succeeded.

Damn it. Why did those women have to make me cry? I'd done my crying months ago, when all those pots and place settings and throws had been divided up between us, and I'd taken the rice cooker and half a Pottery Barn showcase to the spare bedroom in Alice's apartment. That had been the cruelest day of all. Not this one, with its flurry of *sign here* flags and duplicate and triplicate copies. It hadn't even been necessary to see Sean's cheating face today. Why had I let them get me so emotional?

"All right, Egan," I said to myself quietly, ignoring the fact that my powder room solitude was being broken by the swinging door. "Buck up. Eyes forward. Shoulders back."

"Chest out?" I whirled around, startled by the sound of a hopeful baritone in the sanctity of the women's room. A.J. leaned against a stall divider, a hundred-and-ninety-five pounds of chiseled muscle barely constrained by a few ounces of nylon and twill. At my startled expression, he quirked the corner of his mouth. "Don't wet your pad, it was a joke."

"I'm not . . . my pad is none of your business, frankly," I snarled, instantly flipping around and turning on the taps to high. The noise of the water filling the sink brought me back to reality, grounding me in a way nothing else could. My whole world might have faltered in its orbit today, but the ordinary would bring it back to its steady course. "And you're not supposed to be in here."

"Says who?"

"Says . . . says the rules!" When he didn't say anything to that, I peered at him in the mirror. "Oh wait, I forgot. Men don't follow rules. You don't need rules. You do what you want, where you want, with whomever you want, especially if they look good in a tight skirt and drop a pair of panties in your coat jacket for your poor wife to find."

"Hey." A.J. didn't change posture at all, merely shrugging a little. "I'm not Stan."

"Who?" I finished angrily washing my hands and began grabbing for the towels again.

"Stan. The guy stupid enough to dump the likes of you."

"Sean," I corrected, feeling my bad temper erode slightly, much against my will. At the same time, I despised myself for letting a little flattery, no matter how indirect and seemingly sincere, win me over.

"So he left you for someone else, right? Some other chick?" I nodded, trying to make something of my hair and wondering where in the world this could be going. "So what was she?"

I really didn't want to talk about this. "The daughter of one of the partners in his law . . ."

"No," he said, face pained. He propelled himself from his leaning position and shifted over to the sink, standing closer. "On a scale of one to ten. What was she?"

"That is *so* like you!" I sputtered, aghast. "Using some stupid system that reduces a complex woman to a number, instead of—"

"Blond hair?"

"What? No. Not natural, anyway."

"Tall and slender? Like you?"

I ignored his gesture in my direction, instead crossing my arms and setting my jaw. "Hah! Hardly. She's a shrimp!"

"What'd you do, stalk the chick?"

"No!" Grudgingly, I conceded, "Not in person, anyway. On the Internet. Her photo's on the firm's website."

"Oh, hell to the yes, you stalked her! High five!" I left his hand hanging in mid-hair. At last he let it drop. "So you've seen the goods. Hmmm." He nodded, stroking his chin with one of his meaty paws. I half expected to see a caption appear beneath the tableau: *This is what smart people do when they think*. At last he asked, "So probably about an eight-point-five, huh?"

"Six-point-five!" I was surprised by the ferocity of my growl. "Seven, at *most*."

A.J. shook his head. "You see, that's not right. You don't downgrade to an economy model."

"Damn skippy." Paper towels hanging from their dispenser rattled from my sudden, deep sigh. I hated all this hostility, boiling like burnt coffee deep in my gut, acid and just as bitter. It didn't solve anything. It didn't make me feel better—if anything, the contrary. So why did everyone seem to be hell bent on making me wallow in that crap? I didn't need that kind of catharsis. "Wait a minute," I said, distracted from my misery for a few seconds. "Downgrade?"

"Well, sure," he said, smoother than yogurt and with half the aftertaste. "A man doesn't go from an eight to a seven. Definitely not a six-point-five. It doesn't make good sense. Especially when you're already married. You've already invested all the time and good money in the eight, the way I see it." His voice had taken on a sudden professorial authority, and his eyes danced as he spoke. Obviously I'd stumbled onto one of his favorite enthusiasms. "You've cultivated that eight. A guy using The Method knows there's no downgradesies."

"Downgradesies?" Some words you simply never expect to find yourself saying. "But you do . . . upgradesies?"

The look he gave me could have withered stone roses. "Don't mock The Method. Yes, there are upgradesies." He made air quotes around the last word. "But only if she's at least two points higher. So that ex of yours should have gone only for a ten. *Maybe* a high nine. Because at that end of the bell curve, true tens are kind of rare. But definitely not a *seven.*"

"You know," I said carefully, "in a way—your own freakish way—you've made me feel better than any of my girlfriends tonight." It was true. A.J. was ridiculous, but his forays into the calculus of this so-called Method were making me grin a little. Was he the only fool in New York who talked like this, or were all guys this way and he was the only one honest about it?

"Well, *duh!* Those dames want you to be their Lifetime Movie of the Week. Hey," he said to a little Asian girl who poked her highlighted head through the door, "can't you see we're busy in here?"

"But it's the women's room?" She asked the question as though it was obvious enough, appealing to me with her eyes for backup that suddenly, I realized with a bubble of silent laughter, I didn't want to give.

"I know," he repeated in the same voice. "And we've got women's problems to talk about. So scram already." The Asian girl retreated with much eye-rolling and eyelash-batting. "Sheesh. Some people. Yeah. So see, those chicks cast you as a victim. You feel miserable, they get to be the angry sisters-in-arms, everyone's happy."

"Except me." Maybe it was the martini, but A.J. was making a kind of seductive sense. Maybe I was just flattered at being an eight. I'd never really dared to think of myself as anything more than a seven. Maybe a seven-point-five, tops.

"Except you." He nodded. "You know what? I'm seriously going to hold you to that bet we had. We're going out next weekend."

"You can't be serious," I said, letting my head loll back. The small measure of goodwill A.J. had built up over the last five minutes instantly began to crumble. "What is this, some kind of sleazy, disgusting, come-on attempt?"

"Listen, princess," he interrupted, "I'm on The Method. I'm the ten. You're the eight. Two point spread, remember?"

"Ten minus eight *is* two, Einstein." I turned to examine my reflection.

"Tens stick to tens and nines, smartypants. Maybe high, high eights." Though Sean had always been a wash-and-wear type of guy, I'd always suspected that some of his sex were just as vain as the gals. A.J. angled his head like some kind of male model, patted down some imaginary stray hairs, and began inspecting his silhouette and rear end from various angles in the mirror. "Not mid-to-upper eights. I meant we go as buddies. Just head out, get some drinks, work the crowd, let you see what it's like to be having fun instead of being this week's *Divorce Court* highlight." He reached into his pocket, searching for something. "You already lost the bet. Come on, be my wingman. We'll pull off some stings together. It'll be fun."

I didn't even know what being a wingman involved. I wanted to ask, but instead I curbed my curiosity and finished pulling my hair back into place. The brown eyes in my eight-point-seven-five face stared back at me. Maybe I wasn't as bad as I feared, in a lot of ways. "Mmmm," was all I said, and then he pushed something into my hand. I looked down at the professionally printed business card and read the raised, engraved print aloud. "*A. J. DAYE. MAN ABOUT TOWN.*"

"Call me," he said, just as I noticed his phone number nestled underneath. He yanked open the women's room door, dodging the little Asian girl and a friend. "Seriously. We'll have fun. You'll see."

"Done powdering your nose, Josephine?" the tiny girl snarled after him. All I could see of A.J. was a quick glimpse of his hangdog smile. Then the door eased closed.

"Holy shit," said her friend, watching him go. "What a Hottie O'Hottentott."

"What an asshole." The Asian girl slammed her clutch onto the granite counter and gave me the once-over. "Some people!"

I claimed my own bag, turned, and exited before she could call me any more names. It wasn't a hasty retreat, though. I sailed loftily, head held high, the way an eight would when confronted with a couple of six-point-fives. Back at my table, the girls had ordered a round of mineral waters in lieu of any more martinis; Sarah was working on a beer, notebook open again. "Back!" I said, much more cheerful than when I had left.

"You poor thing." We were back to that again. Rani reached across the bar to pat my hand, but at the very last second I grabbed my water and chugged it, to deny her the gesture. I wasn't going to revisit that old routine.

"I'm fine," I said. Then, to Sarah, "What are you scribbling, anyway?"

"Dream journal. My therapist suggested it." She slammed the Moleskine shut once again and thrust it in her leather jacket.

"You're writing down last night's dreams?"

"No." She screwed up her face as if I were crazy. "I'm writing down some crap for the upcoming week so I don't get behind by the next appointment."

I had to get this straight. "You're making up a week's worth of dreams in advance?"

"Let's talk about you: Are you feeling okay? You look down."

"I don't feel down," I protested. I didn't need sympathy from someone making up her own dream journal. These gals were way crazier than I ever could be.

"Yes, you do, darling." Alice was too close for me to evade. Her long hand traced the side of my face, leaving behind a trail of warmth and the scent of moisturizer. "Don't worry about it. It's natural."

"I'm fine!" My insistence drew a round of skeptical glances. "Portia? Portia. Do I look down?" I asked, trying to get the attention of A.J.'s sister.

She, however, was too busy doing the Portia thing with a middle-aged man sporting a Rolex and a wedding ring to respond right away. When she did, her breasts deflating slightly at my interruption, she merely turned to me, blinked as if she'd never seen me before, and said, "Sorry?"

Useless. Absolutely useless. Across the bar, A.J. was leaning against a dark, wooden Corinthian column, drink in hand, arms crossed to show off the depth of his chest as he chatted with a vapid-looking blonde. Beautiful haircut. Long, slender neck. Delicate hands. Definitely a nine. "Now, *she* would have been upgrad-sies," I murmured, only half-aware I was saying it aloud.

"Up what?" Alice asked. From the corner of my eye, I could see the look of concern she shot the others. *Gird your loins, girls,* said that look. *She's about to crack!* I knew that within mere moments I'd be showered with more sympathy and pity than I could stand.

"Never mind." I sighed, digging in and preparing to be made miserable again. As if on cue, from across the bar, A.J.'s eyes met mine, his mouth pursed in crooked amusement. While still listening to the blonde babble on, he lifted his free hand, thumb and pinkie crooked, held it in the vicinity of his ear, and shook it slightly. *Call me,* said the gesture.

Then he raised his glass in a silent toast. Of deep sympathy, I suspected.

THREE

"Eighth Avenue Antiquarian Books." Ethan Reddiker's business voice had always struck me as light and pleasant. Beaming mothers everywhere would have called it well-mannered. Although he made a grand show of slumping over his old roll-top desk and pretending to strangle himself with the phone cord, he continued smiling as he spoke. "No, I'm sorry, we don't have any signed copies of *The Da Vinci Code*. We deal with old books. No, I mean, older than 2003. If you're looking for fiction that isn't a load of pseudo-mystical crap I could suggest . . . Alrighty, then." He replaced the rotary handset, let his hands cup his cheeks, and asked me, "Do you think the word *antiquarian* is throwing people, somehow?"

"Maybe you should answer, 'Eighth Avenue Neglected Dusty Tomes'," I told him. Cars started zipping through the street when the corner traffic light switched to green, but my attention was focused solely on the Starbucks opposite. "Really get the point across."

From the very back of our small and overheated little store came the reedy tenor of Cesar, one of the two part-time students hired to manage electronic orders. "Books and Shit," he called out. "Want me to put it on the Web site?"

"No!" brayed Sarah from her own office. Ethan and I shared a quick grin. No matter what students were working for us in a given semester, it always seemed as if they wanted to see how far Sarah could be pushed. "Don't you dare!" Her head suddenly poked out the door at the top of the landing, cat's-eye glasses glinting. A year ago, before he'd passed away, the office had been her father's; sometimes it was difficult for me to think of it as anything else.

"Sorry, Ms. Markel," Cesar called back. I recognized the voice. It was the same one he'd used the day before, after eating my pudding cup from the staff refrigerator. "Won't happen again, Ms. Markel."

"In London they say *shite* instead of *shit*." Our other student had been with us for close to two years, and I'd never seen her wear anything other than plaid skirts and blouses with lacy little Peter Pan collars that made her look like moments before she'd trotted from St. Agatha's School for Exceptionally Wholesome Girls. Was it a thing? A kid thing? It was too late to ask now without appearing hopelessly out of touch. Apparently during my five years of matrimony, I'd completely lost track of what the fashionable kids were wearing. I might as well have spent twenty years in a nunnery. Despite her sleepy voice and guileless appearance,

Michaela surely didn't talk like a Catholic schoolgirl. "I think that sounds a lot classier, don't you?" she asked, joining me at the window with an armful of leather-bound books in protective polyester sheaths. "Like how they say *arse* instead of *ass*."

"Still means the same thing," murmured Ethan.

"But it *sounds* so much nicer. Maybe if Cesar put *Books and Shite* on top of the Web page . . ."

Sarah countered by yelling from the back, "Maybe I'd fire you both."

"Good idea, Michaela. I'll answer *Books and Shite* next time the phone rings." Ethan's eyebrows shot up in mock surprise when, as if on cue, the decades-old phone began clanging.

Michaela hugged the books to her chest, almost doubled over in horror. "Oh, I dare you!"

"Double-dare!" I heard Cesar call.

The phone rang again. "Want to make it a triple, Becca?" Ethan asked, his short, practical fingers gripping the receiver. He waggled his fair eyebrows mischievously.

"You're not going to do it." I grinned. Ethan's clowning was one of the things that had made the last year bearable.

"Oh, no?"

"No."

"Yes he will!" In her glee, Michaela danced back against one of the ancient bookcases. Ethan reached out his spare hand instinctively, as did I. Not that the store's bookcases were spindly, mind you—quite the opposite. Those literary bulwarks had been installed when the bookstore opened in the 1930s and had survived wars, the 1960s counterculture, a brief career low during the Summer of Love as a head shop, and the upscaling of Manhattan during the last two decades. They weren't going anywhere. It was the books we were worried about, the delicate volumes we'd just gotten in stock from a deceased collector in Connecticut. Any single one of those volumes would have paid our rent for the month.

Only once we'd made sure both Michaela and the books were intact did Ethan pick up the phone. His arched eyebrows shot up beneath his amiably sloppy, sandy bangs. "Books and . . . Eighth Avenue Antiquarian Books," he mumbled, face reddening so quickly that he attempted to hide it from view. "Yes, we sell books. Yes, that's correct, we're on Eighth Avenue. All right, good day now." He hung up the phone, baffled. "Where else would we be?"

Across the street, in the window of Starbucks, I finally caught a glimpse of the guy I'd been looking for. He worked the afternoon shift, one to seven, four days a week. I didn't have a clue what his name might be, or what his voice might sound like, but I did know how he smiled—easily and lazily, as if it came to him without effort. During the daytime I often saw him leaning over the tables nearest the outside windows, removing coffee cups and bussing tables, smiling and having conversations with the customers; on the evenings I worked late, I could see him illuminated by the store's recessed lamps, shining down on his neck-length wavy hair like special effects arranged by heaven's lighting technicians. Right then, he had stepped out of the door to look at the March sky, squinting at it and wiping his hands on his apron as if he expected the gray skies to blow away. I had a catalogue to put together, but I couldn't stop watching. Maybe he had an appointment after his shift? A class? A girlfriend?

Ethan eased his lean frame around the waist-high sale rack until he shared the dusty window well with me. He peered through the backward gold-leaf lettering that spelled our store's name in a gentle arch, and commented, not for the first time, "You know, you could always go over and introduce yourself." He handed me a slip of paper. I unfolded it to find a Roz Chast cartoon from the *New Yorker* featuring a harried high-schooler. Ethan was a compulsive clipper. Ever since he'd begun working at the store after Mr. Markel passed away, he'd brought in cartoons to share with me; the entire inside of his desk was covered with his own personal favorites.

I gazed at Chast's nervous line drawings to disguise the fact that guilty heat prickled at my face and was spreading quickly to the rest of my body. "I'm just looking. I know, I've got to stop looking. You're right, it's silly to look at some boy when I should be working." Some people have enough skeletons in their closet to keep the *National Enquirer* afloat for years. Others have secrets that would shock a hard-bitten madam. Me? You'd think I could find more exotic a source of shame than a cross-avenue crush, but there it was. I was the newly-single woman who worked in a bookstore days and went home to her sister's apartment in the evenings. That was as colorful as my life got. "Oh, God," I moaned, horrified at the realization of how sterile my life was. "Three months from now I'll be one of those menopausal cat ladies."

Ethan's slightly snubbed nose twitched at that non sequitur. "You talk about yourself like you're an old woman."

"I am an old woman."

"You're not an old woman. If you're an old woman, I'm an old man, because we're the same age."

"Man years are different from woman years. Woman years are like dog years. I'm an old woman with an old woman's shriveled old-woman womb."

"Uh-huh. I seem to remember that your birthday cake last November only had twenty-nine candles on it." Ethan's friendly blue eyes didn't help me feel any better. "You talk about that guy like he's half your age. He's not." Across the street, Mr. Starbucks shook his tousled head with disgust, put his hands on his hips, and shuffled back inside. "Go order a coffee and *talk* to him. You know our coffee's swill."

"It's not that simple," I protested, though I knew that really it was.

"Are you bad-mouthing my coffee again?" Cesar, stuck at the computer in the stock room for too long, creaked out of his chair and lurched into the store, his latest experiment in mustache sculpture twitching. "Why do I have to make coffee all the time?"

"Part-timers always make coffee," murmured Ethan and Michaela and I simultaneously. It was a mantra around here.

"Part-timers *always* make coffee." When Sarah stuck her head out of her office door and made the pronouncement, Ethan immediately ducked his head and slunk away back to his desk, trying to pretend he hadn't been imitating her moments before. She hadn't heard us; I doubted she'd much care if she had. "It's the pecking order."

"But why do I always have to make the stuff? I don't even drink it. Why doesn't Michaela make coffee?"

Michaela's jaw dropped, aghast at the suggestion. "That's so not right."

Sarah crossed her arms and said in tones cold enough to give dry ice a run for its money, "Are you suggesting that Michaela make the coffee because she's a girl? Because if you are, I think you and I will need to have a little discussion about gender equity. Is that what we need to do?"

"No 'm." Suddenly meek, Cesar thrust his hands deep into the pockets of his powder-blue hoodie, giving the impression he was trying to make himself as invisible as possible. No easy feat, considering that at two hundred and thirty pounds and six feet and three inches, he nearly stretched the entire width of the aisle of crowded bookcases. "That's not what I meant."

"I should hope not." Sarah looked around the shop, arms crossed and jaw jutting out, challenging anyone to contradict her. There weren't any customers in the shop at the moment—there hadn't been any all morning—but even had there been, their presence wouldn't have stopped Sarah Markel from one of her notorious rants. Only the weekend before, during a shouting match between Sarah and Cesar that had started when he'd told her the Web server had been down for several hours and had worked its way into a long-winded fulmination over why Sarah intended never to buy German products for the rest of her life, had a retired psychologist from NYU wandered into the verbal assault from the store's back room and become so frightened that the store was being robbed that Ethan had to talk him out of phoning the police in the children's fiction section. Currently, Michaela had gone back to shelving the Connecticut collector's books, while Cesar took the opportunity to slink back to his workstation. Ethan was already at his desk, pretending he wasn't a part of what was going on. And me? I was the one Sarah skewered with a single look. "Get in my office."

Only one time in my life had I ever been sent to the principal's office in school, when during a school gym rope-climbing incident I slid down too quickly, burned the inside of my thighs, and let fly with what our chain-smoking, broad-shouldered, whiskey-voiced female gym teacher prudishly called "the brown word." The sinking feeling in my stomach now was very similar. Not that I seriously thought I was in trouble, mind you; despite her penchant for loudly proclaiming other people's faults, Sarah and I had been friends since the days when her father ran the store and she'd been in charge of the same administrative tasks Ethan now performed. He was bent over what looked like a sheaf of bills as I neared the old rolltop desk, smiling to himself. It struck me right then that he surely smiled a lot; it also struck me that I was enough of a New Yorker to automatically find it suspicious. Who smiled like that without a reason? When I passed him, he looked up briefly from his scribbling and graced me with one of his broad grins that showcased the slight crookedness of his incisors. Whatever slight misgivings I might have had about his high spirits vanished in an instant. Ethan was a nice guy. One of the few truly good ones.

"Shut the door," Sarah said, once I'd finally climbed the creaking stairs to the second level.

Her office was a picture of utter squalor, but that was no surprise; it hadn't changed substantially at all since the days when her father had run the business. His old stacks of carefully typed three-by-fives were stacked high along the waist-high shelf running the room's length, representing every book that had passed through the store since it had opened. It was a low-tech system that might have made sense when the store opened during the year of the Bicentennial, but it hadn't been added to during the two years we'd been computerized. A file cabinet bulged with musty folders and carbon copies of correspondence long forgotten by anyone who might still be living. To add to the general decrepitude, a pile of empty sandwich bags from Subway lay piled on the floor around the wastebasket. Those were Sarah's alone. "Sit down," she said.

"Listen." I had my defense at the ready. "I know I wasn't working on the catalogue like I was supposed to, but it's kind of a slow morning and I've been taking it home on my laptop."

The look she gave me could have curdled milk at thirty paces. "Do you really think I'm *that* kind of boss?"

Sadly, it wasn't a rhetorical question. "Well, no, but you were kind of down on Cesar a minute ago."

"That's because if he doesn't make the coffee, I'll have to drink Michaela's. Cesar's coffee might be swill, but Michaela's is the swill the swill leaves behind when it moves out of the starter slum in swillville into better digs. Anyway, shut up. Listen to this." Her chair protested with a mighty groan as she swiveled around and reached for a tabletop radio with a giant dial and a single speaker that probably had been ancient back in the days it was used to tell Paul Revere the Redcoats were coming. "I'm going to kill her. You will, too."

"Kill who?" I said, clearing a stack of sections of the *Times* from the chair so I could sit down. The seat let out a series of high-pitched squeals as I settled.

She didn't say anything, merely turning the large volume knob. From the radio I heard a somewhat muffled male voice saying, "Um, thank you. It's just a . . . I'm not even sure what brand it is, really. It's just a suit. I don't notice . . ."

"It fits so well," said a woman. "The jacket makes your chest look so *masculine*. You work out, don't you?"

"Well." The man on the radio was obviously flustered by the question. "I try, certainly. When you reach a certain age . . ."

"How old are you?" said the woman, whom I had slowly realized was none other than Portia. I'd never had even a mild desire to listen to her radio show, given its endless parade of guests who crocheted their own sexy lingerie, specialized in tantric yoga, and espoused the joys of Swinging After Sixty.

The man cleared his throat. "Forty-five," he said at last.

Portia laughed. Her voice was low and sexy; I felt vaguely dirty listening to it, as if I'd accidentally turned on a walkie-talkie with a twin in her boudoir. "You're quite the silver fox, aren't you? Especially for a hypnotist," she asked. "How old do you think I am?"

"Oh lord." Sarah rolled her eyes.

The man sounded distinctly uncomfortable. "Um . . . well, first of all, I'm not a hypnotist." He laughed slightly. "I'm a hypnotherapist. A licensed therapist with a medical degree. I'm not a cheap parlor magician with . . ."

"Come now," cooed Portia. "Don't be shy. Guess."

"Guess?" asked the baffled doctor. "Your age? Um . . . twenty-five? I'm not very good at . . ."

"Oh yes you are!" Portia said, throatily. "You got it right on the first try!"

I couldn't help myself. "If that hag is twenty-five, I'm—!"

". . . good," the man was saying, laughing nervously. "I would have hated to guess a number that was too high. Are we . . . we aren't on the air, are we?"

"Of course we are. That's what the flashing red light means, silly. If you're listening, you're listening to 'Portia Daye's Radio Show with Portia Daye.' And I'm Portia Daye, of course. I would have forgiven you if you'd guessed twenty-seven, Dr. Vega," Portia purred. Though I couldn't see a thing, in my head I envisioned her uncrossing and re-crossing her legs in a move straight out of *Basic Instinct*. "You're adorable. Especially for a hypnotist."

"Hypnotherap—"

"Why, you're so adorable, I think I could forgive you anything."

Either good Dr. Vega had a bad case of bronchitis or else he'd choked on his own saliva right then, because for a moment I heard nothing but spluttered coughing. "You're very kind," he said, and then added, with careful emphasis, "My dear, dear *wife* forgives me every-thing, too."

Portia's producers must have been going crazy about the good ten seconds of dead air that followed. Sarah didn't even bother to hide the obvious glee she felt at the gaffe; with her dark bob and retro spectacles, and with her nail-biting and hunched-over delight, she looked even more like a scandalized little schoolgirl than Michaela. "Your . . . wife?" Portia asked at last. "Don't nod! You can't nod on radio. No one can see you nod!"

"I'll be celebrating my twenty-third wedding anniversary in a month, yes."

"But you don't have a ring!"

"It's common . . . well, it's not unusual, let us say . . . for married men not to wear . . . especially when my blood pressure medicine causes digital swelling. . . ."

"But you don't have a ring!" Portia repeated, more stubbornly than the first time. Another long period of dead silence followed. I squirmed, pitying the doctor and Portia alike. "Well, then," she finally said. In the background I could hear the shuffling of papers. "You really should have said something before you started coming on to me, that's all."

"I didn't—!"

Portia cut off her guest's squawk immediately. "You wouldn't have gotten anywhere. I have a highly respectable boyfriend, you know." I performed a classic double-take in Sarah's direction. The only love interest I'd ever known Portia to have that lasted longer than one of the *Lord of the Rings* movies was the poor, hapless Kinko's worker she'd stalked for three months before discovering he was gay and partnered. "A professional football player."

Sarah made loops around her ear with a finger. I'd had enough. I didn't listen to Portia's show for many reasons—the way she brought the crazy being first and foremost. "I'm going to get back to the catalogue."

Sarah shushed me and, with a gesture, stopped me from getting out of my chair. "He's very fortunate," said Dr. Vega. "Maybe we could get back to . . ."

"He is fortunate, isn't he?" Portia cleared her throat. "And he loves me very, very much."

"Well, I'm sure he . . ."

"And he'd never cheat on me." Suddenly Portia's voice changed from sullen and pouty to bright and interested. "Oh! Oh! Which brings me back to the question I'd asked before our commercial, doesn't it?" Sarah began jabbing a pen at the radio. Not to stab it, but to indicate to me that I really was there for a reason.

Good Dr. Vega let out a sigh. "Thank God. I mean, yes, yes, indeed. You were talking about a friend of yours with a problem."

The hairs on the back of my neck began to prickle. No, surely not. When I glanced over at Sarah, she had her arms crossed once again and wore a terrible smile. "Yes," said Portia, getting down to business. "You're a hypnotist."

"Hypnoth—"

"That's what I said, isn't it? Now, this friend of mine. Let's call her Bec . . . Kate."

"Beckate?" murmured the doctor, totally bewildered.

"Yes, Beckate, one of my dearest, dearest, dearest friends. Now, let me describe her to you. She's deep in the heart of middle-age." My head lolled back on my neck, as limp as if a puppeteer had cut its string. This couldn't be happening. "Beckate's just gone through a divorce, poor thing. Her husband was cheating on her with another woman."

"Ah, yes, the age-old story. Is she in menopause?"

"No, they don't. That's the problem."

"Er . . . I'm sorry." The doctor cleared his throat. "They who?"

"Who?"

"You said, *they don't.*"

"Yes. The men." Portia managed to make the most ridiculous non sequitur sound absolutely self-evident.

"What men?"

"All of them. Or none of them. They don't pause. They don't look at her or talk to her or anything. Poor Beckate."

Dr. Vega made several strangled noises into the microphone. "No, I said *menopause,* not . . ."

"Oh! I see what you mean now! I didn't say she was *that* old," Portia reproached. "She's one of my best friends!"

"Just a warning," Sarah said, her face red. We'd been listening so intently to the old radio that a live voice nearly made me jump out of my skin. "The thudding noise you'll hear all afternoon? Yeah, that'll be me banging my head on my desk whenever I think of this moment. Why, oh why, do you insist on letting her tag along with us everywhere?"

"Silly." I knew it had come following a lot of misinformation and slander, but oddly, I felt a bit of affection for Portia's calling me a best friend. Mind you, it was far outweighed by the fact that she was trashing me before an audience of twenty on one of New York's most obscure AM radio stations, but it was little moments like these that kept me from drop-kicking her sorry rear end into the Hudson from the 59th Street Bridge. "She's one of Alice's finds. I can't dictate who Alice likes and doesn't like!"

"Ssshh." Sarah waved her hand at me, as if I'd been the one to start this digression.

". . . a bit sad, really, how she sits in the singles bars and drinks and drinks and drinks and hopes that someone will pay a bit of attention to her . . ." Portia was saying.

I gasped. All my affection vanished. "Oh, like I'd have a freakin' chance, with that black hole of flirtation sucking in every man in a three-galaxy radius!"

". . . So I suppose what I was wondering was whether a hypnotist could find out what she did wrong in her past lives to end up this sad. It couldn't have been something very nice."

Now it was my turn to let my head, if not bang, at least rest gently on the edge of the late Mr. Markel's desk. "Oh, God."

"I'm not . . ."

"Murder, maybe. Or adultery. I think it might be adultery. Isn't that what karma's all about?"

"Karma's the philosophical . . . actually, I think we'd better clear up something here, Ms. Daye. Oh. Well, all right, then." Dr. Vega seemed a little surprised that Portia didn't interrupt him. "You seem to be under the misapprehension that I'm a hypnotist. I'm a hypnotherapist. I don't . . . I don't hypnotize people to have them explore

the nonsensical notion of past lives. I'm a serious therapist with serious goals for each and every patient. Let's
put it like this: You come to my office."

"All right," said Portia. "Where is it?"

"My office? It's on Bleecker Street."

"All right. I come to your office on Bleecker Street,"
said Portia, sounding remarkably cooperative.

"And what I'd have you do is to relax on the sofa."

"I'm relaxing on your sofa."

"And it's at this point that what I do as a therapist totally diverges from what a stage hypnotist might do, because my objective is . . . Ms. Daye? Are you sleeping?"

"I'm relaxing on your sofa," Portia repeated.

If Dr. Vega had sounded doubtful he might be in the
company of a crazy woman before, he now had evidence ample enough to put Portia away in a nice little
rubber cell for a long, long time. "And what I'd do now
is . . . what are you doing?"

"I'm relaxing on your sofa."

"Why do you keep saying that?"

"Because you've hypnotized me!"

"No—no, I haven't." Dr. Vega laughed nervously, as if
hoping she was kidding.

Sarah and I both knew it was definitely no joke. "Oh!
How funny! I thought you had!"

"Ah. Hmmm. I think we're probably running out of
time here, Ms. Daye," said the doctor, sounding hopeful. "Basically, my professional advice to your friend,
Becky . . ."

"Beckate," corrected Portia.

"My advice would be that while bars can be a fine
place for socializing of all sorts, from the purely recre-

ational to the pursuit of more serious relationships, shall we say, that if alcohol is a serious problem, Beckate might seek the help of a professional . . ."

"We have loads of time," Portia piped up from nowhere. "A whole half-hour more. Don't worry about rushing."

It was at that point that I stood up, leaned over the desk, and gently switched off the radio. If only I could have helped Dr. Vega out of his misery as easily. "She's horrible," said Sarah. "She's insensitive, she's arrogant, she's completely self-absorbed . . . she's horrible! Shun her!"

Here we went again, with my friends telling me exactly how I should be feeling. It made me dig in my heels a little. "She's horrible, but she's not that bad. Stop sputtering," I added, standing up and crossing my arms. "Yes, the post office probably delivers to her all the dead-letter mail addressed *Center of the Universe*. Yes, she sometimes makes me want to . . . I don't know . . ."

"Beat her around the head with a golf club?"

I acknowledged the impulse with a shrug. "But she's Portia. In her own, brain-addled little way, she's trying to help, just like you are with the portfolio of therapist's cards you've been leaving in my work tray."

Sarah banged her hands on the desk and said, in a raised voice, "Therapy has helped me become a much less angry person!" Almost immediately she buried her face in her hands and murmured, "I've got to stop doing that, don't I? I didn't used to be like this."

"No, you didn't," I agreed.

Here's what I feared other people saw when they

looked at Sarah Markel: the vague start of stress marks on her forehead. Tight, pressed lips. Frumpy clothing. Anger and rage, especially when the subject of men came up. It would be easy for anyone to call her a name, like *bitch* or *shrew*, without knowing the thousand stresses causing those worry lines and tense expressions, or the economies and sacrifices she'd made to keep her little bookstore afloat. "You fret too much."

Wrong reply. Couldn't have been more wrong, actually. Sarah drew herself back, stiffened her neck, and said, "You could be helping me out by not aiding and abetting that childish, solipsistic, *narcissistic* . . ."

"Sarah." I wasn't going to let her bully me into changing my mind. "Despising Portia and A. J. Daye for the way they act is like faulting . . . faulting a feral tomcat for spraying indoors. It's their nature!"

"Tomcats can be trained!" I threw my hands into the air, turned to go, and opened the door. This argument wasn't getting either of us anywhere. *"And neutered!"*

The last two words echoed through the store as the oak door shut behind me. We'd gained a customer while I'd been inside, I saw—a middle-aged fellow in jeans and a sloppy sweatshirt who looked up from his reading with a disturbed expression and a gasp of, "Oh, my!" Since I could tell almost immediately that the schlub was browsing a vintage copy of *Fanny Hill*, it was easy to ignore the old-lady mannerisms.

"Who's she going to neuter?" Michaela appeared in the closest doorway, arms still full of books. Behind her, Cesar poked his head around the corner, chewing on food that he wasn't supposed to be eating in the vicinity of decades- and centuries-old collector's items.

"No one," I assured them all. They weren't buying it. Not even the vintage porn lover. "Just these people. A friend of ours. And her brother, specifically." Ethan raised his eyebrows. "It's nothing."

"Did she sleep with the brother or something?" It was tough to tell, from that sleepy voice, whether Michaela actually thought it was a possibility. "Because she sounded kind of mad."

"No, she didn't," I said, aware that all eyes were on me, including Mr. *Fanny Hill*. "Nobody's slept with him." Were Ethan's eyebrows painted with anti-gravity lotion or something? They couldn't have risen any higher. "He did ask me to be his wingman, but . . ."

Michaela erupted in laughter. "Nice!"

"What?" I watched as Cesar nodded, considering what I'd just said. Ethan simply went back to his ledgers. "Is it bad? What is it?"

"Wingman's like a best buddy. Like the guy you give your car keys to when you know you're going to be out drinking and you'll need a safe ride home," Cesar explained.

Fan-diddly-tastic. "Great. Like a baby-sitter?"

"No," said Michaela. "Much cooler than that. Is he hot?"

"Well, yeah," I admitted. Ethan looked up again, resting his chin on his palm as he listened. "Kind of. Sort of. Yes. In a don't-want-to-go-there way."

"That's great, then!" For the first time in like, ever, she was actually treating me like someone only seven or eight years her senior and not some fusty, middle-aged old crone. It baffled me. The fact that I didn't understand her enthusiasm made her stomp her foot in mild frustration. "He's not going to want to boink his wingman. Right?" She appealed to Cesar, who nodded tentatively. "Guys don't boink their wingmen."

"Because most wingmen aren't girls," Cesar said.

"Shut up. It just doesn't happen. So you could have pure, unadulterated fun without the physical complications." Michaela sighed. "I wish a guy could see me as sexless."

Rarely were words more calculated to make a gal feel like she'd entered cronehood. "Gee, thanks," I said wryly.

"No, not like that!" Michaela shrugged. "But you should do it. I would."

"You could be my wingman," Cesar said to her.

Michaela bestowed upon him a withering look. "Your jet's grounded."

"Hey!"

I listened to the kids bicker as they headed to the back room, thoughtful as I gathered up the folders that I'd been using to assemble our print catalogue. So that's all a wingman was? It sounded like a low-pressure way to get out there and mingle some. That's what I'd kind of been craving, hadn't it? As long as I didn't have to—no, the thought of sex with A. J., even if both of us had been covered head-to-toe in cootie-proof latex—made me shudder. There wouldn't be any of that, I knew.

No, the whole idea was stupid. Why should I hit a nightspot with a letch and a perv when I could go with my friends? My girlfriends. The ones who kept insisting I was depressed and bitter? The ones who stifled me when I protested? Yeah, that was the ticket. We were talking real fun.

I sighed, only to find Ethan still looking at me. "You're thinking about it, aren't you?" he asked. His voice didn't carry any judgment either way, I noticed. Merely a plain statement of fact.

I grinned, embarrassed. "I was. For one hot second. Then it cooled. Not really my style."

"It could be fun," he said, going back to work. "There's nothing wrong with fun." I dumped all my folders onto the large reading table in the store's center, vaguely aware of the fact that this catalogue was the farthest thing from fun possible. Ethan bowed his fair head over his writing, still smiling to himself. When the phone let out another shrill cry, he answered it on the first ring. "Eighth Avenue Antiquarian Books," he said, voice as pleasant as ever. "No, we don't carry Harry Potter. No, not even first editions. Because they're not—hello? Hello?" He gazed at the receiver. "Rude."

I smiled with sympathy, but my mind was elsewhere. He'd been right: There was nothing wrong with fun. Getting in over my head, though—that could be deeply and horribly wrong. Better to go at this thing at my own pace, and as a solo flight.

FOUR

"And one of the really interesting projects I've been working on is the collection of statistical data from the Triborough area on water quality and consumption so that our unit can articulate some consistent, ethical- and evidence-based advocacy positions to local governments." Walter paused in his monologue—mercifully—to take a sip from his wineglass. The sleeves of his corduroy jacket were a little too short, I noticed, and the leather band on his watch was so frayed and cracked that it looked like it might give way at any moment and plop into the mostly empty casserole of chicken lasagna. Fortified and refreshed by his beverage break, he leaned back in his chair, pulled up his knee, and began explaining. "You see, the World Health Organization has declared this the Water for Life Decade, and our position papers are specifically designed to alert officials to the very real threats that arise from . . ."

The guy produced words with the same unrelenting determination of Lawrence Welk's bubble machine on overdrive. Somewhere deep inside, the adolescent in me let out an exaggerated sigh and flounced in her chair, praying for the over-extended dinner to end. I knew full well that I was too old to have my teenaged self still lurking within, but until nature stopped occasionally cursing me with forehead zits, I reserved the right to the same internal hissy fits I'd thrown when I was fourteen.

How did Alice put up with this barrage of self-importance on an everyday basis at the nonprofit she ran? Attentive and alert, she listened raptly to every multi-syllabic word. Even Rani, who was normally the most talkative of my sister's friends, sat next to me absolutely motionless, seemingly rapt. Of course, I'd probably learn to care too, if like them I were raking in a six-figure salary. "Tell her about your theories of how water access affects third-world development efforts," Alice suggested.

"It's fascinating, really." The biggest bore in the world cleared his throat. "The World Health Organization has identified eight Millennium Development Goals, including the eradication of poverty and hunger, promoting gender equality, and universal access to education, that can greatly be speeded by a worldwide approach to improving water and sanitation." Holy Mother of God, was Alice trying to *punish* me?

She might have been. I'd given her reason to, what with my feet-dragging for this particular dinner. When she'd announced that we'd be having special company for Saturday night's dinner, I immediately could tell from the offhand and too-casual way she'd tossed the news out there among the morning breakfast cereal and newspapers that it was a set-up. My suspicions weren't in the least abated when she'd gently suggested I borrow one of her better Lauren tunic sweaters—pink, no less—and slacks so I could, in her words, "make a good impression."

"What, I can't wear my overalls?" I'd retorted.

She'd given me one of her trademarked Alice Looks of Utter Superiority, shaken her head, and replied, "One might think your wit would have more of an edge, given the amount of time you spend among the classics."

I was brought back to present reality when, without warning, Walter leaned forward across the table and addressed me directly. "Did you know that every day, diarrheal diseases claim the lives of over five thousand people?"

"Golly. Do they?" I'd only half-eaten my individual molten chocolate cake, but after looking at its oozing brown center, I let my fork fall to the plate with a clatter and stood. "Maybe I should clean up."

I was already safely in the kitchen offloading my armful of dinner plates when Alice burst through the door and let it swing shut behind her. "Get back in there," she snarled.

"You're always saying I should do more cleaning around here." I plucked a whole black olive from what was left of the lasagna, leaning against the counter as I popped it into my mouth and savored the saltiness of it. "Sheesh."

"I brought home a perfectly nice, good-looking, intelligent . . ."

"Bore."

". . . *single* man for you, and I won't have you skulking in the kitchen like some kind of . . . some kind of . . ."

"Kitchen skulker?" When Alice glared at me in the way that only older sisters can, I sighed, slumped, and came very close to wiping my olive-y fingers on her Ralph Lauren slacks before I stopped myself. "Oh, come on, Alice. When he talks, all I hear is *blasé-blah-blah, blasé-blah-blah-blah.* And what's with trying to get me hitched again? I only signed my divorce papers last Friday! Are you that desperate to get me out of here?"

"You know perfectly well you are welcome to stay here for as long as you need." Alice looked back over her shoulder as if realizing she was staying longer in the kitchen than she'd intended, and called out, "Coffee's on the way, guys!" before stomping over to the fancy espresso maker that had more levers and buttons than a typical space shuttle. To me, she said in a lower voice, "I don't expect you to *marry* him. I don't think it would hurt you at all to get back on the horse, though. Circulate some. Meet some *nice* guys. Like Walter."

"I'm sure Walter Slezak is a nice guy."

"Yes, Walter Slezak, deceased star of stage and screen and star of Alfred Hitchcock's *Lifeboat,* as well as many other classics, was a nice guy. So is Walter Pleziak, the guy from my office who's been trying to get your attention all evening. What's wrong with him?

Is it his scar?" When I immediately looked blank and astonished, she shook her head. "Scratch that."

"He has a scar?" I asked, unable to help myself. I hadn't noticed.

Alice rubbed the center of her forehead the way that our mom had quite frequently done during our teen years. "Forget I mentioned that, please. I remembered too late about Bobby Gunn in high school."

"I did not dump Bobby Gunn because of his forehead scar!"

"You called him 'Scarface' behind his back." Alice had the memory that elephants consulted when they were feeling scatterbrained. "All right, let's level. Walter has the *tiniest* of scars. On his neck," she added, before I could ask. "It's from when he had an emergency tracheotomy. He . . ."

My eyes had flown wide open at that news. "Oh, my God!" When Alice's face grew prim and threatening, I hastened to reassure her. "No, I was just feeling sorry for him. He's so young and all." Was she buying it? Or could she tell that I was nearly reeling inside from a sudden vivid image of a sidewalk operation performed with a nail file and the tube of a ballpoint?

Apparently she bought it, because her expression became less pinched. "The least you could do is spend some time talking to him." Behind her, the espresso machine started to make its death-throes noises. Alice opened one of the narrow cupboards and pulled down her green cups so she could arrange them on a tray. "I'm not asking you to date the guy. Unless you wanted to. Stand up straight—don't slouch."

I pretended not to hear her advice on my posture. "I

told you yesterday, I'm going to the movies with Ethan from work at nine." I will be the first to admit that I'm not the world's best liar, but Alice was so busy adding sugar and spoons and creamer to the little Chinese tray that she didn't notice how unconvincing I was. "So I can't hang around all night listening to him talk about diarrhea."

She sighed, glanced at the coffee machine, and shook her head. "I've said it a thousand times, Becca. You don't know when a good guy is right in front of you."

"I knew Sean."

"Case in point." She backed out of the door with a significant raise to her eyebrows. "Talk to him!"

It was less a request than a command, but I stubbornly turned my back and began clattering dishes around in the sink while I ate the last bite of my cold lava cake. I hated when Alice lectured me; she made me feel like some kind of ungrateful brat who leeched off her bounty without contributing anything in return. Or maybe that's simply how I felt as the unexpected guest in Alice's spare room, in an apartment that had been much grander than anything Sean and I could ever have afforded together. That wench he'd shacked up with might have been a downgradesies in looks, but she'd certainly been a major upgradesies in income. Apparently it had been worth it.

Oh, this was stupid. Thinking about Sean and about my insignificant salary was only a psychological ploy on my own part to keep me from thinking about how nervous I was about my date. Not date; my assignation. My secret rendezvous. The upcoming meeting that had kept me jittery and twitchy all afternoon, and the thought of which had made sitting through serious-minded talk sheer torture. I'd kept telling myself I was looking forward to it, but I really wasn't. Yet I kind of was. Still, I wasn't. Lord, if I was this bad now, a good forty minutes before I was scheduled to go anywhere, what was I going to be when I went out?

I heard the door between the kitchen and dining room swing open behind me. Alice again, to check on the coffee. I was prepared to ignore her completely when I caught sight of a corduroy-clad arm placing dinner plates onto the tile counter. I whirled around and saw Walter standing there. The urge to run was strong. "Cleaning up?" he asked. I smiled, not saying anything, letting the colorful plastic scrubbie in my hand do the talking. Finally he cleared his throat and nodded at the sink. "You know, it's easier on the water treatment plants if you scrape the food from the plates into a waste container."

"Oh, my gosh. What was I thinking?" I smiled brightly, grabbed one of the plates he'd brought in moments before, and let a leftover second helping of lasagna and a chunk of bread fall into the open drain. Then, still cordial-appearing as all get out, I flipped on the garbage disposal until it digested them both.

Maybe it wasn't fair of me to be so outright hostile to Walter. I mean, I could see why Alice was trying to set me up with him. He was tall, for one thing—a good six-foot-three, and taller than I, which was something of a novelty. His hair was fair and straight and fell in a natural part down the middle of his head. He had a nice smile. His clothes were plain. When he spoke, it was with a gentle intelligence. Sure, it made him the world's biggest bore, but it was plain that Alice had picked him because in every way he was the exact opposite of my ex-husband. I was pretty sure that the only thing they had in common were penises and a genetic tendency to leave up the toilet seat after they peed. He could have stomped out of the room right then, but instead he crossed first his arms, then one ankle over the other, and studied me. "So Alice tells me you went to SUNY Binghamton." I nodded. "Good school."

"Thanks." Ordinary people at this point would have returned the favor by asking where he'd gone, but I was rusty enough at small talk that I didn't feel like giving it a go.

"Alice went to Penn, right?" he said, squinting at me.

"And then the Wharton School."

"Oh, yes. The Wharton School." He cleared his throat. "Supreme Court Justice William Brennan went there, I believe. And John Kendrick." When I shook my head, not comprehending, he explained. "Director of the Smithsonian." When still I didn't say anything, he turned his attention to the coffee machine. I wasn't touching the thing; as technologically inept as I was, Alice would have killed me if I'd twisted a knob wrong. Luckily, he seemed to know what he was doing. He pulled a lever and let loose a stream of steaming jet-black liquid into one of the little cups Alice had set out, and put it onto the tray. The aroma of freshly-steeped beans filled the room. "And Donald Trump. You know him, right?"

"I don't watch *The Apprentice*, if that's what you

mean," I said. I knew I should make a move to help him, but I was still mad enough at Alice for trying to fix me up that I couldn't. I really couldn't.

"And she says you studied literature? You like to read?"

Refreshing as it was to have someone ask the question without giving it the same inflection most people would use in the sentence, "You like to pick your nose?" I wasn't moved. "I work in an antiquarian bookstore. My salary's laughable, but my liberal arts degree makes me nigh on unemployable elsewhere. I signed my divorce papers a week ago yesterday. Ain't I a catch?"

There. He knew the deal now, no matter what kind of spin Alice had put on my situation for him. "Oh," he finally said, pulling at his collar with discomfort. "But salary's not an indicator of worth, really. Right?"

"It would be to Donald Tru . . ." I started to say. Then I saw it. When Walter had tugged at his neckline, he'd pulled his sweater vest low enough that his shirt collar parted. The tracheotomy scar Alice had mentioned was nothing more than a fingertip-deep indentation between his collarbones, so undistinguished that I wouldn't have noticed it unless Alice had said something about it.

But she had. And now all I could do was stare at it with absolute fascination as it bobbed up and down while he talked. "I mean, gosh. If that was true, there'd be a lot of worthless people out there." I tried not to ogle. I really did. It was so difficult, though, to tear my eyes away from the sight of that tiniest of concavities at the base of his neck. Every time he spoke, it bobbed up and down between the edges of his collar, mesmerizing me. "My mother stayed at home all her life, but I'd certainly hesitate to call her worthless. Don't you think?"

I cleared my throat faintly, trying to will myself to look anywhere other than his neck. If I looked him in the eye, though, he'd know immediately what I'd been staring at. "Worthless," I echoed, trying to unfocus my eyes and appear merely vague.

"It seems to me you have a lot going for you. You've got an interesting job, you live in one of the most vibrant cities in the whole world, you've got a fantastic sister—everybody raves about her at the office, you know." Vague was good. I could do vague. Spatula in hand, I let my eyes drift away while he spoke, uncomfortably aware that I could still see the mark of his tracheotomy leaping up and down with every syllable. "She's got a lot of heart. I bet you and she have a special connection."

"Mmm, sure." I cleared my throat again and took a deep breath. I felt better. I had my equilibrium back.

He leaned against the counter, arranging the full coffee cups on the tray. "Or, I don't know. I never had an older brother or sister. Maybe she's a pain in the neck."

"Neck!" I squeaked, my sangfroid dashed to pieces. My eyes snapped back into focus where they weren't supposed to be. Hastily I jerked them upward, met his confused smile, wrenched my head toward the dining room, and tried to keep it cool. "I mean, pain in the neck!" Whimpering escaped my lips. I tried to make it sound like laughter. I must have sounded like a lunatic.

Even as I thought it, I could hear Alice's voice in my head: *Oh, now you care what he thinks of you?* When the apartment doorbell rang, I nearly jumped out of my skin. "I'll get it!" I yelled, much too loudly. "You!" I added to Walter. "Take the coffee in! The people need coffee!"

My face flamed hot as the java itself, but I created my own breeze by rushing down the little hallway, away from the kitchen and the embarrassing scene I'd just made. That bell was enough to make me believe in the power of prayer. By the time I grabbed the handle, I had my composure back once again. "Yes?" I asked, opening the door.

"Hey." A.J.'s hand rested against the doorjamb. A vision of gym-built muscles sheathed in an expensive leather jacket and a black silk shirt, he graced me with a slow, lazy smile. "You ready?"

God hated me. God hated me for thinking mean things about Walter's neck. I slammed shut the door, stared at the heavens (or more accurately, stared at the smoke detector in the ceiling with its little blinking light), and groaned, "Why? Oh, why?"

"Who is it?" From a distance I heard the sound of my sister pushing her chair away from the dining room table. I wasn't having any of that. I'd already lied to Alice about where I was going that evening, and I wasn't taking a chance on blowing my cover. If any of my friends found out that I was actually going out with A.J. . . . well, let's just say I'd rather be dead.

Yes, it was that bad.

I willed myself to sound calm. "Nothing!" I said, keeping my voice light. "I've got it. Be right there." Before the pretty monkey in leather outside could ring the bell again, I whipped open the door. He was exactly where I had left him. "What are you doing!" I stage-whispered, shocked. "You weren't supposed to come up here! You were supposed to meet me down in the lobby! You weren't supposed to come up here!" I knew I was repeating myself, but I couldn't help it. "You were supposed to meet me . . ."

"Down in the lobby?" A.J. shrugged, then craned his neck so he could look past me into the apartment. There wasn't much to see beyond the narrow hallway that led to the living area in the back, but I could see him taking in the photographs on the wall, the flowers on the table nearby, and the collection of boots, mostly mine, next to the mat. "I got here early. Shoot me."

I gave him a narrow-eyed look intended to warn him not to tempt me. "It's only a little after eight-thirty!" Did he not know how to tell time? "I didn't want you coming up here! How did you get past the security door? My sister's throwing a dinner party! There are people here!" People who might see him and draw some rather unsavory conclusions about me, I feared. "I'm not ready! You're early!"

I had a dozen reasons I didn't want him at the door right then, but none of them seemed to convince him to step away. "Don't have a cow. So I got here a little early. I sweet-talked one of your neighbors into letting me in. No big deal." Fantastic. The sister I theoretically loved dearly was living in a building where the stupid residents were letting in A.J.'s sort willy-nilly. Of course, I was the one who'd lost the bet and agreed to go out with him as his wingman, so maybe I was the stupid one. While I stalled, A.J. raised his eyebrows in perfect twin arches, waiting for me to do something. "So, do you want to get going now?"

"No!" The resentment I felt at his question was almost immediately squelched when I remembered exactly what a fantastic shindig was waiting for me in the dining room. Coffee and more talk about world water policies, or drinks and an evening's worth of secret amusement at the expense of *Details* magazine's modern-day answer to the old-fashioned court jester? Hmmm. "Give me five minutes," I said, before shutting the door in his face again.

One breakneck hair-brushing, face touch-up, and quick-change later and I was ready to go. Clutch under my arm, I took a few steps down the hallway so that I could be heard when I called out, "I'm going out to meet Ethan!" Then I whirled around and tiptoed toward the front door, feeling both giddy and guilty, like the time in high school when I told my parents I was going to my friend Annalise's house to study when in reality I was rocking out at a Hootie and the Blowfish concert I wasn't supposed to be attending on a weeknight. Hootie and the Blowfish: good lord. What more proof did I need of how pedestrian a life I'd led, even then? I called over my shoulder, "I'll be back when I get back!"

"Will you, now?" Where the kitchen doorway met the front hall stood Alice, carrying a sugar bowl and a cup of coffee nearly as bitter as the expression on her face. She looked me up and down, her glance lingering especially over the region of my chest. I already felt self-conscious about showing more skin than usual—a lot more skin than usual—but her stare made me want to grab one of my typical late-winter cardigans, wrap it around my boobs, and plunge my hands deep into the pockets before shuffling off to old age and obscurity. "Where is it you're going exactly?" she asked in an icy tone that seemed to imply the answer had to be either *To my new job at the whorehouse!* or *To hell!*

"Is there anything wrong with dressing up a little? It's your outfit," I told her, squelching an impulse to fly out the front door while she stood there and A.J. lurked outside. "Like I said, we're going to the movies. I'll be home by two, Mom."

"You know, I was hoping we could have a nice evening at home tonight, with this dinner party. I'm trying very hard to look out for you." Alice sighed, and for a split-second I sympathized. It couldn't be easy, having a smart-ass little sister who rummaged through her wardrobe for almost every occasion and couldn't be trusted with blind dates.

"And I appreciate it," I assured her, trying not to sound as brusque. Starting an argument wasn't going to get me out the door quickly. "I know you only want the best for me." When she gave me a suspicious look, I added, "Honestly! I know I've been dragging my heels over . . . Walter." I could barely bring myself to say the guy's name, and when I did, it was accompanied by an involuntary gulp. "Maybe I'll eventually be ready for that kind of thing. But for now, I'm just keeping it casual. Okay?" This was working. "I love you, Al."

Something I'd said must have mollified her, because her face stopped looking like a flint in search of tinder and softened. She even kind of smiled at me while her lips worked to find words to respond. Finally, we were going to have one of those all-too-rare sisterly moments I'd heard about from friends and had seen in Hallmark TV commercials. I readied myself for a tear. "Is that really one of my dresses?" she finally said, unconvinced. "What was I *thinking?*"

So much for tears. "I won't spill on it," I promised. "Popcorn, I mean. So greasy." I was babbling.

She leaned back and looked at me the way my mom had from time to time, upon realizing I wasn't such a little girl anymore. "Are you interested in this Ethan guy?"

I furrowed my eyebrows, annoyed. "No! He's interest-*ing*, but I'm not interest-*ed*. We're just friends. Friend-time is good. Friend-time helps me keep my mind off things."

"That's just a highly unusual dress for anyone to wear for friend-time, that's all." Was she getting suspicious? I couldn't afford to have her following me out the door. I was pretty sure I was too old to be grounded at this point, but if Alice saw A. J. lurking without, ready to escort me to the sleaziest lounges in town, there was no telling how she'd react. "Who was at the door?"

The abrupt change of topic made my palms sweat. She did suspect. She had to. Why else would she ask that question? "Oh, just some solicitor. I turned him away."

"In this building?" she asked, incredulous.

"I think someone must have let him slip past the security door."

"Weird," she decreed. I shrugged, hoping the moment might pass.

"Do you need any help?" I heard Rani call, from the direction of the dining room.

The urge to be a good hostess overrode any skepticism she might have had. Alice looked at both her cooling coffee and the sugar bowl in her other hand and sidled past me. "Have a good time," she called out, and then added to her guests, "Coming!"

Thank goodness. I counted to ten while I threw on one of Alice's leather jackets, then opened the door. "Sorry," I told A. J.

He had been leaning against the wall opposite, one leg crossed over the other at the ankle, hands dangling by his side in a James Dean-a-licious pose. The only thing missing was the cigarette and the hair grease. "Oh, my God," he said, curling his lip.

"What?"

He looked me up and down, apparently aghast. "What is that?" The distress in his voice was real.

"What?"

"That!" he said, gesturing at my breasts. I tried to pull the jacket over them, but before I could get it buttoned, he'd wrenched back the lapels and exposed the rest of my outfit. "All of that!"

I didn't understand. "I thought we were going out," I stammered. "Isn't this the kind of thing . . . ?" Did I look bad? Had my status as an 8 plummeted?

He dropped the jacket lapels and took a step back. "*I'm* going out. Apparently *you* have been asked to shoot the 'My Humps' video with the Black-Eyed Peas. Get changed."

Still confused, I asked, "Don't you like it?"

"I'd like it fine if you were some bimbo I was trying to use The Method on. Wouldn't even have to take you up the Yes Ladder in those clothes. You're one big checkered flag, girl! If a guy saw you in that, he'd just grab you by the wrist and walk you out the door to your slutmobile." I stared at him in the dim light of the hallway, wondering if there was a roundabout compliment in there, somewhere. "Go get changed!"

"Into what?"

He waved his hand, shooing me. "What you had on before was good."

"But that's so boring."

"Classy is what it was," he admonished. "That was an outfit with real taste. Go change back."

"I—!"

"You're my wingman, not my ho." Apparently that was to be the final word on the subject.

I sighed. "Fine. I'll change." A.J. shook his head, obviously disappointed in me before our night out had even begun. I wasn't relishing the thought of creeping back into that apartment again, but apparently I didn't have a choice. "I thought I looked nice. Different."

"Nuh-uh," he said, pointing at the door. "Sheesh. I can't believe that sister of yours let you out of the house in that."

I glared at him as I slipped back inside. Maybe the two of them were in collusion after all.

FIVE

Apparently the Essex Pub was short-staffed, because the line in which I'd waited an eternity to buy a drink had been five people deep by three people across when I'd joined it. Not that I'd minded spending the last ten minutes with a mean-looking German guy on my right, whose spiky hair, horn-rimmed glasses, and nose piercing weren't half as off-putting as his eye-watering case of B.O. Nor did I mind on my left the perfectly ginormous woman with a platinum blond wig and a glittering powder blue jumpsuit to which someone—a blind someone with lots of time on her hands and very little in the way of taste—had taken a Bedazzler. I didn't even care when, over the third Aerosmith track in a row to play on the jukebox, I had to yell out, "Can I get a vodka and cranberry?" to the bartender in order to make myself heard. Or that he stared at me as if I were a nun in full habit who'd ordered a whole milk, straight up, no chaser.

No, what I resented was that before the scrawny, tattooed scrap of a bartender had even turned away to look for the Absolut, A.J. yanked me away from the bar and out into the middle of the congested room. "What was that all about?" he wanted to know.

I didn't understand why he was so ticked off. It wasn't as if I'd been skulking in a corner, scowl plastered on my lips. I hadn't even complained about the clientele of this particular spot. Yet. "You were in the men's room," I replied, snatching back my upper arm. "Do you have any idea how long I waited in line to get a drink?"

His head tilted to one side as he regarded me with the same exaggerated sympathy an exasperated dad might show toward his exceptionally slow child. "Lesson number one," he said, "never buy your own drinks."

I wasn't about to let him clutch my upper arm again, not when he wore flashy gold rings on both his thumb and forefinger that pinched when he'd grabbed me. Exactly where did bad taste end and sheer bling begin? I wasn't sure. I did go so far as to let him hold the tip of my elbow and guide me away from the crowded bar in the direction of a tall table flanked by waist-high stools in the room's center. It was cluttered with several beer bottles and a tin container of Jiffy Pop, slimy with salt and empty save for a handful of unpopped kernels and a cigarette butt that, by law, shouldn't have been there. "Why don't we buy our own drinks?"

"Not *we,* you dope," he said without any real malice. "You. You, Rebecca. You, a pretty lady." When I showed reluctance to understand, he shook his head but still held out the stool for me to sit. "You were one of those college girls, weren't you? Didn't you ever go out?"

"Of course I went out!" I protested. The stool was still warm. The Essex's clientele seemed to consist sheerly of whoever could drag themselves out of their Lower East Side apartments and down the stairs into the most obscure neighborhood bar ever to have been opened beneath a convenience store. Which evidently meant a bunch of poor-looking students, a surprising number of people who could have been part of a biker gang, a bunch of bored-looking Goths who couldn't afford the train fair to Williamsburg, and quite a few confirmed members of the Hair Club for Men. Considering that, I wasn't sure I wanted to think about who'd sat on the stool before me. "I went out all the time! I was kind of a party girl."

"Kind of a party girl, huh?"

"Yeah!" I asserted, not really enjoying the skepticism I saw in his eyes. "You might say that. A party girl."

Like his sister, A.J. had big, wide, heavy-lidded eyes that gazed at me half-closed. He looked almost asleep, though I could tell by his posture how alert he really was. "Tell me about the parties you went to, party girl."

"Well, I . . . I . . . well . . ." He'd flustered me. I hadn't expected him to call my bluff. I could have been a party girl if I'd wanted to! It's not as if it would take any particular skill to chug down beer, jerk around to old George Clinton hits, pretend that my white girl feet had rhythm, and spend the wee hours of the morning clutching the toilet rim and reeking regret. I said the first thing that came to my mind, which unfortunately was, "Once the Honors English Program had a Michel Foucault masquerade party where we . . ."

"Never mind," he said, cutting me off immediately and looking around the room. "Sorry I asked."

"You don't even know who Michel Foucault is!" I pointed out. It was a bit of a hollow triumph.

"Unless she's stacked, I don't really give a rip." He grabbed his face with one hand and swiped it in the direction of his chin, as if suddenly realizing he was stuck for the evening with a social retard. Then he shook his head.

I'd been thinking about retorting back, but I feared he'd give up on me if I put up too much resistance. And then where would I be? Sitting back at home across from my well-meaning sister and her achingly dull attempts at trying to find me a suitable man, that's where. So pathetic was my impulse to kiss and make up that I'm afraid I wanted to leap all over him like a puppy dog left alone at home all day. Instead, I took a deep breath, smiled, and said, "So, I don't buy my own drinks, right?" He nodded. Was it bad that I found him both incredibly hot and yet repulsive at the same time? Was that even normal? "Then can you get me my vodka and cranberry?"

He tilted his head again. Not a good sign. "No," he finally said, screwing up his face as if pained.

"Then why couldn't I buy my own?"

"I can see we're going to have to start at the very beginning."

"A very good place to start," I added. When his expression remained blank, I tried to jump-start his brain. Assuming he had one, of course. "Oh, come on.

Rodgers and Hammerstein? Julie Andrews? Christopher Plummer? The lonely goatherd? Nazis? None of it's ringing a bell?"

A.J. looked down at his chest, decided his shirt was only showing off 90 percent of the ripples and contours of his torso, and reached down to tuck it in more tightly so the other 10 percent could have a chance. "I've seen *The Sound of Music*, thanks. I rooted for the baroness instead of the nun. The reason I'm not buying you a drink is because you're a chick. One of these other guys will take care of it for you."

When he gestured at the crowd milling around the room, some of them vaguely nodding their heads to the power pop blaring from the CD jukebox, I wanted to run far, far away from the Essex and everyone who'd marched their unwashed bodies through the front door. "You've got to be kidding!" I gasped.

"What's wrong?"

Oh, I knew what he was implying, with that antagonistic blandness oozing from every pore. "You know, I don't care if you think I'm a snob. Maybe I *am* a snob. But these people . . ." Next to us, a pair of boys in their mid-twenties walked by. One of them wore tattered, dirty kitchen-line pants, a filthy beret, and, despite the March chill, a sleeveless T-shirt spattered with brown paint; the other sported heavy plastic glasses so impossibly large and outdated that he'd either snatched them from the shelves of the Salvation Army or else spent hours selecting them from the Geeks-R-Us Trendy Designer catalog, several eyebrow piercings, and a long beard that covered his chin and ended between his nipples. I stopped speaking until they'd passed. A.J. raised his eyebrows. "The guys are . . . A.J., if Sarah were here, she and I would right now be playing a fierce round of 'Hipster or Homeless?' and I'm honestly not sure if we'd have any way of figuring out which one of us was right. Look at that guy." I nodded toward a burly specimen exiting the men's room, who was performing in public the final hitch of his pants that he should have completed in the privacy of the washroom.

A.J. turned on his stool, his heavy forearm still resting on the table between us. He looked the guy up and down, taking in the mullet (complete with rat-tail hanging down the back), the completely vinyl trucker cap, the untrimmed crumb-collector that served as a mustache. He shrugged, not seeming to notice the half-buttoned fly of the guy's jeans or the fact that . . . I gulped . . . he was missing two joints of one ring finger. "What about him?" He was being willfully uncooperative.

"He's wearing a sweatshirt that says he's captain of the U.S. Muff-Diving Team."

A.J. pretended ignorance. "Is that an Olympic sport now? Sit up straight."

"Who are you all of a sudden, my sister?" I asked, annoyed at being chided. "If you think I'm going to let some guy like that buy me a drink . . ." I shook my head and began to rise from the table. This wasn't going anywhere. Obviously I'd been trotted out in my conservative uptown duds—pink, no less!—so I could be humiliated and laughed at. Classic fish-out-of-water material, cleverly choreographed.

Right on cue, a little barmaid appeared by my side,

tray in hand. The only reason I could tell she worked at the Essex was that she wore a dark green apron around her waist and a pen buried in the dyed-red corkscrews she called hair. "Drink for ya, honey," she said.

I wanted to marvel at how anyone could manage to snap her chewing gum so loudly and so frequently when she'd spoken less than a half-dozen syllables in all. Instead, though, all I could do was stare in horror as she lifted a tumbler from the cork-lined tray and set it on the table. The vodka and cranberry left an oval-shaped trail of moisture when she pushed it in my direction. "Who?" I coughed out. Then, more to the point, "Why?"

A.J. was no help. In fact, I was sure that the coughing fit he was enjoying at the moment was little more than a ruse to conceal his amusement at my ordeal. "Want I should say something back for you, hon?" asked the barmaid, still clacking away. My mouth worked for a few silent seconds but nothing came out. Then I had the pleasure of having the woman with the gum-snapping tonsils, the springy curls of near-Bozo proportions, and the general stench of an ashtray hosed down with bourbon look at me in my pink classic Lauren tunic sweater and say in stern tones, "A thank-you is the usual."

"Fine," I managed to gabble out. "Tell him I said thank you. Wait. Who—?" My head jerked in every direction as I stared speculatively first at Eyebrow Piercings Guy, then at Dirty Old Man in a Dirty Old Trenchcoat sitting at a table nearby, then at Skanky White Guy With Rasta Dreads sucking down Coronas by the jukebox, and finally at Six-Foot-Five Hell's Angel in Leather Chaps glowering in our general direction. At last she tapped me on the forearm and pointed over my shoulder in the direction of the Essex's door. A guy stood by himself against the wall, nervously trying to blend in between a glass case of what looked like fly-specked bowling trophies and a mangy moose head adorned with earmuffs, Ray-Bans, and an oversize meerschaum. He looked my way, then hastily turned his head, let his long, shaggy hair fall into his face, and pretended he hadn't just met my eyes. The kid couldn't be any more than twenty-five or twenty-six. He hadn't shaved in a week, and oversized hip-hop clothes hung like tenting from his painfully thin frame. "Holy-moley."

I guess that reaction was enough to pass for enthusiasm in the Essex, where not ten feet away from where I shuddered to myself, a trashed blonde barely able to walk was passing out in the Dirty Old Man in a Dirty Old Trenchcoat's lap head first, much to the amusement of everyone in the immediate vicinity. Minus one, if you included me. The waitress stepped away from the table, waved wildly at my would-be swain, and gave him a thumbs-up so broad that everyone in the bar had to have seen it. "A.J., what the hell am I going to do now?" I asked, turning back to the table and hoping for some kind of constructive, helpful comment that would put everything into perspective.

Save for the vodka and cranberry, my table was empty. A.J. was nowhere to be seen.

"That *bastard!*" I hissed through my teeth, furious at having been deserted during combat. Somehow he'd managed to find a way to sneak away when I'd needed him most. I couldn't see him anywhere. Even with my considerable height on an already-lofty perch, I couldn't see his oily, shiny head in the crowd. Good thing, too, because at the moment I wanted to fling my glass at it.

Did I dare look over my shoulder at my hip-hop boy's silhouette again? Apparently I did, though I was painfully aware of how much I must have looked like Bambi in the monster-truck headlights when I buried my nose in designer pink wool and peeked. He wasn't by the bowling trophies any longer. Which could mean a couple of things. One, that he'd totally been turned off by my disagreeable reaction to his generosity and left. Which was good, right? Only not really, because it meant that he'd probably left believing me a total bitch. Which I wasn't! Or two, it could mean that he was on the move. As in, walking closer and closer to me by the second. He even could be standing next to me, ready to put his hand on my shoulder.

That was enough to make me flinch, but a quick check revealed no stalkers to my immediate left or right. I was just being stupid. Again. I was letting the grungy atmosphere of this dive get to me in a way that it wouldn't if I'd stumbled in for a quick phone call after work, or if I'd agreed to meet friends here for a quick burger before a show. For years I'd walked around a married woman, Mrs. Sean Mulvaney, letting that status act as some kind of invisible force-field that kept the world at bay. I hadn't even noticed that shield until it was gone. Every time I went out now as a certified single, I felt more naked and vulnerable than before. Mind over paranoia. That's all it would take.

I took a moment to inhale a few deep breaths of the

Jiffy Pop–and-beer-infused air and composed myself. A.J. would be back. Like a bad credit report, he popped up when you least wanted. And as for my Wonder Bread P. Diddy—well, I'd probably scared him away. All I had to do was sit still until A.J. got bored enough with his silly schoolboy prank. Or then again, maybe not even that. I'd held up my part of my devil's pact by accompanying the guy here tonight; if I wanted, all I had to do was stand up, walk out the front door, and hail a cab. Then I could speed off somewhere where the leather seats hadn't been repaired with duct tape and the music was more likely to be soothing and VH1-y than to send me to my otolaryngologist for emergency treatment. That, in fact, was exactly what I was going to do. I grabbed my bag, stood up, and at the very last moment grabbed the vodka and cranberry from the scarred tabletop, intending to slug it down as fortification before making my bold move.

I'd raised the glass halfway to my mouth when I saw him, standing not ten feet away. My beau with the baggy streetwear had been concealed behind my friend with the powder-blue jumpsuit and supersized blond wig—not a difficult feat, since she was more than three times his size. He'd stepped out from the woman's considerable shadow, however, and was now loping toward me, his enormous athletic shoes almost a blinding white in the pub's darkness. I froze in place, a pink statue clutching a girlie beverage. "Hope the cocktail's okay." His voice was surprisingly thin and reedy; he was a bleating little lamb with a name-brand baggy track suit and a buzzed head. "I don't know what girls like you drink." As an afterthought, he added, "My ma likes the hard stuff. Damn, you're really tall."

"Well . . ." The only thing making me speak was a dignified kind of propriety. This kid, though he was only four or five years younger than me, was already comparing me to his *mother*. I wanted to run and hide. My shoulders began caving in; only the thought of my sister's voice ordering me to stand up straight brought them back into place. I swallowed. "I guess I am. Thank you. For the drink," I said, mindful of the barmaid's advice. The two of us stared at each other for a minute, both of us looking like frightened deer, alert and wary. Not that I'd actually ever seen a deer on the island of Manhattan. But I could imagine. "Maybe I should . . ."

At the same time I began making my move to go, he blurted, "You don't have to drink it if you don't want it. I just made a guess at what you liked. And you looked like a vodka and cranberry woman."

Inwardly, I groaned. What other choice did I have at that point than to guzzle down a mouthful of the stuff? I'd already been raising it to my lips; to blithely say "Okey-dokey, then!" and put it back down on the table would have been another direct insult. "Mmmm," I said, licking my lips from the slightly sticky drink. "Thanks again."

He stared at me with something approaching disbelief before saying, "You aren't a regular here, are you? I can tell." I shook my head. "You got a quality." When I pressed my lips together, unsure of how to take that compliment, he held out his arms. "Aw, come on. You gotta know it. You've got kind of a high-class, educated thing going on. I mean, that's why the vodka and cranberry. This is a beer and Munchos kind of place. I bet you read a lot."

I'd been about to mention my work, except for my instinctive sense that letting a stranger know where I and my snatchable purse and credit cards spent their time wasn't a good idea. "Yeah," I said instead. "You might say that."

"So . . ." While he'd talked, his eyes had been darting here and there, checking out the other bar patrons, checking out invisible dust on the floor. Only occasionally had he dared to look me square in the face. After that one syllable, he hung his head and stared directly into my eyes. "Maybe we could talk a little? Or are you heading out?"

A half-dozen scenarios played out in my head, like movies on a rack of televisions at the local electronics store. In one of them, obviously directed by Quentin Tarantino, my heels tapped out of the Essex and down the sidewalk and into an alley, where I was chased and eventually attacked by my stalker and left in a pool of blood. In the Sofia Coppola version, the pair of us separated and never saw each other again, instead leading tasteful lives of ennui set against a classic rock soundtrack. Then there was the Alfred Hitchcock screenplay, in which I endured a brief and polite conversation with the guy, only to find him popping up at the most unexpected places in the days following, with each materialization more malevolent than the last. I didn't like *any* of these movies. "Sure," I said, suppressing the sigh welling in my lungs and sitting my pink-clad hiney back onto the stool. I took another swig of the drink. I was going to need it.

I'd had some pretty awkward dates in my life, particularly during the college years, when Alice had used me as a bargaining chip time and time again. *Oh, sure, my sister would love to meet your cousin/brother/ roommate/T.A.! No problem! She'd love to sit across from him staring glumly while you and I enjoy sparkling conversation and then a tussle in the econ grad student lounge while they pick their noses in the vending machine lounge!* "I'm Randy," said the boy, avoiding my eyes again.

"Rebecca," I said, before cursing myself and wishing I'd thought to use a fake name like Porphyria.

"Oh, cool. Like De Mornay. Or . . ."

He seemed so absorbed in the challenge of finding another namesake that I decided to help him out. "Rebecca Pidgeon?"

"Is that like, a cartoon or something?"

"No, she's an actress. She's married to David Mamet. The playwright." Nothing. Not a spark of recognition. "Or there's *Rebecca*, the novel. By Daphne du Maurier." I shut my mouth. I was coming off all high-falutin' and bookish. If this were a movie, it would be one of those avant-garde exercises in tedium by Andy Warhol in which an unmoving camera focused on a dead flower for eight hours.

I swallowed, and in the silence that followed wondered how much conversation a vodka cocktail actually bought. Mentally I'd calculated that I was doomed to sit there for at least three more minutes until I could make a clean getaway, when out of the blue my friend Randy said, "Do you like fortune-telling?"

If I hadn't established myself as a stuffy old fossil moments before, what came out of my mouth next sealed the deal. "I beg your pardon?"

"Fortune-telling. Tarot cards. I learned them at art school a coupla years ago. Great, it'll be fun. Hang on." From his pocket he retrieved a deck of cards, worn around the edges and slightly grubby. While he undid the thick rubber band holding it together, he grinned at me and said, "You know the Tarot?"

I leaned forward and watched him shuffle the deck around a bit. "Well, I know what it is."

"Here. Mix 'em up some." His fingertips grazed my palm as he handed me the deck. I noticed how well-groomed his nails were. "Go on. It'll put your personal touch on them."

"All right." I riffled through the cards a few times, playing along, though not really involved. After a minute, I handed them back without a word.

"Mmmm." He cut the deck, then moved my glass aside so he could lay out the top three cards from the deck. "You ready?"

"Sure." At least he'd thought up a diversion to make the next couple of obligatory moments pass. After he was done, I could get up and leave, as I'd originally intended. No one really seemed to be thrown by the fact that he'd begun his own Psychic Friends Network in our little corner of the room.

"Okay, this first card is like, your present situation. What's going on in your life." He flipped it over to reveal a blond-haired fellow walking along a road, his worldly possession in a little bag tied to the end of a stick. "It's The Fool." That was me, all right. A fool for coming out with A. J. "That's a good card. It means, like, new beginnings. You've just started out on a journey. It's like, leaving everything that's disappointed you and walking down a new path, hoping you'll find something better. Hey, you have, haven't you?"

Was the kid psychic? It took me a moment or two to realize he must have seen the astonishment on my face at his interpretation. "Kind of," I said in a small voice that was nearly drowned out by bar babble, trying to sound casual about it. "In a way. It's a little thing." An affair, soul-deadening arguments, and an earth-shattering divorce that left me basically without a home of my own. A little thing like that. I had to admit that I was hooked, though. "Is that all it says?"

His head bounced from side to side as he considered. "It's a good thing to have. It could mean trying new stuff, making a new friend. . . ." He let loose with a genuine smile, shy and experimental. "Okay, this next card is about what's going to happen to you soon." Randy flipped over the card with his pale-skinned fingers, revealing a dapper medieval fellow with a fancy hat leaning over at the waist, a jewel-studded golden goblet in his outstretched hand. "Cool. The Page of Cups. He's kind of the Fool's . . . hmmmm."

"Wingman?" I popped my mouth shut. I really needed to think before I opened it.

"What? Yeah, kind of, in a way," he said. "They're buddies. The Page of Cups is a little like Cupid. He's saying, like, romance is on the way. He's kind of saying that it's okay to let go and enjoy yourself once in a while. Because the right guy's coming along real soon, if he hasn't already."

Interesting. I studied the Page in his dandified, courtly costume, all bright colors and fine silk. "You can tell all that just from a card? You learned this in art school?"

"Yeah. I came to New York to be a painter," he said, riffling through the deck in his hands. "Went to school for it, worked in a studio for a while . . . it's a tough field to break into, I've gotta tell ya."

I took another swig of the drink he'd bought me. "What kind of painting?"

"I do this . . . commercial art. It's kind of like, street art, graffiti, you know, but these days I mostly do these big paintings on the sides of buildings, out in the neighborhoods. The Bronx, sometimes Brooklyn. Kinda different. I did one for the PSP a couple of weeks ago. That's a game machine." He mimed pressing buttons on a handheld.

Wow. I hadn't expected to find myself actually interested in what the guy had to say. "That's fantastic," I said, leaning forward so I could hear better. "I mean, so many people never really get paid for doing something that excites them."

He shrugged modestly. "Anyway. Want to see what your last card is?"

"Sure!" I wanted to find out, too. Did I believe in the kinds of readings he was giving? Not really, but I'd always enjoyed watching people working up an enthusiasm over something they were good at. During the last year of our marriage, Sean used to whip himself into a frenzy over Sudoku, and though I'd never really evinced any interest in that kind of puzzle, it used to fascinate me to hear him talking about it. Or to watch him. His pencil used to fly over the page, making marks here and there as he filled up the little grids with numbers.

Of course, now I realized he was probably so absorbed with Sudoku because it was easier than pretending to still be in love with in me.

That was in the past, though. Randy picked up the last card in his hand and said, before turning it face-up, "This last one's all about where you'll be farther on down the road. The Nine of Cups." On the card lying on the table, a slightly pudgy, jolly-looking gentleman sat on a chair, surrounded by more of the golden goblets. His arms were crossed; a vaguely smug smirk rested on his lips. "Hey," said Randy, looking me in the eye. "Another good card. Looks like you've got some luck coming."

"It's about time," I muttered softly enough that he couldn't hear it. When he raised his eyebrows, I shook my head. "Nothing."

He tapped the self-satisfied man with his fingernail. "This guy's happy because everything goes his way. He's gotten over all the hurdles and made a success out of things. So what's gonna happen to you is that all these problems you might have had are going to be way in the past, and one way or another, you're gonna be satisfied about what's coming down the road for you." He traced an arc where the cups surrounded the man. "Prosperity. Love. It's all coming." With deft hands, he collected the cards, shuffled the strays in with the rest of the deck, and then started to wrap it up in the rubber band. "So I don't know you very well, but I'm kind of guessing it's not gonna suck to be you real soon."

Once again, he grinned. This time, it was less tentative. Sunnier. His teeth were slightly crooked, but they were white and clean and cared-for. You know, despite the shaggy hair and the voluminous clothes, Randy actually wasn't that bad-looking a guy at all. It was flattering that a younger guy might find me attractive. An artist, even. I had a quick vision of him asking me to model for him, but I discarded that notion when I remembered that his subjects ended up on the sides of brick buildings in the Bronx. Yet he was a nice guy, and I felt moved to say something to show him how grateful I was that he hadn't turned out to be an utter creep. "You have a great smile." He flushed furiously and tried to wave off the compliment. "No, seriously, you do. It shows who you are as a person."

"You, too," he said, flashing me one of his exploratory glances. "I mean, you can tell a lot about a person by the way they smile, can't you? When you deal with these corporate types, you can tell they've got these painted-on smiles like the Blue Meanies. They look like smiles, but they're not real smiles. Not by a long shot. You've got a real smile." He seemed to feel he'd gone a little too far, because he cleared his throat and changed tacks. "You know the Blue Meanies?"

I hadn't minded the compliment. Not at all. "From *Yellow Submarine*? Well, sure. Drawn by . . . don't tell me." I had the name on the tip of my tongue. "Max. Peter Max!"

"It was kind of in Max's style, yeah, but he didn't

draw them. Hey, you know stuff about art," he marveled, cocking his head. "That's amazing. Most chicks can't tell Chagall from Chanel. You must've taken some classes in college, right? Oh, man, you're probably like, this amazingly famous art gallery owner and you think I'm schmoozing you for a show or something. If you are, I'll just melt into a little puddle on the floor. You can step in me if you want." He buried his face in his hands and winced. "You are. I can tell. I'm going to ask the bartender for a Draino mixer."

"No!" I said, grinning at the melodrama taking place across from me. "I'm not a famous anybody. Just someone who took Art History One-Oh-One and whose mom was a Beatles fan from way back." When he peeked out from behind his hands, hopeful again, I couldn't help but laugh. "Seriously. I don't know anything about art."

"Well, I can teach you." We both paused at that. Though I recognized the sentence as the statement of interest it blatantly was, I didn't really mind so much; not now, anyway. He, in the meantime, stared at me frankly. I didn't mind that, either. Finally he nodded in the direction of my almost-empty glass. "Let me get you another drink."

"I—" I'd been about to tell him that I shouldn't, that I'd really only intended to have one and be on my way. The interior of the Essex wasn't quite as frightening now, though, as when I'd walked in. No longer was I in a bar filled with bikers and drug pushers and ax murderers. I was simply visiting a slightly grungy neighborhood dive, mingling with the artists and blue-collar workers and all the regular people I met every day when I went to restaurants and shops. I could stay a little longer. "You know what?" I told Randy. "I'll take you up on that."

"Great." He smiled at me and made a move to stand up. "I'll be right back. Don't run away or anything."

"And . . . *scene!*" said A.J., popping up at the table between us. And I do mean, popping up. It was as if he'd been crouching below table level and had sprung to his feet on cue. His shirt, I noticed, had fallen open by another button, clearly revealing the center of his overdeveloped pectorals. "Excellent work, bro. Hey, you're an amateur still, but you're making it work for you. That's what counts." He grabbed Randy's hand and began pumping it up and down. The rest of the poor kid's arm flapped like rubber.

"Where the hell have you *been?*" All the annoyance I'd felt earlier came rushing back at the sight of that oily mass of muscles and pomade. "And what is *that?*"

Somehow, somewhere in his peregrinations around the bar, he'd managed to accumulate a black feather boa around his neck. Oddly, it didn't detract from his masculinity in the least. He toyed with it. "You like? It belongs to some chick named Rhonda. At least I hope she's a chick." He peered closely at someone across the room.

"No, I don't like!"

"Um." With the return of the prodigal bum, I'd all but forgotten about Randy. Though he was valiantly trying to appear cool, A.J. was unsettling him. "Who's your gay friend?"

A.J. just laughed at that. "Now come on, bro. You know better than to dis another Method man. Come on. I gave you a compliment."

I wanted to take the boa and stuff it in the man's big, fat mouth. "Randy is not a Method man. He didn't use a Yes Ladder. I would have caught that. You're just . . ."

A.J. flicked his forefinger gently on my forehead, astonishing me into silence. Who actually *did* that kind of thing? "The Yes Ladder is a tool. It's not The Method, doofus. You call a locksmith to open something, he doesn't bring one key and hope it fits. He's got a whole ring full of keys, and one of them is going to work. Right?" he asked Randy.

"I—I don't know what you're talking about." Randy had leaned back in his chair, arms crossed, clearly on the defensive. I felt sorry for him. "Is he your boyfriend?"

"No!" I yelled.

"As if," said A.J., rolling his eyes.

"Your brother?"

You know, I could see how Randy might have thought that. A.J. and I had been acting like contentious siblings. "He's not my brother. I don't have a brother. He's my . . . I'm his . . . we're . . ." My hands flew up in frustration. "It's complicated. And weird."

"Maybe we could head out somewhere, if you want," Randy suggested, leaning forward and trying to ignore the fact that A. J. was leaning over the tableside railing and listening to every word we said. "Somewhere quieter." His eyes slid in the eavesdropper's direction.

"Excellent!" A.J. broke into applause.

I gritted my teeth and growled, "He wasn't inviting *you.*"

A.J. gave me a pained look. "I *know.* I'm talking about a smooth, nay, classic implementation of Step

Five initiation. Skin!" He raised up a hand to Randy for a high-five that, from Randy's expression, would be long in coming. "She doesn't believe me," he said, finally shaking his fist as if that was what he'd actually meant to do. "So let's review the various steps of The Method. Step One: Identify the quarry. Hard to miss this one from across the room, huh, bro?" he asked in that frat-boy, confidential, icky tone that men use as a substitute for actual intimacy. "Can't keep your eyes off her? Think she's pretty?" Though it was impossible to ignore A.J. as he nudged and smirked and prodded his elbow against his biceps, Randy at least made a valiant effort. Finally he jerked his arm away, keeping his eyes fixed on the ceiling. "Then Step Two: Make the opening gambit. *Here's a vodka and cranberry! I was listening to you order it from the bartender, but I'm going to pretend I read your mind and ordered it for you and then say you look like a vodka and cranberry girl!*" Over the bar ruckus, A.J.'s falsetto imitation could easily be heard.

"That's ridiculous." When I looked at Randy for some sort of similar denial, his eyes were still fixed on the ceiling, and his arms remained crossed.

A.J. continued ticking off his fingers. "Step Three. Oh, the all-important Step Three: Make sure she knows you're a value-added attraction. *Did I mention I'm a real, live artist?* Ladies dig that, right?"

I hated A.J. at that moment. Mostly I hated him because so much of him was so wrong—the super-tight clothing, the confidence that oozed seamlessly into arrogance, the boa and the leopard-print shoes—while my instincts told me that he was absolutely, 100 percent right in what he said. The fact that Randy just sat there and pretended none of it was happening didn't do much to convince me otherwise. "You're hateful," I told A.J.

"Reading your cards, too. Shows that he's got a deep, mysterious, spiritual side. Am I right? By the way, bro, I've got to commend you. The Tarot cards? Excellent chick crack!"

I had to know. "What's—?"

"Chick crack. Stuff chicks can't get enough of. The stuff you pull out and they all come flocking. Tarot cards, personality tests, ESP experiments, dream analysis . . ."

Randy opened his mouth and spoke. "Your friend is crazy." He sounded openly hostile.

A.J. didn't notice or care. "I never went with the Tarot cards. Too much memorizing. What I do sometimes is something like this." He cleared his throat. " 'Hey, I've been taking lessons from this palm reader. Can I practice on you?' " Somehow he'd managed to make his voice sound both innocent and earnest, while his brown eyes had become round and wide. I didn't even protest as he maneuvered my hand between his. His index finger brushed against my palm as he traced the longest of the lines there. " 'This is your life line. See those crosses? It looks like you've had some trouble in your past. And see how it's broad and clear, here? That's smooth sailing ahead, because you find someone you trust and want to be with. And this is your love line. Wow. I can see that under the surface, your feelings really run deep. Amazing!' " He turned to Randy. Almost immediately his voice reverted to the dopey frat-boy talk. "See? You get the same mileage without all that shuffling. *And* you initiate physical contact, which otherwise you don't get until Step Six or Seven." Instantly I grabbed my hand back. "I'm just explaining," he protested, unapologetic.

"I . . ." I didn't know what to say. I seemed to be protesting just because I didn't want to admit that I'd been had again.

"Step Four's setting up the similarities. *Oh, hey, do you remember this movie? Oh, sure, I remember that movie. Hey, we both remember the same movie! It gives us an excuse to move ahead to Step Five!* Which is when the Method Man makes his move to Step Five: Isolate the target from the outside world. As in, *Wanna go someplace quiet so I can get you away from friends who might talk you out of this?* Which leads to Step Six: establishing an intimate connection. Hand-holding. Head in the lap. Touching the face. Which leads to my favorite, Step Seven: taking the target to a seduction location!" With his hands he performed a complex motion involving crashing one fist into his palm while simultaneously snapping his fingers. "Badda-boom!"

"This whole Method thing is cynical and just plain annoying," I pointed out to him. Oddly, I wasn't taking any of this personally, but more as an intellectual challenge. "How many ways are there to get to know a perfect stranger? Of course when you see people you like you approach them. Of course you talk to them and try to impress them a little. You try to talk to them and get them on your side. As a matter of fact," I said, warming to my diatribe because I knew I had a point to make, "I'd venture to say that most people—most sane, sensible, intelligent people—actually enjoy positive, mutual communication, unhindered by manipulative, calculated attempts at . . . at . . . you know." The sheer amount of electric guitar solo blaring from the CD jukebox seemed to be erasing my vocabulary, syllable by Latinate syllable. I held out my hands in the direction of Randy's chair. "You look at Randy and you see a Method Man. I look at him and I'm willing to give him the benefit of the doubt that he's a nice guy who's not on the make and is looking to meet someone for the long haul. What?" I challenged the skepticism of A.J.'s thick, raised eyebrows.

"In for the long haul, huh?" I didn't know what he meant until I looked at Randy. Or more accurately, at Randy's empty chair. He'd snuck away while the two of us had been arguing. "Good eye, Egan."

Ouch. I couldn't see Randy's cropped head anywhere, even when I shakily stood up on the rungs of my barstool to peer over the crowd. "I wasn't serious about him, anyway."

"He totally suckered you with that chick crack."

He'd scored a point there, but I didn't let it show. "I don't know why I'm sitting here listening to you abuse me. I don't know what you do for a living. I don't even know what your initials stand for. The only thing I know about you, and it's the one thing I most dislike, is that you've got this world view that every man is on the make and every woman is a victim to his games. I don't want to be that jaded, thank you."

"Listen up, wingman." A.J. rested both elbows on the table and leaned forward so that his forearms swelled to Popeye proportions. "My goals and yours aren't all that different. You want to meet someone nice. I want to meet someone nice. You want to have a friendly conversation. I want to have a friendly conversation. You want to get to know someone better. I—"

"Want to get someone naked." When he cocked his head and seemed disappointed, I sat back in my chair. "Deny it."

"You know something?"

"What?"

How in the world would he attempt to justify a hedonistic lifestyle not seen since the fall of Rome? Or, at least, the last episode of *The Jerry Springer Show*? I couldn't wait to hear. Much to my surprise, though, he shook his head. "I don't let that many women into my bed, Becca. I *could*," he added hastily. "Don't get me wrong. I could have to be changing the sheets every morning if I wanted to. Hoo boy, could I ever." I sat and waited for this display of piggery to end. What, was I supposed to be impressed that he actually *changed* the linens afterward? When I didn't soften, he sighed and rested his chin on one meaty hand. "I'm like a judo master."

"Sensei," I corrected.

"Bless you!" he joked. I rolled my eyes and let it pass. "You've got this judo master who's got all the moves. He can kick. He can take out bad guys with a single karate chop."

"An expert in judo would scarcely take out bad guys with a single *karate* . . ." At the sight of his stern expression and wide-open eyes, I closed my mouth. "Sorry."

"Thank you. So he's got all these skills. But does he spend all his life going all The Bride in *Kill Bill* on people? No. Does he use the heel of his hand to drive his enemy's nose into their brain tissue, bringing about their instantaneous and fatal deaths, even though he could? No. What he does is teach his students, so that they might have the benefit of his wisdom and experience. Not every guy is a pickup artist. But if you're determined to hit a lot of these downtown joints, you're going to run across a lot of them who are. Don't you want to be able to tell one from the other?"

At the end of his long speech he waited for me to answer. I hesitated before I croaked out, through the suspicion that seemed to have corroded my throat, "Why would you do that for me?"

"Because it's fun," he immediately replied. Then, grudgingly, he added, "And because you could be very useful to me."

I thought about it, and decided I could envision A.J. as the kind of guy whose ego might be flattered by a veneer of generosity pasted over a whopping edifice of self-interest. "What would I have to do, sensei?"

He raised a single eyebrow and, in a dramatic and mysterious voice, murmured, "Wait and see." By now the sound of the crowd, the jukebox, and the tinkling of glasses across the bar had all melded into a continuous white noise that I barely noticed above our conversation. I bit my lip, considering. I couldn't say I exactly liked A.J., but things were much more interesting when he was around. There would be a certain utility to learning a little more about these Method Men and how to spot them, wouldn't there? As if knowing I was vacillating, A.J. reached out, picked up my empty glass, and shook it to set the ice cubes rattling. "Come on. You won't have to pay for your own alcohol."

"All right," I finally said, then made a quick clarification of my own. "Not because of the free booze."

"Ah so!" A.J. put his hands together prayerfully, then bowed in my direction. "The master, he have new pupil."

He probably didn't hear the snort that issued from my nostrils at his smug satisfaction. "Every death is fatal. You said 'fatal death' a minute ago," I explained, when he appeared confused. "It's redundant."

In his terrible Hollywood Asian accent, A.J. bowed again and crooned, "Confucius say, 'When in doubt or uncertain, use either redundancy or that which is inessential.'"

The apothegm made no sense whatsoever. Suddenly I narrowed my eyes. Was he having me on? "What did you say you did for a living, anyway?"

"You have much to learn, grasshoppah." He hopped down from the barstool with his paw still cupped around my glass, his mood jaunty once more. "Such as, too many questions spoil the broth. Vodka and cranberry, right?" he asked, shaking the tumbler. "My treat, this once."

"Gee, thanks," I called out, wondering what I'd done to deserve such an indulgence.

"And Egan?" he called out from several feet away, making a face at me. "Try not to pick up another dozen guys while I'm gone, would ya?"

SIX

"It's AM 1470," Sarah said to the old man hunkered over the table in the Chess and Checkers House, deep in the park's interior. She glanced at her watch nervously, then reacted to my silent rebuke with a defensive, "He doesn't mind!"

The boom box sitting on the concrete table had seen better days. Deep scratches marred almost every surface, as if it had been used in a game of keep-away between two heavy throwers wearing sandpaper mittens; the speakers were covered with white splotches that I sincerely hoped were old paint. Despite its age and battered condition, it filled the pergola with sound, though it was interrupted by static as its owner rotated the dial. "And that brings me to my first question." The dulcet tones of Portia Daye's voice echoed across the floor, around the checkerboard-topped tables, and out into the wan spring daylight. "Are you ready?"

Portia's guest cleared her throat and replied, in a well-modulated voice, "I suppose you want to know about the abstract my research partner and I recently submitted to the *Journal of Micromechanics and Microengineering* that caused such a kafuffle in the scientific community!"

"What?" Portia sounded utterly taken aback. "No."

"I wouldn't *think* so," grumped Sarah. March had decided to tease us a little by giving us the tiniest taste of spring after so many gloomy afternoons: a sprinkle of sun, a dollop of temperatures in the lower fifties, and just a hint of the green, moldy smell that always tickled my nose during my walks in Central Park. Though Ethan and I had been strolling with our coats open, fooling ourselves that warm weather lay just around the corner, Sarah remained stubbornly bundled up in a downy pink winter coat, hood pulled up, her hands stuffed into a pair of matching gloves. Shivering on the bench, she looked like a strawberry Popsicle.

She might have had a point. The shade of the chess and checkers house seemed almost icy, as if the sun wouldn't penetrate the cool here until the height of summer. "I thought we were having a nice walk," I felt compelled to point out.

Sarah shushed me and leaned more closely toward the boom box. Its owner, an elderly man with skin the color of coal and a grizzled white beard, didn't at all seem to mind. Portia's guest had begun talking again. ". . . probably want to hear about my work with the Manhattan College board of trustees to educate teachers willing to involve young students in the areas of science and mathematics education, then, because it did—though I don't like to boast—it did bring me the Philip G. Winters Award for Outstanding Contribution to . . ."

"No." I could just imagine the expression on Portia's face—blank and uncomprehending, as if I'd just told a literary anecdote about Boswell and Johnson. "They told me you were going to be a *good* guest."

"Well." The woman cleared her throat once more. "I got in the *Times*."

"I used to get in the *Post* all the time," Portia complained mildly. "It's really not that difficult. You open up your apartment door and there it is, on the mat. You don't even have to bend over if you're not in the mood."

"That's not what I—"

"You just pull it in with your foot." I distinctly heard Portia sigh and rustle some papers. "If you're just tuning in, you're listening to 'Portia Daye's Radio Show with Portia Daye.' And I'm Portia Daye."

Ethan sat on the railing with me, his blue-jeaned knees scissoring with delight as he laughed silently to himself. "She's crazy! And you know her?"

Sarah shot him a look of hatred. "She's a friend of my sister's," I explained to him. Then, in a stage whisper I added, "Some people have lately been obsessed by her."

"Obsession is such an ugly word." Sarah dismissed me with a wave.

"I think the word suits someone who interrupts a perfectly nice lunchtime walk to hijack someone else's afternoon music, don't you?" I asked Ethan.

My cohort in crime nodded solemnly. "I do, indeed."

The old man playing the red chess pieces lifted his queen and moved it diagonally across the board. "I don't mind at all."

"You're the one who should be obsessed!" Sarah snapped back, her head low to the table where the elderly black man played a thoughtful game of chess with a wizened little dried apple doll of a fellow who suspiciously resembled Jerry Stiller.

"But I'm not," I told Ethan, before Sarah began shushing us again.

"So, if you don't mind, Marcia—can I call you Marcia?" Portia was saying, sounding slightly more peevish than before. "I'd like to get on with my question. *My* question."

"My name's Martha, but of course. . . ."

"My show."

"Of course it's—"

"*Ssssh!*"

Portia's professorial guest zipped her lip at the sudden silencing, then waited for her to proceed with the question. We all waited. For long, long seconds, nothing came out of the radio save for silence and dead air. Ethan turned to me and raised his eyebrows, his mouth open wide, ready to laugh. I gave him a shrug—this was Portia's show, after all, and she did pretty much what she wanted with it. Sarah moved her head even closer to the commandeered radio, as if that might coax more sound from it. She moved so close, in fact, that her hair threatened to sweep a castle from the chess board. "I might have lost that there signal," said the box's owner, finally, making a move to adjust the knob.

For a second I thought Sarah might slap at his hand. Luckily, at the very last second, Portia's guest spoke up, obviously nervous. "Are you going to ask? Your question, I mean."

"But I did."

"I didn't hear it. . . ."

"Of course you didn't. I asked it in my head." Portia made the statement sound like the most reasonable and obvious thing ever. "Didn't you hear it?"

Beside me, Ethan was snickering with helpless laughter. I swatted him. "No," said the professor, wonderingly. "I didn't."

"I don't mean this as a criticism," said Portia, smug. "But if you can't read my mind for the question, you're not a very good psychic."

"I . . . I'm not . . . that is, I think you might be . . ." The guest sounded so flustered that she couldn't even form the most tentative beginning of a sentence. "I'm not a psychic. I'm . . . you seem to . . . I'm a physicist."

Sarah looked as if she might bang her forehead on the chessboard. Ethan, on the other hand, snuffled in wild delight. When I looked over at him, he was slightly flushed and red. I couldn't help but grin right back in his direction. "I beg your pardon," said Portia, "but you're not. It says here on my sheet that you're Marcia Holmes, the psychic."

"It says . . . I hope you don't mind, but I can see it from right here, Dr. Martha Holmes, physicist." Even the boom box's owner was shaking his head at that point.

"I love her," declaimed Ethan, jumping down from the railing like a little kid. "I want to marry that woman."

"I'll kill you," I swore. "Ethan, you're too nice a guy to fall into her clutches."

"Is she pretty?" he wondered aloud. "She has a sexy voice. I bet she has long, long legs that won't quit. And lips like honey."

"I can fire you, you know," glowered Sarah, shushing us both. Ethan winked at me and went to stand by the table where the two old men had been playing a solitary game of chess before Sarah had begged to listen to their radio.

"Who booked you?" Portia was asking. "Who booked you on my show?"

"I—"

"Which one of the assistants booked you? Was it Marlon, the boy with the squeaky voice and pimples, or Fawn, the lesbian with the short hair?"

"I didn't see her hair. . . ."

"Fawn, then. Thought so. Hmfph." Portia's sour tone turned sweet and practiced once more as she murmured into the microphone, "Thank you, Marcia, for stopping by! You're listening to 'Portia Daye's Radio Show with Portia Daye,' and we've just had on Marcia Somebody—"

"Holmes," said the guest, trying to get in a last word edgewise. "I didn't get a chance to talk, really, I . . ."

My hair began to stand on end when I heard what followed. "—who is definitely *not* a psychic. Next up, our new regular feature: 'Portia Daye Helps Beckate,' in which I, Portia Daye, turn to you, my listeners, for suggestions on helping my friend, 'Beckate.' . . ." Even without a visual, one could practically make out the air quotes.

I didn't need to hear the rest. "Oh, no," I said, easing myself off the railing. I stuffed my hands deep in my pockets and shook my head.

"I've been trying to get you to listen." Sarah sat up from her hunched-over position, finally, and pulled back her hood so she could swipe her bangs from her eyes. "She's been doing this every day since last week."

Once had been bad enough. Once was a quirk of Portia's personality, a misguided act of charity, a mistake that with a little bit of stoicism I could shrug off with a chuckle. "So you're Beckate?" Ethan asked, thankfully drowning out the sound of Portia's voice. I was under the influence of too many emotions to trust myself to answer; Sarah managed to grunt out an affirmative. "And Portia Daye, the star of 'Portia Daye's Radio Show with Portia Daye,' she's the sister of the guy you've . . . ?"

I'd given Ethan a brief outline of my adventures with A. J., since he'd been my cover the weekend before. Although my eyes had been set in full glower, now they flew wide open. I jerked my head abruptly to tell him to *ixnay*. Luckily, he caught the gesture before Sarah noticed. "The guy who makes every girl's life a living hell," she said. "Honestly, you've got to wonder about the loins they sprang from."

"Now Charles in Soho," I heard Portia say from the mucked-up speakers. "Charles, it was nice of you to send in a photo for Beckate, but lonely as she is, poor thing, I don't think she's quite *that* desperate. Sorry, but that's how it is."

I ran my hands through my hair, squeezing my temples and ears with my palms so I wouldn't have to hear more. Too much. It was all too much. "Enough," I told everyone, indicating to Ethan that he should switch off the sound system. For a moment his long fingers scrambled atop the box until at blessed last, Portia's voice shut off with an electronic squawk. The radio's owner turned away from his chess game and gave me a resentful stare that I tried to ignore. "Just let go of it, Sarah. I have." When she opened her mouth to protest, I plowed right ahead. "Neither of us has to listen to her show. I'll be a hundred and fifty percent happier if I don't know what she's saying. You'll be that much less stressed if you're not trying to whip up righteous anger on my behalf. I thought we were getting out of the store for a couple of hours so we could clear our heads on a nice afternoon!"

Unexpectedly, the Jerry Stiller look-alike picked up the aluminum cane leaning against the concrete table and jabbed it in my direction. "Your friend is only trying to look out for you, young lady!"

"Damn right I am," Sarah muttered.

"I don't know who you are, coming into my baili-wick and using language like that," said the other old man to Sarah in a deep, sonorous voice that he possibly could have stolen from James Earl Jones. He crossed his arms and regarded her sternly.

Sarah mumbled, "Sorry."

"Your friend Beckate is trying to take the high road here," he informed her. "You should respect her choice."

"Three cheers for that," I said, crossing my own arms and squaring off against Sarah. "Three cheers!"

"What's the use of keeping her head in the sand,

though?" asked the shrunken head. "Things don't go away just because you wish them to." He pawed at a plastic Baggie sitting next to the game timer and pulled out a large water cracker that, when he chomped into it, exploded into crumbs that fell all over his rumpled jacket. Poor guy. He'd probably be buried in that suit.

"The world's an unpleasant enough place as it is," my defender explained. I nodded vigorously. "Why wallow in it when one can choose to let it be?"

"But if you have friends willing to be there for you in a time of need, why not let them?" I wanted to run over and brush those crumbs from the guy's blue blazer. But no, he plucked another of the crackers from the Baggie and proceeded again to attack it with his gums, all while saying, "That's what they're there for."

"Well, that *is* a point," said my advocate, nodding thoughtfully. "Why don't you?"

I felt the growing sensation of being backed against a wall. Sarah joined in the round of accusatory stares, asking, "Yeah, why not?"

"Checkmate," Ethan announced to the cracker king, pointing at the board. "If you move your bishop there, anyway."

The elderly African-American man stared at him with resentment; the victor peered through his glasses as if he couldn't quite believe his luck and shakily pushed forward his red bishop.

One of the things I learned in my divorce is that endurance only took a girl so far. There came a point when throwing in the towel was the only sensible thing to do—and in this situation, I'd reached that point five minutes earlier. "I'm going to finish my walk," I announced firmly, keeping myself under control. "See you back at the bookstore."

"Rebecca, don't . . ." Whatever she'd been about to tell me, Sarah cut off with an exaggerated sigh.

The pergola's high-ceilinged acoustics carried the sound of the crumby man's voice as I walked across it. "Hiding her head in the sand again."

"You leave that girl be," chided his friend. The words grew fainter with every step. "Every mama's child knows what's best for herself."

"That doesn't make sense at all!" I heard the other man say, before I stepped out onto the path. Outside of the refrigerator chill of the chess and checkers house, I felt much more comfortable; I let my jacket fall back open as I strode back in the direction of the carousel. I didn't have to let Portia get to me, I reminded myself— or Sarah, either. I could enjoy this moment. I could enjoy this sunshine, this promise of future warmth, if I concentrated. "Crazy," I heard myself saying aloud.

Once I was free of the shade, I closed my eyes and inhaled deeply, letting the smell of the wet earth and the grass fill my lungs. In the middle of the park, it was almost easy to forget the surrounding canyons of concrete, steel, and glass. At this time of year I wanted to ignore the city and focus on the bare tree branches, the crocuses that grew in small and surprising clusters, and the faint hints of yellow buds in the forsythia bushes. Never mind that at heart I suspected that if banished to the countryside, I'd complain constantly about the mosquitoes and worms and the lack of anything to do; for a few days a year I could walk into the park and pretend I was a girl of simple tastes, low-maintenance and enviro-friendly.

That's all I'd wanted from the walk today. I certainly hadn't asked for a lecture on my faults and shortcomings. "Is it so bad to prefer to taste the sweetness in things?" I didn't know to whom I was saying the words. Myself? The world? A bearded Old-Testament God peering down from the clouds, forever in my mind resembling the line drawing of George Bernard Shaw from my parents' album of *My Fair Lady*? In the wide outdoors, among the grass and scrub, my question vanished almost instantly. No one would ever hear it, or care that it had been asked.

"I don't think so. What's a world without optimism?" I heard a rustle of feet in the grass behind me. When I opened my eyes, the sunlight made them water. I decided to pretend I hadn't been addressing the ether, and waited as he came closer. "It sounds pretty grim to me."

"Where's Sarah?" I asked, once he'd finally caught up. It seemed natural to keep on walking, so we paced forward slowly, not in any obvious hurry.

He jerked his head in the direction of the pergola. "I think she's telling the history of your marriage to the seniors."

"And not seeing the irony of broadcasting my personal history far and wide, while getting angry at Portia for the same thing," I griped. "Sorry. Being dragged into the middle of a girl fight was probably the last thing you wanted to do with your afternoon, huh?"

A small flock of sparrows flew from the grass and

fluttered up into the air; the birds circled around and around each other in a cyclone of chattering and flapping wings. "I'm the one who opened his big fat mouth about your other friend. A.J."

I shrugged. It wasn't really his fault. "He's another sore point for Sarah. Plus, if she or any of my sister's friends found out that I'm hanging out with him . . ." I threw up my hands and let him draw his own conclusions.

"He's a real bad boy, huh?"

"Hmmm. He's good-bad. But he's not evil." Ethan let out one of his curious snuffles of laughter. I looked over, and when I saw his blue eyes alight with pleasure, I explained, "Sorry, that's a quote from a Shangri-Las song."

"Yeah, 'Give Him a Great Big Kiss,' I know. I love the Shangri-Las. They're so depressing."

"You love something that's depressing?"

"They're funny-depressing. Somebody dies in just about all of their songs." He leaned in my direction and held out a hand so he could count off fingers. "'The Leader of the Pack dies after one of the Shangri-Las dumps him. There's another song, um, 'I Can Never Go Home Anymore,' where one of the Shangri-Las runs away from home and her mother dies. Then there's 'Long Live Our Love,' where the Shangri-Las are singing to a soldier who's overseas, and praying that he won't be hurt."

"And he dies?"

"You *know* he will. You know he probably gets a bullet to the neck the minute the singer opens her fat mouth. It's the curse of the Shangri-Las!" His mock–

Vincent Price impression made me crack up a little. "It's like the curse of Jessica Fletcher."

We were only a few dozen feet away from the carousel gates. I began meandering toward the wrought iron. "Who?"

"Jessica Fletcher? Jessica Fletcher? Oh, my God." He jogged in front of me and stood still, crossing his arms and tucking his hands into the armpits of his red-and-black flannel jacket. "Cabot Cove? Queen of mysteries? *Murder, She Wrote*?"

"All right, all right." I grinned and started walking again. "You've jogged my memory. What about her?"

"What *about* her? Didn't you ever watch the show?"

I shook my head. "Once or twice, maybe." In my defense I added, "It was a long time ago!"

"Oh my gosh, it was my favorite show when I was a kid. All right, then you've seen the curse of Jessica Fletcher in action. What happens every show? She shows up to visit some poor schmoe of a niece or nephew. Someone dies. The hapless relative gets arrested and Jessica has to go to work to prove that the C-list celebrity guest star of the week is the real criminal." We'd reached the carousel gates. He leaned against them heavily. "If I were one of Jessica's relatives, I'd hightail it out of town the moment I saw that wispy dyed hair of hers. And there you have it: the curse of Jessica Fletcher."

"And the curse of the Shangri-Las." I grabbed hold of the closed gate and leaned back on it a little. Seeing the carousel animals woven into the fence always cheered me up. Today was no exception. The sight of them made me realize something. "Are you trying to cajole me out of a pissy mood, by any chance?"

He tossed his shoulders quickly. "Is it working?"

"The curse of Rebecca Egan." I let the words roll out, trying them on for size. "Every friend she has turns into a shrieking harpy."

"Yeah, okay. It's good that you're not dipping into the Enchanted Well of the Drama Queen or anything," Ethan said, letting his finger trace a stylized monkey on the fence. He wiped the tip on his jacket sleeve. I laughed a little bit. I knew how histrionic it had sounded. "I can't claim to be the most educated expert on the opposite sex, but I thought you girls got through that bad-boy stage in your teens."

"Apparently not!" I started walking around the fence's circumference, letting my fingers strike the iron pickets. They made a satisfyingly hollow sound. "It's not—we're not—" I didn't know how to explain. I'd told Ethan a short version of what I'd been up to with A.J., simply because he'd been a good enough guy to go along with me using him for a cover story. I hadn't at all gone into my motivations, though. Perhaps because I wasn't exactly sure what they might be. "We're not *dating*," I finally managed to say. It sounded lame.

"Is he the total opposite of your ex, maybe?" Quickly, almost too quickly, he added, "Sorry. That's a personal question."

"No, it's okay. I'd never really thought about it in those terms." I meditated on the question for a moment. "I don't know. Maybe. A.J. . . . he's crude and totally on the make, twenty-four/seven. Big alpha male. Sean was an alpha male too, but in a different way. He wanted to be the provider for the two of us, for example. In his little Seaniverse, it didn't matter if I didn't bring home a lot of money, because I was the woman and he was the big bad man." I remembered, much too late and with a pang of awkwardness, that Ethan's salary was even less than mine. Hastily I moved on. "It was a little arrogant, but I thought it was cute, back in the day."

"So they're more similar than not?"

"It's tough to explain. Sean was—" Why was it, I wondered, that whenever people talked about their exes, they referred to them in ways that made them sound deceased? Even at the height of the divorce proceedings I hadn't seen Sean, thanks to a number of hermetically sealed envelopes delivered by couriers, but he was still living somewhere out there—possibly not even a half-mile from where I stood right then. "Sean was this guy who came off as having an high-minded moral system three miles wide and a half-mile deep. It was one of the things that attracted me to him when we met in college. He was a lawyer to the core, even then, standing up for unpopular issues on the debate team, writing fiery editorials for the school paper. A.J.'s a total bozo. He saves up all his money for super-tight shirts, drinks, and hair gel. The guy wastes more time in a weekend waxing his eyebrows that I spend on makeup all year."

"So they are total opposites."

I was confusing the poor guy. "Yes, but . . . you see, the guy who was supposed to be irreproachable turned out to do something totally random, like hooking up with the boss' daughter and divorcing his wife.

And the sleazeball has this ethic, this Method, that's more honest than anything my ex-husband turned out to have." Old leaves from the autumn had collected between some of the pickets. I kicked a few of them loose with my foot before we moved past the carousel altogether. "I don't know. Maybe they're different enough that I need the change."

"Listen, you deserve a little bit of novelty." I don't know why I hadn't talked like this with Ethan before. Oh sure, we said things to each other. We'd gone out on lunches and talked about movies and books and occasionally swapped little tidbits of gossip about our coworkers, but I couldn't recall ever having talked to him much about Sean, even though Ethan had started working at the bookstore at about the time everything had started unraveling. "You're cooped up all day with someone who should be the founding member of Shrink Addiction Anonymous, some ditzy part-timers, and an old-maid account keeper."

Meaning himself, of course. I felt outraged on his behalf. "You're not an . . . oh, hey!" I stopped in my path, whirling around to regard him square-on. A pair of young, would-be Frisbee players walked by, tossing their discs into the air and catching them as they talked. One of them wore shorts. While I admired the optimism, the thought of all that bare skin in the chilly air made me shiver a little. "Brilliant idea!"

He raised his eyebrows. "Oh?"

I looked him over. With the clear blue eyes, the broad shoulders, the tousled hair, the even, white grin, and the little dimples that appeared in his cheeks when he smiled, there was a lot of good raw material there. Sure, his clothes were a little shabby, but I'd known many guys to do a lot more with less. "You're an attractive guy."

His eyebrows remained raised. "Thank you?"

"No, you are." I studied him from a number of angles. Beneath that terrible plaid coat and sweater and the baggy corduroys that were his staple winter-wear, it was tough to tell what kind of shape he was in. My memories of the previous summer were mostly of the numbness I felt after Sean had announced his affair, but I seemed to recall Ethan wearing some retro bowling-style shirts to work that had framed a pretty decent torso. "I think we should get you some girls."

The laughter that issued from Ethan's nostrils wasn't exactly the happy chortles of grateful glee that I might have hoped my offer would inspire. He sounded downright alarmed, in fact. "Girls?"

I was so confused at his reaction that I paused. "You are straight, right?" I'd always assumed he was, but he had called himself an old maid, after all.

"You've worked with me for months and this is the first time you've made the slightest inquiry into my personal life, you know." Now it was his turn to start walking again. It almost seemed as if he was trying to escape me. "Yes, I'm straight, and I'm single. But I'm not really looking for *girls,* plural."

Ah, now I understood! Ethan was as upstanding and decent and old-fashioned as they came, these days. "One girl, then. We'll find you one special girl. The girl who makes your face light up and your heart pitty-pat."

His mouth curved upward, Cheshire catlike. "And how do you propose to do that?" he asked, not looking at me.

"Isn't it obvious?" I danced along beside him, genuinely excited at the idea forming in my head. "I'll observe everything I can about A.J.'s so-called Method when I'm out with him. Then I'll teach it to you. We'll turn you from Clark Kent into Superman in no time." Hastily I added, at the sight of the pained look on his face, "Not that there's anything wrong with you, mind. It'll be a make-better, not a make-over."

"Rebecca, I'm not at all sure . . ."

"Oh, come on. How hard can it be? So far The Method seems to consist mostly of wearing some dumb accessory as a conversation-starter, insulting the girl you're interested in, and a couple of basic techniques straight out of the Psych 101 textbooks."

"So even I could do it?"

"You betcha!" I didn't know why I felt so giddy at having a project of my own. Turning Ethan from chump to champ would be a blast. Something about the prospect made me want to skip through the grass like a spring lamb. No, lambs gamboled. What gamboling was, I had no clue, but I'd give it a shot if I had to.

Ethan appeared to be considering my offer seriously at least, though it was plain from the look on his face that he thought I was crazy. "What kind of dumb accessory?" When I told him about A.J.'s tiny little monkey hat and his feather boa, he looked up at the treetops, laughed, and shook his head. "No."

"Oh, come on!" I urged, teasing him. "You'd look fabulous in feathers."

"That's exactly what I'm afraid of!" He laughed again. "So if I agree to this scathingly brilliant idea of yours . . ."

"You want to do it!" I crowed. "We're going to get you a girl!"

"I said *if*," he pointed out. "And no dumb accessories."

I considered for a moment as we stepped back onto the path that would eventually lead us out of the park and back to the bookstore. "How about a fancy gold necklace with your astrological symbol on it?" He narrowed his eyes. "Big belt buckle emblazoned with the word STUD in rhinestones?"

"This A.J. has unleashed a monster upon an unsuspecting world, hasn't he?" Now that we were in the full sunlight, we stopped. For a moment, Ethan wrestled with his plaid jacket, grumbling to himself as he pulled it off. The sweater followed, leaving him in his shirt-sleeves, which he promptly rolled up. "That's better," he said. While he had been removing his clothing, I couldn't help but notice the veins running the length of his forearm. He really was a lanky guy. There probably was a very nice, lean body beneath those clothes. It wasn't until he said, "Um, are you checking me out?" that I realized he'd noticed my not-subtle attentions.

"Ah," I began to stammer. "I was . . . I was just thinking that you're about an eight. You'll do pretty well out there, I think."

"Well, gee whiz," he said amiably, walking on ahead so that I had to catch up to him. "Thanks for objectifying me."

"With a little monkey hat, you'd be an eight-point-five, easy."

"I'm so flattered."

This walk had turned out to be better than I'd expected after all. "How about leather pants with red and yellow appliquéd flames licking up from the cuffs?" I teased.

"You frighten me, Becca," said Ethan, shaking his head. "You really do."

SEVEN

The old-school funk playing over the dozens of loud-speakers strategically hung in the After Ten Lounge's upper reaches thrummed so loudly through my every joint that, when my phone began to vibrate at my side, I at first thought that the inescapable beat had shaken loose a rib. I dug into my sleek black bag—okay, Alice's bag—and pulled out my cell. "What?" I asked, recognizing the number immediately.

In order to hear I had to press one hand against an ear, while mashing the little phone against the other. "I've spotted the girl." Oh, yes, we were at Step One of A.J.'s foolproof Method to git it, hit it, and forget it: identifying the target. If I'd been able to wrap a cheesecloth around that masculine voice and give it a good pressing, I could've extracted several bottles full of extra-virgin smug oil. Cancel that: There was nothing remotely virgin about A.J., much less extra-.

"Where?" I asked, vaguely grateful that I'd shaved my

armpits, since they were both exposed to the several hundred people who'd braved the March night chill to get into the latest bar of the moment. We hadn't had to stand in line at all, like most of these poor schmucks; A.J. had simply walked around the velvet rope to the front, nodded at the sour-faced bouncer, and walked us in. Part of me was still riding high from that moment, which had left me feeling slightly supercilious and naughty, like I was meeting Liza and Andy and Halston for drinks and blow at Studio 54.

"To your right." I swiveled in a clockwise direction, only to wince when A.J. barked directly into my eardrum, "Your other right!"

"That would be my left and *your* right," I pointed out, shooting a glare in the direction where I'd last seen him, at the other end of the vast room carved out of one of the Meatpacking District's seemingly more cathedral-like warehouses. The After Ten's owners had draped saffron-colored panels of fabric from the ceiling to soften the industrial overtones, and they'd laid down a rich rosewood floor for the dainty leather soles of their patrons, but they'd left the brick walls bare and hadn't bothered to cover the iron-and-chicken-wire skylights at the ceiling's peak. I couldn't find A.J. anywhere in the mass of people seething around the edges of a dance floor where only the most disaffected couples gyrated with each other.

"Just turn the other way," commanded A.J. I looked to my left. Not surprisingly, I saw a hundred pretty girls: blondes, brunettes, redheads, and one striking dark-skinned woman with no hair whatsoever. "See her?"

"Help me narrow it down a little, would you?" I was developing a crick in my neck.

"She's the only ten!" Nope, didn't do anything for me. I brushed hair from my eyes and coolly tried to figure out which of these glamazons might have an edge over the others. "Okay, fine, but we're going to have to work on your eye. She's the itty-bitty kitty with the pretty, pretty—"

"If the word *titties* is next," I warned him, "I'm going to hang up." The chick standing immediately next to me crinkled her eyebrows, then dismissed me from her mind as she went back to conversing with a slick-ster wearing a pukka-shell necklace only half as white as his smile. Another Method Man, I was guessing from the general air of confidence and the blinding choppers.

"I was gonna say *rack*, potty mouth." A.J. cleared his throat. "Blond hair. Blue dress. See her?" It took a moment, but when I scanned the area, I saw a pretty young thing matching that vague description occupying a sofa near me. With her straight, thin hair, a stick body that resembled a praying mantis, and a general air of disorientation, she seemed more worthy of pity than envy. Then again, a lot of guys went for that malnourished, model-y, attenuated, Chloë Sevigny-y look. "Yeah, there. Don't look too obvious. You remember what to do?"

"Yes, I remember what to do."

"Then get cracking. She should have a space opening up next to her on the sofa in five, four, three . . ."

"*Jawohl, mein Kommandant!*" I would have done

the heel click, but I didn't want to risk the chance of scuffing Alice's pumps. Instead, I clicked off the phone, stuffed it back into my bag, and made my move.

The art of the pickup is like a game of chess, A.J. had told me during the lengthy lecture that preceded this particular outing. Well, if that was the case, this queen knocked over two bishops, a rook, and a couple of knights in her hurry to make speed to one particular pawn. "Oh, my gosh!" I exclaimed in a loud, girlish voice as I collapsed next to my mark on the over-stuffed sofa with a Moroccan-themed fabric. "I thought I'd never find a place to rest!" It was a bold lie, since I'd had a stool not moments before. "No one's sitting here, are they? Good."

She seemed prepared to ignore me, but that was fine. A.J. had told me she probably would. Instead of waiting for a reply, I launched into a monologue as I removed my shoes. "*Every* time I come to this joint, my feet end up killing me!" I reached down and rubbed them ostentatiously. "Did you just get here?"

The blonde shrugged. Up close, she looked even more as if she'd suckled on sour milk as a kid. Her eyes were so pale green, and they seemed almost empty. And I'm sorry, but when you can see the hollows beneath a girl's collarbones, it's time for her to eat a cookie or ten. "A while," she said at last. Though she kept her thin eyelids lowered, I could tell she was casting glances at my shoes. "Where did you get those?"

"Oh, Via Spiga. In Soho?" She shook her head. "You've got to go sometime. They've got gorgeous stuff, and it lasts longer than a single season."

"Really?" she asked, interested at last. In her hands

she cupped a wide glass with a vaguely yellow-looking cocktail that smelled of bananas; she sipped from it and considered. "Where in Soho?"

"Right on Broadway, near Spring Street. I buy a *lot* of my shoes there." Oh, I was so glad that I didn't have a Pinocchiolike jinx on me, because my nose could have been used simultaneously by forty-seven limbo contestants, including a few out on the sidewalk on Gansevoort Street. I had, in my defense, accompanied Alice to the store several times, enviously watching her try on pump after pump and turning down her offers to buy me a pair. "Give it a try sometime."

She swung her hair back and watched as I tucked my toes into them once again and worked the backs behind my heels. "Did you have to wait long in that awful line?"

Get the girl thinking of you as a friendly face, A.J. had instructed. *Talk about girly stuff. Bras and things. I'll take care of the rest.* Did men really think that we gals sat around talking about our lingerie on a regular basis? I didn't want to know the answer to that. Knowing A.J., he probably envisioned us doing it half-clad, then having giggly feather pillow fights that culminated in girl-on-girl make-out sessions. "Oh lord, no," I said, leaning back, then immediately popping back forward again. *Body position is everything,* was another of the rules I'd memorized earlier. *Sit or stand so that she's open to the rest of the room. Specifically, to me.* I tried to sound like the jaded kind of New Yorker who, like a debilitating case of mono, had long ago gotten over standing in lines. "I know the guy at the door. He lets me and my friends in."

It was a tricky line I was walking. Either she could think I was a pretentious ass, or, as I hoped, the kind of woman whose definition of *friend* was as slippery as pashmina on well-oiled skin. "I stood in line for an hour and a half," she finally said. I didn't miss the note of envy. "And it was fucking *cold* out there."

"Oh, no!" I oozed sympathy. "Next time, if you see me walking by, just grab me!"

"Really?" She seemed astonished that I'd offer. I felt a stab of sympathy for the poor thing. "Why would you do that?"

Ooch. Good question, and exactly the type a typically suspicious denizen of Manhattan isle would ask. I thought quickly. "Because you're a member of the Good Shoe Club. Why else? Besides, it's no skin off my back. Hey, what kind of drink is that? It smells . . . strong."

She looked at the glass in her hand with obvious disdain. "Some loser bought it for me. As if."

I snorted in sympathy. This one might be a tough cookie to crack. How much longer was I going to have to spin this out? "Doesn't that drive you *insane*?" I asked. Not that I'd had more than one experience with the phenomenon, mind you.

"Hey." Thank God. Seemingly out of nowhere, A.J. strode up. Tonight he was wearing a flimsy cotton designer shirt of a brown so dark it was nearly black, spotted all over with tiny pastel blue and pink polka dots. Somehow he'd managed to tuck it into a pair of black jeans and wrap his narrow waist with a belt sporting a buckle fashioned like the yin-yang symbol. He spoke to me. "I've only got a couple of minutes because I've got a bet going. You look smart. Can I ask you a question so we can settle this?" Ah, yes, Step Two . . . the opening gambit.

I glanced over at my new buddy, eyebrows raised, as if to say, *Here we go again*. Since A.J. was looking only in my direction; she was free to look him over. And look him over she did—from head to toe, lingering especially around the contours of his backside, all while pretending to appear disinterested by sipping from her drink. "What question?" I asked.

"That thing over there. On the other couch." He jerked his head at the sofa set perpendicular to our own, where a clutch of women shared laughter and drinks. "The last one on the left. Is that a man or a woman?"

It was a stupid question, but it didn't matter. Like the expert Method Man he was, A.J. had thrown down several of his unique strategies already. He'd made clear he was under a time limitation, to reduce the amount of threat he might project. He'd spoken to me and not to the blonde for the same reason. What's more, he didn't even appear the slightest bit interested in her; his body language was all for me, the one woman in the room thoroughly resistant to his so-called charms. "The one in the red dress?" I asked, looking her over. There was absolutely nothing out of the ordinary about the woman, though she was a little bit older and tanner than the twenty-somethings and thirty-whatsits crowding the After Ten. "I think she's a woman."

"That's what I said. I'm a doctor, and I should know." he continued, smoothly perching on the sofa arm next to me and placing his hand on the furniture's back, so that it surrounded my shoulders without touching them. If he'd been after me, it might have been clumsy and obvious—but I wasn't the object of his attention. I supposed we were on the step that involved promoting yourself as a value-added attraction, but it was difficult to suspend my disbelief at the thought of A.J. as an actual physician. "But my buddy swears up and down that she's a man."

"Is your buddy a tranny chaser or something?" When the blonde piped up next to me, it seemed pretty apparent that she wasn't fond of being left out of the conversation. Though she still pretended not to look in A.J.'s direction, her eyes kept dancing over his muscles with obvious interest. "I mean, she's got no Adam's apple."

"Excellent point. I guess you guys know best. I owe you a drink for that one. Won't be a sec. I know the bartenders here." A.J. jerked his head in the blonde's direction. "Is she always this hostile?" he asked me. Nice way to work the 'sult in, I noticed. But wasn't he walking a dangerous line? Couldn't she just as easily decide he was an asshole as find him irresistible for ignoring her?

Before I could answer, he was gone. The blonde didn't say anything, but her head turned as she watched him disappear into the crowd. "I'm *pretty* certain that's a woman," I said, leaning back as if I intended to stay for a while.

"That guy has some pretty strange friends, that's all I can say."

Oh, she didn't know the half of it.

A.J. couldn't have been gone for more than a flat sixty seconds when he reappeared, a hefty drink in each hand. He balanced them with a long-practiced grace as he wove his way in and out of the crowd, staring at me the entire time. "I hope you like this," he said, once he'd settled his hiney on the sofa arm again. He gently lowered the martini glass. "Thanks for your help. My buddy's still not convinced, but his loss."

"No, thank you!" I said, trying to sound for all the world like a girl who was meeting him for the first time. "What is it?"

"It's passionfruit, vodka, and a shot of sour grape schnapps. They're calling it the *Desperate Housewives* Martini."

"Hah!" I said, genuinely amused.

The blonde next to me had crossed both her arms and legs upon A.J.'s return, expecting to be ignored again. "Oh, yeah," he added, seeming to remember he had an identical martini in his other hand. "Thanks to you, too."

"Oh." Upon realizing she hadn't been forgotten, the woman's attitude changed immediately. She uncrossed her legs, leaned forward, and, after discarding the foul banana concoction, accepted the *Desperate Housewives*. "Thanks," she said, unfreezing enough to give him a smile that didn't show any teeth.

"Uh-huh." He turned immediately to me again. According to A.J.'s theories, focusing on me should be upping the blonde's interest factor a thousand-fold. While I wasn't sure of the exact magnitude of her absorption, it was pretty clear she did find him interesting; she leaned forward and tried to listen to what he said as she took a sip of the sickly-sweet cocktail. "I'm A.J."

"Catriona," I said, graciously putting a hand to my chest. I was rewarded by A.J.'s slightly shocked look. What, he didn't think I could come up with an alias?

"Melanie," said my couch companion.

"So Catriona, Melanie, you two are good friends, right?"

Before the blonde could tell him anything different, I swiveled my head, looked at her, winked, and then turned back around and said, "Sure we are."

"Want to see how good?"

I shrugged, pretending to teeter on the brink between active interest and a simple desire to pass the time. "What do you think?" I asked Melanie.

She shrugged. We were exactly like bored high school girls being courted by some geeky guy. "All right."

"Excellent." In one smooth move, like a chess knight gliding between two more powerful pieces, A.J. managed to ease himself from the sofa's sturdy arm and between the two of us. Honestly, if I hadn't been mindful of the techniques he was employing, I would've sworn that he'd been sitting in the middle, beside me, the entire time, and furthermore, that I'd invited him there and liked it. He leaned forward from the waist, forcing us to turn a little to see him. "Hold out your hands," he said, again reserving all his attention for me. He barely appeared to notice when Melanie slipped her slim fingers in his meaty paw. "Now: Do you both wear the same perfumes?"

I had no idea how I was supposed to know. I

glanced at Melanie, and she did the same to me. "I don't really wear a lot of scent," she said.

"And I like citrus-y smells," I volunteered.

"Okay. Question two." His hand was warm around mine. "What's your favorite color?"

"Green," I answered, immediately glancing her way.

"Orange," she said.

"Mmmm." A.J. appeared noncommittal. "Last question: I'm thinking of a shape. What is it?"

She raised her eyebrows at me, then said to A.J., "Triangle."

"Kind of an ovoid with spiky lines going throu . . . I mean, plain old circle," I amended when A.J. gave my fingers a vicious squeeze.

He appeared to think for a moment. "We didn't agree much, did we?" Melanie asked, while waiting for an answer. She seemed totally interested in the questions; but then again, she probably thought of the *Cosmo* quizzes as something akin to gospel.

"You know what's important about your answers?" We both shook our heads. "It's not that your answers were different, but that you looked at each other before each of them. There's a bond there—you're communicating. That's important for a friendship." After all that schmaltz, I looked longingly at my *Desperate Housewives* Martini but refrained from reaching for the glass. A.J. turned to Melanie for the first time and said, off-handedly, "It's interesting that you like orange and that you mentioned a triangle."

She was all attention. "Why's that?"

Slowly, subtly, he shifted his body so that it pointed

toward her. Her own legs were angled directly perpendicular to his now; they'd become quite the cozy little pair without Melanie even realizing it. "Well, a lot of people say green. It's a safe color, green. Naive. Circles are kind of the same thing. Safety. No edges. You're different from that, aren't you?"

Melanie smiled a little bit, and if she didn't outright look in my direction and say, *hell yes, I'm better than that hussy on your other side,* there was something about the congratulatory way she sipped her martini that certainly implied it. She looked altogether like a cat who'd just eaten a serving of bacon off its owner's plate and wasn't in the least sorry. "I like to think I am," she said, removing the plastic toothpick from her drink and popping the maraschino cherry on its end into her mouth.

"Scientific tests show that people who answer *orange* tend to be more adventurous and outgoing, and crave a lot of stimulation. I mean, it takes a bold kind of person to appreciate orange, don't you think?"

"Mmm-hmm." She nodded in agreement.

"More sexually adventurous, too," he said, managing to sound quite serious without transgressing into sleazy. Me? I was all but forgotten, over in my sofa Siberia. "People who answer *triangle* tend to be very sensually oriented. They like massage, for example."

"Oh, I love massage!" murmured Melanie. Privately, I rolled my eyes.

"They enjoy tactile sensations more than other people. Like hand-holding." It was only then that Melanie looked down and realized that A.J. still held her hand. Mine, he'd dropped a while before. "Or, when they're with a lover, they enjoy things like—oh, I don't know, having fingertips run over their skin—but not tickling." Melanie shook her head. A.J.'s message might have had a different effect if he hadn't been so clinical about it. Heck, *I* might have bought it if I hadn't known him any better. "Triangles tend to feel pretty deeply about social issues, too. I bet you're like that."

Whether or not Melanie had any clue what he meant was totally up in the air. She certainly hadn't given any indication of it. But I could see through to the diabolical cleverness of A.J.'s scheme: who was actually going to come out and say they didn't give a damn about social issues? "Of course," she said.

"I'm a triangle, too, you know."

"Really?" she asked, with intensifying interest. *Set up the similarities.*

"So, anyway," he said, dropping her hand like a hot potato and looking around the room as if searching out his friend, "that's what the personality test said about you."

"What kind of doctor are you, a psychiatrist?" she asked, obviously loath for him to leave.

"Not a psychiatrist, no," he said. "But I find the human mind fascinating. Don't you?"

Up the Yes Ladder she went, one more step. "Absolutely!"

He held up a finger. "For example: Say the first thing off the top of your head to my next question. Ready?" She nodded. "Name a number from one to ten."

Without hesitation, she said, "Seven."

A.J. nodded ruefully, as if that hadn't been the answer he'd expected. He shifted his weight to one side, reaching around to his back pocket with one hand, managing to slide a little closer. He retrieved a folded slip of paper, which he twiddled between his second and third fingers. "Check this out."

Melanie set down her martini on the little glass-topped table nearby, then took the paper and opened it up. Wonderingly, she displayed it to A.J. It had the numeral 7 written on it. "Oh, my God!" she gulped. "Are you a mind reader?"

A.J. laughed with as much self-deprecation as he could muster . . . which, to me, didn't seem like much. "No, though some guys would try to pass themselves off as one. Do you know that it's human instinct to answer with the number seven when asked that question?" He tapped at his temple. "Scientists—like me—think it has to do with the brain's hardwiring. You enjoy hearing about that kind of thing, don't you? I can tell."

"Well, sure!"

"Excuse me," I said, standing up with my drink. "I think I see a friend."

I could have told them I was about to pass a kidney stone in my martini and they wouldn't have noticed. I was effectively shut out. They were up to the next step: *Isolate the target from the outside world.* I'd done my work, and A.J. had certainly done his. Mission accomplished.

It was funny, but I felt giddy as I left them and made my way over to the quieter side of the bar—and by quieter, I meant the side where people were merely talking at a louder volume than usual instead of caterwauling at the tops of their lungs. Yes, I actually felt giddy. Light-headed. Shaky legs. Fluttery stomach. The whole nine yards and then some. Some part of me felt as if I'd taken part in some marvelous caper, or as if I were a gamine Audrey Hepburn in an old-fashioned, clever movie comedy in which I'd gotten to wear dozens of pairs of Jackie O–sized sunglasses and more than a few disguises. Was this what criminals felt like after they'd broken the law and gotten away with it? Minus, of course, the mug shots, the fingerprinting, the MOST WANTED ads in the post office, and the threat of possible incarceration?

Because if it was, I liked it. I, Rebecca Egan, dressed up like some little kid in my older sister's clothing, liked being a gender outlaw. Did that make me sound like some kind of cross-dressing, sex-change candidate? No matter. I'd led a fellow female to the slaughter with no regrets. I felt sorry for the poor thing—I mean, how many people could fall victim to A.J.'s dubious charms and still look at themselves in the next day's cold, harsh light of morning? But as for my own part in her demise? It didn't affect me in the least.

A gentleman at the bar offered me his stool when I approached, seemingly intending to use the act as an opener to get to know me. I thanked him politely, then spun away so that I faced the softly underlit bar itself. So these guys wanted to play chess? I knew chess. I'd played it with my dad three times a week after school in my youth, and I knew full well that once you got your most valuable piece safely protected, nothing could bring it down. I crossed my legs, sipped my free drink, and continued to glow.

With a little bit of thought, I realized that maybe I

was wrong. I hadn't enjoyed leading poor Melanie down the garden path to seduction. That was simply an unfortunate side-effect. It sounded corny, but what I'd really loved about that escapade was getting out of myself for a few minutes and getting a good, scary glimpse into the male psyche. I mean, my God! The time and effort A.J. had put into his Method! The rules! The theories! The strategies! If A.J. and his ilk harnessed some of that energy for good instead of for lechery, they could have solved the ills of AIDS and cancer and world hunger and even the Third World water access thingie that Alice and her organization were always going on about.

And what amazed me was that it worked! If someone had come up to me on the street and asked me, the average, underpaid, overworked, Manhattan woman, if I'd thought a handful of mildly manipulative artifices could have a woman eating out of a guy's hand, I would have answer with a hearty *Hell, no!* We like to think of ourselves as a tough and hardy breed who've seen everything, not pawns that can be moved around at will. Yet I'd been one of those pawns all through my marriage, I realized. My abortive attempts at mingling as a single had nearly resulted in the same end-game.

It wasn't going to happen again. A.J. had bestowed upon me a gift: free and clear sight. I wouldn't be taken in again.

Newer, better Rebecca was still feeling exultant when, a few minutes later, A.J. sidled up to her. "Nice work!"

I'd been savoring the triumph of the evening; I hadn't seen him in the vast mirror affixed to the warehouse brick. "What are you doing here?" I yodeled, nearly jumping out of my skin. "I thought you'd be in a cab, halfway to Melanie's place by now."

"Who?" he said, feigning forgetfulness. I swatted him. "I know, I know. No offense to the gal—she's cute and all—but she's not bed-worthy." He raised a finger to one of the bartenders, who instantly stopped his trek for another patron to pour a shot of scotch and hand it to him. "Thanks, Benny." He took a sip, seemed to wash a bad taste out of his mouth with the stuff, and swallowed as he looked around the bar. "But I've got to say, hats off to you. Especially for a first-timer. You leaped in there, you did your spadework, and when I swooped in for the kill, you drove off like a banshee."

"How many metaphors are you going for, there, big guy?" I asked.

"How many who?"

"Forget it." Emboldened by success, I grabbed the shot glass out of his hand and took a swig. I wasn't a scotch fan, but the *Desperate Housewives* Martini was a little cloying. The stuff seared my pipes on the way down, leaving me slightly breathless. "But I don't know why you didn't seal the deal."

"She was attractive. Doable. Just not what I had a taste for."

"Hmmm." I cleared my throat—or tried to, anyway. "You're not *really* a doctor, are you?"

"I just play one on TV." Smartass. I'd find out what he did for a living one of these days.

Everything had been going so well that evening. I'd been having such a great and giddy good time. So of course something had to come along to mess it up.

"A.J.?" asked someone behind me. Then the voice added, with surprise, "Rebecca?"

Oh, no. A.J., already all smiles, held out his arms before I could even turn around. I knew, though, whom I'd find standing behind me: his little sister, staring at the two of us with happiness and bemusement. "Baby girl!" A.J. said, cocooning my nemesis in his arms and rocking her back and forth in a touching display of fraternal affection. Over her shoulder, he opened his eyes and made a face that, in a very close toss-up, could have read either, *Whoops!* or maybe, *Get her off! She's choking me!*

"Becky!" The human anaconda came for me with arms outstretched. Since falling to my knees and crawling away wasn't a real option—honest, I checked—I found myself accepting one of her strangulating hugs. Once we'd separated, she appraisingly looked over my outfit, my shoes, and my hair, apparently couldn't find anything negative to say about them, and settled for, "What in the world are you doing here?"

"Well, you know." I laughed lightly, trying to make it sound as if the After Ten was my usual little hole-in-the-wall bar where everybody knew my name.

She laughed along with me until we'd run out of false hilarity. Then her face fell slack. "No, really."

I looked at A.J. He looked at me. Portia watched the two of us exchange complicit glances, her eyebrows ever-so-slightly knit, though not to a degree that actually might risk a future wrinkle. "Well . . ." I started to say.

My colluder, for once, had lost all his usual aplomb. "Yeah, you see . . ."

"A.J.?" Portia had been holding a rum and Coke, but she placed it down on the bar beside us and stood with her hands on her hips. "What's going on here?" She looked from him to me and back again. "There's something you're not telling me."

I tried to laugh again, but she'd pulled her pretty and smooth face into something resembling a stern schoolmarm's and had crossed her arms. It silenced me immediately. "Okay, Portia, look: Here's the truth. The utter, unvarnished truth." Could she tell I was stalling? "Okay. The truth. I was feeling kind of . . ."

"We're dating." You know what? A.J.'s explanation was *nothing* like mine was going to be. My jaw actually dropped open as I gaped at what he'd said. Portia's did as well; she regarded us both with shock and, my pride was hurt slightly to see, a little bit of apparent nausea. The big stupid lug to my right in the meantime nodded solemnly. "Yep. We're an item." He grabbed me around the shoulders and pulled me close, rubbing my arm. "Aren't we, honey?" I literally couldn't answer, so shocked was I.

"But . . ." Portia hadn't gotten over the bombshell either. It took her a good few seconds to work up an answer. I sat there in silent suspense, waiting for her reaction, before I even attempted to join in the dialogue. I didn't have too long to wait; she at last broke out with a broad, sunny smile and almost yelled, "But that's *fantastic*. Oh, my God!" Still in awe, she grabbed one each of our hands with hers, jumped a little on her heels, and repeated herself. "That is *fantastic!* My big brother! And one of my old, old, *oldest* friends!"

I smiled weakly, not totally onboard with either the lie or the way she made it sound like my teeth could be carbon-dated to the Mesozoic era. "Hey, now."

"I'm so happy for you! Oh, I bet your sister is, too!"

A.J. and I stared at each other with the same panicked countenances on both our faces. "But you can't tell anyone," he said at last, drawing his index fingers to his lips to indicate a confidential shush. "It's got to be a secret."

"But why?" Portia wanted to know. Of course. Who wouldn't ask?

"Because . . ." In a circumstance as rare as the appearance of Halley's Comet, A.J. seemed at a loss for words. He appealed to me silently. "Because we . . ."

"Because of Alice," I found myself saying. Portia moved her attention from her brother to me. Her unwavering stare made it even more difficult to construct a plausible lie. "Because she . . . set me up with this guy from her office. He's an incredible goober. And it's not going to go anywhere. But you know how controlling Alice can be. Plus, of course, she would worry that if A.J. and I split up . . ."

"Like we ever would, sweetheart!" A.J. mugged nuzzling my neck until I dug my nails into his thigh.

"But if it didn't work out, she would worry about your friendship. The friendship you guys have! Because you know, you're her best friend."

"I know I am!" Oh, yes, I had her now. She had been nodding in sympathy the entire time. "And I *completely* understand." Could she hear our twin sighs of relief? I certainly felt them. "But honestly, Rebecca. I would never hate Alice because you were a thoughtless bitch!"

"And that's why it's got to be our little secret, sis." As he spoke, A.J. practically had to hold me down. "At least until things are more settled between us."

Was she going to agree? I held my breath until at long last she nodded, biting her lip. Then she broke out in glee once more. "But I still think it's wonderful. And I'm so happy for you both! My two favorite people in the world! Well, my favorite person in the world, and one of my other favorites. Though there is our mother and father, of course. And Alice. And Rani. And my producer. And . . ."

A.J. cut her off before I discovered that in Portia's universe, I ranked right between the guy at the Chinese grocery and her third grade teacher. "But you can't tell anyone. Remember?"

"Our little secret!" she agreed, giggling.

"That's right! Our little secret! All right, sis. Bye-bye, now!"

I have to admit, A.J. certainly knew how to handle that sister of his. I'd thought she might stick around for the rest of the evening, but at his farewell she curtsyed at the knees. "Oh, I see. You want some *alone* time!"

"That's right!" I said, playing along. "Don't we, honey?"

A.J. took my hand in his, then brought it to his lips and kissed my fingers. It was all I could do to keep from wrenching it away and shaking off the cooties. "We sure do."

"Naughty!" She laughed, then mimed zipping shut her lips as she backed away. "I won't say a thing."

"Mum's the world!" I caroled, pretending to be blissfully happy

"Bye-bye, now!" A.J. waggled his fingers and talked in a high tenor. "Bye-bye! Bye-bye! Bye . . . all right, she's gone." Almost immediately he flung down my hand and grabbed for his drink.

I managed to keep my knuckles from hitting the bar's stone front just in time. "Gone?" I repeated, voice raised to a shriek. "She's going to blow this whole thing!"

"She's not."

"She is!"

"There's one thing you don't know about my sister." A.J.'s voice was so confident and calm that I stopped whipping myself into a frenzy to listen. "She does *everything* I ask her to. Everything." I must have looked dubious, because he added, "If I tell her to stay quiet, she'll stay quiet."

I considered that. I could see it happening. I'd always noticed how much Portia worshipped her big brother. Already I felt 100 percent calmer. "And do you do everything she asks you?"

"She's only asked me to do one thing."

"What?"

"Listen to her show every day."

"And do you?"

He laughed instead of answering. Or rather, I suppose it was answer enough. "Let's get back to the game, shall we?" Chugging an ice cube into his mouth, A.J. sucked on it as he considered the room. "Let's see. You know what I have a taste for?"

"What?" Weird, but I was already recovering from the

close call we'd had with Portia. Pretending to be A.J.'s secret girlfriend was, in a lot of ways, just another layer of deception atop the game we'd already played earlier that evening. I was a naughty girl—and the realization made me tingle from my head to my toes.

"Hmmm," he said, looking around. Then, without hesitation, he swung around to a girl with a short, dark bob and a mildly conservative suit who looked as if she'd come to the bar straight from a show. She scarcely came up to my chest. Although she'd been talking to a pair of women a few feet away from where I stood, A.J. tapped her on the shoulder. "Excuse me—sorry to bother you," he said, leaning down and speaking loudly and distinctly. "But have you ever owned a parrot?"

"What?" asked the girl, crinkling her face as she gave him the once-over. "No!"

"Oh, sorry." He straightened up and appeared to study her for a second. "I guess you don't look like a pet person, after all. This woman, here, was just telling me that she was thinking of getting a parrot and wanted to know if they were high maintenance."

Now the girl looked at me as if I were the crazy one. "Birds stink!"

A.J. nodded slowly. "That's what I thought. They stink and they have lice. But this woman—what was your name again?" he asked me.

Showtime. I sighed deeply, crooked my wrist, and affected the pose of a weary would-be parrot owner. "Hedvig."

Was that a glare I got from A.J. in return for that? "Yeah, Hedvig says she thinks they're way more sanitary than cats or dogs."

"She's a lunatic." I was beginning to gather that A.J. liked the targets who weren't shy of sharing their opinions. "Cats are *much* cleaner, and they don't poop on the floor like birds do. I mean, disgusting!"

"Are you a cat owner, too, then?" said A.J., turning ever-so-slightly away from me.

"I have three." The girl crossed her arms and swayed from side to side, obviously in no hurry to end the conversation. She looked up and down A.J.'s massive body, ending her study at his interested, broad, white smile. "Do you?"

"Well, no," he said, sighing. "Sadly, my landlord won't let me. That's why I volunteer at the animal shelter twice a week. Just so I can see the animals."

"Re-ally!" said the woman, melting a little.

"Oh, sure. I hope you got your cats from a shelter. There are so many helpless pets who need a loving home, you know." She might not have known it, but the woman had been turning away from her friends and the vast majority of the After Ten's patrons so she could focus solely on A.J. He glanced at me over her shoulder and gave me the slightest, the most imperceptible of winks.

I knew my cue. Grinning broadly, I picked up my drink and skedaddled. Once again, the knight had captured the queen, and I'd loved watching every move it had taken.

and when he played Albert #3 in *The Six Faces of Einstein*. I'd even been there for his potentially biggest triumph that turned out to be his most notorious flop, in which—courtesy of an aerosol can of white hair spray—he'd appeared as The Grandfather in a musical adaptation of *Flowers in the Attic*.

On this particular night, though, we were there because we'd endured Alan's performance as Jason in the Jean Anouilh adaptation of *Medea*. Normally I'm up for a good classic Greek revenge tragedy as much as the next divorced girl, but this production had turned out to be unusually trying. The director had decided to go with a marriage-as-oppression angle and subsequently designed the sets and costumes to imitate those in old episodes of *Leave it to Beaver*. He'd also apparently cast his girlfriend, a flaxen-haired temptress billed as Charlene—no last name, of course—as the mute onstage Greek chorus. At least, that was my interpretation of what she was doing as she stood silently upstage on the Formica kitchenette table with her hips jutted out in a number of irrelevantly sexy poses. Throw in the mix a number of hard wooden seats with no cushions and a theater so far Off-Off-Broadway that we were actually in Hackensack, and you've got the most tortuous evening every known to mankind. After an hour and a half of it, I'd begun thinking that Medea's murdered kids were getting the better end of the deal.

Afterward, of course, we were part of the select opening-night group of 200 invited to mingle with the cast and crew, so we could laud them with compliments and bemoan the state of commercialized theater these days when gems like whatever we'd just seen were unjustly overlooked. "Alan!" I cried out when he approached us in what used to be the fellowship hall of the old church-turned-theater. "God, you were wonderful. Really, really, really, really good."

I was never good at lauding. He saw through me right away. "That bad, huh?" Onstage, Alan was always called upon to play super-masculine roles that took advantage of his broad shoulders, deep and resonant voice, and uncanny ability to play gruff, bluff brutes able to show their inner marshmallow. Offstage, he was gayer than a double-feature of *Whatever Happened to Baby Jane?* and the Garland *A Star is Born*, with a chaser of strawberry-kiwi daiquiris. "Sweetie, look at you!" he said, kissing me on both cheeks and leaving a little of his makeup behind. He let his hands wander down my sweater, pulled out the side hem of my skirt, and then checked out my shoes. "You're letting your sister dress you again!"

I flushed; it was true. Save for my undies, every ounce of clothing on my back was Alice's yet again. "Do you never change?" I asked. "It's sick, how young you always look. Are you still with Phil?"

He accepted the compliment with a giggle, then smoothed down the Ward Cleaver tie he was still wearing fresh off the stage. "Phil moved to L.A. But thank you for the flattery. You always tell the best lies. Do you like the hair? I've decided to go super-short, since male pattern balding is such a bitch. Who's your friend?"

"Oh." I'd almost forgotten that I had a date myself. Rather, I wished I could have forgotten that I was there with someone. "Alan, this is Walter Sle . . . hang on, I mean . . ."

"Walter Pleziak." My companion reached out and pumped Alan's hand so vigorously that to the casual outsider it might have appeared he was trying to loosen the actor's arm from the shoulder joint. "Gosh, that play was swell. A real thought-provoker. I've been trying to think all evening what it reminded me of."

Alan bestowed upon my so-called date a genuinely warm smile and then cocked his head and plainly pitied me. "Maybe the classic Greek play *Medea* by Euripides?"

"You know"—Walter pointed at my old friend as if he'd come up with something—"that might be it."

"Ah." Alan paused, then smiled. "Good, then." Poor Walter. I was so loath to be with him that I couldn't even look at the guy. It wasn't just the bobbing tracheotomy scar, either. His L.L. Bean outfit was certainly no worse than the majority of my own clothes, and probably considerably better, even though I still couldn't stand the corduroy jackets that seemed such a ubiquitous part of his wardrobe. I'd unfortunately come to think of Walter as some kind of romantic golem, a Frankenstein's monster of dating pieced together from unknown donors and animated solely by a passion for water access rights. It didn't in the least surprise me that Alan couldn't see a connection between us either. "Where is your sister? She and I have so much to catch up on. I'm so glad *you* came, though. You never miss anything of mine! Look at her," he added to Walter. "I can tell just what she's thinking to that: *more's the pity!*"

"Get out," I grinned, swatting him. "I think she's over by the puff pastry."

"I must see that fabulous bitch posthaste. Back in a few." He sailed away in a cloud of grease paint and Brylcreem.

I mourned, mostly because I knew it meant that Walter would begin talking to me. "So, he's an old college friend?"

"Didn't Alice explain any of this to you?" If I sounded a trifle impatient, it was only because I was. A dose of Walter felt a little like a teaspoon of itching powder in my bra. "Alan is her ex. Her ex-husband. She was married to him for six years." I missed those six years, too. No matter how bad the play he was in, Alan had never ceased to be entertaining during its run and eventual death.

"Wait a minute." While I waited for Walter to process the information, I spied Alan greeting Alice across the room. She beamed at him with genuine affection and leaned over to give him a hug, her long and elegant neck resting on his shoulder in an old, familiar way. He thumped her several times on the back, and then they began to gabble excitedly while still holding hands. Walter, in the meantime, had finally worked it out. "Your sister was married to a gay man?"

"Yes." Was it bad that half of me hoped he'd trot out some not-so-subtle intolerances? It would be the perfect excuse to have an argument and high-tail it away from him, rather than having to continue pretending I could abide the guy. We weren't even on an official date—I'd merely told Alice that I'd be attending to-night's performance stag, and she'd decided to give one of the comp tickets to my shambling, tweedy nightmare man. I felt guilty enough, though, that I'd allowed him to tag behind me all evening. "My sister was married to a gay, gay, very gay, super-gay man."

"Wow." From our hors d'oeuvre–less position against the wall, near the door through which people were still filtering from upstairs, Walter studied Alice and her ex. "And she didn't know?"

Typically, my answer to that kind of question would have been along the lines of "How could she *not* know?" but in this case I felt particularly defensive on Alan's behalf. "She knew. He didn't hide his orientation. It wasn't one of those *Brokeback* situations. They were friends for a long time, and it was just an arrangement they decided to try, and when it didn't work out the way they thought, they decided to end it like civilized adults."

If my speech sounded a tad defensive it was because I was relating it to a relative stranger whom I really didn't want to entrust with much in the way of personal family information. Walter, though, seemed to take it like a man. He nodded and observed, "I've noticed that your sister always seems to manage her affairs like the most civilized of adults."

What, that was it? "You think it's bad that she married a gay guy?"

"Bad? Of course not." He furrowed his high-and-mighty forehead. "I suppose they both had their reasons."

"You don't think it's *unusual?*" Why I was so challenging, I wasn't clear. Maybe I really did want to provoke a fight.

Walter wore the beatific look of a man at peace with the world and his own sexuality. Damn it! "From what I

understand, it's not uncommon. Statistics seem to indicate that a significant percentage of the population
has admitted, in surveys, to . . ."

If there was anyone who deserved to be battered
with talk of statistics after trying to bait Walter into an
argument, it probably was me. I'd just belted myself
down and prepared to take my bumpy and long-
winded penance when through the hall doors walked
Portia Daye, looking stunning as usual. My first instinct
was to scamper away as fast as my legs could take me,
but I was so surrounded by Anouilh lovers that flight
was impossible. Besides, I was taller than just about all
the women in the room and most of the men, so she
could have tracked me down like a bloodhound. "Rebecca!" she exclaimed in her sleepy soprano.

It wasn't as if I hadn't seen Portia during the play.
She'd arrived late—as usual—and made quite a
scene—as usual—as she crawled over person after
person stuffed into the old church pews with a date
we'd never seen before—as usual—in tow, until at last
they'd reached a space in the row ahead of us. Over
Medea's anguished railings at her poor womanly fate
and Charlene's awkward gyrations on the kitchen
table, she'd mimed contrition and regret to everyone
around her, though with Portia it was difficult to tell
whether she was rueful about arriving ten minutes after the curtain had gone up or whether she was sorry
that not everyone else in the audience was as fetching
as she. I was lucky enough to be right on the aisle, so
that the moment Alan and Charlene and the woman
playing Medea had taken their bows, I managed to
lose Portia in the crowd. Yet I wasn't deluded enough

to think I could avoid seeing her all evening. Toughing it out was the only thing I could do. That, and praying she wouldn't blab a word about her brother.

"Portia!" I exclaimed as she grabbed my hands and gave me an air kiss. I used the same blithe tones as moments before when I'd greeted Alan. When her cheek was close to my mouth, I reined her in and begged, "Please don't say a word about A.J. Please." When we separated, my eyes kept up the pleading that my mouth couldn't do.

Walter had noticed my strange behavior. "Rebecca? Is something wrong?"

"Yes, Rebecca, is something wrong?" Portia leapt into action, pouting and swinging our arms as if we were six years old and going 'round the mulberry bush. "Are oo mad at Portia?"

Oh, lordy. "No, of course not." I kept my face perfectly blank and simulated an expression of puzzlement and surprised. "Why would I be?"

She kept up the baby talk and, in a Portia-sized effort to remain subtle, winked at me so broadly that there might have been a few people in Connecticut, all blind from birth, who missed the gesture—but I doubt it. "Because Portia was a naughty girl and talked about oo on her radio show." Without missing a beat, she resumed her normal voice, extended a hand to Walter, and announced, "Hello, I'm Portia Daye. You've probably heard me on 'Portia Daye's Radio Show with Portia Daye'."

Walter seemed utterly nonplussed at what to do with her hand, which hadn't been presented to him as a handshake but rather in the manner in which royalty and popes traditionally have expressed a desire for sycophants to kiss their rings. After staring at her curled digits for a moment, he finally shook them up and down. "Walter Pleziak." When she continued staring at him, he added, "I'm escorting Rebecca this evening."

And if that wasn't the most milquetoast way of avoiding the use of the word *date*, I didn't know what was. Portia looked down Walter's pale blue sweater and the blue, button-down shirt that lay beneath, the brown corduroy jacket, the gray slacks, and the penny loafers, and then back up at his square-set face, finishing off with an inspection of his fine, thin hair. She let out a little laugh. "No. Be serious!"

I loved her a little right then.

While Walter was trying to figure out exactly what she'd meant by that remark, Portia immediately went back to her favorite topic. "Rebecca," she pleaded, almost lapsing back into baby talk again. "I only do these things because I want to help. I hope you understand that. Don't be mad. As an established member of the media community I have the ability to reach out and change lives. It's a dangerous power, Rebecca, but when I can use it for good, I feel it's my duty." All through her speech she'd held her hand to her chest to indicate her absolute sincerity, apparently not realizing that the Academy Award was only bestowed upon the best performances committed to film, not those executed in the basement of the old Hackensack Second United Methodist Church.

"I'm really afraid I don't know what you're talking about," I said, laughing lightly. I could see Sarah, dressed up in her usual evening-out ensemble of black slacks and billowing black blouse, beetling her way in our direction, Dixie cup of wine punch firmly in hand. "Did you do something?"

"You really don't know?" Portia said, cocking her head. She never could conceive of anyone not listening to her show. "Really?"

"No, I don't." I dug deep and made myself sound firm. "Really?"

"Nope."

Portia wasn't the kind of woman who took no for an answer. "Really?"

I was about to repeat myself for a third time when Sarah finally edged her way forward. "Portia, Becca is really upset about all the things you've been saying about her on your show."

In a move straight out of a Three Stooges short, I actually slapped my hand to my forehead, but not before I noticed Portia widening her eyes in my direction. Any gloating to which she might have felt compelled, however, was more than discounted at discovering she had another fan. "Have you been listening?" she asked Sarah, delighted to a broad smile. "Chaz, did you hear that? Everybody loves me. Chaz doesn't have a radio," she explained. "He's never heard my show. Poor thing!"

I think we'd all forgotten the floppy-haired fellow with the piercing blue eyes standing behind Portia, although during our conversation he'd been smoldering with a number of male-model stares that apparently he'd picked up from repeated viewings of the movie *Zoolander*. In fact, with his narrowed eyes and his jutted jaw, I was pretty sure he was right then treating us to his version of the Blue Steel pose. "I don't have a radio," he said, nodding with great solemnity.

"Silly. I just said that!" Portia swatted him.

"Oh, my God," Sarah said, aghast. "She's found someone on her same mental level."

"Sarah, aren't you *sweet!*" Practically glowing with delight, Portia grabbed Chaz's hand and bounced a little, as if she'd just announced they were engaged. She looked at him fondly. "We do feel a certain kinship. Chaz is an actor. I'm going to help him break into the business. It's amazing how we seemed destined to meet. It's like Serengeti."

Sarah had been spoiling for a fight, but like me, she was flabbergasted at the random mention of Tanzania. "Serendipity?" she finally asked, gesturing with her drink.

"No thanks." Portia smiled, then beckoned to Sarah with her index finger, crooking it to draw her closer. "I think when it comes to alcohol we should be setting a better example for you-know-who," she said in a confidential tone pitched somewhere between a stage whisper and a yodel. In case no one knew who you-know-who was, Portia nodded in my direction.

"I really don't have a drinking problem," I felt compelled to tell Walter for some odd reason. "She just has this . . . idea."

"Oh?" He blinked rapidly.

Portia straightened up and grabbed her date's hand. "Well, we've got to go see darling Alan. I want to introduce Chaz to him and see what he thinks." Knowing Alan, the reaction would be something along the lines of *Hubba, hubba!* "I'll see you all later. Well, not you, probably," she added to Walter, "but it was nice to meet you anyway. Oh, Rebecca!" she said, remembering something. "My brother said hello." Once again she let loose with one of those broad, vaudevillian winks.

My insides clenched so tightly that I could have sat down on a penny and picked it up. Portia might be keeping her end of the secret bargain, but she was going to give me a myocardial infarction in the process. "Oh, did he?" I said, fearing my attempt at nonchalance wouldn't fool anyone. "That's nice."

Chaz tightened his jaw muscles and gave us a fierce expression copied from the pages of a Calvin Klein editorial. "It's been great," he said, before Portia led him away by the hand through the room's center.

None of us spoke for a moment until Walter broke the silence. "Who is she, again?"

"One of my sister's friends," I groaned, for what must have been the thousandth time in my life.

Any hopes I had of escaping scot-free were dashed when Sarah turned to me with her arms crossed and demanded to know, "Why in the *world* would that simian of a brother of hers send a message through her?" I shook my head helplessly, certain that she'd guessed about my assignations with A.J. and mere inches away from confessing all, when Sarah said, "You know, I give up. It's like trying to come up with a system for roulette when you know that the whole thing is completely random and the odds are overwhelmingly against you. You're absolutely right," she said to me, ignoring Walter's presence. "You're right. My psychiatrist is right. When it comes to Portia and the absolutely crazy, mental things that go on in that fallen soufflé of a brain of hers, I just need to let go. I just need . . . to let . . . go."

Since that afternoon in the park the week before, Sarah and I hadn't been quite the friends we'd been before; I'd gone out to lunch with Ethan and sometimes Michaela instead of the usual brown-bag chatterfests in Sarah's office, and we'd even skipped our regular Monday night *24* Kiefer love-in in front of Alice's television. Oh, we'd been cordial, but I don't think either of us would have denied that the slightest of chills had descended over the relationship. "Really?" I asked, hopeful. "Because I honestly don't think she's being malicious. She's just . . . the way she is."

"You keep saying that. I know. But the way she is drives me utterly crazy, and I've got enough on my plate without her. First thing tomorrow, I'm going to take my dad's radio out of my office," she swore, "and give it to Cesar to use in the server room. If you see me inching toward it in the afternoon, I want you to slap my hands." Her guilty eyes looked into mine for a minute, then away again. "I'm sorry."

It was a handsome gesture. Knowing that Sarah disliked emotional scenes, I merely laid a hand on her elbow and squeezed. "Did you really talk to your psychiatrist about her?"

"In both my regular session and an emergency weekend session," she confessed. "And then again yesterday. I sounded crazy even to *myself*."

Asking even a close friend to divulge what's gone on beneath the shrink-patient cloak of confidentiality is always an iffy proposition, but I didn't have to wait long to find out what he'd said, thank goodness. "You know what he did? He listened to me for all of those three sessions, then right before I left yesterday he gave me an assignment. He said, 'Sarah, I want you to write an essay about redecorating your living room.'"

"That's it?" Almost immediately I knew how unsupportive I sounded. I might as well have said, *What, he didn't offer you Prozac?* "I mean, why?"

"That's the thing." She took an extended sip of her punch. "These guys don't give you random assignments for no reason. It means something, and I'm going to figure it out."

I'd never been in therapy; I didn't really know how it worked, other than that you shelled out your cash, talked for fifty minutes, and occasionally learned something from the experience. "When's it due? Are you redecorating your living room for real?" Sarah's efficiency flat didn't even *have* a formal living room.

"It's due whenever I finish it, and with what money am I going to redccorate?" She shrugged, then finished off her drink. "It's a metaphor for something. I'll figure it out. Who are you?"

For a startled second I thought she was throwing out another metaphor, but then I realized she was talking to Walter. The long-suffering guy had stood there silently while we'd talked, no doubt wishing he were anywhere but with the woman with all the crazy friends. Well, I could hope, anyway. He reached out his hand and pumped Sarah's. "I'm Walter Pleziak," he announced. "I'm—"

"He works with Alice," I said hastily, before he

could tell anyone else we were dating. "And speak of the devil!"

Although I didn't at all mind being surrounded by a group of people who would dilute the amount of time I'd have to spend actually talking to Walter, I'd actually kind of hoped we could have done it a little closer to the refreshment table. After a lengthy spell of French-authored drama, I was famished, and the little Costco mini-quiches on the warming plates looked as if they would hit the spot perfectly. Alice carried a paper plate with several of them that she balanced as she tiptoed toward me, Alan straggling behind. ". . . Sorry!" he was saying. "I gave my mailing list to the theater staff and he was still on it. I didn't mean . . ."

Even when she was in a mood, Alice always managed to come off as damned elegant. I could tell something was up by the way she carried herself, but to anyone else she seemed as cool as the cream and camel ensemble she sported like a professional runway model. "You don't have to apologize twice, Alan," she groused.

"I just don't want her thinking . . ." The actor smiled at me and stopped dead in his tracks. "Hi!" he said brightly.

Too brightly, in fact. "Thinking what?" I asked, suspicious. Alice and Alan had reverted to that chipper, resilient facade they'd adopted during their showcase marriage. It might have been effective at convincing strangers that nothing was wrong beneath the surface, but I knew better. "Want her thinking what!" I repeated.

Alice reached out and put her hand on my shoulder. Uh-oh. This was going to be bad. "Sweetie."

"Is there something wrong with Dad?" I asked, alarmed. "Mom? Is she okay?"

"They're fine." All the visions of ambulance lights and hospital gurneys I'd been having allayed, she squeezed me reassuringly. "Everything's fine. You're surrounded by friends who love you." Was I mistaken, or did she give Walter a meaningful look? I didn't dare glance his way to find out. "And I love you."

"Alice . . ." I growled.

"Just tell the child!" Alan was no more than thirty-five, mind you.

My sister looked over her shoulder, fretful. "Well . . ."

I wanted to shake her. "Tell the child!"

"Oh, my god," said Sarah, beside me. "Sean."

The name galvanized me like a cable running straight from an electrical transformer. "Is *he* in the hospital?"

"No, sweetie, he's—"

Sarah pointed to a corner of the room. "He's right over there."

I couldn't speak. I couldn't even blink the fuzzies from my eyes to see clearly.

"I was trying to explain to your sister—"

Alice shut Alan up with a single finger. "There's been a little mix-up," she said in tones that would have soothed even an irate pair of new parents informed that the baby they'd taken home didn't belong to them.

"He's here? Sean is here? *Here?*" I repeated, over and over again, knowing that I sounded like I needed a session or three with Sarah's analyst. "Where?"

"Let's not prolong this," said Alice, the eternal peacemaker.

Sarah, ever helpful, pointed. "Right over there by the emergency exit."

Thanks to an obstructed view, it was Portia I saw first, head cocked so that her long, straight hair fell to one side, gloriously shown to full advantage. Her lips were moving: big surprise. Her lips never stopped moving. She gestured to Chaz, talking about him for a brief moment before returning to the eternal subject of her own self. Then the crowd parted and I caught a glimpse of short-cropped brown hair, of sideburns leading down to the chin, and then, as the man turned, of Sean's beard, mustache, and trim features. It really was him, standing across the room from me for the first time in more months than my memory cared to divulge.

When was the last time we'd communicated? I seemed to remember talking over the phone about our apartment's security deposit a couple of weeks after my lawyer had sent his lawyer the keys. We'd kept it businesslike and simple. So simple and clinical, in fact, that I didn't remember a word we'd said, though I did remember swapping cheery good-byes at the end that implied we'd talk again. I'd left our apartment nine months ago; he'd stayed there for another two and a half. So it had to have been a good six months.

I became vaguely aware that, as I'd watched Sean from across the room, "He *had* to have known you were going to be here," Sarah was saying. "You attend all of Alan's opening nights. We always have. I can't believe he'd have the nerve to show up."

"I'm sorry," said poor, confused Walter. "But Rebecca's ex-husband is here as well?"

Alice sighed. "It's a night of exes, it would appear. Sweetie, are you all right?"

"I can get rid of him," Alan said, so nervous that he didn't even appear to notice the would-be fawners trying to get his attention to the side. "This is all my fault, after all."

"I hope you take him off that mailing list of yours!" Alice was as vexed as she ever got, which to an outsider might not seem like much, but to anyone who'd experienced her slowly corrosive wrath was instantly recognizable. She crossed her arms and glared. "Honestly."

"We're right at the door," Sarah pointed out. "Let's just ease her out. You won't mind, right, Alan?"

"No! Not at all!"

"I'll lead her out," Walter suggested. I felt his hand on my shoulder.

"Guys." I was tired of all of them trying to be so damned solicitous of my feelings. Walter's touch had been the last straw. Of all the living people I wanted playing the solicitous white knight, he was definitely near the end of the line, after the Unabomber and maybe Richard Simmons. I stepped sideways to clear myself of them, nearly running into a hipster beatnik chick wearing a black turtleneck and a beret, who apparently had confused the evening's proceedings with an audition for a remake of the Audrey Hepburn musical *Funny Face*. I excused myself to her and tried to calm everyone down. "Stop fretting. It's only Sean. I'm not furious at him." Alice gave me the subtlest kind of look that only sisters can exchange. "Anymore," I added. "Don't drop him from your mailing lists, don't shun him, don't hiss at him on the streets, don't feel like you have to hustle me out of here just because we're in the same room. We're not a split atom. We're not going to explode and leave Manhattan radioactive."

I thought I sounded perfectly self-contained and reasonable. And I really must have meant what I'd said, because after the initial shock, my heart rate was returning to a normal level and I didn't feel quite as sweaty-palmed. No one else seemed convinced, though. "You've never had to cope with an ex before, Bec." At Alice's assertion, Alan's mouth began to twitch. "Oh, come on," Alice told him. "You know it was awkward those first few times."

"But we got over it!"

"We did."

I envied that look of fondness between the pair. One of these days, I wanted to be able to smile that way with Sean. Not that I really wanted him back in my life, the way that Alan and Alice had stayed together. They shared a certain peace that at this point I could only imagine. "And we will, too, I'm sure. In fact"—I straightened my shoulders without any prompting from my sister, lifted my head high, threw out my chest and took a deep breath as I made up my mind—"I'm going over there." My announcement was met with a number of expostulations from the chorus, from Alice's and Alan's simultaneous *Sweetie!* to Walter's concerned mumbling to Sarah's disapproving clucking. I'd made up my mind, though. "Don't try to stop me."

"Of course I'm going to try to stop you. I'm your friend. It's hardwired into my programming!" said Sarah.

"Let her go," said Alice, sighing. "I keep telling you, she's stubborn. She always used to rip off her Band-Aids in one go rather than peel them back a little at a time."

"Exactly! Why prolong the pain?" Bag tucked beneath my arm, I readied myself to go. "All right, then."

I was vaguely conscious of everyone trailing behind me as I pushed my way around the room's edge to avoid the crowd. It still wasn't a quick trip, however; the prospect of free canapés and watered-down liquor was enough to turn the most hardened, budget-challenged skeptic into a sycophantic fan. Charlene, in particular, seemed to be getting a lot of attention from the younger, male-er audience members, but I scarcely noticed her as I and my entourage swept by. One minute later and I'd reached my target. But what was I going to say? I hadn't thought of a snappy opening line. Should I be jaunty and launch with a snappy *Hey, you!* Should I feign surprise with an *I didn't see you standing here*? Should I tap him on the shoulder and just smile mysteriously?

In the end, I didn't have to do anything. Portia, still monopolizing Sean's attention, smiled broadly and squealed, "Rebecca, how sweet! You came looking for me!" And that's when Sean turned and saw me.

My first thought was that he looked the same. Silly, I know; it wasn't as if we hadn't seen each other in years. He'd had that identical beard when I'd first met him, and I'd thought it an exotic thing for a budding lawyer to have, back in the day when the law schools were churning out cookie-cutter, clean-cut corporation drones. His eyes were the same muddy brown. He was even wearing the same type of clothing he'd favored for nights out—an open-necked, jewel blue formal shirt with a white T underneath, flat-front slacks, shiny black loafers. Why was I surprised at how little he seemed to have changed?

"Becca, you remember my friend Sean Mulvaney?" Portia said, jerking me out of my reverie and back into the real world.

I stared at the gracious hostess and her inattentive consort for a moment before I heard Sarah hiss beside me, "They were *married*, jackass! Remember?"

Portia blinked, then recovered. "Well, I knew that."

Sean, trying not to laugh, opened his mouth to speak. "Hello, Beck." He greeted me pleasantly, as he might an old but slightly distant friend. I suppose that summed up our relationship.

"Pssssst." Sarah made a noise and a come-hither motion in Portia's direction. Our dim-witted friend made a face of incomprehension, so Sarah repeated the gesture.

"What?" Portia asked, turning to Chaz for clarification. Sarah grunted and motioned one more time. "What!"

"Just *come here!*" Sarah's bellow attracted attention from as far away as the mini-cheesecakes at the refreshment table; Alan and Alice hastened to escort a baffled Portia a safe distance away so that Sean and I could be alone.

"I'm friends with the Keystone Kops," I said lamely while we watched the antics subside.

He chuckled a little. "So I recall." He teetered back on his heels, hands deep in his pockets, while he looked at me with raised eyebrows. I remembered that routine well. Sean used to do it all the time when he was feeling awkward. The notion that he might be more nervous than I gave me ballast. "You look great," he said at last.

"I know!" I hadn't intended to sound so arrogant—it had just come flying out. But what did he expect, the very picture of misery? "You, too." Neither of us made any effort to say the next sentence. Sticky, sticky, sticky. But again, what did I expect? "How's work?"

"Excellent. You? Still at the bookstore?"

"Yes, I am, and work's dandy. How's your new place?"

"Great." He cleared his throat. "Yours?"

"Oh, you know Alice. It's an *Architectural Digest* showcase in the making." What came out of my mouth next even I didn't expect. "How's what's-her-face?"

"Mary is fine," he said, emphasizing the name. "And we're not together anymore."

"Oh?" I couldn't help myself, but I really, really wanted to smile right then. I managed to control the corners of my mouth, however, and force out, "That's too bad."

His eyebrows furrowed. "Don't gloat."

"I'm not gloating!"

"You're gloating."

"What do I have to gloat about?" I asked. Inwardly, I must confess, I was riding a tidal wave of gloat while dancing the Scottish reel on the poop deck of the Good Ship Gloatinpop. I must have seemed convincing, though, because he backed down and seemed less defensive. "We're divorced, not mortal enemies."

He seemed to accept the truth of that, shrugging. "So, are you seeing anyone else, then?"

"No!" he said, offended, as if I'd implied he was a big male he-slut. Which I hadn't, not at all. "You?"

Why were we going here so quickly, so soon after we'd first laid eyes on each other? "Well," I admitted, folding my arms, "I've been going out a lot."

"Out? Where?"

"You know. The Venetian Club. Mmm, where else? I was at the After Ten last weekend. A couple of other places, too." I named a few of the other hotspots I'd hit with A.J. the previous two weekends, deciding to omit my adventures at the Essex Pub.

"The After Ten? The After Ten Lounge, Becca?" He laughed. I hated that tone of voice he'd used—during the days of our marriage, it had always made me feel like a silly little fool. "Oh, come on. It's like, the most hopping place in the city. I tried to get one of the partners in there a few weeks ago and we ended up standing in line for two hours before giving up." My shrug and bland smile must have had the same maddening effect on him. "How did *you* get in?"

"Didn't you say just now that I looked good?" I asked, feeling like a stubborn adolescent pointing out the obvious.

"Well, yeah, but—"

"It's not that hard when you know the right people, Sean." I tugged at my sweater and made sure I was still standing up straight. "What do you need, Mr. Attorney? Should I produce a matchbook so I can prove I was there? Do you need corroborating photographs?"

"Don't be silly. But—" He was stuck on that *but*. He shook his head. "How are you affording all this skylarking?" What an old-fashioned word, that. And who did he think he was, my father? "I know your salary, remember? You can't buy many drinks at the After Ten, and God knows at the Venetian, on what you make."

"Oh, Sean," I said. My once-dear, ever-predictable Sean. I looked at him in all his unchanging glory and smiled, feeling for him in the first time in months a pity I'd never thought I'd have the opportunity to experience. "What makes you think I have to buy my own drinks?" While he fumbled for an answer, I decided the time had come to leave, while I still had the upper hand. "You be good. I'm really sorry about . . . Mary." When I walked away in the direction of my waiting friends and family, he was gawping at me still.

You know, I kind of liked leaving him hanging, for a change.

NINE

The party was in full swing at @72, and I was still wriggling in my seat from having moments before rubbed shoulders with an actual member of *NSYNC. He'd asked me how things were going, just like he was a normal person. Not the most famous *NSYNC guy, whose name I couldn't remember. And not Lance Bass, whose name I could. The one who always had the little goatee and spindly mustache. Actually, come to think of it, maybe I'd met a Backstreet Boy. It's not as if I could really tell the difference.

Or cared. What mattered is that I, Rebecca Egan, had landed in one of the most exclusive, members-only rooftop clubs in Manhattan. The entire seventeenth story of one of the most expensive boutique hotels in all Soho, if not the entire city, had been converted into an Art Deco playground of pastels, silver leaf, and elegant wood furniture with elaborate geometrical inlays. All the outside walls were fashioned from glass, so no matter where I looked, I saw a beautiful view of either Midtown or lower Manhattan, a pool of thousands upon thousands of tiny little lights stretching in every direction. In fact, I could barely make out where the cityscape ended and the stars began—it was that kind of night.

And was I leaning against the glass and enjoying that spectacular view? Was I sitting alone, contemplating the mystery of the night and enjoying that excited, trembly feeling I always got in the pit of my stomach whenever I stared at the sky and contemplated infinity? Was I shivering out on the expansive patio, looking over the balcony on the car-flooded streets below?

No, I was losing at five-card stud, the only woman at a table that included a wealthy Texan who, between the unlit cigar on which he chomped throughout the game and his ten-gallon hat sparkling with rhinestones and a tribal feather, made sure no one forgot his proud state. The game also included a skinny, nervous native of the city who twitched so much that either he was taking our little game too seriously or else he was going through substance withdrawal right before my eyes. And, finally, there was the fellow who'd fronted the money for me to play, Ricardo by name. I didn't know him from Adam, but when he'd noticed me hanging around pretending to watch the game while really I was staring at the *NSYNC member who wasn't Lance Bass, he'd grabbed a handful of chips, thrown them on the table, and nodded at me before saying, "Play for a couple of hands."

It was a game I hadn't played since college. "Check," I opened, looking at the pitiful nothing in my hand.

The Texan regarded me with disdain. From under the brim of his hat, he announced, "There's no checkin' at this table, li'l lady. We bet like men."

"Check," said my patron, curving his lips into a broad smile at both me and the Texan. He was the kind of guy, had I seen him out on the street bundled up against the torrential rain we'd been having for the past two days, I would have assumed to be a slightly geeky, unthreatening IT technician who'd cut off all his hair to minimize the signs of premature balding.

All that might have been true, but up here in the exclusive environs of @72, he was wearing expensive gray slacks, a crisp white shirt with French cuffs, and cuff links that sparkled in the flattering indirect light. Up here, he was god of the poker table. The Texan looked as if he might challenge him for a moment, but after taking a glance at the lion's share of chips neatly stacked in front of my financier, he changed his mind. "Fine," he said. "I'll open." He flicked a red chip on the table.

"Call." The enervated hipster was a man of few words.

To some people, it might seem that I was underprepared for gambling in a posh private club with only four years' worth of late-night dorm room poker for experience, but let me tell you, those had been some pretty intense games. Some of those girls had grown up with Gameboys with Vegas simulators, and they'd been pretty tough to beat. Despite the fact that I'd won more than I'd lost during those misspent years, I had no illusions that I was anything more than a competent player who was stuck with a pair of sevens in her hand. After Baldy and I both called and swapped in our cards, my hand wasn't much improved. I checked again.

Mr. Yellow Rose looked absolutely disgusted with me. His cigar even went flaccid, but he said nothing. "I'm in," said my friend with the chips. He tossed in two blues and a red. Since no numbers were printed on the things, I had no idea how much it meant.

"Call and raise, big boy," said the Texan, grinning. He flicked three red chips into the table's center. His eyes met mine and glinted. I stared right back at him.

The skinny fellow flicked his cards back and forth, obviously nervous about the stakes. More nervous, in fact, than Mary Catherine O'Malley, who'd gnawed off more fingernails during our college games than I cared to think about—and we hadn't even been playing for pennies. "Fold," he said at last, slamming down his hand.

My turn. I looked at the Texan again. His cocky arrogance reminded me of Sean at his worst. Nothing against Texans, mind you: My mother had come from Denton, after all. But what kind of guy was so obstinate about letting others know what state he was from that he felt he had to wear a cowboy hat wherever he went? You didn't see people from Wisconsin toting around wheels of cheese, did you? "Call." Before the guy at my left could open his mouth, I spoke again. "And raise." I added two more red chips to those I'd just thrown in the middle of the table. It nearly cleaned me out of the starting stakes I'd been lent, but what the heck? It was just for play.

"You sure about that, li'l lady?" the Texan asked me.

"Yeah, I'm sure about that, pardner," I drawled, meeting him stare for stare. He was bluffing. I knew he was bluffing. If there's anything a recent divorcée can spot, it's a man who's trying to convince her he's honest while hiding a subterfuge. "You gonna call?"

"Actually, it's my turn," said Ricardo, clearing his throat. He looked at me, exhaled a column of air through pursed lips, ran his hand over his head, and at last put his cards on the table. "I'm out."

The Texan stared at me, trying to read my face. I stared right back. @72 was the first hotspot we'd visited where the music wasn't thumpa-thumpa-thumping its way into my bone marrow. I wouldn't have been surprised, though, if while the Lone Star State's favorite son and I were enjoying our face-off, the theme song from *The Good, the Bad, and the Ugly* had started playing. "Call," he said at last, insolently flipping his chips toward me. "Show 'em."

"Ladies first," I said, as an invitation. That got a grin out of my banker, at least.

"Fine." He tossed down a jack, a queen, a king, and a ten, all of different suits, while my heart provided the thumpa-thump that the sound system lacked. Finally, grudgingly, he threw down his last card . . . a four.

I wanted to giggle, but I didn't want to give the guy the satisfaction of seeing me do something especially girly. "Nice," I said, throwing my cards face up and, with what I hoped looked like a practiced move, swept all the chips in my direction.

"Sevens!" crabbed my opponent, pushing up his hat so he could rub his forehead. "Shit."

I, in the meantime, pushed the chips back in the

bald guy's direction. He hadn't stopped grinning at me since I'd challenged the Texan. "Hey, don't go," he said. "Sit in for a few more hands."

I shrugged. "Aw, I don't want to take you bitches for any more than I have to," I said, with a private wink in his direction. "Have fun!" The last cheery directive I'd tossed at the Texan, who I could hear grumbling as I rose and moved back across the room. It had been fun, but if there's anything I'd learned from A.J. in the previous three weeks, it was to always leave them wanting more.

And where was A.J., my sensei, the Henry Higgins to my Eliza Doolittle? Right in the room's center, in the middle of a sofa with two vapid blondes on one side and a Winona Ryder look-alike giving him big, longing eyes on the other. A small crowd had gathered around them, laughing at something he'd said. Other than the patrons still standing around the bar pretending not to letch after the boy band star, it was the largest gaggle in the entire place.

"No, really," the Winona-alike was saying when I passed, "don't kid around. Because I take this stuff very seriously." I paused for a minute to listen, blending in with the crowd.

"So do I," A.J. reassured her. "Scientists have discovered that certain people generate different electrical fields from others. Have you ever known anyone who made wristwatches stop?"

"Oh, my God," said the girl. "My mother! Her watches always broke down."

A.J. nodded as if he wasn't at all surprised. "There's a

lot of stuff out there that can't be explained. You seem like the kind of girl who knows that."

She nodded vigorously. "So can you see my aura, too?"

Nobody noticed my hearty guffaw, thank goodness. Nobody, that is, except for A.J. He blinked his sleepy, bedroom eyes, shifted them in my direction, and slyly acknowledged my presence in a single, smooth move that no one else would have noticed. "I can see anyone's aura," he assured her, touching a finger to his lip thoughtfully, "when the atmosphere is right. It's got to be quiet, you know. Too many energies conflicting, otherwise. That kind of thing. I want to be sure that I'm reading *you.*" He followed up the statement by taking the index finger that had been resting against his lips and gently tapping it against the girl's exposed collarbone. She broke into a smile.

Well, that deal was certainly sealed. If I'd been hearing this sorry tale from a friend of mine, I would've been sympathetic. *Oh, my gosh. He really told her all that crap about auras, just to get her phone number? What a schmuck!* But let's face it. I don't care if you're male or female, young or old. When it comes to someone who'll accept at face value the claims of total strangers in a bar, my emotions are going to skew more toward the pity end of the scale than compassion. Was that bad of me? Well, I didn't have a lot of commiseration for people in giant SUVs who, when the only thing between them and a rolling death is their own foot on the brake, open their driver's side door and lean out to pick up a newspaper, either. Instead of watching any more, I returned to the bar of diamond parquet wood, ordered myself a fruity, girly drink from the solicitous bartender, and settled down to make best friends with a blown-glass dish of cashews. Obviously A.J. was way too busy to notice that I was breaking the rules by getting my own drink.

It was a couple of minutes later, in the middle of the bartender telling me that Shannen Doherty had been staying at the hotel all week and had twice come up to the bar, whipping me into a frenzy of star-struck anticipation that was totally out of proportion to the lack of interest I had in Shannen Doherty herself, that I heard a voice at my side. "Hey, big winner," said Ricardo.

"Well, hello there," I said in a friendly manner— though not too friendly. As subdued as the lighting was in @72, my poker-playing friend's noggin was so closely shaved that it gleamed like a freshly polished bowling ball. Worse, from my perspective anyway, the top of his head only came up to my clavicle. And I'd always been put off by the whole soul patch issue, that exquisitely groomed facial hair feature occupying an entire square half-inch right below the center of a man's lower lip. As well-dressed as the guy was, and as much as I liked the little cuff links he wore filled with colorful water and a single bubble each that could have acted as levels in a carpentry emergency, I wasn't buying what he was selling. "Thanks again for letting me sit in."

"Cowboy hat's still a little pissed he got beat by a pair of sevens." When Ricardo grinned, it could light up a room, so white and even were his teeth. A.J.'s smile was a lot like that, too. Did these guys practice beaming in a mirror? "He's still talking about it. Speaking of which, I've got to get back in a minute. You know, so I can win the rest of their money." He cracked another of his toothy grins. "I didn't get your name."

"Gretchen," I murmured amiably. "Gretchen Hoorst."

"Gretchen. I like that name. Your heritage must be what, German?" I nodded at his question. "Minus my stake, you netted about one-fifty, you know."

Somehow I suspected he wasn't talking about six shiny quarters. "You're kidding."

"Any way I can talk you into accepting it?"

Thank goodness he didn't actually proffer the money; I would have felt like some kind of hooker, accepting cash from a stranger in a bar. "Oh, please," I said, laughing a little. "I've never played for money. Pepperidge Farm Goldfish. In college, that's what we used as chips."

He narrowed his eyes. For a second I thought he was going to proclaim me a strange girl. Instead, he merely asked, "Which were the dollar chip? The plain?"

"You know it," I said, taking a bite of the pineapple speared on my drink's toothpick. "Cheddar stood for five dollars apiece, and the pretzels kicked in at ten."

He nodded, as if I weren't talking absolute nonsense. "And the pizza-flavored?"

"Ew," I replied, not wanting to dignify that kind of question with an answer.

"So are you sure?" he asked. "About the cash?"

I turned on my chair so I could face him fully. "Yes, I'm totally sure."

"Fine. Just you know, though, I'm going to be giving it to Big Brothers/Big Sisters. The charity? I do a lot of work with them."

"Oh, my gosh, that's really sweet of you!"

He shuffled modestly, kicking his foot on the floor. "I didn't think you would take it, honestly. I bet you never took candy from strangers as a kid, either."

I acceded the point with a nod, though I did feel I had to qualify a little. "Except on Halloween, naturally."

"But of course!" He leaned against the bar's edge, then nodded at my Slurpee-colored beverage. "Okay, I'm going to go out on a limb here and guess that you were more of a fruit-flavored candies girl than a chocolate craver. Am I right?"

"Well," I drawled, prolonging the suspense, "every girl loves her chocolate. But I did have a thing for Starburst, so you might very well be . . . hang on a sec." I'd heard the tinkling effect of my phone's ring tone in my purse, so with an apologetic smile I dug through the essentials I saw fit to carry on my excursions with A.J.—a minimum of cosmetics, a small mirror, my wallet, and a cherry-colored condom I'd taken from Alice's dresser—retrieved the vibrating, melodious object, and looked at the screen. I knew the number calling me. I couldn't quite understand how I recognized it, however, until I mouthed the digits and realized that for five years I myself had given them out to countless clerks across the city whenever I'd written out one of the checks with *Mr. and Mrs. Sean Mulvaney* across the top. It was our old home phone number. Sean must have transferred it to his new place, rather than get a new one.

Ergo, Sean was calling me. My heart did a quick double thump in my chest. Why in the world would he be doing something like that? My screen flashed.

MISSED CALL, it told me. Missed call? My whole marriage had been a missed call. What in the hell had he wanted, anyway? It couldn't have anything to do with the divorce itself—that was settled and done with. Had someone in his family died, and he'd thought I would want to know? They'd always been nice enough to me, after all.

My poker buddy was still talking to me. I slowly returned to awareness. "Have you tried the appletinis here? They're amazing. Oh, wait, you know what's better? A caramel appletini. I want one of those. Maybe, since you won't take your winnings, you'll let me buy you one, too?"

Ah, so he was making the move. I'd been wondering when he might. "Don't you have to get back to your game, Ricardo?" I asked, nodding at the table at the floor's far end, where the cowboy and the skinny guy were attempting to show each other how to shuffle cards in a show-offy way.

"What?" He checked out the table. "Oh. They'll wait for me. It's not like they've got much of a choice, is it?" Again he presented me with that smile, that charming, charismatic smile. That Method Man smile. "So, is that a yes to the drink, Gretchen?"

"Yes Ladder." At first, Ricardo thought I was agreeing to the drink, but his face seemed to shrink and change when he realized I was calling him out. "You're trying to hustle me up a Yes Ladder. I'm not going to sleep with you, you know. I'm not even going to give you my phone number." Mean of me? Maybe a little, but I'd spent enough time being the agreeable, nonconfrontational girl. A.J. had been right; learning to spot the emotional con artists was saving me a lot of time and false hope. What surprised me, though, was how *funny* I was finding his predicament. The guy had never had a girl challenge him face-to-face this way. It was probably the first nonmanipulative conversation he'd ever had in this kind of setting. "Come on, see the humor in it! Every magician knows that there's going to be one person in the audience who sees through his tricks. You should be glad I stopped you before you wasted a lot of energy on the whole routine. Heck, I didn't even cost you a caramel appletini."

"Tricks?" he repeated faintly. His laughter was utterly without hilarity. "Come on, Gretchen, I don't use tricks. . . ."

I ticked off my fingers, one by one. "False time constraints, just to reassure me you're not going to hit on me. Throwing cash around to show me you're a value-added attraction. Pretending you work for Big Brothers/Big Sisters for the same reason. Step Four: candy similarities. Oh, come *on*." I reached my pinky. At no time had my tone been angry or upset. If anything, I felt a bit like a triumphant Nancy Drew, flush with excitement upon confronting the perpetrator of the *Mystery of the Missing Spider Sapphire*. "And finally, the ubiquitous Yes Ladder."

His jaw hung slightly slack. The dust-up seemed to have sapped the crisp from his shirt. "How . . . how's a girl like you know about Yes Ladders?"

"I'm no ordinary girl, my friend. No ordinary girl at all." I pantomimed imaginary grime from my hands, then shook them dry. "All right, you've officially been schooled. Run along." I dismissed Ricardo with a wave. "Run along, now. Shoo. And you just be careful next time you try to use that Method of yours, you hear?"

I sounded just like a mother talking to a slightly pesky son, and that's about the way I regarded the guy—affectionately, but recognizing the need for firm discipline. Though he walked away, Ricardo still looked back over his shoulder as he stumbled hard into one of the Art Deco sofas, his expression drawn somewhere between astonishment and reverence. I waggled my fingers, smiled, and watched him go.

After he'd made his way around the apparently tricky piece of furniture, limping slightly from where he'd banged his knee, he finally spoke. "I do work with Big Brothers/Big Sisters, you know."

Aw, that was nice. It didn't make me change my mind about him or the games he played, but I was glad that he hadn't lied about that one thing. "Good for you!" I said encouragingly. "I'm sure they'll enjoy that contribution!" With one final, cheery smile, I waggled a quick bye-bye and swung back around.

One Method Man down, thousands more to go.

Speaking of Method Men, where was mine? I hadn't seen him in the lounge area when I'd been dismissing Ricardo. In fact, that little coterie had dissipated into couples and small groups who drank and talked and flirted with each other in their small sets. Sipping from the sweet drink in my hand, I scanned what I could see of @72. They weren't at the poker table, where Ricardo was regarding me still as he dealt a new round of cards. They weren't on the outdoor patio, shivering and sneaking smokes in the dark, the way a few brave couples were. I didn't see them examining the locked individual vaults in the glass-enclosed wine cellar near the entrance, looking for celebrity names. Nor did I spy them near the glossy ebony grand piano, where a musician had just sat down and begun to play a tongue-in-cheek semi-classical rendition of Britney Spears's "Toxic."

He hadn't left me, had he? I mean, it wasn't as if I didn't know my own way home or anything like that. I'd just kind of assumed that if Big Cat A.J. seriously wanted to hook up with one of the mice he caught and toyed with, he'd at least find a way to slip away and let me know he'd be going. Common courtesy, after all. No, he had to be around here someplace.

Now I had two things nagging at me—A.J.'s whereabouts and the reason behind Sean's phone call. At least one of those I could solve readily. After I'd downed the last of my drink and smiled and pushed the glass in the bartender's direction, I stepped down from my stool, tucked my bag beneath my arm, and pushed the redial button on my cell phone. Half of me hoped for the voice mail to pick up. The other half was glad that I was at least a little bit fortified with alcohol for the experience, because I was really dreading whatever the bad news might be. What if it really was something dire? What if his mother was in the hospital? She'd always struck me as one of those dedicated hausfraus who, after years upon years of servitude in the kitchen and garden with only Friday-night bowling and passive-aggressive game-playing with her children to break the tedium, would one day burst a blood vessel in her brain and keel over in a batch of her famous homemade mayonnaise. Would Sean even be able to call from a hospital?

In mere milliseconds, while the line continued to ring on the other end, I'd progressed from that scenario to one of my ex-husband, both his parents, and their two adorable Ridgebacks having a high-speed collision on the West Side Highway, when Sean picked up. "Hello?" he asked.

"Hi there!" I said a little too loudly and brightly, mainly from trying to mitigate back to reality from the vision I'd just had of Sean lying on the asphalt, frantically dialing before his gory demise the one person in his life to whom he owed more amends than anyone. I cleared my throat and tried to calm down a little. "Is everything okay?"

"Where are you?" He sounded peculiar. Not my-family-is-dead-can-you-hold-my-hand strange. More like I've-got-a-frog-in-my-throat-and-it-won't-go-away weird.

"Is everything okay?" I repeated, delineating my syllables more distinctly. "Is it your mother? Did someone die?"

"No, everything's fine. Why?"

The puzzlement in his reply irritated the hell out of me. I'd wasted an entire twenty seconds whipping myself into a panicky frenzy of the imagination and it turned out that nothing was wrong? "Then why did you call?"

While dialing, I'd walked from the bar over to a north-facing window where the wonders of midtown Manhattan were spread out before me. The night was beautiful and clear; the neon and lights from the city's center cast a glow I could warm my hands over. I leaned against the glass as he said, "Where *are* you? I hear some kind of music."

I took a deep breath and calmed myself. Still looking for A.J., I slowly began wandering along the room's perimeter. "I'm at a club. When you called, I thought there was some kind of emergency. Someone sick."

"No," he said. Was he *eating* something while he talked to me? I had a vision of his old pre-bedtime ritual, in which he would shuffle around the apartment in bare feet and pajama bottoms, munching on enormous, salty pretzel rods that brought a new dimension to phallic imagery. "Everything's okay."

"Then why did you call?"

"You're at a club? What club?"

And that was five years of our marriage in a nutshell: me asking questions, him not answering them, and the two of us going around and around in circles until he cheated and we both fell down. Perversely, I decided to tell him the truth. "It's a little place called At Seventytwo. You probably haven't heard of it—it's a private club. Very exclusive." I was passing the piano then, excusing myself as I slipped by the people in suits and expensive sportswear who'd congregated nearby to hear the musician's slow and elegiac piano arrangement of a U2 standard.

"You're kidding," he said in a flat voice. "That place has been written up in *New York* magazine. I think *Time Out New York* did a special feature on it."

"Did they?" I kept my voice as lively as he managed to make his sound inert. "I missed that. Oh, sorry," I said, as a smiling middle-aged gay couple wafted by in a cloud of cologne. "One of the *NSYNC guys is here."

"What?" Sean was beginning to sound exasperated—which was fine with me. "Which *NSYNC guy?"

"I didn't ask his *name*." A.J. wasn't anywhere near the small booth where I guessed a DJ occasionally spun tracks other nights of the week, nor in the little conservatory of actual orange trees, though I did manage to interrupt what looked like a clandestine exchange of illegal substances. I beat a hasty retreat.

"The pretty-boy one?"

"No."

"The one with the little brother who has a solo career?"

"No. And see, that's what I thought, but I'm pretty sure he's a Backstreet Boy."

"Lance Bass?"

So far I'd established that A.J. wasn't in any of the public areas, by the bar, in the much-vaunted wine cellar. Avoiding the poker area, where Ricardo appeared to be pulling on a leather jacket and taking his leave of his fellow card sharks, I peeked out the doorway into the area by the building elevators. Nothing. "And I met Shannen Doherty," I lied, simply to pay him back for making me panic earlier.

"Wh—?" Ah, sweet gratification. My star-chasing totally irritated him. "Becca, what is going on with you? I was calling because I thought it was nice seeing you Thursday night, but I'm finding it hard to believe how frivolous you're becoming."

"Frivolous?" My, how nice it was to hear the voice of

jealousy speaking from a mouth other than my own. "So, when *you* stand in line at the After Ten, it's being a smart businessman. When *I* actually get in, I'm frivolous. Oh, it's clear now. Thank you for elucidating."

"No, it's . . . I didn't . . . you're. . . ." I leaned against the wall and enjoyed the moment. "You didn't used to be like this when we were married."

"That's because I was married." Right then, Ricardo passed me, waving at the bartender as he headed for the exit, coat in hand. He stopped at my side. "Hang on," I said into the phone. This was going to be interesting.

"Gretchen." Once he had my attention, Ricardo leaned in close, resting his weight with a hand on the wall beside my head. "Whatever you think of me? I think you're a pretty cool lady." Without any encouragement on my part, he leaned in and gave me a quick peck on the cheek. "And a damned good poker player. Good night."

With a wink and a rustle of leather, he was gone. I returned to my phone call, where Sean was saying, "Gretchen? Who's Gretchen?"

"I'm Gretchen." I sighed. "I just told this guy that was my name. Sometimes I go with Natasha."

"And you were playing *poker* with him?"

"Sure. I won fifteen hundred pretzel goldfish for that guy. Hey, Sean?" I asked, suddenly inspired.

"What?"

"How about you don't eavesdrop on my private conversations in the future?" A stunned silence was my reward for that little question. "That is, if we have conversations in the future. A prospect about which I'm not too certain. And now, if no one is dead—"

"Everyone's fine. Becca, I didn't mean to be a prick. I'm just not used to how different you are. I guess I'm just not sure where it came from."

"I can tell you one thing," I said, wishing I'd been different a long time ago. "It sure didn't come from Pottery Barn, like most of our marriage. And on that note, I've got to go." Over his protests, I explained, "I'm here with a friend, and I've lost him. It was good hearing from you, Sean. Do take care."

Before I pushed the button to release the call, I heard Sean ask, "You're there with a him?"

Yes, Sean. I was there with a him—a big, beefalo of a him who drew stares from the women—and several of the men—wherever we went. I walked down streets with the him, shared cab rides with the him, and had been seen by perfect strangers with the him on our quick dinners before the clubs so many times that I was sure several of them thought we were an item. And no one had ever asked questions.

I was there with a him in theory, anyway. In practice, I seemed to have lost the guy. But you know, that was fine. I'd send him a quick text message on my phone to let him know I was leaving, then make my way back to Alice's place. First, though, I'd attend to the call of nature.

@72's restroom was as elaborately themed as the rest of the place, managing to give the impression of a classic movie palace while still maintaining a hip, clean look. Vases flanked both sides of the vast, mosaic-framed mirror, filled with stalks of a blue flower that I'd never seen before but that filled the room with a sweet scent. I set my bag on the granite counter and, using that strange system by which punching on numbers somehow converts them to words—usually mangling them in the process—typed out the briefest of messages to send to A.J.'s cell. After I pushed the SEND button, I picked up my bag again and walked across the burgundy-and-royal-blue tiles in the direction of the toilet stalls.

A few seconds later I heard a familiar noise coming from the direction in which I walked, echoing between the metal partitions and filling the room with a chirpy, electronic chime. Was that A.J.'s phone? It certainly sounded like it, and I had just sent him that text message. "A.J.?" In the echoing restroom, my voice sounded weak and tentative, as if I were in a haunted house by myself on a dark and rainy Friday the Thirteenth, instead of treading the tiles of a swank private club where Shannen Doherty had probably planted her butt in one of those very stalls. No answer. "Are you there?" I asked, pushing open the first of the three open doors.

The door swung open, colliding with his leg right before it hit the wall. A.J. sat on the toilet, thank goodness with his pants not around his ankles, hands braced against the walls, as a single-minded succubus attempted to retrieve his soul through his mouth. Okay, so it was only the Winona Ryder look-alike from out in the lounge sitting on his lap and straddling him, her legs wrapped around his hips and the back of the john. But seriously, her tongue was so far down his throat that she could have checked for tonsil inflammation.

A.J. saw me first, of course; I'd banged the door right into the inside of his knee. He didn't seem the least surprised, or embarrassed, or discomfited by the position in which I'd caught him. His eyes had been shut when I'd pushed open the door, but they remained open now, watching me as he continued to make out with the woman. If anything, he seemed to enjoy me watching. It was just a spicy little embellishment to the act.

The girl, though, seemed to notice the sudden influx of air on her backside. She disengaged her three feet of tongue from A.J.'s epiglottis, swung her head around, and glared at me. It was then that I noticed her blouse was open in the front, and that a stylized tribal tattoo of a lizard slithered down her left side of her chest and into her baby-pink bra. The message in her eyes was utterly unmistakable: I'd trespassed on her territory. Her property. Her man. And I wasn't wanted. She slammed the door shut. I heard one of them fumbling at its latch.

Out in the hallway, I took what felt like my first breath in a couple of minutes. I was dizzy and light-headed from what I'd seen, and more than a little . . . what? Shocked? Not really. I'd seen more action at the post–drama club knockdown parties in high school, where a lot of the guys had gotten to second base in Samantha Middleton's parents' cellar. Appalled? How could I be? I'd been the one who'd told all my friends they couldn't fault a tomcat for following its nature. Jealous?

Oh, please.

No, what I felt was unconditional, 100 percent amusement at the whole thing. A.J.'s stings were the silliest and most basic system of barter I'd ever seen. Pure, simple, and easy. Just the way relationships should be, right? Certainly not the way mine had been. A.J. had gotten exactly what he'd wanted, after throwing around that alpha male smile, the practiced stories, and all that chick crack nonsense. And the girl? Well, she sure was getting an aura reading, inside and out, from one of the most sought-after guys in Manhattan.

I leaned back against the wall by the restroom door and laughed, tucking my phone back into my bag as I got ready to go home. I didn't care if anyone saw me enjoying a moment's private amusement—I was having fun. That was the point of these outings, wasn't it? Fun? Well, mission accomplished. For that evening, anyway.

It was when I walked out @72's door that I realized I had one question still burning in my mind: What was it with A.J. and women's bathrooms, anyway?

TEN

I don't have a living room. I live in a 500-square-foot efficiency with a convertible sofa, a television that belonged to my father before he died, a stack of bills on a rickety wooden desk, and books. Too many books. I have more books than I have bookshelves, many of them my dad's. I haven't read all of his. I haven't read many of them, in fact, because they're all on topics like the War of the Roses or the Battle of Algiers or the Crimean occupation of whatever-it-was, and I'm kind of a Jane Eyre person.

I have books piled on top of my two bookcases, and I have books lined up on the floor along all the walls, and books sitting on top of those. In the little kitchen area, I have books on top of my refrigerator. They're mostly cookbooks.

So what I picture is this: clearing out all the books. Every single one of them. What I do NOT want is for them to go to a used book store, where they'd putrefy and accumulate dust and mold and clutter up some poor sod of a bookstore owner's inventory, swelling the ranks of their stock like they'd been plunged into water and left to bloat. Otherwise, I don't care what happens to them—they could be incinerated, or sent to the shredder and turned into wood pulp, or recycled as toilet paper for some backwoods Appalachian family.

What I wonder is how much more space I would have if I didn't have those books there. So that's how I'd start.

"Wow," I said once I'd finished reading aloud the handwritten page in Sarah's Moleskine. She had stared at me all during my recitation, nervously eating cold tortilla chips and waiting for a reaction. Sarah certainly had managed to give a pretty accurate description of her apartment, for one thing. With the thousands of volumes she'd managed to accumulate, it did have the air of a mad monk's disorganized scriptorium. As with all of Sarah's psychological exercises, though, I was always uncertain when she was actually wanting feedback, or merely asking because she felt she ought. "That's quite an essay. Didn't you think?" I asked Ethan, sitting to my left. Let him take some of the burden of this particular conversation.

"Mmmmm." The schmuck. Seeing a question flung his way, he'd leaned over like a ten-year-old and, hands-free, begun sipping through his straw at the fishbowl-sized margarita in front of him. It was obvious he intended to keep sucking away until he didn't have to answer any longer. I envied him not having best friend status. I really did.

Sarah still looked at me with big, vulnerable eyes. "I think it's great." I tried to make myself sound authoritative and cheerful, but after an enormous dinner of fajitas and too much chips and salsa beforehand, the small pauses I kept having to take to conceal small belches made me sound hesitant, I feared. "Concise and to the point." Her head dipped so low that I feared it would absorb what was left of her enchiladas. Ethan reached across the table and gently moved the finished plate to the table's edge for the waiter to take when he swept by. "What?" I'd said something wrong.

"That was only the first page!" she said, jerking up her neck again. "I had seven more!" Before either of us could stop her, she yanked a handful of pages out of the little notebook and crumpled them into a ball. She proceeded to throw it onto the floor so that it skittered and bounced under the table of a surprised older couple sharing a plate of fried ice cream. She didn't even notice their arch reaction. Ethan sent them sympathetic smiles and looked as if he might get down on all fours and dive after it. After two of El Zocalo's strawberry margaritas, I was woozy enough that I knew staying planted in my comfortable seat was probably the best plan. "You're right." She buried her face in her hands. "I should start over."

"Haven't you been working on this assignment for the better part of a week?" She nodded at my question. "Why don't you just turn it in as is? There was nothing wrong with what you wrote, silly. If that's how you would redecorate, that's how you would redecorate." Sarah seemed to be struggling with something; she kept shaking her head with every sentence I spoke. "What? I don't get what's so hard about it. Your first instinct's probably the right one."

Over in the restaurant's corner, a number of employees had come out with another of the fried ice creams, this time sporting a birthday candle, clapping and singing as they sidled through the aisles and finally set it down in front of a kid who looked all of ten years old. Watching her delight gave me an excuse to keep from observing Sarah's obvious discomfort. "You don't . . ." she started to say, and followed it up with, "It's hard to . . ." I smiled to let her know that she could talk to me. Maybe it was Ethan's presence hampering her, but I didn't really think so; she hadn't objected at all to me reading the excerpt aloud a few moments before, and she seemed to accept his more frequent presence at our after-work dinners as a given. No, something else had been bothering her over the last few weeks, and more especially in recent days. She sighed. "I can't go with my first instinct! You don't understand how therapy works."

"Maybe I don't." If I had to be truthful, I was slightly irritated to have the therapy card played on me for the thousandth time. "You know I love you to bits, okay? So no offense?" Even from my mouth, that meant something offensive was sure to follow, and from the way she sat up and crossed her arms, I knew Sarah realized it. The liquor had loosened my tongue, though, and what flowed over it was straight from the heart. "But I hate that you-just-don't-understand, us-versus-you superiority thing."

"I'm not like that!"

Oh, but she was. "If someone spends a good portion of their salary and time on something like hiring a personal trainer at Crunch, I don't like it when they lord their body over lesser beings." Like A.J. with skinnier, smaller men. "But at least everyone can see the results. You go into a therapist's dark office and came out, week after week, and . . ." Here's where I should have stopped. I didn't, though. "I don't see much difference."

If she was planning to be offended, now was the perfect time. Ethan even looked slightly apprehensive at my comparison, and obviously disliked being caught in the middle of yet another argument between the two of us. Sarah, however, merely nodded and sighed. "No offense," she agreed, making my heart glad. "But you still don't know jack about therapy. Every stupid little assignment he has me do is a cruel and calculated exercise designed to give him insight into some area of my life that I don't want him to have. This guy's not looking for essays. He's looking for a toehold into my psyche."

"Isn't that kind of like the fellow's job?" Ethan asked with raised eyebrows, looking to me to see if I felt the same.

I did. "Yeah, it seems like you'd kind of want to cooperate. Right?"

"No, God damn it!" Sarah's response was hotter than the chile relleno sizzling in a cast-iron skillet that our waiter was delivering to a neighboring table. He swooped back by and retrieved our plates. By the time he'd vanished, she'd calmed down somewhat. "That's the *last* thing I want to do!" At our blank and bewildered stares, she leaned forward and explained with both elbows on the table, her hands making fierce gesticulations. "Look, let's say I write this essay over. And I say that I'm going to paint my living room red, or something. Dr. Carter's going to raise an eyebrow and say, *Hmmm, is zat zo? Why red, Sarah? Is it ze color of ze passion you are lacking in your zad unt zorry life?* If I say I'm going to paint it green, he'll be all, *Oh-ho! Green is ze color of envy, is it not? Of what are you envious? Is it ze cars, ze fancy apartments, ze lovers you don't possess? Is it ze money your friends have zat you do not?*"

"We're your friends," I pointed out. "And you pay us crap."

Ethan, on the other hand, was mystified by something else. "Your doctor's German?"

She'd ignored my statement, but Ethan's made her looked pained. "No, he's from Kentucky, but Freud was German."

"Freud was Austrian," Ethan and I said in unison, then smiled at each other, delighted at the coincidence.

"Work with me, people!" Sarah suggested, slugging down the rest of her Corona. "If I talk about the bed, he'll think I have sexual problems. If I talk about the kitchenette, he'll be quizzing me about why I let food be a substitute for love. It's safer to talk about my books. They don't mean anything that I can think of! God forbid I mention the bathroom, lest he bring up the whole anal retention thing."

"He's Freudian, then?" Ethan asked, before I could shake my head at him.

"No, he's more of a gestalt-y, behavioral science-y, Maslow-y . . ." Sarah sighed and capitulated. "Okay, I don't know. I don't let him talk much. This is ridiculous. Not you guys. You guys are great. I mean this whole redecorating my living room thing." Into her massive shoulder bag went the Moleskine and out came her wallet. She counted silently on her fingers, then pulled out a ten, a five, two ones, and thirty-five cents in change. "I'll just have to tell him I've been thinking about it carefully. That's always safe."

"Will he ask?" I wanted to know.

She shook her head. "They never ask anything. They wait for you to say something, then they pounce, like feral cats." Sarah glanced at her watch, grabbed her puffy coat, and began to stand up. "I'm going to be late. Which means a lack of commitment on the client's part, if you ever decide to get an analyst of your own." She gave her watch a second glance, then leaned over to give me a quick peck on the cheek. "Take this for my part of the bill, okay? See you tomorrow?"

"We're both off tomorrow," I reminded her.

"Oh, crap. It'll be me and the kiddies, then. Thrill." And with those final words, she was off, beetling between the tables in the direction of the exit, pausing only to apologize to the couple nearby as she retrieved the balled-up first draft she'd tossed beneath their table.

Ethan waved at her back. "Bye," he said, not really expecting her to hear him. Once we were totally alone, he said to me, "I'm just glad I'm not in therapy."

"Ditto." He seemed to be trying an experiment in facial hair this week; a mossy growth had accumulated on his cheeks and chin over the past few days. "What's going on with this stuff?" I asked, drawing a little air circle around the affected area. His hands flew self-consciously to his face. "And with your hair?" It seemed different somehow. Was he using product? "Mr. Reddiker, are you turning into a fancy boy?"

Ethan didn't have enough hands to cover both his burgeoning beard and a head full of tousled hair. He opted to duck his face shyly and change the subject. "Have you ever noticed how, even after you've stuffed yourself until you're bloated at a Mexican restaurant, there's always room for more chips and salsa?"

"Are you avoiding my question?"

He flagged down the waiter again. "One more of these, *por favor*," he said, gesturing to our strawberry margaritas. "And the bill. That good for you?"

"I don't know about another drink."

"Have to get home to your sister?" he challenged.

"She's out at some work-related reception at the Met, thank you, with all her friends. Won't be home until the wee hours of the morning. So, is it crispy?" I asked, tentatively reaching out and touching the top of his head. "Oh, good." His hair wasn't, thank goodness. He'd obviously used some kind of goo up there but had left his style malleable. I took a few seconds to move my hands from the sides of his head toward the center, bringing his thick locks to a point in the middle. After a little fluff here and a smoosh there, I was satisfied with the result. "This is what you should be going for. The faux hawk. The omnipresent head fixture of the straight male nightclub *cognoscenti*," I announced in the confident tone of a Discovery Channel documentary narrator. Then, in classified tones, I added, "Which is why all the gay boys are totally over it, by the way."

"You're embarrassing me," he said, swatting my hands away and patting the top of his head to see what I'd done.

"Don't fret. I've only enhanced the whole scruffy hipster thing you were going for."

"I wasn't going for a scruffy hipster thing." He leaned back in his chair. "I'm a scruffy person. And my hair's getting long. My neighborhood barber closed shop and I haven't found a new place I can afford yet." Ethan's fingers ruffled through his hair, trying to smooth it back down. "It's not a hipster thing. Not everyone's a hipster."

"Aw, come on," I said, raking the stuff through my fingers again until it stood up. "Live it up a little. Let your inner blue-eyed hottie out for the night."

"Is that what you've been doing?" he asked. "Letting your inner hottie out?"

The waiter returned right then with another fishbowl filled with reddish slush for us to share, each topped off with a orange slice. Two straws lay against its rim, rendered sticky by sugar. "Enjoy, *amigos*," he said, before dropping the tab, grabbing a few unused utensils, and vanishing again.

I wasn't quite certain how to answer his question. Two major doses of tequila-laced icy drinks had both chilled and numbed my wits a little. I stared happily at the new round. "You're the only guy I've ever known who really got into the fruity margaritas."

"I'm a girl-drink drunk," he informed me quite seriously. "No, really. I don't like alcohol unless it comes in a form that resembles a Slurpee. So, frozen margaritas, daiquiris—those are fine. Scotch on the rocks? I'm just not going to put myself through that kind of torture for the sake of appearing masculine."

"But you don't." I'd just taken a deep, cooling swig from my drink and suffered a bit of brain freeze. "That came out wrong. You don't not appear masculine, I mean. Note the double negative." I shut up and wrapped my lips around the straw, where they couldn't make any more noise.

"Duly noted." He leaned forward and sipped as well, looking directly into my eyes. We looked like some kind of post-modern, mildly alcoholic satire on the "Bella Notte" scene from *Lady and the Tramp*. All we needed was for our lips to meet in the middle as we tried to slurp up the very last traces. The mental image of that made me blush furiously. Maybe I shouldn't have accepted a third drink, when I'd already consumed roughly two pounds of ice, syrup, and distilled agave. "But you didn't answer my question." When I appeared ignorant, he reminded me. "About letting out your inner hottie lately."

"Don't be silly," I said, laughing in a self-conscious way. "It's all been innocent fun. I'm not slutting my way around town!"

"I didn't say that." Relief washed over me at his words. I'd have hated for Ethan, of all people, to carry a mental image of me as the wanton Jezebel of the Upper West Side. Right now, he was the only person I could trust; he was certainly the only one who knew all about my extracurricular activities. "You've just been totally alive lately. A few weeks ago you were mooning over the long-haired guy over at Starbucks and worrying about becoming a dried-up cat woman, and now you're, well . . ." He held out his hands in my direction. "Look at you."

"What?" I was flushing from his kind words. Or perhaps it was the alcohol. Or a combination of both. Either way, I felt as red as the slush in my margarita glass. "Oh, shush."

"I'm not the only one who's noticed."

"Who else has?"

"Cesar, for one. He said the other day . . ." My curiosity grew while Ethan paused to recall the exact words. "He said that he didn't know you had a great figure before. Don't worry. Michaela swatted him for saying it. With a first edition Zora Neale Hurston." He made a rueful face.

"I guess that's nice." I settled back from another sip of my drink and realized I'd let my shoulders cave in. I pulled them back and sat up straight, my sister's constant admonitions playing in my head. We needed a change of topic. I hated talking about myself. "Oh, gosh. You know what we should do? We should go out and pick you up a girl." Ethan looked abashed, and hung his head at my suggestion. "No, seriously! Oh come on, it'll be fun."

"I don't *like* bars." He laughed at my broad pantomime of exasperation. "I don't!"

"Fine," I said, inspired. After checking out the final cost for our excursion into indigestion, I dug through my purse and pulled out some bills that I added to Sarah's contribution and left them in the leather wallet our waiter had kindly provided. "Settle with me later," I commanded when he shifted weight to reach for his wallet. "We're going to the closest bar."

"Rebecca . . . !"

"It's right over there," I said, pointing across the room. El Zocalo had its own street-side cocktail lounge in a separate, open area of the building. It might have been a little heavy on the antiqued, battered tin advertising signs and adobe tiles, but hey, it was only twenty-five feet away, and we already had our drinks. "Are you game?"

He was, but with qualifications. "I'm not going to go thrusting myself at the girls here," he announced, once we'd moved our coats and drinks to stools by the bar and settled ourselves on the leather seats.

"There's no *thrusting*," I countered. "We don't *thrust* ourselves at the girls. I don't know what kind of weird, thrust-happy places you've been going." Ethan's blue eyes rolled at my would-be witticism. "Now: Do you see a girl you're interested in?" He looked at me for so long that I assumed he was refusing to play along. "What?"

"Nothing," he said, shaking his head and exhaling. "Do we have to do this?"

"No, we don't have to. But we're going to. Because it's fun. So tell me. What kind of girl do you like?"

"All right." He turned to me on his stool, crossed one leg over the other, and settled in. "You want to know what kind of girl I like? I like hot, sassy blondes. Hot sassy blondes with big . . ."

He seemed unable to get the word out of his mouth, though the hands he held out cupped in front of his chest gave me a good idea of what he was saying. Since

Ethan had never said the slightest off-color or explicit thing during the entire time I'd known him, I thought I'd help him out with a suggestion. "McFloppities?"

"Popinjays," he said at the same time.

My mouth flew wide open. "You've been reading entirely too many Victorian novels," I commented. "Proceed."

"Hot sassy blondes with big McFloppities," he continued, running with it. "And a lot of junk in their trunks." I raised my eyebrows at that, but let him continue. "And they've got to be dwarfs. Three-foot-five of sassy blond stackitude."

"Are you quite done?" I asked, buying none of it.

"Isn't that the way your trained chimp talks?"

"Well, yeah. But he's not into little people."

"And you like that? You don't find it derogatory?"

He sounded so incredulous that I paused, curious about the hostility. "He's not serious. He just says that kind of thing to try to get me going." Ethan tilted his head, dubious. "It's true. Anyway, he doesn't talk about me that way. I'm not on his list of stings."

"So it's okay if he talks about other women that way, as long as it's not you."

This conversation was getting way too heavy. I shook my head fondly at him. "A.J.'s a diversion. Nothing more. He's harmless."

"Hmmm." I hadn't convinced him, I could tell. "Even tigers will roll over and pretend they're harmless before they maul you."

We were getting way off track. "Seriously: What kind of girls do you like?"

"Smart ones," he said almost instantly. "Independent ones. Girls who read. A girl who knows the difference between *Jane Eyre* and Jane Fonda."

"You're not going to find any of those in here." I scanned the after-work crowd milling around the El Zocalo bar and saw mostly big-haired Jersey women stopping off for a drink before boarding the trains back home, a few touristy-looking types, and a group of people in suits having some kind of office send-off for one of their colleagues. "There're some pretty girls here. Does she *have* to be a literature major?"

"Why are we doing this?" His voice had taken on a plaintive tone.

"Because we want to get you hooked up, that's why. How about that one?" I nodded in the direction of one of the office workers, a sweet-looking Asian girl with a heart-shaped face and adorable dimples whenever she smiled, which she did quite frequently. "She's very pretty."

Although he'd followed my nod, after studying the girl he turned back around and pretended to yawn. "Maybe I'd better get home."

"No! I'm on an educational mission here!" I began picking out people at random. "The big buxom blonde? The one in the boots? The one in pink?" I reconsidered. "Strike that. She's only a six."

"Six?" Ethan blinked. "You mean, on a scale of one to ten?" He cocked his head and narrowed his eyes at me. "Tell me you don't really do that. You called me an eight once. I thought you were joking."

"Of course I was!" I lied, feeling slightly embarrassed that I'd gotten into the habit. I tried to change the topic.

"Come on. Pick out a girl. I'll show you how to end up with her number. It's a sure-fire thing."

He was having none of it. "What's a guy have to do to be a ten with you?"

"Stop! I don't really . . . I'm not . . ."

I said, a little too quickly and with a little too much heat. Maybe I'd ranked him a little too low that other time. Who wouldn't find him thoroughly adorable? Well, besides a girl whose physical ideal was the A.J. type, who might find his musculature lacking and his brain overlarge? I mean, sheesh. Any woman who put up resistance if Ethan sweet-talked her would have to have rice pudding for brains. "How about the one over there with the long ponytail? She looks intelligent."

"Rebecca, what exactly am I supposed to do if I did see someone I liked here, in the middle of a cheap Mexican diner?" While he talked, I took refuge in the depths of my still-cold margarita. "Go up to them and talk?"

"Exactly! No, seriously," I said, when he reacted with disbelief. "Once you pick, you have ten seconds to make your move."

"Ten seconds?"

I nodded, swallowing the slush in my mouth. "Any more than that and you psych yourself out. That's what A.J. says." Ethan, like my sister, had the talent of being able to raise a single eyebrow to express his disbelief. I reacted to it in the same way I did with Alice. "That's the ten seconds or less rule! He lives by it. Honestly! Once you've made up your mind that you see some-one you like, the countdown starts. You've got to get in there and make your move, or the moment passes. The ten-second rule is what distinguishes . . ." I suddenly became aware that I'd been parroting one of A.J.'s lectures and fell silent.

"Distinguishes what?" Ethan wanted to know.

I cleared my throat and, still reddened from embarrassment and tequila, murmured, "Distinguishes a real pickup artist from a wannabe."

"Somehow, I don't mind falling in the latter camp."

I grinned at him.

"What?"

"Nothing," I said, still smiling from ear to ear. What a nice guy. It had been too long since I'd sat around with a nice guy. I wouldn't have traded this moment for rubbing shoulders with all the *NSYNC guys at once. "You just don't know how glad I am to hear you say that."

An odd expression passed over his face; he laughed a little to himself with his usual soundless huff of amusement, eyes looking off to the side. After a while, he sat back in his chair and asked, "So, if I were to find someone in here I wanted to take home with me, what would I do to get her?"

Hah! Maybe he was interested in taking a short seminar in Smooth Techniques 101 after all. "Well." I moistened my lips and got down to business. "You remember me telling you about the pickup line and the opening insult, right?" He nodded. I smoothed down my blouse and sat up straight. "Okay, pretend I'm a strange girl."

"You *are* a strange girl."

I ignored the witticism. "Pretend I'm an *unknown* girl sitting alone, drink in her hand, and you've picked me as your love interest for the night. Try to pick me up." I faced the bar and looked up at the ceiling in an innocent, unaware manner, slightly whistling to myself, while I waited for him to say something. "Ten seconds," I prompted from the corner of my mouth. "Go."

He cleared his throat. Patiently I waited until he finally said, with a bright smile, "Hi, there!"

"No!" I dropped my I'm-a-stranger-here-myself pose and went back into instructive mode. "You don't say 'Hi, there.' You say something that's attention-getting and that can lead right into a conversation. Like, 'Hey, how much do you know about competition ballroom dancing?' or 'Was Spike Lee still filming down the street when you walked in?' 'Hi, there' is a dead end. Okay. Proceed."

I heard a sigh, but at least he tried to play along. "So, hey . . ." His voice, always quiet, was firm and friendly. That was good. "I don't suppose you know anything about track and field?"

"No, why?" I tried to keep my reply slightly imperious, like some girl in a bar might.

"My little sister is trying out for the high school track team. You look like you run."

Oh, very nice—a fitness compliment wrapped up in an opening line. Han Solo with my Yoda very far will go to be a Jedi knight, yes. I tilted my chin and gave him an appraising glance. "Well, I do jog in the mornings."

"She thinks she's an endurance runner and wants to go for the sixteen-hundred- or maybe the thirty-two-hundred-meter runs, but I kind of see her more as a sprinter. The two-hundred-meter races, definitely. Maybe the hundred-meter sprints. I can see her doing those. I think she'd be good on the hundred-meter high hurdles, too, so long as she . . ."

"Wait a minute, wait a minute." I waved until his mouth shut with a clamp. "That's way too much information for any woman to evaluate all at once. Unless she participated in the last Olympics, anyway." His abashed expression was so adorable that I wanted to laugh at him, but my old experience with Sean's tissue-thin ego warned me that I might want to hold off. "Let's move on."

Without warning, Ethan suddenly blurted out, "Your face looks like a peanut."

I stared at him for a second, and then at my drink, wondering if I'd had so many strawberry margaritas that I was having auditory hallucinations. But no, I was pretty sure he'd actually said it. "What?"

"Sorry." I'm glad I wasn't the only one who turned red. Ethan had ripened to the shade of a plum tomato. "I was trying to give you an opening insult."

"Ohhhhh!" That made more sense. Wait, though. "You think I look like a peanut?"

"No!" Over in the corner, the office party erupted into wild laughter as someone opened up a gag gift of some sort and began to pass it around. Ethan waited until it was quieter before he answered. "It just kind of came out."

"Well . . ." An odd sort of insult it had been, for sure. "Not bad. For a first try, anyway. I'd stay away from peanut comparisons in the future, though." Moving right along! I took a long sip from my melting margarita. "Let's try the Yes Ladder. You remember what that is?"

"Where I ask a lot of questions that can be answered

with yeses, so that eventually she'll say yes when I pop the big question?"

"You're not going to ask her to marry you, I hope, but you've got the idea. Like, um . . ." I thought a second. "So, do you really have a sister?"

"Yes. Three of them, all younger. The baby's fourteen years younger than me. I don't get to see much of her, since she's still back in Pittsburgh."

"Wow!" I exclaimed, feeling pangs of sympathy for his poor mother. "But she's trying out for track?"

"Yes. We all did track in high school."

"You, too?"

"Me, too. I still run. Every morning."

Accustomed as I was to rolling out of bed forty minutes before I was due at work, hopping into the shower, grabbing a train to the bookstore, and arriving fifteen minutes late, the thought of actually rising early to exert myself elicited an involuntary shudder. "No, really."

"I do! You should try it with me sometime. It's exhilarating."

"You're insane." I grinned. "Oh, shoot. I'm sorry, I was supposed to be playing the Yes Ladder with you."

"I think I have the general idea." Ethan rested his bristly chin on his hand as if trying to keep his head steady. That seemed a good idea, actually. I matched his pose and gazed back at him, my eyelids heavy. "Do you really think this Yes Ladder thing works? It sounds corny."

"Absolutely! I've seen it work. It's simply a psychological technique. I remember studying it when I had a psych class in college. It's a theory of escalation—if you ask someone for a very small favor, you'll be more likely to grant them a larger favor the next time around."

Ethan seemed to consider that information for a moment. "So if I ask you for the time of day, you'd be more likely to let me buy you a drink?"

I laughed. "Something like that. Maybe a few more steps in between. People like saying yes."

"Is that why you keep saying yes when A.J. asks you to be his wingman?"

Here we were, back at A.J. again. "Sure, I get a lot of amusement out of it. You said yourself that I should be having fun. Anyway," I added briskly, "we're supposed to be practicing the Yes Ladder for you."

He smiled. "Who says we aren't?"

When I thought back to the questions he'd just asked, I had to give the guy credit. "Slick. Very slick."

"So, have I earned the right to ask you something serious?" We'd been so playful and mock-flirty during the last few minutes that I was caught off guard by his sudden change of tone. "Nothing embarrassing, I promise." I nodded, thinking he was going to ask something about the Method, only to have my heart sink when I heard the question that followed. "Don't take this the wrong way, but you seem awfully self-conscious about your posture."

Automatically I straightened in my seat. "A little," I admitted, after a long internal struggle. I hated talking about this subject.

"Is that because of your height? I'm sorry," he said immediately, sensing how uncomfortable I was. "After I said it wouldn't be embarrassing, too. Skip it."

I slurped the last of our drink while he watched me

with those kind blue eyes. Done at last, I slumped back into my chair before remembering to keep my spine erect. "It's silly." I tried to laugh. "It's a silly, stupid issue, but it bugs me, yes."

"Why?"

I met his querying gaze. "You don't know what it's like to be enormously tall."

"I'm taller than you!" He laughed.

"Not by much! What are you, six-one? I'm almost six feet tall, Ethan. For a woman, that's colossal." He didn't believe me, I could tell. Men never did. They belonged to a gender in which guys came in three sizes—small, average, and potential awesome basketball buddies. "In fourth grade I was a head taller than everyone. In sixth, the boys were calling me 'string bean.' It wasn't until I was in eleventh grade that a few of the boys began catching up to me in height. And not very many, even then. We read *Gulliver's Travels* in one of my English classes and got to the part where Gulliver's among the Lilliputians, and everyone in the classroom began to snicker. At *me.*"

"Everyone has something in middle and high school that makes them stick out. I had acne. Bad acne. I mean, acne so bad it looked like my face was melting."

"So you understand." I felt a pang of sympathy for him. We'd had a few of those kids in our school, too. "You know what we tall girls do when we're surrounded by shorter people? We stoop, Ethan. We stoop." He was quiet now, listening to words I'd never said aloud to anyone. "We blend with the pack and hide what makes us different and special. My mom and sister barked at me for years to straighten up. But after a lifetime of hunkering down, I'm so used to doing it that I need to remind myself still that I don't have to stoop anymore."

After a long moment of silence, he finally spoke. "Wow."

"I'm being melodramatic."

"No." I felt a pressure on my hand; he'd reached out and taken it with his own. In my boozy haze, it felt warm and reassuring. I didn't have the slightest desire to pull away. "Thank you. For telling me," he added, when I shook my head, not understanding. "I've known you a whole year and I never knew you had those kinds of doubts about yourself."

I laughed more bitterly than I intended. "You're kidding."

"No, I'm not." He pulled my hand toward him, cupping it between both of his own now. "You probably think I'm just that work guy who brings you clippings and bitches about the coffee with you, but I admire you. A lot. I mean, to me you've always seemed so smart, so *confident.* You know what has to be done and you go after it. I never realized . . . I think a lot of people stoop, you know. Not . . ." He pantomimed hunching over. "I mean, we pretend to be less intelligent than we really are, so no one says anything. Or less talented. It's stupid, isn't it? Ah, shit, this isn't coming out right. I really am a girl-drink drunk."

"No, I get it," I told him. All four of our hands were entwined, now. The tips of my fingers stroked the downy hair decorating the backs of his wrists. I'd never realized how large his hands were before—large and soft, though I could feel a callus between his middle and index finger from where he held his pen. "You get it, too."

When I smiled, he cocked his head and returned it. I felt like we were bathed in a comfortable, warm, strawberry-flavored glow that I wanted to last forever and ever. I'd had a good dinner. I'd had good conversation and laughs with friends. Best of all, I'd discovered someone who saw me in the way I wished everyone would. The world was very good to me that night. "I do get it," he said, very quietly. "You don't ever have to stoop around me."

I knew that now was probably the time I should take my leave. I didn't know why I felt that way, since I was enjoying myself so very much, but it seemed the correct and conventional thing to do, somehow. "I really should get home," I murmured.

"Don't." Had I been hoping he'd dissuade me all along? Maybe I had, because at that one word, and his squeeze of my hands accompanying it, my heart seemed to beat twice as fast. My lungs caught a breath and held it, waiting in suspense for something to happen.

I wanted to make that something happen. I wanted to do something to thank him, and the first thing my foggy brain conceived of was to lean forward, pull my hands from between his, and lay them on either side of his prickly face so I could draw his lips to mine.

They tasted sweet and sticky from the sugar-rimmed margarita glasses we'd been raising for the last two hours. I was surprised at how Ethan didn't at all resist my impulsive move. If anything, he kissed me back, prolonging what I'd intended to be a short, sweet peck of thanks into something more passionate, something more eager and hungry—something *more*.

We separated for a brief moment, looking across the short space between us into each other's eyes. Then, as if by mutual consent, we leaned forward and began to kiss again, his hands running through the length of my hair, mine gripping the back of his head as if fearful he might try to escape from me. Right there in the middle of the El Zocalo, two of the most mild-mannered people in the entire city began making out with each other as if our lives depended on it. "Oh, God," I moaned, astounded at how hard I was breathing. I thought my heart might try to beat its way out of my ribcage, so desperate were each of its thudding impacts.

"You said your sister's out?" Ethan asked, taking a quick taste of my lips after his question.

I nodded, hoping he was thinking what I was thinking. "Until late."

He seemed to sense my urgency. "If I were doing the Yes Ladder right now, would this be an appropriate point to ask you home?"

"Very," I said, wanting more of him.

"Want to go?" he asked, grabbing blindly for his coat.

"Yes, do you?"

"You bet I do."

By now I had my coat in hand and stuffed one hand down an arm, even though my lips were still hovering in the vicinity of his as we continued to steal swift kisses from each other. The wrong arm, unfortunately. "Let's go, then," he suggested.

"We're going." The two of us were peeling out of there as if we were conjoined twins attached at the face, one of whom had her coat on only halfway, and upside-down at that. I didn't care. At least I knew, when we galloped out of there, fingers intertwined tightly, that I was leaving with my shoulders back and my head held high.

Somehow I had a suspicion that for the first time in my life, I was going to be one of those New Yorkers who made out in a taxi cab all the way home.

ELEVEN

"You're sure your sister's out?"

"It's not even nine." Our voices echoed in the hallway while I fumbled with the key to let us in. "Her reception's barely gotten started." The key wasn't cooperating—or maybe my hands were shaking too much. I steadied myself by wrapping both sets of fingers around the key and very carefully inserting it into the knob. We both sighed with relief when it finally fit and twisted. "Okay," I said, leading him in.

The instant the door closed and we were left in the darkness, he was on me, pushing me back against the tasteful Ansel Adams knock-off photos hanging on the wall by the coatrack and gripping my by the shoulders even as I kicked off my shoes and reached for his head. I pulled him down to me so we could kiss once more in a way that had made our display at El Zocalo look like timid pecks between disinterested cousins. I'd worried that his prickly beard would leave my face raw and red, but by now I didn't care. All the little things I usually fretted about in the presence of guys had faded away. Whether we both had salsa breath no longer mattered, nor whether my face was properly applied, nor the fact that all those margaritas were threatening to give me a bad case of the fajita burps. I just wanted him close to me; I wanted to feel his mouth over mine, enveloping it with his soft lips, and his tongue darting purposefully in and out of my mouth.

"Is this bad?" he asked, not for the first time. He'd thrown out the same question several times in the cab ride home.

Resenting that he'd take his lips away from mine for even the few seconds required to make that query, I gasped out the same answer I'd already given him. "No. It's not bad. It's good. It's very, very good."

He mashed his face against mine, dragging me to the side and throwing the photos off-center. Lost as I was in the moment, I still somewhere in the back of my mind made a mental note to fix that before the evening's end, lest it offend Alice's anal housekeeping sensibilities. "Good. I'm glad it's good."

"Good." It wasn't the kind of dialogue I was going to find in the august literary love scenes of D. H. Lawrence, but somehow that didn't bother me either. Our cool-weather wear, however, weren't giving us the kind of flexibility I would have liked. "Let's . . ."

"Okay."

He read my mind. We backed away from each other and struggled out of our coats, staring at each other in the gray-blue light from the city that was filtering in through the kitchen window and out to the vestibule where we stood. Once we'd thrown our jackets onto the floor, I tossed back my hair and tried to control my heart's pounding. Ethan stood motionless, breathing heavily, his silhouette broad, his shoulders back and arms curved slightly behind him, like a tango dancer about to lunge at his partner and, in the heat of passion, dip her low to the dance floor.

When it came to lunging, though, I'm pretty certain it was me who charged first. This time it was my turn to knock him back. We narrowly missed the ceramic art tiles hanging next to the hallway, instead landing against the edge of the kitchen door. "Ow," he complained as our lips met again.

"Oh, God!"

"No, just . . . corner. Back."

"Sorry."

"Don't be."

"I'm not really." Though I knew it was wrong to compare Ethan's kisses to those of other men I'd known, it was impossible not to. Sean had been—well, who cared what Sean had been, really? I didn't, not at that moment. What I did know is that Ethan didn't hold back. He didn't appear to be trying to be overthinking what we were doing, or taking off in the opposite extreme by simply going through the motions; he wasn't trying to impress me with his smooth moves, and he wasn't showing off. He merely wanted me, and wanted me badly. At least, that's what I judged by the way he pushed himself off the wall and propelled me backward in the direction of the living room, our lips still firmly locked. I gasped as simultaneously his mouth moved to my neck, causing me to shiver uncontrollably, and I crashed into the wall behind me.

Another mental note: I had to remember to pick up the antique chess pieces after I'd caused them to fall from the little shelves on which they'd been perched.

"Shoes?" he asked, kicking off a pair of Doc Martens oxfords onto the floor.

"And sweater." I took the liberty of sliding my hands underneath his woolly henley and yanking it upward.

Unfortunately, with the remnants of three margaritas' worth of tequila sluggishly working its way out of my system, my dexterity wasn't at its highest. He responded with a surprised yip of "Ow ow ow ow ow!" when I caught him in the neck hole. His arms were still entangled in the sleeves, as well. In my haste to undress him, I'd turned Ethan into some kind of headless scarecrow who was blundering back and forth across the hall trying to find his hands in the voluminous folds of cloth. "God damn it," he said, at last yanking the sweater back down over his body. I started giggling. "What?"

"Whack-a-mole," I told him, pointing. "You look like that carnival whack-a-mole game with your head popping up like that." It was a silly observation, I knew.

Ethan crossed his arms and unsheathed his sweater in the normal way. He threw it on the floor to join the trail of other clothing we'd left behind. "I'll show you whack-a-mole."

I didn't know what in the heck that actually meant, but when Ethan grabbed me by the shoulders and determinedly pushed me in the direction of Alice's living room, I didn't really care. "Just a second," I told him when we seemed about to make impact on the sofa. His hands lingered on me when I turned around, roaming over my back, my hips, my rear end, seeming not to want to let me go. I defogged my lust-crazed brain enough to grab the TV remote from between the leather cushions and toss it onto the coffee table, where I also moved a half-consumed glass of water I'd left before heading out for dinner earlier that evening. I also had the presence of mind to quickly remove Alice's dangly earrings so they wouldn't get bent or lost. At last, all my preparations complete, I sat down on the sofa. "All right. Go."

He laughed silently at my command and perched at the couch's other end. His shirt had come half-untucked when he'd taken off his sweater and coat and his hair was the messiest I'd ever seen it. Not seeming to notice his disarray, however, Ethan sat up very properly, hands on his lap, as if he were the chaperone we were so sorely missing. "Go where?"

"Come here," I breathed, from my end of the sofa.

"What for?"

"You know what for." I loved that he teased me; I'd never before had a man stop in the middle of a passionate make-out session to be playful.

Though it was still shadowy, I could make out the skeptical tilt of his head through the gloom. "No, what for?"

I could be coy, too. "I was thinking we could, you know. Make out some more. And maybe other stuff."

"Other stuff?" Considering how we'd been all over each other for the last half hour, it was amazing how virtuously we were behaving now. "Hmmm. I think there's talk of 'other stuff' in our store's vintage erotica section. Not," he hastened to add, "that I've read any of it."

"Of course not," I agreed decorously.

We sat there in silence for a moment, no doubt grinning at each other, though I couldn't see it. Suddenly inspired, I leapt up. "Music."

I didn't hear the swoosh of his khakis against the leather until I'd already taken a couple of steps. "Crap!" he yelled, right after I heard the glass-topped coffee table give a little leap.

"Are you okay?"

"Yes," he said, annoyed. "I didn't know you had moved. It's just my knee."

I flicked on the stereo, which was visible by the stand-by light over on the entertainment center. "I'm coming back."

"Hurry."

It took a moment for the receiver to warm up after being switched on. I was already back to the sofa and edging my way around the coffee table when a male voice began speaking from the stereo at the room's other end. ". . . Thanks for that, caller. If you're just tuning in, this is Bob Gittel on WMDX, fourteen-seventy on your AM radio dial, all talk, all the time, taking your calls on the topic of your choice tonight. And if you haven't been listening to our other shows, such as 'Love Line Express' or. . . ." He laughed a little before proceeding. "Or 'Portia Daye's Radio Show with Portia Daye,' tune in to WMDX during our drive time and afternoon shows for some of the most controversial and . . ."

"Shit," I growled. I'd just reached Ethan, only to have

to turn back. I'd been expecting something bluesy and jazzy—the kind of bland, nondescript background music it's appropriate to enjoy with your nooky after you've reached a certain age. And here I was getting a constant reminder of the damned Daye family. "Let me switch that." Mostly, I admit, I was annoyed at finding proof that apparently my sister had been listening to Portia's radio show when I wasn't around.

"Stay." I felt a tugging at my back. I didn't resist. I sank down onto the couch and felt Ethan's hands gently peeling clothing from my shoulders. I didn't resist that, either. Neither did I notice the talk show host's voice any longer. Once he'd thrown my sweater aside, Ethan's fingers traced down my front, outlining my collarbone through the silk blend of the twinset's shell. His other hand touched my side, just below my rib cage. Involuntarily, I shivered. "I hope you know I really like you."

Even though he whispered, I could hear him plainly. I nodded, only realizing too late that he probably couldn't see me. "I like you, too," I whispered.

His index finger moved down to the side, drawing a crescent around the side of my breast that ended in a curlicue around my nipple, causing me to let out the smallest of breaths. A moment later, I felt the same sensations on the other side. "We're going to be okay after this, right?" he asked. "No weirdness?"

"Nuh-uh," I promised, sounding sure of myself. This all felt so unreal—like the kind of hazy erotic fantasy I might have in the dozy moments before waking in the morning. The fact that I couldn't see him clearly only added to the dreamlike sensation. "No way."

I would have said anything to keep him touching me

right then. After our furious wall banging a few moments before, this subdued, soft approach seemed almost too slow and serious, yet I couldn't get enough of it. I felt a tug at my waistline. Without any more warning than that, his fingers slid up along my abdomen beneath the surface of my top. The sensation of his warm fingertips gliding along my stomach, my tender sides, and around to the small of my back nearly made me want to yell out with pleasure. Instead, I bit my lip and whimpered.

I couldn't let his sensual salvo go unanswered, however. I tugged at his shirt and, raising my mouth to his once more, undid one button after the other, starting from the top. I'd reached midway down when I stopped. Reaching in with my left hand, I let my palm brush against the planes of his chest. The contained growth of fur on his pectorals surprised me. His nipples were hardened and taut. Though his chest was neither as overinflated as A.J.'s or as conspicuously trained to look good in a business suit as Sean, it didn't matter. I wasn't envisioning the models from a fitness magazine when I undid his final three buttons and yanked the shirt over his shoulders.

"Arms," he murmured, his mouth against mine. He pulled away to tear off his shirt, whipping a part of it in my face. I felt something hard—probably one of the buttons I'd just unfastened—nearly hit my eye. "Are you okay?" he asked, hearing my little squeal.

"Fine. Let's each take off our own clothes," I suggested. "We keep hurting each other."

His soft gasp of excitement seemed to fill the darkness. "How much should I take off?"

"Everything. No, not everything. Almost everything." By then I'd shimmied out of the blouse and was undoing my pants.

"Watch?" I heard the sound of his metal wristband tinkling as he removed it and dropped it onto the coffee table.

"Okay."

"Socks?"

"Definitely socks." I was having a little bit of a problem with my legs. Ordinarily, when there was no pressure, I had no issues whatsoever getting dressed or undressed. Somehow with the sexual heat on, I'd reverted to preschool days, when a jumpsuit and a pair of Velcro-laced sneakers seemed the most baffling creations in the world. At last I resorted to scissor-kicking my legs violently to shake the things off. From the sound of things, they landed somewhere on the room's other side, bringing one of Alice's ceramic vases down with it in a heavy, thankfully muffled thud—one more thing I'd have to remember to pick up when we finally moved to the bedroom.

Ethan paused. "That didn't sound good."

"Nope." I adjusted my bra and pulled my panties, readying myself for what came next.

"Should I go check on it?"

My answer was the same as before. "Nope."

In another lunge I was atop Ethan, pushing down and straddling him on the sofa. He'd taken off everything but what felt like a pair of boxer briefs. Wherever our nakedness met, my skin seemed to flush and warm and tingle. It was impossible not to notice how aroused he was; his hardness filled with blood and pulsed against my pelvic bone, where it rested. I deliberately ground into him, receiving an instant response. "Are you having fun?" he asked, once more moving down to my neck with his mouth, then letting it travel to my shoulders. "Please tell me you're having fun."

"Yes!" I exclaimed. "Fun. I like fun. Fun is good. Are you?"

"Ye-es!" he gasped, when I ground my hips against him again. "Just don't . . . if you don't want to . . . I'll understand if . . ."

Being on top was something of a novelty to me, given that I'd always been used to Sean weighing me down, Saturday night after Saturday night. I could see why the guys liked it. I shifted my weight to increase the pressure on his hard penis. "If what?"

All he could do was let out a helpless whimper. That was fine. It was my turn to explore.

I started with the underside of his jaw, letting my mouth slide down his neck to the middle of his heaving chest. When I lay my ear against it, I could hear his heart jack-hammering at the ribcage. I had to hold down his forearms to keep them from wandering over my own body—I needed this particular moment to be under my control. His stomach leapt and protested as I rubbed my lips and chin over its slightly hairy, flat surface. The aroma of laundry detergent and fabric softener filled my nostrils when I ran my cheek over his briefs, down the length of what lay within. I let go of one of his arms so my fingers could slip beneath the elastic waistband, teasing it back and darting down to the naked flesh below, before letting it slap back. His breathing was even more labored now. Impulsively, I reached inside and wrapped my fingers around his curved shaft, which was thick and surprisingly hot to the touch. The tip was already slightly sticky.

"Tell me you don't have a nickname for it," I whispered, giving it a squeeze.

"No." The single syllable was ragged from the torture I was applying. "No nicknames."

"Nothing like Little Ethan? Red? Mini-me?"

"No. Please . . ."

I let go, struggling to a rising position so I could yank his shorts down. We didn't need them any more. He surprised me, though, with a counterattack that flung me against the sofa's chilly back and then onto the warmed spot where he'd moments before lain. I put a hand on his back, but he removed it; I put the other onto the smooth skin of his buttocks, but he pushed it off. "Nuh-uh."

"I'll touch you if I want."

"Nope."

"Why not?"

He seemed to consider the question for a moment before answering. "Because it's my turn."

The sensation of his face against the tender skin of my stomach made me gasp and nearly try to squirm away, like I might from an unexpected ice cube on my neck on a hot summer afternoon. It didn't take me long to realize, though, that the sensations he was arousing were far from uncomfortable, and that to make me wriggle was definitely his aim. His burgeoning beard scratched against the inside of my thighs, making my legs flail, and then with intense deliberation moved up to the most sensitive area of all.

I felt his face nuzzling outside of my panties, lips spread wide. Then came something I hadn't expected—a great heat that spread from his mouth to deep within me. Was I on fire? No, he was merely breathing, slowly and with great concentration, through the fabric, inflaming me with the air from his lungs. "Bring your legs together," he instructed. "Lift up." There was no way I would refuse, especially when I felt his hands skim up my hips to grasp the hem of my panties and gently pull them down.

And then I felt his mouth on my thighs once more, tickling and teasing and raking the flesh with his teeth.

I can't say how long we spent on the sofa after that. I honestly lost track of the clock. For all the things we did with each other, it should have been hours . . . though with the sweet way time seemed to zip by, it might have been mere minutes. All I knew was that at one point, when I was back on top of him, gently rolling my hips back and forth as we giggled and he tried to clear his mouth of my hair falling into it, my vision was suddenly bleached white by a blinding supernova. And that immediately afterward I heard my sister's voice saying my name. "Rebecca? Oh, my God, are you all right?"

It took several seconds for me to get my eyesight back to normal in the overhead light. "Oh, hi," I said, realizing that I sounded like I'd just woken up. My sister stood there holding my shoes, Ethan's sweater, and the ceramic vase I'd brought down with my pants, looking absolutely frantic.

Alice wasn't by herself, either. In fact, she'd brought home quite the little party. First there was Walter, standing there with a baffled expression on his face. Then there was Rani, big eyes wide open and mouth agape. There was Portia, who waggled her fingers at me as if she hadn't noticed that I was wrapping my arms around my nude torso like some shy Renaissance nymph, and the good-looking but dopey boyfriend she'd brought to the show the other night. Then, just because some malevolent deity hated me, there were an additional two or three suits from the non-profit that Alice presumably had brought home to her showplace apartment for a nice drink. Somehow I suspect they'd never expected the showplace apartment to be more of a burlesque theater.

"*Hi? Is that it?*" Alice sounded none too happy. "Are you *okay?* I thought the place had been *robbed,* what with the way . . ." She paused, joining the others in the general gaping as Ethan slid his sticky body across the leather and sat up. Startled, he gave them all a sheepish wave.

"Everybody, this is Ethan," I said in my best little-sister-of-the-hostess voice. "Ethan, this is . . . everybody."

I'm not sure who was more mortified—them or us. I would have put down a few dollars on it being a dead heat. Actually, I was kind of hoping that Alice would come to her senses soon and move everyone out, so that I wouldn't have to stand up and show off all the goods to Walter and the boys. Those dreams were dashed when the one unembarrassed person in the room took a few steps forward, peeked over the top of the sofa, and saw exactly what I'd been hoping to hide. "Becca," said Portia, as matter-of-factly as if she'd been reading the weather report on her show, "you've been having sex with this Ethan man."

I couldn't deny it. Neither could he. In the cold overhead light, we looked at each other and blushed. "Yes," I finally told her, suddenly chilly.

"But you're dating A.J.," she announced. "I think he'd want you to have sex only with him."

"What?" If Rani opened her mouth any further she could probably have comfortably fit a basketball within. She slapped her hands over it in shock.

"I—"

"She's *what?*" Alice demanded. I got ready to duck, just in case she threw the vase at me.

"She and A.J.," said Portia, as if it were the most obvious thing in the world. "Dating. Having a thing? Doing it?" She illustrated the point by thrusting two fingers of one hand into her other closed fist. "She said you were trying to fix her up with some impossible guy who was an incredible dork." I cringed, genuinely horrified for Walter's sake. He didn't even flinch, but I winced for him.

"I . . ." I couldn't finish the sentence. "Um."

It was Alice who finally saved the situation. "Coffee in the kitchen, everybody!" she said, voice bright and artificially cheery. "Let's go. Let's move along." The strangers filed out first, probably grateful for a reprieve. Walter followed, then Portia's boy toy, and a reluctant Rani finally followed the pack. "You, too," Alice told Portia, trying to grab her elbow while simultaneously avoiding seeing anything over the sofa's top.

Portia shook her head. "A.J.'s not going to like this,

you know." Her tone changed and grew warmer as she gestured in the direction of the forgotten radio, which was still playing softly. "But thank you for listening to WMDX!"

Ethan cleared his throat and coughed. She'd obviously been addressing him. "Absolutely. Love the show."

"Oh, do you! That's so sweet. Alice, did you hear? He listens to my show."

Portia continued babbling as Alice firmly shoved her in the direction of the dining room and kitchen. My sister returned a moment later, looked at the mess we'd made, and had three words for the both of us. "Clean up. Now." Then she swiveled on her heels and clacked to join her guests.

Neither Ethan nor I had much to talk about as we scampered across the floor, collecting bits of clothing, straightening furniture, and picking up the tchotchkes we'd knocked over. "I'd better go," he said.

"Yeah, probably," I told him. Running about with my arms over my breasts, bent over at the waist, made me look awkward and ungainly. He'd been all over me for a long time, yet I couldn't bear to let him see me naked in the light like this. "Listen, I'm sorry—"

"No, it's my—"

"No, mine." I had a hard time even looking at him, or his pretty face. "I shouldn't have—that is, I loved it, but . . ."

"No, no, I get it," he assured me. He had on his pants, one sock, and half his shirt now. "It was kind of a surprise, and we were both—"

"Yes, exactly!" I said, as if I'd let him make a point.

"But it's not weird, right?"

"No! Not weird at all!" I handed him his other sock. "I'm going to—"

When I jerked my head in the direction of my bedroom, he understood. "All right. I'll see you . . . well, not tomorrow, unless you . . . I mean . . ."

Frantic to get him out, I draped Alice's sweater over my chest. "We'll talk," I assured him.

He stopped me before I fled the scene of the crime for good. "Rebecca, you're sure this isn't weird for you? Because I'm getting a vibe of weirdness, and I'd hate—"

"No, we're good." I nodded. "Honest. We'll talk."

"Okay." He breathed a sigh of relief, and made an impulsive dive in the direction of my face. At the last moment I turned my head so that his lips landed on my cheek. "Good night, then."

" 'Night!" I said, finally making a run for it.

It wasn't until I'd reached the solitude of my room and managed to wrap my robe around my naked body that I sank down onto my bed, rested my head on my hands, and considered the whopper of a lie I'd just told. Because that moment with Ethan, standing there naked and exposed beside him, had been very, very weird. And I really couldn't say why.

TWELVE

There's a certain kind of woman, independent and optimistic, who when struck by adversity that makes her divorce look like a Sunday cakewalk, bravely rises to the occasion. She swallows her pride, admits to her mistakes, and struggles to make things right.

I was definitely *not* that kind of woman. Apparently, I was the kind of woman who, when the mythological Fates looked down from their Corinthian plinths—or whatever it was that Fates sat on—and saw a girl having a little too much fun, and after a little consultation between themselves decided to take her down a peg or two by having her flop around naked on a sofa with a guy her sister and chums had never seen before, reacted by calling in sick to work. And who moped. And who got sucked in far too easily to marathons of *The Partridge Family* on cable.

There were two common phrases heard in my sister's apartment over that weekend. The first was a plaintive "Couldn't you at least have put down a throw? That was fine Italian leather!" against which there was no good argument. It's not as if the sofa was ruined, exactly, but Alice couldn't exactly bring herself to sit on it until I'd wiped it down with a damp sponge and chamois.

The second was a little harder for me to counter. "I can't *believe* you were dating A. J. Daye. Of *all* people."

"We weren't dating." I sighed. I was sprawled on the much-abused sofa, while Alice perched primly on a love seat that had been spared the touch of anyone's naked rump. The pair of us were a study in contrasts— she in a dressy business suit with her blond hair perfectly groomed, taking little bites from the takeaway salad she'd brought home for her Monday lunch, and me in my sweats, unshowered, with an empty plastic bowl of microwaveable noodles filled with a handful of KitKat wrappers in the middle of the coffee table. "We were never dating."

"And the thing is, she was *dating my brother*." The little Bose stereo atop the entertainment center reproduced Portia's voice as clearly as if she'd been in the room with us. As if that statement proved everything, my sister held out both hands at the speakers, then glared at me as she savagely stabbed a cherry tomato until it bled on her fork. Then she devoured it. "Out of the goodness of my heart, I, Portia Daye, allowed one of my best friends to date my brother—a sensitive, intellectual man—only to find out that she was sleeping with another man. How was I supposed to know she was a big, enormous, lying slut?"

"Um." Whoever Portia's guest du jour might have

been seemed to be having difficulties answering that particular question. "That's a valid point."

I wouldn't have thought it possible to slump any farther back, but with a flop of my head on the couch's back, I managed. "Oh, God." I tried to rally. My sister was a rational person, if nothing else. "I lied to Portia. I was never dating her brother. I'm not a slut." Alice's raised eyebrow didn't exactly make me feel confident about my defense. "I'm not! What you saw the other night was . . ."

How could I finish that sentence? What she saw the other night was some of the most passionate, most untamed, most feral sex I'd ever enjoyed. I'd had to slap myself mentally several times to keep from falling into daydreams about it. Good as it had been, though, I couldn't let it happen again. I'd egged Ethan on! I was as bad as A.J., goading the poor guy into practically assaulting me. I wanted to blame it on the drinking, or the full moon—anything that would help explain away that unexpected feeling of raw, instinctive need I'd felt when we'd sat close to each other at the El Zocalo bar. In the end, though, I only had myself to blame. Why in the world would Ethan want to dally with someone who'd been off the market so long that her date stamp had expired?

"It was an anomaly," I said finally, after thinking it over. I couldn't bear to meet Alice's eyes.

"So. When you told me that you were out on 'friendly dates' with this guy from work, this . . . Ethan . . . you were actually . . . getting more serious about him?"

Something about the way she said Ethan's name with roughly the same enthusiasm she might have pronounced the words *festering canker sore* irked me. "No," I said, without thinking it through first. "I was out with A.J."

"Okay." Whenever Alice was angry, she didn't get so much irate as swiftly and quietly chilly. If she'd been plunged in her current state into the north Atlantic after the *Titanic* sank, the survivors clinging to scraps of wood and lifebuoys might have agreed that the icebergs they'd previously been swimming among had been toasty by comparison. Through gritted teeth, she attempted another approach. "So on the nights you claimed to be with Ethan, you were really seeing A.J.?"

Any other time I might have taken consolation in the fact that if Ethan had been a mere canker sore, Alice pronounced the two initials of my good-time buddy with roughly the same loathing as *scorching case of herpes*. "Yes." I sighed.

"Thus, you were dating." Alice had always been awfully good at those logic proofs in high school geometry.

"No, we weren't—we were going out, but we weren't—argh!" I ran my hands through my hair in frustration.

While Alice waited for me to explain myself, Portia continued her radio interview. "So, let's get your opinion. Do you think sexual addiction is a real issue?"

"Well, certainly," said the woman, who sounded authoritative and calm. I wondered where Portia's staff had managed to find her, and how much they'd had to bribe her with to get her to sit in that chair. "All addictive behaviors can be damaging if they're allowed to get out of control."

"Exactly."

"In fact, I'd say your friend Beckate might need to see a counselor if she's really suffering from a sexual addiction. A good counselor can provide the kind of behavior therapy she might need."

"Absolutely," said Portia. "Beckate, if you're out there listening, this is an expert speaking."

Alice echoed, "See? An expert!"

I rolled my eyes.

"And I'm very sorry about your brother," said the expert.

"Why, thank you!" Portia sounded genuinely touched.

The woman cleared her throat and, with the greatest of civility, inquired, "And now, maybe we could talk a little about dog shows? That is why you asked me here, I believe?"

I couldn't resist glaring at Alice and commenting, "That's one doozy of a material witness you've got there."

She rose from her seat and walked across the room to turn off the stereo. "I'm worried about you, Rebecca." Alice crossed her arms and gave me the stern older sister expression she'd been practicing since she first hit double digits in age and decided I was going to be the burden she bore for the rest of our lives.

This was all ridiculous, though. "Don't! There's nothing to worry about!"

"There's plenty to worry about. You managed to insult Walter the other night, who's a perfectly nice guy."

"Portia insulted Walter. Not me." The distinction was specious, I knew, but it was still a distinction.

Alice didn't care. "You've been getting more and

more erratic. You've been telling lies. Look at you: You're miserable."

"I just wanted to shake up my life a little!" My protest was loud and heartfelt. I stood up and faced her, aware that my height gave me a more imposing presence. More imposing than melting into a sofa, anyway. "You guys have decided that A.J.'s a vile little troll. But he's one of the only people I know who hasn't thought I should be wearing sackcloth and a hair shirt because I'm not wearing a wedding ring anymore! If I'm miserable, you should be happy! That's the way you'd prefer me, miserable and holed up in my little room with a book!"

"I have never wanted you to be miserable," she countered, still angry. "Never."

To insist otherwise would make me sound like a petulant fourteen-year-old. Alice had always been good to me. She and I were merely very different people—that was all. "I know," I sighed, suddenly tired again. I sank back down onto the sofa, capitulating. She at least uncrossed her arms and went back to her chair, reclaiming the remnants of her salad and placing the plastic tray in her lap so she could pretend to pick at it. I could tell from her stiff neck and exquisite posture that I'd hurt her feelings, yet at the same time I was stubborn enough that I wouldn't hand the entire argument to her on a silver platter. "Just . . . don't judge me too harshly, would you?"

She chewed for a while, prolonging the swallow so that she wouldn't have to speak right away. At long last, she gave me a quick little nod. We hadn't completely hashed this out yet. We might never get around to it.

But at least for now, we'd managed to agree not to intrude on each other's space. Thus had things always been done among the Egan sisters, ever since we'd had to share a room for most of our juvenile lives. So grateful was I for the reprieve that I decided to toss her a concession. "A.J. *is* kind of a little troll."

"You think?" she retorted. Then, curious, she asked, "Are you *really* sick or is this like when Mom gave you that bad perm in sixth grade and you didn't want to go to school for the entire week after?"

"Definitely the bad perm thing. Do you want your baby carrots?" She held out the tray and let me pluck them out. They were nearly the first food not grown on a KitKat tree that I'd eaten in forty-eight hours.

While I crunched, she shrugged. "And how serious are you about this Ethan guy?"

"Well . . ." I'd called sex with him an anomaly moments before. I could use more anomalies like those. If there were a universe where I could have my cake and eat it, too, I would want to be able to keep Ethan as both a friend and a lover, because I had the vivid impression that a couple of vigorous hours hadn't at all exhausted our sexual repertoire. I liked Ethan. I liked him an awful lot. Part of me, deep inside, tingled whenever I wondered whether what I'd experienced Saturday night might have lead to more than liking, nurtured the right way.

Hadn't I always thought that some girl would be lucky to have Ethan as a boyfriend or husband? Hadn't I always felt a fond, easy envy for the woman who'd get to wake up to those blue eyes every morning? I'd felt so weird about what we'd done because we'd gone about it the entirely wrong way. A normal girl did not try to pimp out a guy in a bar and then take him home for a romp when he struck out. That kind of thing just didn't happen.

I'd been avoiding going into work so that I wouldn't have to see the hurt in his eyes. Or maybe I was afraid I might see hope there. I wasn't sure which might be worse.

"Never mind." I'd been silent for so long that Alice had closed her salad. She stood up and crossed in the direction of the dining room and kitchen. "I think I can figure out the answer to that."

I watched her go without saying a word. If she knew the answer, I wished to hell she'd tell me.

Alice had been right about many things, but one in particular bugged me: Walter. Much as I wanted to shunt the very thought of him from my brain and concentrate on the very special episode of *Saved by the Bell* playing on one of the cable rerun channels, the notion that I'd hurt his feelings, however inadvertently, made the tiny core of misery deep within me throb with pain. The guy couldn't help being a double-D—dopey and doughy. The entire time I'd known him, he'd been unfailingly polite and gentlemanly. I needed to make amends there.

That's why, within a few moments, I found myself asking his assistant at the non-profit if I could be patched through. Yes, as Alice had once said, I was indeed the girl who ripped off her Band-Aids in one mighty swipe. If I had to take my medicine, I might as well get it over with quickly. Waiting for him to pick up seemed like an eternity, but at last I heard a series of clunks as he answered his line. "Rebecca?"

"Hi," I said. At the sound of Walter's amiable—if confused—voice, the bluff resolve that I'd had when I'd picked up the phone faded.

"Rebecca Egan?" he asked. Oh, no. He was going to give me the stiff and hurt routine. Not that I didn't deserve it. I had been the one who'd told Portia that horrible half-truth about Alice trying to fix me up with someone who was out of the question.

I grit my teeth and plunged forward. "Yes, that Rebecca. I'm sure I'm the last person you expected to hear from, but . . ."

He interrupted me immediately. "Is something wrong? Is Alice all right?"

His voice had become so loud that I had to hold the receiver away from my head, slightly. "She's fine," I assured him. "She's on her way back to the office. Listen . . ." Medicine time. I held my breath and plowed through the speech I'd tried to prepare in my head while I'd punched out the number. "The other night was embarrassing for us both. I wanted to call and make sure, you know, you understood that in a sticky situation, things sometimes get said that are a distortion of the way—I mean, things sometimes get said that aren't really a good reflection of the reality behind them."

"What?"

I can't say I really blamed him for being puzzled. I didn't understand my self. "Let me try again: The other night—"

"Oh! Saturday night." Finally, the light had dawned.

Maybe he was playing me. Maybe he wanted to make this apology as difficult as possible as a balm for his wounded feelings. Fine. He deserved at least that much. "Yes, Saturday night, when you and everyone else kind of walked in on . . ." I stopped, unable to go on. Wouldn't he help me out, even a bit? Meet me a quarter of the way?

Hope flickered in my chest when he coughed and spoke. "Well . . . It is your apartment, too, of course. I know Alice feels strongly about that."

I didn't exactly know where he was going with that, so I tried to steer the train back onto my track. "I wanted to apologize for what you saw, that night, first of all. And . . ."

Walter's voice was kindly when he said, "We must have really surprised you, coming back to your place hours before the party was over."

What a *nice* guy. And I'd missed it all that time! Maybe he was going to let me off easy, after all. "Yes, it was a surprise. And second, I wanted to apologize for what Portia said."

"Portia?"

"Dark hair, olive skin, big eyes?"

"The television . . . ?

"Radio."

". . . anchorwoman?"

"Talk show host. AM radio." This Band-Aid should've been off already. Now that we'd gotten her identity out of the way, I went straight to the point. "Anyway, what she said was hurtful, and I wanted to make certain . . ."

"Let's see." His voice sounded distant, as if he was

trying to dredge up the exact words Portia had used to damn him. "She said something about you dating her brother. And something about your sister trying to set you up with someone." Here we were. He was going to blast me verbally next. "Which I've got to say, is very nice of Alice. She's a great girl. She really is."

He was going to make me repeat Portia's hurtful words, wasn't he, merely to add to my torture? "Yes, but . . ."

"Can I ask you a question?" This conversation was totally not an iota the way I'd expected. I shifted on the sofa, looking longingly at the empty KitKat wrappers and wishing we had a 7-Eleven in the building's ground floor instead of the stupid formal lobby. He coughed again and plunged ahead. "Well, it kind of seems to me that you Egans can't really tell when a guy is interested in you."

Ouch. "It's not a matter of not liking you!"

He didn't listen. "So—I don't mean to be offensive— does your sister only like gay guys? Or would a straight guy qualify?"

"Of course she . . ."

Wait a minute. My mind reeled and backtracked a hundred steps. Was it at all remotely possible that Walter wasn't merely pretending that he hadn't heard Portia's insult but that he hadn't taken it to heart because he didn't think it applied to him? Was he perhaps utterly unaware that my sister had meant him as possible date material for me . . . because he had other ideas?

"Of *course* she likes straight guys," I said smoothly, sitting up straight. Suddenly I wished I had on real clothes that would have made me sound more confident. Then, more coyly, I murmured, "Why do you ask?"

Poor guy. The dam burst loose. "I don't know what else I can do to get Alice's attention. I'm on company time, but damn it, I'm entitled to a personal life, too. I'll tell them to deduct this call from my check if they don't like it!" I was slightly awed by the new, reckless Walter and his work-be-damned attitude. "We've had lunch together every day. I spent a lot of time getting to know her family because it's all she talks about. She's obviously very fond of you." In other words, he'd put up with me and my obvious disdain because he thought it would move him one step closer to my sister's heart. I was off the hook! "I thought that our first real date the other night—the night we saw you, uh, gamboling with your—anyway, I thought it might end in something romantic between Alice and myself, but there were too many people around. I even asked her to work on my medical waste dumping initiative! I'm not so sure I'm willing to go gay just to get her attention."

Mere words could not describe my elation. He who was voted Most Likely to Put a Clinical Insomniac to Sleep liked my sister! Not me! In a way, it almost felt like I was being rewarded for trying to do the right thing. Heaven knows that happened rarely enough. "I know Alice thinks very highly of you," I said in a diplomatic tone. "She's always telling me how wonderful you are."

"Really?"

"Really." Of course, it had always been in the context of her trying to convince me that Walter was the perfect guy for my post-divorce rebound romance, but hey, I wasn't lying.

"So there's hope?"

I'd seen several sides of Walter—most of them dry and academic, with his passion reserved only for topics like the World Health Organization—but I'd never before heard this plaintive, yearning bleat come from his thin lips. I had no idea how my sister felt about the guy, but I'd already been let off the hook once from quashing his romantic aspirations. I wasn't about to give it a second try. I told him, "Isn't there always hope?"

It was a question I had to think about when I hung up the phone a little later.

THIRTEEN

I've always loved the smell of coffee. For one thing, it's one of just a few aromas that can't be mistaken for anything else. In the old days of my marriage, when I used to take solitary Friday evening shopping trips for the both of us, I used to linger over the bleached barrels of the coffee section, each lined with muslin and filled with shiny, deep brown beans. I'd flip up the lids atop two or three, pausing at each to plunge its silver scoop deep into the mound of beans, lift it up, then let them tumble from its tip in a staccato rain so I could inhale the dark, rich bouquet. For the life of me, I couldn't tell the difference between the Arabicas and the Robustas, or the Costa Rican beans from those grown in Vancouver. Even drinking the stuff was something of an afterthought—the real pleasure was in that heady, overwhelming first rush of scent. That's what always perked me up.

While I'd never dared venture into the Eighth Avenue Starbucks across from the bookstore, it seemed much like any other of the branches I'd visited in the past: brown woods, a wall full of beverages I could order from a chalkboardlike menu, a brightly lit case full of biscotti and sweets, acoustic music on the speakers, and a rack of CDs I could buy if I cared to reproduce the entire Starbucks experience in the privacy of my own home. The heady jolt I got from the coffee aroma, however, was what got people inside the doors. Luckily for me, my work day started after the morning business rush, so when I reached the counter, I didn't have to compete for his attention.

" 'Lo," said the clerk, nodding at me and letting loose with one of his effortless smiles. "What can I do ya for?" JAKUB read his nametag. Like *Jacob*, except with a spelling that indicated either illiterate or terminally whimsical hippy-dippy parents. Or maybe he'd changed it himself, in a bold gesture of idiosyncrasy. Either way, it was as cute as Jakub himself. Funny—how many months had I been spying on the guy from across the street without daring to come over and see what he looked like? Three? Four? In all that time I'd known him as the guy with the big smile and the long, wavy hair but I'd never been able to see the little details that were more apparent up close, like the pale green of his eyes, or the sprinkling of fuzz that was supposed to pass for facial hair in the general vicinity of his mouth. After I ordered and paid for a mocha, he grabbed a paper cup from the stack in front of him, made a mark on it with his pen, and regarded me curiously. "I know you from somewhere."

He had startled me. I hadn't come in here with any

agenda, other than finally seeing what the Starbucks guy looked like up close. "Um, I don't think so."

"Yeah," he said, pointing at me with the cup's rim before he began fiddling with the coffee machines. "I know you. You're . . . do you go to MisShapes?"

A little embarrassed at getting any attention at all, I shook my head. "Afraid not."

"Dude, I know you." He leaned in close and raised his eyebrows with meaning. "Do you dance somewhere?"

Oh, my God, this guy was so young. I mean, I wasn't any more than a couple of years older than him, tops, but he was *so young*. "No, I don't dance anywhere," I said, grinning despite myself, then looking around to make sure no one else had heard. If anyone had asked Alice if she stripped for a living, they would have had to quarantine the twelve-square-mile area surrounding the ground zero of the nuclear explosion following. Me, I just rolled with it. Hey, it wasn't as bad as being called a slut on AM radio. "I'm glad you think I could, though."

He didn't reply to that statement immediately. Instead, he lifted his eyes and looked at me, trying to place my face while a curtain of steam rose between us from a nozzle. "So where do I know that face? Come on, help a guy out. Did you come to one of my band's concerts? Is that how I know you?"

I had a sudden vision of Jakub's life right then—the cramped and squalid apartment shared with five transient roommates who grunted and called each other *dude* while boiling their ramen on the hot plate, the nights of partying, the late-night three-chord noodling on the guitar while writing earnest and heartfelt songs that would be over-amped and played at top volume by the equally earnest band in some dank venue. "I work across the street," I told him, deciding to let him off the hook. I pointed at the storefront opposite. "At the bookstore."

"Ohhhh, shit, yeah!" He looked at the bookstore, as if expecting to see me over there. "That's right. That crazy little bookstore. One of the gals here went over there to see if you had that *DaVinci Code* book and you guys didn't. Crazy."

"Yeah, we get that a lot," I said, wishing I was back in the comfortable shelter of that bookstore instead of over here. Some dreams are better left unexamined closely, aren't they?

"I bet you could tell some stories, huh? Working in a bookstore?"

Was he under the impression that I worked in an *adult* bookstore, perchance? I wasn't going to ask. "It's pretty quiet. I bet you get more stories over here."

"Oh, man, you've got no idea." He shook his head while he finished mixing up my drink. "It's wild in here a lot of times. All types, too. Businessmen, hookers, regular people, homeless . . . bookstore girls." I heard him snap a lid on my drink while he grinned at me again. I'd always wondered what it might be like to be the recipient of one of those grins. At least now I could say I knew, even if I wasn't looking forward to repeating the experience. "My ex-girlfriend used to come in here and stalk me all the time. If I talked too long to a pretty customer or something, she'd come over and make a scene. Like, *Oh honey, who are you talking to? Hi, I'm his girlfriend, bitch.* Only she wouldn't say *bitch.* What a total cockblock."

If he was demonstrating value, he certainly wasn't adept at it. "That's a shame."

"Here ya go."

The drink he handed me was so massive and heavy that I had to reach out with both hands to steady it as he passed it across the counter. "Hey, I didn't order an extra-large," I told him, envisioning a morning traipsing back and forth between my table and the restroom.

Jakub winked. "Yeah, I know. Enjoy your medium. Hey, maybe I'll come over and visit your place sometime."

It was easy enough for me to give him a wink back. A harmless gesture. "Yeah, do that!" I told him, as I raised the cup in thanks.

But I wouldn't be holding my breath.

When I walked in through the front door of the bookstore, Ethan was on the phone, the pair of glasses he sometimes wore instead of contacts perched on his nose. He did a double-take at the sight of me, a smile lighting up his face. "Yes sir," he said, into the receiver, while he pushed a slip of paper onto the top of his desk in my direction. I could tell from the uneven edges that it was one of his clipped magazine cartoons. "We do sell antiquarian books. Why yes, we are on Eighth Avenue. Yes, we—what?" He raised his eyebrows at me quickly, while I set my bag and mocha onto the table that was my usual workspace. "Ah, I'm wearing a brown cardigan, a white shirt with kind of blue checks on it, and some tan slacks. Why do you . . . ?" After a moment, he held the receiver away from his face, stared at it with disgust, and then gently replaced it in the cradle with only one comment: "Ew."

"Hi," I said.

Or tried saying, anyway, because as Ethan rose to greet me, surprise and expectation in equal measures on his face, Michaela wandered in from the back, cushioning an old oversized atlas in her arms. "You're back!" she said, obviously glad to see me. She looked at my stuff on the table. "Did you bring me coffee?"

"Are you bad-mouthing my coffee again?" From the back room, Cesar yelled threateningly.

"Shut up!" Michaela yelled back, ignoring the fact that Mr. Rothenberg, a bowed and gray older gentleman who had been one of our more regular customers for the better part of three years, had stepped out from between the two high bookshelves leading to the naturalism section. He bore a volume he'd admired before, which I recognized as a Victorian book of marsh bird engravings, handsomely bound in roughly half a cow's worth of leather. The book weighed as much as he did, poor guy. Before I could move, Michaela automatically put down what she was carrying, tripped over to Mr. Rothenberg, and said, "Let me take that for you!"

"Thank you, my dear," said the old man, grateful not to lug the thing any farther than he had to.

Cesar was still miffed. "Because you can make all the coffee you want, you know!"

Michaela dropped the part of the sweet schoolgirl long enough to yell back, "I said, *shut up!*" Then she smiled sweetly and began looking up the book's details on the PC. "I'll have this ready in no time," she told Mr. Rothenberg, who was still blinking at the girl's split personality. Cesar grumbled something inaudible.

The door to Sarah's office opened. "What the f—" At

the rare sight of a customer, she shut her mouth just in time. Her eyes flickered over to me. "Oh, there you are. Welcome back. I've got to talk to you all in a few minutes. Important stuff." She cleared her throat. "Hello, Mr. Rothenberg!" When he raised a wavering hand in her directly, she smiled, looked suspicious at the rest of us, and went back to her sanctum. Had it been my imagination, or had she given me raised eyebrows before vanishing? I'd known that sooner or later she and I were going to have to have it out over the A.J. affair. If she'd been listening to Portia again, it was going to have to be sooner.

Ahh. Rancor, courtesy, and all the pleasures of a dysfunctional, tight-knit family. It was good to be back at work.

I can't say I'd minded Michaela's interruption, because as much as I knew it was necessary to clear the air with Ethan, I was in no way looking forward to it. What was I supposed to say—that I'd loved the night we'd spent barking like dogs on my sister's couch? It was true. That my second reaction, for some reason, was to run away from him and never do it again? That was also true, but hurtful. At least when I'd been A.J.'s wingman, I knew what my function was supposed to be, and what part I was supposed to be playing at any given time. With Ethan, I was floundering. I hated being scriptless.

Now that no one stood between us, I turned to Ethan and waved. I really was glad to see him; so many times had I mentally re-created his features in the last three days that actually seeing them was something of a relief. He hadn't changed. No, that wasn't true. He'd trimmed off that scruffy growth on his face and was clean-shaven once again, but everything else that made him uniquely himself remained—the eyes, the gentle slope of his nose, the way he nibbled his lip as he looked me up and down. "Hi," he said.

Seeing him in the flesh was more difficult than I'd anticipated. In the protective nest I'd made of terrycloth and candy wrappers, it was simple to swear off future thoughts of carnality. With him around, it was hard to stop looking. And remembering. "What news do you think she has?" I asked at last, to break the ice. My fingers scrabbled for the cartoon he'd left me. Without looking, I stuffed it into the pocket of my sweater.

He must have thought I was keeping it a little impersonal in front of Michaela and our customer, because he gave them both a glance, cleared his throat, and responded in a less intimate voice, "Gosh, who knows. Didn't we do some kind of inventory last year at this time?"

I groaned. Sarah was a Type A personality at the best of times. During a messy inventory, she turned into a micromanager of such proportions that she made Martha Stewart look slovenly. "It can't have been a year already!" He probably was right.

"So, are you feeling better?" he asked, keeping his voice low. I curved my lips into a small smile, nodding, receiving in return a flash of his teeth. "Oh, thank God. I spent all yesterday worried that you were having second thoughts. I mean, you said you were okay with—" He looked over at the counter again, where Michaela was chattering to Mr. Rothenberg as she slid his new purchase into a protective plastic case, then hushed some more. "With what we did. And I know how weird it got at the end, there. With your sister and all. And her colleagues. And everything."

He was talking to fill up the awkward space between us, I felt. And the reason for that awkwardness was all me; I should have been reassuring him, or agreeing. I should have been saying something. Anything. Or no—I should have been telling him the truth. "Can we . . . ?" I jerked my head in the direction of the store's other end, where at least we wouldn't be under anyone's immediate scrutiny.

I left my mocha to cool on the table but picked up an armful of the antique sheet music I'd been cataloguing the Friday before, as if heading off to put it in our bins. Why I needed to cradle something to my chest I don't know, unless it was to keep myself from letting something happen with him that I worried shouldn't. He followed until we were around the corner, where the weighty and musty-smelling volumes of our encyclopedia section faced off against the wooden boxes where we kept ephemera. "You don't know how much I want to touch you," he murmured, standing next to me in the aisle

He was making what I had to say even more difficult. "Ethan," I started, getting his attention. Well, I already had his attention. I just needed it on my face, rather than wandering familiarly up and down my body. "I can't lie to you. It was weird. And I wasn't sick, yesterday. I was . . ." I bit the bullet and said it: "Scared."

See, that's what happens when someone too quickly rips off the mother of all Band-Aids—that stunned, stricken expression that spread across his face. Only the one who had the prickling tears afterward was me. "Well, sure," he said, trying to rally. "I mean, come on, Becca. I was a little freaked out, too. All my life I've had those nightmares, you know the ones, where you're in a train station and you're the only one with no clothes on."

"I know, but . . ."

"Up until then you were enjoying yourself. I know you were. I might not be some kind of magical Method Man, but trust me, a guy can tell these things."

He wasn't angry, exactly. Insistent was more like it. "I know." My voice, my posture, everything about me was like a limp rag doll, waiting to be picked up and shaken. "I really enjoyed it. I enjoyed you."

"So what's the problem?" Around the corner I heard the tinkling of little bells that hung above the old oak front door. Mr. Rothenberg leaving, most likely. "Is it really that A.J. guy? Are you seeing him, like his sister said?"

"No! Ew. I told you that was the lie we told her to keep her from blabbing to everyone." At least I'd been honest there. "The A.J. thing is done with."

"Is it the Starbucks guy?"

"Oh, good lord, no." He had to guess my sincerity from the scornful tone in my voice. "You don't really think that."

He shrugged. "For the first time since I've known you, you came to work with a Starbucks cup in your hand."

"I did go to Starbucks. To lay that particular curiosity to rest." Lay it in a coffin and drive a stake through its heart, more like. "That was a symptom of my need to move on, Ethan. I'm over that particular obsession."

"And now you're over me? We didn't even get a chance to get obsessed."

"No! Listen." Frustrated, I chucked the sheet music into the bin, not even bothering to alphabetize by composer. "I didn't plan for you, Ethan. I didn't expect you. You weren't in the script."

"So?"

"So we've worked together for only a year and it wasn't until a few weeks ago that I knew much of anything about you at all. So we got a little bit drunk and stuff happened. It was good stuff! I liked the stuff!" I said, before he could point out again how obvious my enjoyment had been. Had I heard a noise? I waited a moment before speaking again, this time at a lower volume. "I loved being with you. I really did."

"I did, too!"

"I know! It's just . . ." I sighed, overcome by the enormity of it all. "You don't want me, Ethan. You don't know what I'm like."

"I don't know what you're like." He accompanied the statement with a sharp laugh, then put his hands on his hips and paced down the aisle before turning. Back in the store, I heard the bells tinkle once again. "I've worked with you 'only' a year. Only the worst year of your life. I only saw you come in some mornings looking like the living dead, pale as a ghost and eyes red from crying before you got here. I saw that drag on for months, while you were a living zombie." Emotion choked him for a few seconds, but he coughed and continued. "Maybe there were some things I 'only' could do back then. Like, the only way I could help was to tell a joke once in a while, to see if you might smile. Or I could only hope to cheer up your day a little with a cutting from the paper or a book you might like."

"Stop," I told him. Somewhere in my throat was a golf ball I'd swallowed. At least, that's how it felt. Those little kindnesses had convinced me to trust him across the months. An idea, unwelcomed and unfair, formed in my mind right then, and before I knew it in my confusion, it spilled from my mouth. "When you say that, it makes me think you had your own version of the Yes Ladder, being good to me so that I'd be good to you back. I know!" I protested, when he opened his shocked mouth to respond. "I know you're not like that. But that's how I think now! Anyone who's pleasant, anyone who's nice, all I wonder is whether or not there's an ulterior motive behind it. I'm tainted."

"You're not tainted." He put a hand on my shoulder.

"My thinking is!" He might have been trying to soothe me, but the feel of his warm hand through my blouse only confused me more. Even though it had been the highlight of my last year—or hell, my entire sexual life—I couldn't help but wish that none of the previous Saturday had happened. How can you express that to someone without devastating him? "You don't want someone like that."

"I'm sorry." At the sound of Michaela's voice, I slipped back, bumping into the tottery bookcases and adding a few inches of space between Ethan and myself. His hand dropped to his side as we both turned to see the girl leaning in the doorway at the room's other side. How long had she been there? How much had she heard? "I didn't mean to interrupt."

"It's okay." I didn't sound okay. Ethan didn't look okay, with the frustrated expression on his face and his hands still planted on his hips. He swung around to conceal his face. "We were just checking on something."

From the slow, knowing way Michaela looked from me to the back of Ethan's head, then back to me again, I knew she wasn't buying it. "Sure," she said, obviously drawing her own conclusions about the pair of us colluding among the encyclopedias. To me, she added, "Um, there's someone here to see you."

"Who?" The only people who specifically asked to see me were the vendors I worked with to put together our print catalogue, and they usually only showed up at delivery time.

"He's out front." Michaela sailed away, probably to tell Cesar exactly what she'd seen between Ethan and me, peppered with her own hypotheses of what it all could mean. Of course, if she'd listened to Portia's radio show, she'd know all about it. I could only pray she hadn't.

I turned to Ethan, who refused to face me. "Let's talk about this later. Maybe after . . ."

"Yeah," he said. Strange, to hear his voice without being able to see his expression. We'd never had a phone or e-mail relationship; every time we'd interacted, I'd always been able to see his smile and the way his blue eyes danced. "Okay. I got it."

"Don't be mad," I begged, even though I knew he had every right.

"Just . . ." He sighed and shook his head. "Just go do what you have to do." Without a word more, he suddenly swiveled, edged past me while still facing away, and walked back into the main room. Until I couldn't see him any longer he kept his hands held up, palms out, in the same position someone might if they were being kept hostage at gunpoint. Or giving up on something in disgust.

Which prospect distressed me more, I couldn't say.

My visitor had his back to me, but I could identify him from the posture alone—the cross-armed, aggressive air he projected while he regarded the old bookstore as if he was contemplating where first to splash the gasoline before lighting the match. He wheeled around at the sound of my footsteps. "This place hasn't changed a bit."

As far as I could remember, my ex-husband had only visited the bookstore once, shortly after I began working here. Sarah's father had welcomed him, given him a cup of coffee, talked to Sean about his job with more interest than my own father had shown, and had then given me an unexpected afternoon off so I could spend it with my fiancé. In return, Sean had called him *that crazy old geezer you work for* the four years that followed. "Sean." At the one syllable, Ethan's eyes flickered up to take in my former spouse's details: the quietly expensive sports coat and shirt, the braided belt and tasseled loafers that connoted a casualness that came only at great expense and with meticulous planning.

I was not at all happy to see him. Almost instinctively I began to pull out a chair and sit down to begin por-ing through another estate sale listing the bookstore was considering bidding on, but at the last moment I remembered something I'd learned from A.J.: being seated is akin to being trapped in these situations. It was better to remain on my feet. Sean kicked the battered radiator near the door. "I mean, Christ. You'd think after the old man died, that friend of yours might have made some changes to the place. Brightened it up a little or something. You've probably got lead paint. Asbestos."

"So glad you care." I sounded snappish, but at least I was smiling. "It comes a few years too late, but hey, at least it got here."

Michaela, by the counter, and Ethan, at his desk, both seemed awfully absorbed in their tasks. Michaela, in particular, seemed particularly captivated by a 150-year-old treatise on phrenology, not seeming to mind that it had been written entirely in German. Sean, sensing my hostility, opened with a big fake smile and a heartfelt, "Sweetheart!" A single daggerlike glance squelched that approach, startling him into a honeyed, "Becca—it's about time we both got over our ill-will and started acting like adults, don't you think?"

I merely stared at him, analyzing everything he was saying through the Method Man translator—it wasn't merely for seductions, I'd learned. "By which you mean, you want me to do something for you. I know this technique, Sean," I said, fiddling with the papers on the table. "A guy lays down a mild insult to prove that he's not out for anything, then starts in with the wheedling. I'm immune. How about you come out and just say what you want?"

Why had I never noticed how much taller I was than Sean? "Boy," he said, taken aback. "Palling around with Shannen Doherty has really changed you, hasn't it?"

"Oh, my God, you hang out with Shannen Doherty?" blurted Michaela, unable to contain herself any longer. She pressed the tips of her fingers to her mouth. "Oops. Sorry."

"Maybe we could go . . . ?"

"Michaela, could you give the two of us a moment?" I asked. The student looked up guiltily from her book, her eyes wide. Then she sidled into the back room with Cesar, where the two of them could probably hear everything clearly, even above the hum of the server. That was fine; I didn't care. Sean twisted slightly, glancing back in the direction of Ethan's desk, while he waited for me to clear the room completely. I didn't intend to give him the satisfaction. For one thing, no matter how we stood at that moment, having Ethan there made me feel better. Stronger, even. Maybe some of that was the energy I felt at having to prove something to him. I didn't know. "Just say what you have to say," I told my ex.

"All right. Fine. Listen. No games. I know that lately, in your fancy reinvention of yourself, you've been . . . hitting some of the more exclusive clubs in town."

Why deny it? "A few."

"Okay. So. I'm thinking, for old time's sake, you could help me out. I've got someone I need to impress. I've kind of told him I can get him into that place you go—the After Ten." Oh, by all that was holy. This was too much. I laughed a little and waved him away. "Oh, come on, Beck. You don't know what's at stake here."

"What's at stake?" I asked, genuinely curious. It had to be something big for Sean to swallow his macho pride in this fashion.

For a second he was genuinely helpless, throwing up his hands in the air and aspirating garbled syllables. "I want to get in good with this guy!" he said at last. "He's one of the partners! Even he can't get in this place, and he's got clients on the Fortune Five Hundred!"

"The same partner who fathered the blond Munchkin you left me for?"

He didn't like that question, I could tell. Good. Maybe I would never be grown up enough not to take pleasure in stinging him now and again, but at least I'd reached a point where I didn't feel like hurling the nearest heavy object at his head. That was progress in my book. He winced. "Her name is Mary, and no, this is another partner."

"Ah, another partner." A partner less likely to question Sean's ulterior motives, or at least to let them align with his own.

"Yes, another partner," he said sarcastically. Then his shoulders collapsed. "Oh, come on, Beck. How many favors have I asked you for? Since the divorce," he amended with haste.

"You know what?" The sound of his voice was giving me a headache, a pinpoint of pain directly between my eyebrows that threatened to throb and burst if he pushed it any further. "Fine. I'll see what I can do."

"Is that a yes, or are you putting me off?"

"I'm not—" I started to snap. Then I backed off. "I'll do what I can. That's not a put-off. It might have to be on an off-night, like tonight or tomorrow, but I'll get you in." Even though his posture didn't change behind his desk, Ethan had some definite opinions about what was going on, I could tell. Did he disapprove? Dislike me? Or did he not care at all, and I was merely projecting my insecurities on him?

"You," said Sean, back to his confident, slightly abrasive speaking style, "are a doll. You. Are. A. Doll! Yes." He punched a fist into the palm of his hand, as if he'd just scored a point at racquetball. Why had I never noticed before how remarkably unsubtle Sean was? He'd always worn his emotions close to his skin—which I supposed would at least have a certain degree of honesty of its own, if he hadn't been, you know, secretly cheating on me with one of the partner's daughters. "This is going to be fantastic."

Fantastic for him, anyway. For me, it was going to mean calling in a final favor with A.J. "Are we done here?" I reached for my mocha, which was still vaguely warm to the touch.

"Yeah. Absolutely. Hey. You're amazing." Instinctively, I reared back when he lunged in my direction, but my reflexes weren't quick enough to keep him from grabbing me by the arms and pulling me to him. Sarah's door opened at the top of the little landing right as he nailed me with a kiss on the cheek. "I love this new you!"

"Sean?" Sarah, seeing me in mid-clinch with my ex-husband, didn't bat an eye. "Nice of you to stop by! Don't tell me you've learned to read."

At least he didn't linger in my vicinity, once he'd shown his gratitude. Just as quickly as he'd grabbed me, he let me go. "Sarah!" he said, dangerously pleasant. "Yeah, I just finished my literacy class, thanks for noticing. Thought I'd check out some books as old as you. Whaddaya say?"

"Oh, hah, hah, hah."

Before Sarah could launch into a tirade, I stepped in. "Sean, I'm not usually inclined to do favors for people who insult my friends."

He got the message, holding up his hands to call a truce. "Whatever. I'll get out of your hair, then. But you'll be in touch today, right?" He crooked his thumb and little finger in the universal sign for *call me,* shaking it a little. "The sooner the better would be great." I nodded, arms crossed so that he wouldn't be tempted to kiss me again. "Excellent. Sarah, lovely as ever. Beck, we'll talk. Other people, later."

He didn't exactly leave a Sean-shaped hole in the wall as he shot out of the premises at Road Runner speed, but there definitely was a wake of dust in his departure. I looked expectantly in Ethan's direction for a reaction. What exactly did I hope for? I wasn't sure, exactly, but his utter concentration on his work disturbed me more than anything I might have expected. I'd all but asked for him to forget about me. Why was I disappointed that it appeared to have happened so quickly? When finally I was convinced he wasn't going to throw in his two cents, I heard Sarah say, in her sweetest and most syrupy voice, "Rebecca, may I see you in my office, please?"

"Uh-oh," murmured Michaela in a singsong beneath her breath as I passed by. I silently echoed the sentiment. Sarah, when at her outwardly most kind, was invariably in a foul, vindictive mood. She'd probably drawn her own conclusions about the clinch and wanted to give me an earful about it. Not that the truth behind it was much better—she'd tell me that Sean had manipulated me into doing his bidding yet again, and that I needed to stand up to him and cut him free from my life, and all the other things I already knew so well.

In fact, I was in no mood to put up with one of Sarah's frontal attacks. I'd had a shitty morning. A shitty week, in fact, and it was only Tuesday. I don't know what I'd done to deserve this kind of cosmic karma in that past life Portia had accused me of having, but it must have been something pretty rotten. Anything short of actually ordering the Hiroshima bombing, however, had been amply paid back by the pain and embarrassment I'd suffered lately. I didn't have to endure anything more. As I strode up the stairs that led to the landing and Sarah's office, I thrust back my shoulders and walked like I wasn't in the least apprehensive.

"Close the door." Sarah flicked her finger, still sounding like a particularly joyful Sunday school lady. "Take a chair!"

"Thanks," I told her, stiffly sitting down.

She intertwined her fingers and lay them on her abdomen, leaning back and smiling at me. "Feeling better?"

"Much, thanks," I said, saying as little as possible.

"Oh, good. Good weekend?"

I shrugged. "It was fine."

"I bet it was. You big, enormous, lying slut." The words were like a wet slap across my face; I hadn't been prepared for that. My mind whirling in outrage, I scrambled to find some kind of dignified, sharp response. Sarah, however, was almost cackling with laughter. "Oh my God, get over yourself once in a while and learn to laugh a little, you big sissy!"

Odd advice, coming from the woman who, love her dearly as I did, could have done public service announcements for Chronic Cudgel in the Posterior Syndrome. "Excuse me?"

"Sweetheart, I know the whole story. All seven of us who listen to Portia's radio show heard all about it."

So that was it. "Listen. . . ." I thumped my clenched fists on her desk, clarifying carefully. "What she said about me and A.J. . . . it's not exactly the way it sounds. In fact . . ."

"Becca!" she interrupted me by leaning over and putting her hands on mine. "Don't. Don't explain. I don't care."

Sarah was such a liar. "A.J. and I had an agreement, you see. . . ."

"I don't care!" she repeated. "Seriously, I don't. It's your life. Play by your own rules. If you want to be with A.J., fine! I'll try to love him for your sake. If you want to be with your mystery man on the sofa, great! Good for you for getting some." I stared at her, trying to figure out whether she was being facetious or not. Strangely, it didn't sound like she was. "If your mystery man is Sean . . . is it Sean? No, don't tell me. I don't want to know. If it's Sean, God bless and good luck and I hope you'll ask me to be your maid of honor because that I care about."

"It's not Sean!"

"Well, good, but even if it had been, I don't care!"

Her Halloween pumpkin grin was so broad that I

couldn't help but sit back, stunned, and grin a little myself. "Are you on drugs?"

"No." She planted her elbows on the desk, obviously excited about something. "This is a great story. I had a big breakthrough in therapy after I left you guys, Friday. I mean, major. You know that essay I had to do?" I nodded, staring. A Sarah who allegedly didn't care about me hanging out with A.J. was a changed Sarah indeed. Or maybe an alien Sarah who was going to turn me into a pod person. "On the cab ride down there I wrote another essay. It was fantastic. It was all about how I wanted to buy all these shades of paint from Sherwin Williams and try them, one at a time, on my walls. And how I knew that no matter how thick I painted any color, the ones underneath would bleed through and influence it somehow. Then it ended with me talking about how, in the end, painting would be all about layering on a new skin and learning to live with the blend between the new circumstances and what lay underneath. I mean, it was kind of sloppy, but the sentiment was there, right?" I nodded. "So I read it to him, and he nodded, and thought about it, then he told me I'd done a great job and asked if he could have a copy to show to his other patients."

"Excellent!" I said, happy that she'd finally, finally accomplished something on that therapist's couch. I didn't even want to contemplate how much money that revelation had cost, over the years. "So that was your big breakthrough?"

"No! Not at all!" I blinked, taken aback. "That's when

I ripped it up and told him it was all bullshit. Because it was. Total bullshit!"

Her euphoria was infectious, but I felt like an outsider looking in. "I don't get it."

"I should have been happy at *finally* psyching him out, but I wasn't. It felt hollow. I admit it. You were right! I should have gone with my first instincts—that stupid draft about the books."

"What?"

"The one I tossed across the restaurant. I had it in my pocket, so I smoothed it out and read it to him." I obviously still wasn't getting it. She sighed. "The one that talked about all the books."

That wasn't the part I didn't get. "I know which one you're talking about. You almost beaned those poor retirees with it. What do you mean, I was right?" The mere notion that I could have been right about anything last weekend was beyond me.

She laughed. "Sweetie. My books. These books. My father's books." Sarah threw up her arms and indicated the glorious mess of the office and the shop surrounding it. "That's all I've ever wanted, was to get rid of them. I worked for my father because it was easy, not because it was my heart's desire to surround myself with old Bibles and atlases and biographies of clergymen that no one has thought of in two centuries. I never wanted this. I like to read, but I never wanted *this*," she emphasized, indicating the shop once more. "This was my dad's dream. And the thing of it is—and my therapist agreed with me—that I've been letting it chew away at me. I've been an angry person, Becca.

Don't deny it. I was getting angry at everybody except myself."

"Wow," I said, breathing the word more than actually saying it. "That was some session."

"I know!" she exclaimed, relishing my reaction. "The old me might have gotten mad at you for doing whatever it was you're doing with A.J., because he's every Creationist's living proof that apes did not fully evolve into mankind, but the new me doesn't care that he's a knuckle-scraping mouth-breather!" I couldn't help but laugh a little. "You did say you weren't involved with him, right?" she added, more seriously.

"I'm not. Honest."

"Good enough for me." Sarah paused then, and brushed her bangs from her eyes.

"I'm really glad for you." At least someone was having a good day; if there was balance in the world, all I could do was hope that very soon there'd be some ups to give equilibrium to the extreme lows I'd endured recently. "I really am. Do you need me to come over and help you clean out your apartment?"

"Oh." My question, innocent as it was, seemed to put Sarah into a somber mood. "Didn't I make that clear? I'm not cleaning out at home. I'm . . ." She sighed, then spoke gently. "I wanted to talk to you first, before I told the others this morning. I'm giving this place up, Becca. I'm going to sell out. If I can find a buyer in the next month and a half, great. It's theirs, lock, stock, and barrel. If not, I'm going to sell off the books to our competitors, see about getting out of the lease, and find something new to do."

"Wow," I said, happy for her for a split-second.

Then my vision blurred and my eyes watered. When I realized what was going on, it left me feeling as if she'd just tackled me in an alley with a two-by-four. "Oh, shit."

She studied me for a minute, disappointment on her face. "Don't be like that. This is a big breakthrough for me. Try to be happy."

She thought I was angry with her. "Sarah!" It seemed that the pattern of my life was always the same: Before I could learn anything, I first had to hurt someone. I'd done it with Walter, with Alice, with Ethan, and now with my best friend. I rallied to the occasion, before it got any worse. "I am very, very glad for you. It's simply that most people don't hear about their friend's break-through in the same breath in which they learn they're being fired."

"Fired. Yeah. There is that." She sucked in her lips, now that the ugly word was out in the open. "You know I hate that part, right?"

None of this could be easy for her, I realized. "It's okay," I said, giving her my heartfelt blessing. I stood up and walked around the desk so I could bend way down and give her a hug. She received it gratefully, squeezing me hard. "I'm so glad you're happy. I need a little time to . . . you know. Process."

"You're okay? Really?"

"Yeah," I told her. "Really."

"Don't tell the others. Let me do it," she said, right before I left.

As if I could. When I stepped out, Ethan had moved to the counter, where he was poking at the computer keyboard. He looked at me briefly as I angled myself down the steps, clutching onto the iron rail to steady myself. It touched me that he watched with concern for a few seconds. Then he seemed to remember that he was supposed to be giving me the silent treatment and looked away. Inside my sweater pockets, I curled my hands into fists. My fingers crushed a slip of paper; too late, I remembered that it was the clipped cartoon he'd given me earlier.

When I got back to my table I pulled out the chair and sat down before I uncapped my mocha. The whipped cream that Jakub had sprayed liberally on top had all but melted away. I gave it an experimental sip. The liquid was cold and bitter.

"So," said Michaela, sliding down into the chair opposite mine. Her voice was confidential. "Is she in a mood? Did she go off on you? Was it the same old, same old?"

Sarah's office door opened again. She stepped out, a bright smile on her face, rubbing her hands together as she prepared to rally the troops. I didn't envy her this moment, not at all.

"No," I said, putting the cap back on my cup and pushing it away. "Definitely not the same old, same old."

FOURTEEN

I'd heard the *thumpa-thumpa-thumpa* from the After Ten Lounge a full block away from the insanely long line running down the alley to its entrance. Inside, the Euro-trance beat was drumming its way into my every limb; my feet and fingers tapped away in time with the music's insistent pulse. "Another of these, please," I said to the bartender as he passed my spot at the glowing counter. I shook the remnants of my cranberry-and-tonic so that the ice cubes tinkled.

"Let me get that." A Method Man eased in next to me, brandishing a fifty in the bartender's direction. I recognized him by the blinding smile, the relaxed stance, and the tight shirt that displayed carefully worked pecs, guns, abs, and quads—complex muscles reduced by a grunting tribe to single syllables. His chosen conversation-starter was a shiny purple star the size of a pencil eraser, affixed to his chiseled cheekbone.

My arm was longer and quicker and my tender just as legal. "I'm paying for my own drinks tonight. Thanks, though."

He registered surprise by smiling more widely. The guy's dentist must love him when those yearly whitening treatments come around. "A pretty girl like you?"

I lolled my head to the side and gazed at him frankly, plainly conveying the message, *Seriously, I know you.* "Thanks, but no," I repeated. When he didn't move, I waggled my fingers. "On your merry way." My would-be schmoozer slunk off, tail between his legs, into the vast and seething crowd. I honestly had thought that getting this chore over with that night would have been the simplest and most painless of all the days of the week. After all, it wasn't Hump Day, and it wasn't anywhere close to a weekend. But here they were, the bronzed and beautiful of New York, clutching cocktails and laughing maniacally at each other's jokes as they exchanged mating calls. From my jaded point of view, it was a little like Viagra day at the zoo. "I had no idea this place was so busy on a Tuesday! It's crazy!" I called out to the bartender when he returned with my refreshed drink.

"Tuesday is the new Thursday," he said, leaning over so he could be heard. I shook my head, not knowing exactly what that meant. He explained further. "Thursday is the new Friday!"

Ah. It made no sense, but I wasn't that invested in the conundrum. What I was interested in were the locations of my two male escorts. They'd met outside the club less than an hour before with the same wary pride of two strange male gorillas introduced into the same cage for the first time. There'd been a great deal of hearty helloing, vigorous hand-pumping, biceps-slapping, head-nodding, and all the other rituals used to establish dominance. Since we'd escorted Sean and the partner from his firm, though, my two little alpha males had kept a safe and discernable distance from each other. Over the heads of the crowd I finally located my ex near the bank of sofas close to the ceiling-to-floor banners hanging from the old warehouse's air ducts. A.J., on the other hand, stood near a second bar at the opposite end of the vast warehouse space, a stretch of translucent stone underlit so that it glowed like living ice. Trust him to pick out the spot with the better lighting.

There wasn't any competition between whom I'd rather visit first. There wasn't any ill will between A.J. and me, for one thing. Maybe I sensed that my brief reign as his best wingman was coming to an end, but there weren't any hard feelings between us. He let loose with a flash of his teeth when I approached, drink clutched to my chest to avoid spillage. "What's up with you tonight?" I asked almost immediately, jostled on every side by men and women pushing by. I had to move in close to make myself audible against the crowd.

"Whaddaya mean?" He was down to the bottom of his glass—something clear and minty from the smell of it. Perhaps a mojito. "You're the one who's having the last fling, drinking and going out late on a work night. Not me."

"What's going to happen if I show up late tomorrow? Is Sarah going to fire me?" You know, we'd never gotten

to the bottom of that particular issue of his employ-
ment. "What *do* you do for money?" He shook his
head, once again refusing to tell me or even admit
he'd heard the question. "Fine. Whatever. I'll find out
one of these days. But there's something about you tonight." While he shook his head and dissembled, I
tried to pick out what it was. Despite the heavy-lidded,
sleepy eyes and the lazy, casual way he spoke, usually
A.J. was a bundle of energy, a dynamo of sexual elec-
tricity that crackled to the touch. I wasn't picking up
sparks from him, tonight. "Are you not feeling well?"

"No, I'm great." He nodded his head to the *thumpa-
thumpa* and stared at the ceiling.

"You big liar!" My day had been so lousy that the
noise and liveliness around me acted like a tonic. I
needed to forget all the crap that had happened earlier. "You're not scoping out a single girl here. It's true,"
I accused, when he gave me a scoffing look. "Don't tell
me they recalled your testosterone."

"No, it's still intact." He rolled his eyes and shook his
head, then slugged back the rest of his drink. "It's . . .
never mind."

"Come on."

"Nah, it's not important." He turned his head away.

"Come *on*."

"Fine. It's stupid, though. It's just . . . I'm gonna miss
having you as my wingman. There. Happy?" His glass
hit the stone with a sharp enough crash that several
people, myself included, took a quick look to make
sure it hadn't broken. "I told you it was stupid."

"Aw, that's not stupid!" It struck me then that I'd never
disliked A.J., the man. His methods I found irksome,

but even they'd provided me with an insight I might never have otherwise had. Impulsively, I reached out and gave his arm a squeeze, briefly resting my head against his shoulder. "That might have been the first moment of genuine sweetness I've seen from you. Not that you haven't been nice to me from the start."

"Well, I'm glad you realize that." The formality in his voice mocked me a little. "I've enjoyed having you around, too. You've been a good wingman. It's kind of like having a little sister to hang out with. A little sister with brains," he amended, then added, "Oh, and by the way, she's around tonight. Hey, at least I warned you."

I'd slumped at the news, but you know, once a girl has already been served a heaping serving of crap on a dirty plate, the little hardened poo garnish atop the whole stinkin' slab really doesn't make that big a difference. "Put on your paramedic hat and rescue me if she backs me into a corner, would you?" I begged.

"I'll be your white knight, all right. Hey, that rhymed!"

Loud and frenetic as these nights out had been sometimes, I was going to miss going out with A.J. I kind of wished there was something nice I could do to show him how much I'd appreciated the liberation. What did guys like? Flowers were probably not masculine enough. A bottle of wine in a velvet bag, much the same. Hard booze? Booze in a nice wrapped box? Booze in a brown paper bag? "Let me go find my ex," I told him, waving my fingers. I knew I had to make a duty appearance at least once in the evening, if for nothing else than to make sure he knew I'd fulfilled my promise and wasn't likely to kowtow to his requests again. I'd sacrificed a marriage for that damned job of his—I wasn't going to lay evening after empty evening on the altar as well. "I'll be back."

"Hey," he said, grabbing me before I left. "I just wanted to say that it's been fun for me, too. All of this. You and me." He nodded, as if he'd been about to say something else. Instead, he closed his mouth and jutted his jaw as far as it could go. "Just so you know."

My heart melted a little. Weird as our relationship had been, at least with A. J. things had mostly been *simple*. I was grateful for that. I grabbed his hand, gave it a squeeze, and left him with a smile.

Sean's business cohort had the unlikely name of Mr. Saltina. At least, that's what I'd caught when I'd met him outside briefly, though he'd followed it up with a quick "Just call me Phil." At least, I thought it was Phil. I was pretty sure that his pretty young wife's name was Jessica. As in Simpson. Or Rabbit. She was about as curvaceous and air-headed as either. And hoo, boy, talk about curves—she put the *ay-yi-yi!* in *trophy wife*. It didn't take much in the way of brains when she stood next to her older, slightly paunchy, gray-haired husband to figure out who really had wanted to hit the After Ten so badly. "Everyone enjoying themselves?" I asked brightly when I approached their little circle.

Just-call-me-Phil had been standing there with his hands plunged deep into the pants pockets of a suit so conservative I wanted to check the cleaning label to see if it had been stitched together from skinned Rush Limbaugh fanatics. Don't think that getting him past the After Ten's hard-assed bouncer had been an easy task either. Only A.J.'s unctuous sweet-talking and a

gander at Jessica's two best attributes had gotten
Sean's little trio out of the line and in through the door.
Sean, doing his best to make everyone happy—at least
the everybodies who had a direct say in any future
promotions at the law firm—instantly grabbed me
around the shoulders and gave me a sideways buddy-
to-buddy shake. "Fabulous," he said, brandishing a
scotch. The same scotch, I couldn't help but notice,
that Mr. Saltina held in his own hands.

"Absolutely!" yelled Phil at the top of his voice. "It's
smoking, as they say. Isn't it, darling?" Jessica graced
Sean and me with a wan little smile, bestowed a marginally larger one on her husband and sugar daddy,
and then looked around for someone better to talk to.
Her husband reached out and grabbed her hand. "Do
you kids come here often?"

Was it my imagination, or had Sean hugged me a little closer at the sight of the older lawyer making a public display of affection with his designer wife in the
designer clothes? I was going to have fingerprints on
my shoulder, come the morning. "Actually," I volunteered, "Sean's never—"

"Now and then." Sean looked at me. "Now and then,
right? I've always got so much on my plate that it's tough
for me to party like when we were kids. Right, Beck?"

"I guess." I shrugged. "It's not like I've seen you in
what, five months?"

The explosive laughter from the boys that accompanied this statement baffled the hell out of me. I hadn't
intended to make a joke. "Apparently you've got to really be somebody to get in here," said Mr. Saltina. By
then, Jessica had managed to slither her hand from

NAOMI NEALE

Just-call-me-Phil's clutch; he looked at her with an apology in his eyes. I wondered exactly how much she'd nagged him to find a way to get into the lounge, just so she could stand around and sip her blue martini and pretend she'd been there a hundred times before. "You don't know the strings I've tried to pull. You'd think I was a puppeteer. Har! Har! Har!"

Mr. Saltina's laugh was loud and explosive and sounded so much like an barking seal that instinctively I backed away. Sean kept me from escaping altogether, though, holding me firmly by his side. "Well, Rebecca's a go-getter. The kind of gal who makes things happen."

Oh, the things I could've said then. Since I was willing to tolerate a certain amount of bullshitting from my ex-husband merely because his affairs no longer concerned me, I just gave the old guy a Jessica-style smile. I was sure he was used to those. "She's kind of an in-the-know, finger-on-the-pulse kind of girl. Always has been. Right, honey?"

Honey? "Excuse me?" I asked, feeling every muscle stiffen.

"Isn't it great," said Phil, putting his arm around his wife's waist and dragging her to him, "I said, isn't it great to come home to a woman like that every night?" He gave Jessica a fond-ish ogle. "We're lucky men."

"Yes, Phil. We certainly are."

Something in Sean's smug, almost condescending tone brought me out of the passive and polite posture I'd assumed to endure this conversation and set me standing upright. "Hang on a second," I announced, yanking myself out of Sean's death-grip. Then I addressed the partner. "Are you under the impression that

292

the two of us are together? Because I would like to assure you that we certainly are *not.*"

Sean grabbed me again, perhaps sticking to a shoulder clench because he knew that if he dared put his hand on my waist I'd elbow him in the solar plexus. "You know, Phil, it's no secret that Beck and I have been having our share of problems, but we're working through them. We're working through them," he repeated through gritted teeth, for my benefit. "Aren't we, honey?" Just-call-me-Phil winced sympathetically.

"*Honey,*" I growled, wrenching myself away yet again, "can I talk to you for a minute?"

"In a minute," he said to the bottom of his glass before tipping its contents into his mouth. "Okay, dear?"

"How about now, *sweetums?*" I suggested in the same dangerous snarl employed by feral pit bulls moments before they lunge for the throat.

Mr. Saltina might have been a dirty old man with a taste for young blondes, but at least he was sensitive enough to know when he wasn't wanted. "Why don't we go refresh your drink, my dear? We'll be back in a few moments," he promised, guiding his wife barward.

"Can't wait!" My cheer was as real as Jessica's implants. The moment he was out of earshot, I whipped around and looked down at Sean, certain that I felt steam billowing from my ears and the small blowhole that had probably formed atop my head. "Do you know what I'm about to say to you?" I shouted, aghast.

Luckily, in that crowd I could have screamed bloody murder and it wouldn't have been heard. "That you're disappointed in me and that I should have known better?"

"Yeah," I told him, irate, "Only I was going to word it more like, *what the fuck?*"

"Get off the high horse, Beck." This was the Sean I remembered most vividly. Full of put-downs and self-righteousness, particularly when it came delineating his vast superiority to me. "What the hell harm would it do you to play-act for a little bit? None, that's what. It's no skin off your back. All I'm trying to do here is paint a little portrait of myself as a well-rounded, stable . . ."

"*Married* son of a bitch!"

"So what! So fucking what?" He knocked back the last of his scotch and looked around, as if he wanted to slam it down on a tabletop. There were none nearby, so I was spared the dramatic gesture. "You're not allowed to do me any favors now that you've got your . . . your . . ." I waited for him to finish the sentence. "Your steroid-fed homeboy?" Hah. That took the wind out of me. I let out a whuff of laughter, unable to get enough air to summon the real thing. "Honestly, Beck. You look ridiculous together."

This conversation was so rich in paradox that it could have supplied an entire mining company with irony nuggets for years. I couldn't believe we were having it. "Things aren't always what they seem on the surface, Sean."

"Don't give me that crap. I *saw* you all over him, over there. Thank God the Saltinas were facing the other way, so they could be spared." I shook my head and crossed my arms, unable to believe I was having to put up with these ridiculous recriminations. He'd become the resistible force to my immovable object, and something in my uncaring expression must have driven that fact home because he resorted to wheedling. "Oh, come *on*. I'm not asking you to do a whole June Cleaver kind of thing. You never have to see these people again. You never have to see *me* again. What's the big deal?"

Sean was a tiny man. Why had I never noticed that, during our five years together? I knew exactly why: because during each of those five long years, I'd stooped low enough not to notice. I'd stooped low enough not to stand out. "No," I said simply. I refused to stoop any longer. "No more favors. No more nice. Just go away, Sean. And stay away."

"Beck!" he yelled to my back, but I'd already started to walk away. "We're not done here. I'm going to—"

Whatever it was he planned to do, I didn't stay around to listen. Tall girls had long legs, and I used mine to take as big steps as I could away from the guy for a second time in my life. I mean, how dare he? On a certain level it was classic Sean, the prototypical bull charging into a porcelain shop and expecting everyone to arrange the china so it wouldn't interfere with his exercise. On another, it was exploitation so crass and so *obvious* that it made me prefer the Method Men. At least their manipulations had a certain science to them, instead of being based on instinct and sheer bluster.

And there was my Method Man now, making his way toward me through the crowd, concern in his eyes. I didn't even care that he had his sister with him. "Hey," he called out when within hailing distance, towing a stern-faced Portia on his arm. "Are you okay? From where I stood, it looked like you and buddy boy over there were having some kind of dust-up."

"Yes." I was touched my Lothario Lancelot had sprung onto his white charger and dashed over. Of course, he'd brought Morgan le Vague with him, but beggars couldn't be choosers. "He—oh, he's just an idiot."

"What?" A.J.'s sensitive side was something I hadn't really beheld in its full splendor, though his behavior had hinted at it in the past. "Come on."

Portia had adopted that same cross-armed, prim-mouthed, hip-askew stance most commonly seen on the women of Jerry Springer's show right before they screeched "Oh, no, you di'int!" and tried to rip off their rival's weave. She didn't say anything, but I knew that talking frankly in front of her would be a chore. "Sean let that guy in his firm think that we were still married. That he and I were still married," I hastened to emphasize, when Portia looked as if she thought there was a tiny matrimonial detail we hadn't bothered telling her. "Or that we were reconciling. Have you ever heard of something so sleazy?"

"Oh hell to the no, he didn't. I could tell that guy was bad news." A.J. stood on tiptoes, trying to pick out Sean from the crowd. "Want me to go talk to him?"

"No." I sighed and dismissed the fully satisfactory mental vision of A.J. intimidating the louse I'd married. Or even roughing him up a little. "Leave it alone."

While A.J. nodded, acceding to my wishes, Portia finally spoke up. "Rebecca," she drawled. She was in possession of one of those voices that managed to be heard over the babble and the pulsating music without raising it overmuch. "I am very, very upset with you."

My silent appeal to her brother didn't go unnoticed. "Aw, come on, baby sis," A.J. said, giving her a squeeze. "We went over all that. Becca and I were never a real item."

I played along, chuckling. "No, never. I mean, can you imagine?"

"Yes, I can imagine!" Portia, after a moment's consideration, added, "Well, I can't imagine dating him myself, because that would be against nature. But I think any wholesome, sweet girl would be lucky to get him." Since I'd turned somber and was nodding to show my agreement, I at least was appeasing her somewhat. A.J., in the meantime, was grinning at my discomfort, damn him. "No, what I'm upset about is that you didn't trust me enough to confide in me. Your best friend! I mean, how long have we known each other? Forever. And how many times have I always been there for you?"

Adding to zero was a fast and easy exercise. "I'm really sorry, Portia," I said, trying to sound sincere in my apology. "You know how private a person I am. *Too* private. I have to get over that." She nodded, agreeing. Knowing that a happy Portia would be a Portia I didn't have to worry about, I continued in the same vein. "I'll try to do better in the future."

"You will?" she asked, a bright smile on her face.

"See, sis?" A.J. interjected, making nice by hugging us both around the shoulders. "I told you it would all work out."

"Of course I will." I smiled and gave Portia's hands a quick squeeze.

"Oh, you're so sweet!" Now that she had me back on her side, the younger Daye was all smiles. She tossed back her long hair. "That's a relief! I've lost sleep worrying about you, Rebecca, I really have. I would hate for our close friendship to suffer!"

Considering that our social intercourse had consisted mainly of not talking to each other in the presence of my sister, it seemed that Portia played fast and loose with the definition of *best friend.* "You know I'd do anything to avoid that."

All at once her face grew cunning. "Anything?"

And that's when I knew I was trapped.

When she'd finally named her price and exacted an inevitable promise from me and walked away, triumphant and smiling, I goggled at the wench's brother, unable to speak. "Don't be hating because she got the better of you." A.J. laughed. "It's in the blood."

"In the blood? Who spawned you two?" I demanded. "Lucretia Borgia by way of Attilla the Hun? My God!"

"Come on, let's get you a drink," he suggested.

I'd thought that with their magnetic poles shoving each other away that A.J. would have chosen the bar at the room's far end. Instead, he led us to the closer of the two, not far from where Sean still seethed by himself in a position near the wall. "Vodka and cranberry," he told the bartender there. Then he added, "Hey, there's the square and his wife."

The Saltinas stood less than a dozen feet away. He still looked awkward, as if he'd been teleported from Planet Uptight into the middle of a churning orgy; she still seemed as if she wanted to be anywhere else except by his side. "Don't . . . !" I warned when A.J. raised his hand to greet them.

Just-call-me-Phil, grateful for any familiar face, immediately gravitated in our direction, much to my dismay. "Ah, yes. The young man we came in with. And Rebecca, of course." He gave us a smile and looked down at his refreshed scotch as if wishing it were a double. "Having a good time?"

"Sure thing, man. Cheers."

A.J. raised his glass in an informal toast that Mr. Saltina quickly echoed. "Cheers!" From her position behind his elbow, Jessica raised her martini glass to her lips and sipped, devouring A.J. with her eyes. I mean, honestly, she looked like a fan boy's comic book fantasy of desire, all curves and cleavage and half-lowered eyes, poured into a skimpy outfit and tressed with long and flowing hair. I could practically see the thought balloons of lust popping out of her head.

To his credit, A.J. didn't show the slightest interest in the woman. He didn't even appear to see her. On an ordinary night as wingman, I would have laid odds on him not only ending up with Jessica in some quiet corner or restroom stall with their tonsils adjoining, but managing to do it without her husband batting so much as a suspicious eyelash.

"So," said the lawyer, smacking his lips, "is this your gentleman friend, then?"

A.J. and I looked at each other. It was up to me to set the story. "We're friends," I said diplomatically. The last time I'd pretended that A.J. and I were seeing each other, we'd ended up in enough trouble.

"Ah. Yes. Well, I didn't know about your marital trouble, my dear, I can tell when a man's still in love." He slammed back the rest of his drink and laid it on the bar, waiting for another. "And it seems to me—no offense, son—that our Sean is hoping for a reconciliation."

"No offense taken, sir," volunteered A.J., grinning broadly at my discomfort.

"Well . . ."

"Marriage is hard work." Just-call-me-Phil's syllables were beginning to take on the woozy slurring of a man who's about to have the one-too-many of the evening. I accepted the drink the bartender brought and got to work catching up with him. "I should know. I've been through two wives already. Though I'm on the best one now." He beamed proudly at Jessica.

Well, gosh, didn't he know how to make a girl feel special? "I know, sir. But Sean's married to his work." Much as I disliked what he'd done to me that evening, I could at least go that far. "That's always been his first love."

"Ah, yes. Well." Mr. Saltina looked first at me, then at A.J., as if trying to figure out our exact relationship. "Enough said, then. You seem like a good girl. You'll figure things out. Ah, where is Sean, anyway?"

"Right there, sir." A.J. kindly took the older man by the arm, turned him around, and pointed. "Fourth banner from the left, right underneath." If one knew where he was, Sean was plainly visible. I could understand why Mr. Saltina had been confused, though.

"Ah! There he is! We couldn't find him, before. Madness, this place is." He gave A.J. a quick salute and me a wink. "You kids have a rocking good time, then."

"You bet!" A.J. saluted him with his own drink as

the pair began to weave their way toward their goal. "Nice guy."

Not a word about she of the over-inflated bosom and come-hither eyes? Had he been totally desexed? "How about her?" I asked, in the same conspiratorial voice I'd used over the past weeks when I'd been trying to get him to check out some of the hotter babes around. "Good stuff, huh?"

He shrugged, looking after her. "I've seen less plastic in a bathtub full of Legos. He's looking at you."

"Who?"

"Your husband. Play it cool." When he pivoted back around, I glanced over his shoulder to see the Saltinas reaching their destination. Sean, who had worked himself into a nervous frenzy during their absence, greeted them with smiles, but his attention was firmly on A.J. and me.

Now that Portia was gone, I could explain more. "He went ballistic earlier. Said you and I were all over each other."

"What a knob." A mischievous grin crossed A.J.'s full lips. "Like this?"

"Stop!" I laughed, when he leaned in and gave my earlobe a quick nip. A second later, the sensation had disappeared, but my entire body reacted with a shivering convulsion. "You clown!"

"What, are you ticklish?" He dove for my lobe again. When I backed away and swatted him off, he poked at my rib cage with his fingertips. "Ticklish, huh?"

"You're being silly!" Trust me to point out the obvious after I'd had a couple. Dodging his tickle attacks had left me a little unsteady on my feet. On the positive side, Sean's face had turned from its normal shade of pasty white to a virulent red. "You *are* pissing him off," I said with admiration.

"How about now?" He grabbed me around the waist, pulled me in, and nuzzled my neck.

It felt good to laugh out aloud after the day's frustrations. It felt utterly wrong to let A.J., of all people, manhandle me in front of a crowd, but I couldn't deny I liked the reaction I was getting from my audience of one halfway across the house. "You're going to give him an embolism if you keep this up."

"It'd be pretty funny if this was our final sting." His words were spoken directly into my ear as he pretended to nibble his way around its perimeter. "Poetic justice in a way, don't you think?"

I slitted my eyes and pretended to be enraptured. To be honest, it was fairly easy; all the experience A.J. had with women had made him an expert of eliciting the sensations he wanted. Shivering, I let him take my hand in his. "And how," I said.

Across the room, Sean was trying to engage in light conversation with the Saltinas, but his eyes kept darting in our direction. "Okay, get ready for this."

I had been about to ask what, but then A.J.'s hands skillfully swung me around so that I faced him, and he laid his lips on mine. At first my eyes bulged; I honestly hadn't expected it. But then some little part of me giggled, deep inside, to think of how absolutely crazy Sean must be to witness it. And it served him right, too. "How was that?" A.J. asked, his forehead against mine once the long kiss concluded.

What, he wanted a critique? "Fine, I guess." Honestly, when we'd been kissing I hadn't been thinking about anything other than its effect on my former husband.

"Just fine!" Not really offended at all, he asked, "What, is that Ethan guy you like better?"

I felt a slight pang of regret at the sound of the name. Ethan wasn't up for discussion with A.J. Not now, not ever. "It was fine. It was good. You're the best kisser in the hemisphere. The playboy of the western world. Is that any better, you big egomaniac?"

"That's definitely a start in the right direction. Sheesh." Both his arms were around my waist, now, just as mine encircled his neck, resting my drink glass against the nape. To anyone else we might seem a perfectly plausible couple, though to ourselves we bickered like brother and sister. "Hey, are you having fun here?"

"Doing this?" I asked, playfully swaying against him to the music. "It's okay. Why?"

"I meant here. This place." Before I could figure out what he was talking about, he continued. "Because I'm not really feeling it. Plus I think the very best thing you could do right now is walk out that door with me, like you're going back to my place."

"Without even saying good-bye?"

"Nuh-uh. That would be the perfect part. Just heading out like he wasn't on your mind. Snap! Good-bye." He studied me. "You like?"

I had to admit, I kind of did. Leaving would spare me no small amount of misery, standing around and worrying what Sean might attempt next. "Yes," I murmured, knowing he could hear me at such close range. "I like a lot."

"Let's go, then." A.J.'s hand pressed against the small of my back as he began to escort me across the floor of the After Ten in the direction of the cloak room. I cast my last look at Sean when we passed within mere feet of his entourage, pretending I didn't see him even as I checked out the cool anger on his every feature. It shamed me a bit that I cared even a little about striking back at him, but after his shameful manipulation that evening, I figured I could live with it. Still, wondering exactly how long he'd resent me for the humiliation kept my mind occupied until we were out the door, past the line of people still waiting for admittance and glaring at us with envy for having been within, and into a taxi.

It kept me so occupied, in fact, that I didn't even notice that the address A.J. gave the driver wasn't mine.

FIFTEEN

"You *live* here?" It was the third time I'd asked the question, I realized, but it was coming from a woman looking forward to living a lifetime in her older sister's spare bedroom. Here we were in front of a classic five-story brownstone in the East Sixties, less than a block from Park Avenue, with A.J. inserting the key in the front door and punching a code in the beeping security panel just within. "You *live* here?"

"No, I'm a professional cat burglar and this seemed as good a place as any to camp for a few hours." To make sure I knew he was kidding, he looked over his shoulder and added, "I live here."

"Really? All this belongs to you?" We were talking about serious Manhattan real estate, here—the kind of house that every city-dweller secretly dreams of owning but knows deep in her heart she never will.

The cab had already driven away; I really had no other choice than to follow him inside. "Nah," he admitted, tossing his keys into a lavish blown-glass bowl in the hallway. The house had been modernized within the last decade. Light from the amber, hand-crafted wall sconces cast a warm glow on the drywalled interior, highlighting the garish modern paintings hanging on the walls. The entryway floor was a pretty terrazzo; ahead of me, a flight of stark white cantilevered stairs lead up to the second floor. A.J., in the meantime, had stepped sideways into a living room, completely painted white and furnished with ultra-modern, expensive white furniture and glass tables. It felt a bit like I'd wandered in for worship in a Temple of Mammon. Or maybe stumbled onto a set from *2001: A Space Odyssey*. "I'm house-sitting."

A thought occurred to me. "House-sitting? For whom?"

"For a friend," he said simply. When I gave him a look, he explained further. "A lady friend."

"Are you a kept man, A.J.?" That certainly would explain a lot.

He laughed. "God, no. My friend—*friend*—Lydia is in Europe three-quarters of the year, so I look after the place. Someone's gotta. Come on upstairs," he suggested.

"You know, it's late." I didn't quite know what I was doing at A.J.'s place anyway. Whenever we'd tackled one of our stings together, when fleeing the scene I always felt like some kind of modern-day Bonnie and Clyde, holding up a bank that had been funding the battle of the sexes. I'd been so giddy from psyching out Sean that it had come as something of a surprise when the cab had turned into a neighborhood nicer even than Alice's. "I should probably get home." I pointed at the front door, as if it was my intention to head in its direction.

"It's not even ten-thirty. Besides, it's like you said earlier . . . what's going to happen if you sleep in a little tomorrow? Is that friend of yours going to fire you? You'll be collecting unemployment in six weeks anyway." He began walking up the stairs, so elegant in their construction it looked as if they were weightless. "Come on up. I'll show you Club A.J."

Club A.J., huh? I started to giggle. I'd had a little more to drink than I'd planned, though nowhere near as much as my margarita binge the Saturday before. The less I thought of Saturday, though, the better. "Okay." I grabbed on to the handrail to steady myself as I climbed. "Coming."

I had to admit to a certain curiosity about Club A.J. I'd gotten to know how the guy thought, over the last weeks. He'd taken me into his full confidence; I was the only woman he'd ever trusted enough to give a glimpse into the shadowy demimonde of the guild of Method Men. I knew so little about the particulars of his life, though, at least beyond the fact that he had a sister he humored in a way her alleged closest friends couldn't. Now I was being given a privileged, rare look into A.J. Central. I felt a little like a Bond girl being admitted into British Secret Service headquarters.

When I reached the landing, soft music was playing on some kind of high-tech stereo that was affixed, like some futuristic work of art, onto the wall. Recessed lighting cast long spires of light onto the walls, again making me feel as if I'd walked into some sort of cathedral. At least this largish room, which sprawled across most of the second floor and appeared to be a den of some sort, sported a little more color. The ultra-modern furniture was a shade of retro mustard yellow, as was the fuzzy rug occupying the space between the seating area and the high-def, thin-screen television hanging on the wall. The original fireplace had been stripped down to its brick and painted white. Behind its screen glowed what looked at first like several candles on a candelabra. On closer inspection, they appeared to be electronic pillars that glowed along their entire length. One of the latest iMacs sat on a sleek workstation toward the back of the house; papers cluttered its surface, giving the only lived-in impression I'd had of the place so far.

A.J. stood behind a bar that ran beneath the staircase leading to the next floor, uncapping bottles and pouring liquids into a pair of glasses. "Yeah, I know, this place looks crazy to clean," he said, measuring a cap of something and dumping it in. "That's what everybody says when they first see it." All the girls he brought back, I interpreted that as. "Lydia's got a service that comes in twice a week, and I'm not really much of a slob, so . . ." At last he got the drinks just right. He held out the glasses to make sure they were both at the same level fluid-wise, and then walked out from behind the bar and brandished one of them at me. "To liberation," he suggested.

I went along with it and took a sip, staggering back at the sheer amount of alcohol within. "Good lord," I protested, every orifice puckering. "Are you trying to get me hammered?"

"I've gotta get out of this monkey suit." A.J. gestured

down at his outfit, a pair of too-expensive navy-tinted jeans, sharp black shoes, and a shirt of violent black-and-blue stripes on a bias. "Check out the lighting system," he suggested, pointing to a panel at the back of the room. "Punch one button and you've got lighting for any situation. It's crazy."

"Interesting." I assayed another taste of my drink, finding it just as deadly on a second sip. He padded up the stairs to the next floor, where I heard vague creaking through the ceiling.

I could see what he meant, once I investigated the lighting pad. A number of touch-pad sliders controlled the intensity of the banks of lights around the staircase, the edges of the room, the floor lamps, and the bar. Touching any digit on the number pad, however, brought up all kinds of combinations, from a full brightness to an arrangement that focused on the bar to a low and romantic setting through which I could barely see. I cycled through a couple of settings meant for a casual evening at home or a party before finally I returned things to the way they had been before.

If A.J. was living here more or less rent-free, it occurred to me, he had a pretty sweet setup; small wonder he could afford the fancy duds and the rounds of drinks for both himself and his targets. I had to give it to him: He'd managed to land himself the perfect seduction pad. If I'd been one of his average, brainless marks for the evening, I would have had a hard time resisting the combined charms of his pulchritude, interior decorating, and prime real estate. It was like an evening of HGTV with the promise of an orgasm at the end.

I knew I shouldn't, but I couldn't help but take a few steps in the direction of the desk. The flat-screen iMac whirred away, its screensaver displaying the latest headlines whirling in front of a hazy blue background. A stack of opened envelopes that had contained what looked like bills and invoices sat on the desk's right-hand corner. My eyes flicked to the logo on the topmost paper, which boasted the services of one of the most secure Web site hosts available. What followed was a bill, addressed to A.J. Daye, for three months' worth of hosting at one of the premium bandwidth schedules. Huh.

I quietly lowered myself into the desk chair and set down my drink, uneasily listening for footsteps on the stairs. Funny thing, the way one's personal ethics work. There was no way in the world my moral code would allow me to peek at any of the other bills beneath, but I really had no qualms about checking out the topmost. I supposed it was much the same as if I'd gone home with a guy and, while taking a break in his bathroom to freshen up, I noticed that he kept some personal grooming items by the sink. Specifically, a tube of tough-actin' Tinactin and a family-sized tub of jock-itch cream. I might draw some conclusions—but I wouldn't go digging in his medicine cabinet to see what other ointments he might have.

I didn't know. Even having found out through peeking at a private bill that A.J. was running some kind of Web site gave me misgivings. What kind of site was it, anyway? Internet porn? And why was that the first thing to pop into my mind, rather than Web design or computer support or something esoteric like independent DNA research? Because I was a bad person, that's why. I shouldn't have come around to the desk at all. Maybe that Web hosting bill had listed a domain name? Gingerly I peeked at it again, reading through the details of the agreement renewal until I found what I'd been looking for: *embracethemethod.com*.

He was running a Web site about The Method.

I grabbed my drink and stood. One of the two motions jostled the wireless mouse sitting nearby, which jolted the iMac up from its CNN-fueled sleep. The screen blinked to life. Guiltily, I looked toward the stairs. I honestly hadn't intended to wake the thing, nor had I deliberately planned to have an *oops!* moment that might shed a little more light into my friend's mysterious private life. The best thing I could do at that moment would be to keep on walking and not look back. I knew the difference between right and wrong.

So imagine the shame I felt when I found my body sinking back down into the chair and staring at the screen. Fascination soon anesthetized that sensation, though. The last time he'd used his computer, A.J. had been logged in to his Web site's message boards. *WELCOME, A.J!* said the greeting at the top. *YOU ARE MODERATOR OF THIS BOARD.* Blinking text in the upper right-hand corner told me he had 42 private e-mails. I kept reading the text entry box in the screen's center.

Members-Only Area
Replying to: Re: The Longest Sting
Thread originated by: A.J. (137 messages in
thread)
Latest post by: chicago37_method

[quote]chicago_method wrote:
So when are you taking it to step seven, bro?
We're all cheering you on here but the waiting's
tough![/quote]

Hey chicago37, I think I'm gonna

That's where it ended. Silently and trying not to so much as breathe, I stood up and tiptoed away from the computer back to a love seat in the room's center. I hadn't disturbed anything. I hoped the screensaver would pop back on in a moment and cover the fact that I'd been snooping.

I felt like a criminal, and not the carefree scofflaw variety I'd been when A.J. and I worked the clubs. I'd stooped low. So low. My hands were so shaky that I had to put my glass and the 200-proof concoction within onto one of the tables so I didn't spill any of the contents onto the expensive mustard-colored fabric. Yet what had I done, really? Discovered that A.J. ran some kind of website for Method Men? I wasn't at all surprised there was such a thing. It made sense. A legion of pickup artists on the make, from all walks of life across the country—hell, all over the world—all of them tapping busily on their keyboards, sharing the strategies they'd discovered, discussing the best opening lines, sharing shopping tips for organ-grinder monkey hats and feather boas. And there was A.J., presiding over them all, given his rightful due as King Dude. What else did he do, write weekly columns about his conquests? Or did he merely sit back and collect thousands of dollars in monthly subscription fees?

At the sound of footsteps, I decorously arranged myself on the sofa, not daring to look at the computer far behind me. "Hey A.J., it's been fun, but I really should be going."

"What's the rush?" When he reached the bottom of the stairs, I saw that he'd changed into a simple gray T-shirt and a pair of flimsy trousers that weren't quite pajamas, yet weren't gymwear either. They both managed to hug every muscle of his body, showing off the width of his shoulders, the flatness of his abs, and the sheer protrusion of his butt, in a way that his club animal uniforms had only hinted at. His feet were bare, and he carried with him an apple that he crunched into. "Want a snack?" Without waiting for an answer, he jumped slightly into the air and landed onto the sofa's other end, curled up into a ball. "We could play Scrabble." Without seeming to care, he tossed the apple so that it bounced on the coffee table, leaving behind droplets of juice.

What was this, a slumber party? Were we going to put each other's hair in curlers next? "Tempting, but no. I've got to . . . what're you doing?"

While I'd been talking, he'd reached down and lifted one of my legs onto his lap. As if deftly skimming the skin from a banana, he'd removed my shoe and had begun to press his fingers into the flesh. "I give a hell of a foot massage."

He did, I could tell. It was one of those massages that not only made the soles and tops of my slightly sore feet feel incredible but managed as well to work some kind of magic along my shoulders and spine, making it hard to talk or think of anything other than the firm and pleasurable palpitations. "I didn't ask—not that I don't like—oh, wow."

"I told you." He grinned.

"You don't have to," I said, protesting. Or trying, anyway. The next thing I knew, my other foot had joined the first, and another shoe joined the first on the floor. Massages had not been a part of my plans that evening. "A.J., seriously . . ."

"You know what you need, Becca? You need to be good to yourself once in a while. You've got this mental block that doesn't allow you to receive pleasure." What, was the pickup artist a therapist, now? Maybe I should let Sarah know that I'd found a cheaper alternative to . . . oooh. He did something to my heel that made me want to squirm out of my skin, even as he continued lecturing. "There are some things in life you should just accept, without wondering if you deserve it or earned it. And one of them is a free foot massage. Don't go anywhere," he ordered my left foot, while turning his attention to its mate.

As if it could. It tingled so thoroughly from the freshly circulating blood he'd sent coursing through every square inch that it was content to remain where it lay on his upper thigh. "That is so—oh!—unfair," I managed to get out between pulses.

"Oh, come on." He regarded me frankly, holding my leg like a folk singer might hold his guitar as he tuned it. "All those times we went out together you could've had your pick of the men, anywhere we went. All you did was flirt a little. Sounds like a girl who's scared, to me."

"Listen, I don't judge . . ." I had to pause for a moment as he did something particularly thrilling to my instep. "I don't judge you for the games you play, or the ends you play for. So don't make assumptions about me just because I didn't make out in the bathroom with every cutie who bought me a drink. Holy crap. You don't have to do thi—" I shut up, knowing that what was about to come out of my mouth would only add fodder to his theory.

"Different styles, I know, I know." He began moving up to my right calf, running his hand over it and letting the heel of his hand rub deep into the tissue. "Doesn't sound like you had any problem enjoying a good time with that guy my sister found you doing it with, at least."

I stiffened at that remark, but his firm grasp soon had me lolling back against the cushions once more. "I thought you didn't listen to her show."

"She tells me stuff." He smiled at me to soften his next words. "Unlike you."

Was that a reproach? I opened my mouth to say that I wasn't any less of a friend merely because I didn't get onto Internet message boards and boast about my conquests. At the last minute, I thought better of it. "That was kind of a personal thing," I settled on saying. It was true: A.J. and I might have shared confidences, but I wasn't going to let him sully the part of my life where Ethan was concerned. Ethan wasn't as muscular, didn't have the clothing or the moves, and he certainly didn't live in a veritable Manhattan palace like this one. A.J. would only have laughed at him. I'd been hoping he hadn't heard a thing about Saturday night, and here he was tossing it down at my feet in a challenge. "Let's not go there."

"You went there." Suddenly I wasn't enjoying the foot massage as much, but A.J. wouldn't let go of my leg. From the depths of the mustard cushions I glared at him, but he didn't appear to notice. "I knew I could teach you something. Git it, hit it, and forgit it, right?"

No, wrong. Totally wrong. At least . . . that's what I'd done, at least on the surface. But that's not what I wanted. "What happened that night wasn't part of any Method." I struggled up from the depths of the sofa with all the grace of a floundering sea cow, but I didn't care. I wanted my leg back. Only when my feet were out of his paws and safely on the floor did I speak again. "Just drop it."

"Oh, come on, wingman." A.J. gave me a playful punch on the arm. "Don't tell me you fell for the guy. That's against the rules of the bro-hood."

This crap was only making me seethe. "I need a cab," I said, stuffing my still-thrumming feet into my shoes. "I need my bag."

"Hey." Before I could stand, A.J. took my hand in his and scooted even closer, resting on his knee so that he loomed over me. His eyes bored into mine as he said in a soft voice, "Don't fall for that guy."

Weren't snakes supposed to mesmerize their prey before they struck? "Why not?" I whispered, unable to move.

So unable to tear my eyes away from his was I that I didn't even see his hand approaching my face until it cupped my cheek. He closed the distance between our faces, staring at me with meaning while he murmured, "Because I've waited for this for so long." His lips, when they closed over mine, were plump and soft to the touch. They smelled of vanilla, as if he'd applied lip balm in the last few minutes. He backed off, gazing once more into my eyes as he murmured, "I've waited for you the longest of all, Becca."

He was handsome, and persuasive, and eager to make love to me. Yet the idea didn't arouse me in the slightest. When he brought his mouth to mine for a second time, the actual kiss did even less for my libido. I simply sat there, stunned, wondering how events had come to this. I wasn't disgusted, exactly. I simply didn't know how it had all started, or how I could make it stop. The thought that he'd actually had a thing for me all this time was simply inconceivable. Surely the man with the ten-second rule would have made his move long before tonight. I wasn't even a good candidate! Even that first night we'd really talked, he'd taken the time to explain to me that I was a mere eight to his ten. And now I was supposed to believe that he'd waited for me the longest of . . .

Hang on. My brain shifted out of its sluggish, enthralled gear into overdrive, racing through everything I'd gone through with the Method Man. For weeks I'd been driving blindly down an unexplored road without knowing my destination—and now I realized with certainty that not only had the terminus been handpicked for me from the start, but that A.J.'s hands had been on the steering wheel the entire time. "Oh, my God!" I cried, pushing him off me with adrenaline-fueled force, so that he landed on his backside on the sofa's far end, nearly falling to the floor. I stared at him in disgust. "I'm the longest sting!"

The fact that he didn't even deny what I'd said, or

ask me to explain, told me all. He rested the back of his hand against his mouth, then brought it away and examined it. "I think I bit my lip."

"Oh, my God. Oh, my God!" I paced around the room frantically, piecing everything together, repeating those three words over and over again. It all fit. Everything I knew fit into one giant puzzle I hadn't even known I was supposed to solve. "The Seven Steps of The Method. Step One: Identify the target. Easy enough. Pick on the woman who's sitting by herself at the bar, the night of her divorce. Step Two: Make your opening gambit. Maybe give her a 'sult so that she's thrown off-guard and doesn't suspect you've targeted her. *You're an eight. I'm a ten. Tens don't go for eights. Maybe a high eight, but only if nothing better's around.*" My A.J. imitation consisted of a dopey voice and a bobbing head, my chest artificially expanded to bigger proportions.

"Rebecca. . . ." A.J. shook his head. "You're imagining things."

He had the audacity to give me a fond smile, but I wasn't tolerating any more of his line of bullshit. Still whirling around the room like an imported dervish, I went down the checklist in a high, shrill voice. "Step Three: Show you're a value-added attraction. *Oh, yeah, I'm a master of manipulation. I've got The Method. Wanna learn all about it? Stick with me, chickadee.* Step Four: Establish similarities. *We're kind of the same person. We're both optimists, you and me. We should hang out.*"

"Rebecca," A.J. repeated. "Don't do this."

"Of course you don't want me to do this, A.J.! Because I'm right and you know it. Step Five: Isolate the target from the outside world. *Want to go out with A.J.? Don't tell your friends, Rebecca. They'll hate you for it.* Oh, my God." I threw my hands in the air. "I fell for it hook, line, and stinker."

"Sinker," he corrected.

"Stinker!" I yelled, thrusting my finger in his direction. "Because that's exactly what you are! Step Six: Establish an intimate connection. *You're my best wingman!* No wonder you didn't take any of those women past first base! They weren't even your target!" Even in my loud rage, I couldn't help but consider what a compliment that was. A few of them had been real babes. No, I was getting off track. "I was!"

A.J. offered nothing but silence this time. I had him and he knew it. The evidence, though scanty, was irrefutable. "Step Seven: Remove the target to a seduction location." I gestured to the townhouse's elaborate interior. "Lights! Camera!" Shaking my head, I concluded, "No action."

Still he regarded me with a maddening expression, completely devoid of shock or dismay or any guilt whatsoever. If anything, he still looked on me dotingly—not as if besotted with my charms, but in the same way a parent might at a child who'd presented a particularly good report card. I wanted to kick him. No, I just wanted a response I could understand.

"This whole thing has been one Yes Ladder to you, hasn't it? This whole relationship, a cat-and-mouse game that I wasn't supposed to have a chance of surviving." I put my hands on my hips, then briefly considered grabbing the drink he'd made me and tossing it in his face. I rejected the gesture as overdramatic, but it had looked so good all those times I'd seen it in the movies. "Yes, I'll talk to you. Yes, I'll let you save me from some anonymous jerk. Yes, I'd like to know The Method, please. Yes, I'll be your wingman. Yes, I'll pretend to be someone I'm not so you can maybe get laid. Yes, I rely on you. Yes, I like you. Yes, yes, yes, yes, yes, take me home so you can bang me. That's it, isn't it? Let the target think she's on the inside of the game, when she's still the pawn." My throat was raw from shouting, but I didn't care. "The longest sting, that's me."

A.J. hadn't taken his eyes off me the entire time, though now he was leaning forward, his elbows on his legs. "Where did you hear that phrase?" he asked, his eyebrows raised.

"Oh, no, no, no." I laughed bitterly, shaking my head at him. "You don't get to be morally superior to me. You know perfectly well where I saw those words. On your computer. On your *Web site*. Yes, I looked. It was an accident, believe it or not. I saw enough, anyway." There was no way he could deny the post. I'd seen the words plainly: *I think I'm gonna . . .*

He nodded. At his expression, patient and still benevolent, I paused. Gonna what? What was he gonna do? Gonna consummate the act this very night? Gonna get her good?

Gonna give up the idea?

Something struck me that I hadn't thought about before.

He'd never posted that reply. He'd left it unfinished. Incomplete. Why? For that matter, why hadn't he shut the computer down altogether? Why leave that particular post on the screen? Why leave me alone at the scene of the crime, where I could nose around to my heart's content?

Because he'd wanted me to see it, that's why. He'd done all those things for the very same reason he'd invited me to toy around with the light switches by the desk. Because he wanted me to figure out what he was doing. So I could stop it, on my own. Maybe he had strung me along for all these weeks, teaching me the rules of a game in which I didn't know my true role. Maybe he had intended to seduce me. In the end, though, he balked. Even the clumsy kiss he'd given me, he knew I'd resist.

"Oh, A.J." I sighed, sinking down into a chair. But why, at the last minute, had he decided to give me the push?

"I couldn't do that to you," he said quietly. No tricks. No glitz to distract me. He paused, nodding to himself. "So, do you like this guy?"

Why was he so adamant about—? Oh. He hadn't been pushing me away. He'd decided to push me toward something. Now I understood. After a moment, I nodded shyly. "I think I do."

A broad grin transformed his face from sheepish to rakish. "Then what're you doing going out to the After Ten with me, you big dope?" he said in the voice I knew so well. From the street, I heard the sound of a car horn, sounded twice in rapid succession. He nodded toward the stairs. "G'wan. Get out of here already."

"You called me a cab?" I asked, so astonished I rose to my feet again.

My bag lay on the bar, where I'd left it when I'd come upstairs. A.J. rose and retrieved it for me, along with my leather jacket, which he'd hung on one of the barstools. "When I was upstairs," he admitted. Then, in a louder and infinitely more cocky voice he added, "Never let it be said that A.J. Daye doesn't know what a woman needs!"

"That is one thing I promise I'll *never* say," I told him, tripping down the stairs. The car horn sounded once more, but it could wait. I wheeled around and ran back up the stairs, impulsively leaning forward to plant a quick kiss on his cheek. "Thank you," I told him, cupping his face as he had mine a few minutes earlier. "Thank you so much."

"Not a problem." He yawned. "Now get out of here so I can make a booty call."

"Vile man," I called back over my shoulder as I danced down the stairs.

The last glimpse I caught of him before I unfastened the latch and let myself out was of him standing at the top of the stairs, bowing at me from the waist, hands pressed prayerfully together. "You have learned well, grasshoppah."

It was a blessing I could live with.

SIXTEEN

As many times as I'd heard Portia on the radio, I'd never actually attempted to envision what she looked like during the show's broadcast. Sadly, it was likely to be a picture I'd never be able to get out of my head. When she talked, Portia leaned forward in her chair, silky hair tossed back over her shoulders, her breasts practically falling out of the front of her skimpy spring dress. A pendulous black microphone sporting a bulbous foam covering hung directly in front of her; her neck craned in its direction and her lips practically touched the tip as she said, "Thank you, caller. That is an interesting question. Beckate, *have* you stopped sleeping around with strange men like a nasty skank?"

Yes, this was my penance, the price she had exacted from me the night before—a one-hour appearance on the radio. I'd secretly hoped it might close this particular chapter in Portia's chat-show career. I'd imagined us talking together and smoothing everything out. Instead, I was being treated to questions like that one. "Well, to be honest, I've never slept around with strange men like a . . . you know." Portia made a circular motion with her hand to let me know I had to keep talking. "Like a nasty skank."

"So you *have* stopped, then."

"I haven't stopped, because—"

"There you are, caller. She *hasn't* stopped." Portia's voice was low and sexy as she moaned into the microphone.

"No, I mean, that's not a proper question," I said, confused. The whole array of equipment in the studio was overwhelming enough as it was. Being battered on every side with questions from callers and by Portia's bland incomprehension was turning what I'd expected to be a minor atonement into a major exercise in self-mortification. "It's like me asking you if you've stopped beating your wife."

"But I don't have a wife." Portia smiled into the microphone as if it could see her. Perhaps she thought it could.

"No, of course not. But it's a false—"

"I'm not a lesbian." She giggled slightly to herself. "Though if I were, I'd be a very pretty lesbian."

Was she for real? I couldn't decide whether or not she was kidding around. "You see, you're saying . . ."

"A lipstick lesbian is what they call them."

I had a sudden surge of sympathy for anyone else in the show's history who'd had the misfortune to sit in this very chair. I cleared my throat and tried to explain. "The question's not fair because . . ."

Portia cocked her head at me and, in disappointed

tones, proclaimed, "It's a yes-or-no question, Beckate." She followed it up by winking at me broadly to congratulate herself for remembering to use my pseudonym successfully.

I sighed. "I don't sleep with strange men."

I'd thought it was the definitive declaration, but Portia interpreted it otherwise. "Are *you* a lipstick lesbian, Beckate?" she asked, making my jaw drop. Before I could stammer out an answer, she leaned in and said, "We'll get back to that in a minute. Let's pause for a word from our sponsors." She leaned forward and flipped a few switches, then gave me a thumbs-up before saying, "You're doing fantastic!"

Yeah. Fantastic.

My morning had already started badly. Three hours earlier I'd scampered into the bookstore with a light heart, words of reconciliation ready on my lips for Ethan, and a consolation bag of bagels and a tub of cream cheese for everyone. The place, however, had been deserted. No sign of Ethan or Cesar. Michaela wasn't draped over the counter reading the *Times* as she usually was in the early mornings. Yet the front door was unlocked and the open-for-business sign flipped over. Who was watching the stock?

Ethan's desk, once I'd rolled back its top, was as neat as a pin. Something had changed. Though he'd left the ledgers and invoices in apple-pie order, tidily stacked so that anyone could have sat down and found all the records for the fiscal year. Yet the little *New Yorker* cartoons with which he'd decorated his tiny workspace had vanished. The desk now felt sterile, unused.

"Hello?" I'd called into the chill, feeling both disappointed and a little bit creeped out by the silence and change.

"Back here!" Sarah's voice had echoed from the side room. When I'd set down the breakfast I'd brought for everyone and walked back there, I found her lying on top of one of the immense wooden reading tables. Her arms were flung out, her short hair fanned around her head, and her knees pointed to the plaster ceiling. "I've always wanted to lie on these, ever since I was a kid," she'd explained. "Funny how I never did until now. Actually, I always wanted to make a fort under them and hide out from my dad and all the customers."

I'd had only one question on my mind. "Where is everybody?"

She shrugged. "Let's see: Cesar got some kind of job doing the Web site for . . . let me see if I can get this right . . . his brother's wife's sister's law firm. Yeah, that was it. So he won't be coming back. Michaela is at home, crying. Still. Poor kid." My heart went out to Michaela. Unlike Ethan and Cesar, who'd received the news in a stony silence that had persisted throughout the afternoon, she'd not taken the idea of the store's closing very well at all. I'd not even had a chance to talk to her afterward. She'd spent an entire hour alone with Sarah in her office and then had been bundled out, still crying, in one of Sarah's cardigans into a waiting cab to take her home to Brooklyn Heights.

"Well, we're like a family to her."

"A highly dysfunctional family, but you're probably right." As if she were making a snow angel, Sarah had begun flapping her arms and legs across the table's smooth and battered surface. "This is great. You should try it."

I'd felt a lump in my throat as I asked the question most important to me. "And Ethan?"

She'd shrugged again. "No clue. Hasn't shown up. Didn't call."

"His desk is empty," I'd said, feeling hollow. He'd moved on, then? Without a word? I'd really hurt him so much that he felt he had to disappear without saying a word? I couldn't imagine how badly I'd have wounded him, for him to do something like that.

Sarah had sighed, then reached out for my hand. "I'm glad you're not leaving me." Oh. That had reminded me. When with a heavy heart I'd told her about my promise to Portia, she'd sat up from her relaxed position, screeched out an ear-piercing *"What?"* and then almost immediately lain back down again, murmuring something to herself as she'd performed deep-breathing exercises. "Letting go. Let-ting go. No, I'm fine. Everything's fine. Good for you. Take the rest of the afternoon off. It's not like we have customers, ever. Get closure."

Only closure wasn't what I was getting from this particular experience. Humiliation aplenty, yes. Closure? Not so much. During the short station break, Portia turned and motioned that I should take off my headphones so she could say something personal. "You're doing so well!" she said, leaning across the console to pat me on the hand.

"But they *hate* me," I pointed out. Ordinarily the scorn of people I didn't know wouldn't have given me a lick of worry, but my mind was still trying to assimilate the damage I'd done to Ethan. In every one of the caller's questions I'd heard his voice, challenging me to justify the hurt I'd caused.

"No!" Portia said, nodding at her producer's signal. "They don't hate you in particular. They just hate what you stand for. And we're back," she said pleasantly into the microphone while giving me more heartening smiles. "If you're just tuning in, you're on New York's finest, WMDX, 1470 on your AM radio dial, all talk, all the time, and you're listening to 'Portia Daye's Radio Show with Portia Daye.'" Sullen and numb, I waited for it. "And I'm Portia Daye. Next on the line we have Brian Connecticut," she said, after consulting her computer screen. From the control room, her producer began shaking his head. "Hello, Mr. Connecticut."

In my headphones, I heard the caller's tinny voice correct, "No, it's Brian *from* Connecticut."

"Well, isn't that a coincidence. You have the same name as the state you live in! Isn't that funny, Beckate? If everyone in this state were like that, they'd have to call me Portia New York. Actually, come to think, we'd all be named New York. We'd all be related then, wouldn't we?" She grappled with the thought. "Which would make dating difficult." I privately wondered if I'd damage anything too badly if I banged my head on the console.

"Um, yeah," said the caller, not really following her logic. "It's about dating that I'm calling."

"Go on, Brian Connecticut."

The caller coughed so loudly that he nearly blew

out my left eardrum. "Yeah. Well. If Beckate isn't dating your brother—"

"No, she certainly is not," interjected Portia.

"And if she's available, I was thinking that maybe she and I could be a good match."

You know, if the electronic console was too valuable to bang my head against, maybe I could resort to the low-tech solution of beating it against the wall. "That's very nice of you," I began to say, only to hear myself interrupted.

"There, Brian Connecticut, she thinks it's very nice of you. See, Beckate? There's hope! There's always hope, isn't there, Brian?"

"Sure."

"And what do you do for a living, Brian?"

"I work in a Best Buy."

Portia nodded, impressed, as if he'd answered her question with *stock broker* or *highly paid plastic surgeon.* "I do like those blue shirts. Tell me, what do you like to do in your spare time, Brian?"

"Well, I like collecting and painting miniature metal fantasy figurines," said the man I knew from the start I was going to be unable to resist. "And I'm on one of the largest raiding guilds on World of Warcraft, the Perenolde server. That's a computer game. And last year I was one of the people who helped organize KingCon."

"That sounds lovely." During his recitation Portia had been nodding at me and all but mouthing *what a catch!* "And what's KingCon?"

"Kind of a *Star Trek* convention. You should come. You'd be popular."

"Oh!" Portia accepted the compliment gracefully. "I know I would!"

"You know . . ." I said, breaking in. She was going to have me going out on a blind date with the pimply nerd in seconds flat if I didn't say anything. "Thanks for your offer, Brian, but I'm not really looking. That is, I am looking for someone. Not just anyone." I took a deep breath and tried again. This moment was the real reason I'd decided to go through with the interview today. "I had someone, and I think I've lost him. I want him back. That's what I wanted to say. I want him back."

"Thank you, Brian Connecticut." Portia extended one of her long fingers and cut loose the call. "Now, this is interesting, Beckate." She gave me another of her winks at her use of my pseudonym. "You say you have someone in your life?"

"There's one person I'd like to have in my life." I was glad I'd taken the gambit. I knew the chances of Ethan listening were slim to none—surely he didn't want anything else to do with me after I'd repudiated him the day before. Yet deep inside I hoped that someone might hear. Sarah, maybe. Alice. Walter, even. Maybe Ethan's little sister. And maybe one of them might know how to get in touch with Ethan and tell him to turn on the show, or at least tell him what I said, after. I didn't know where he was, or what he was doing at that moment. All I wanted was for him to hear me say the things I should have said the day before, if only I hadn't been so frightened. "Someone very special." Portia nodded, encouraging me to go on. "Someone I like very much. Who's been there for me for a long time, in a lot of little ways."

"Is he handsome, Beckate?"

I nodded. "I think so. Even when he's unshaven."

"Awww." Portia had been making sympathetic noises, wriggling in her chair like a little girl. "Does he make you squirmy inside?"

Having Portia as my unexpected ally was a genuine pleasure. "Yes," I admitted. "He does. A lot. But I'm afraid I hurt his feelings." Across the console Portia pouted. "I know. I've gotten so used to thinking of myself as off-limits, lately, because . . ."

"Because of your age?"

I glared at the radio host as I firmly sailed on, "Because of my *divorce*. And after you begin to think of yourself as off the market, it's tough to realize when someone . . ."

"Wants to buy you? Mmmmm."

She was making me sound like a hooker or a pound of ground chuck, but I wanted to get out my message as quickly and plainly as possible. "The point is, I was wrong."

"It's so rare that someone can really say that," Portia said, leaning in. "And I think it's a lesson that a lot of my listeners should learn. We all need to learn to say when we were wrong, don't we? Yes. Now, Beckate, have you told my brother about your feelings for him?"

"A.J.?" I squawked. "I'm not in love with A.J.!"

"But you just said you were," said Portia. The porcelain expanse of flawless skin above her eyebrows crinkled ever so slightly. "Are you going to break his heart again?"

And here I'd thought she was following me. "I'm not in love with A.J.," I repeated. "I never was in love with

331

A.J. A.J. and I were friends. We still are, even though I don't know what A.J. means."

"You don't know my brother's name?"

I was taken aback at Portia's shock. No, of course I didn't know. He'd avoided the question every time I'd asked it. Wasn't he like that with everyone? Of course, his own sister would take his real name for granted. "No," I confessed. Then, in a sharp moment of clarity, I had the presence of mind to ask, "What is it? Aaron James? Alexander Jason? Abraham . . . Joseph?"

"Ashley," she said, as if everyone should know it. "Ashley Judd." After the stunned moment of silence that followed, where I tried very hard not to guffaw on the air, she finally added, "Oh, I know what you're thinking. But that was his name *way* before she got popular. He shortened it so people wouldn't confuse them."

Wouldn't confuse them. Right. I could see how people might confuse a hundred and ninety-five pounds of beef with Naomi's daughter and Wynonna's half-sister. "Well, I like Ashley Judd very much," I said carefully, any smudge of rancor I might have had at the memory of being one of his stings erased for good. "But not that way."

"Who is it you like, then?"

At last, a simple question from her mouth. Hell must have frozen over. "Eth . . ." I stopped. Maybe Ethan wouldn't like his name spread on radio—even AM radio. ". . . ward," I finished. "Someone I work with."

"Ethward?" In the studio, Portia blinked several times. "What an odd name. And who is he?"

"You know." I really didn't want to say it on the air,

but she shook her head, leaving dead air space that I felt compelled to fill up. "Ethward. You met him." When she didn't comprehend, I growled, "You *saw* me with him!"

"Ohhhh," she said, suddenly understanding. "The naked guy. Well!" Her voice became bright as she carried on. "I'm very happy for you, Beckate, and I'm sure my brother is happy as well. For the narrow escape, at any rate. Now, Ethward, if you're out there listening? Why don't you give me, Portia Daye, a call. I'm sure we'd be glad to hear from you. And now, let's pause for—"

Before she could finish, I leaned forward and sent the sound panel into the red zone as I blurted out, "I'm sorry, Ethan. I'm really, really sorry. You're the only guy I've ever known who would never ask me to stoop. I shouldn't have asked you to stoop for me, either. My first instinct on Saturday was to be with you—I should've listened to that, instead of second-guessing myself after. So please forgive me."

"Station identifi—"

"Plus I think you're adorable," I blurted out. "Always have. Always will. Okay. Done. No, wait! Listen. If you don't come back, who else am I going to get my cartoons from? Okay," I said, mortified at my own mouth. "Now I'm done."

"—cation," Portia finished, giving me an odd look. Yet once I heard the promotion start playing, she again gestured for me to remove my headset. "Doing really well!" she assured me, giving a thumbs-up.

No, I wasn't, I mourned. I'd made a huge fool of myself on the air. More than Portia, even. At least she had the excuse of the vast quantities of helium filling the gaping spaces of her cranial cavity. I'd wanted to be eloquent, to say something that would make him realize . . . well, that he was necessary. Instead, I'd babbled. Fantastic. I was going to go straight home and crawl into bed when this hour was up.

"And we're back," Portia said, seconds later. "We have a caller on the line . . . oh, my producer tells me we have quite a number of callers in the queue . . . Ethward from Manhattan." At the sound of that not-quite-a-name, my heart did an Irish jig. "Go on, Ethward."

"Eth . . . ward?" I amended, my voice full of hope. Every woman holds out hope for a fairy-tale ending, even when she doesn't really expect it to come her way. "Oh, my gosh. You heard me? You called?"

"Yeah, I heard you, baby," boomed a *basso profundo* in my ear. "I gots cartoons for you. Wanna know what they're of?"

"No thanks," I said, before Portia could ask. I should have known that having Ethan phone the show was too much to ask. "That's not Ethward," I said into the microphone.

"How odd," she murmured. "He said he was. All right, then, our next caller is . . . Ethward from Queens. Hello, Ethward!"

A reedy tenor sounded into my ears, but it wasn't Ethan Reddiker. "Hi, Portia. I wanted to know what Beckate's wearing today."

"Oh, Ethward, you'll only be disappointed," said Portia, making me look down at my jeans and sweatshirt in dismay. "Unless you happen to like bag ladies, of course," she said, smiling my way.

Pervy Ethward gave up on me. "You have a nice voice. Are you as pretty as you sound, Portia?"

"Oh, Ethward." Portia let loose with a laugh. "I'm far prettier than I *sound*. Thanks for ringing us up, now!" She peered at the computer screen. "Oh, look, another Ethward. I suppose it's not as uncommon a name as I thought. Caller? Are you there?"

I looked at the clock. I grit my teeth, took a deep breath, and prepared to suffer.

Sometime during the sixty minutes I'd spent in the studio, clouds had moved into the city. After being raked by the spires of its tallest buildings, they'd opened up and begun pouring rain. I had no umbrella, naturally. And try as I might to stay dry under the downtown studio's minuscule awning, after a good five minutes waiting for a cab while enduring the driving wind and the passing vehicles splashing into the ever-deeper puddles, I looked like the proverbial wet cat. No, not a wet cat. A particularly grumpy, mangy feline who had been dunked in ice water, hauled out by the neck, and promised a nice blow-dry, only to be tossed into a barrel of brine. By the time I reached home, the rain had soaked through to my underclothes. I left puddles behind me in the lobby, not caring that the custodian glared at me when I squelched by.

Bed. That was what I needed. Every ounce of youthful optimism I'd ever possessed had vanished, sucked away by a dozen Ethwards hell-bent on getting my phone number. I needed to get out of my clothes, towel off, and as quickly as possible crawl between my flannel sheets and begin contemplating my hopeless future existence as an unemployed, professionally depressed leech to my more successful sister.

Maybe if I was good and kept her apartment clean, she'd let me have a small allowance. Enough to go out to the second-run movies once a month. That was all I needed. After all, with my newfound life skills I could always go someplace like the Essex Pub and scrounge free drinks and beer nuts off total strangers. That would be a small savings, I thought bitterly as I plunged my key in the lock of my sister's door.

Alice exited the kitchen the moment I stepped in, a cup of coffee in each hand. It was so early in the afternoon that the sight of her caught me off-guard. "Oh, honey," was all she said at the sight of her baby sister.

I knew she didn't mean the clothes that had become glued to my cold and clammy skin. I knew she wasn't referring to the wet hair plastered to my face. She bent over to set the cups upon the little table just within, then held out her arms for a hug. She didn't even care that I was about as comfortable to hold as pneumonia. At that moment, I was suddenly convinced I had the best sister in the entire world.

"I caught you on the radio during lunch," she said, stroking my hair. I wasn't crying, nor was I about to. I simply needed a big hug, and the feel of warm arms around me. Alice was a good second choice of whom I really wanted it from, but I was in no position to be picky. "I thought you might like someone at home when you got here."

"It was horrible," I told her clavicle.

Poor Alice—a normal-sized woman having to support her behemoth of a sister was no easy burden. She withstood the assault as long as she could and then helped me back up to my feet. "Now, now." The way she stroked the hair back from my face reminded me of my mom. The notion that someone cared warmed me more than a half-dozen fires. "It wasn't that bad."

"You're being nice." Invigorated a little, I dropped my bag onto the plastic mat by the door so it could dry out. "Oh, you *are* nice," I said at the sight of the still-steaming cups. I grabbed one and took a deep sip. Already I felt toastier, and drier, and safer. "Hot chocolate would have been better, but I'll drink anything that's warm."

"Actually . . ." Alice began to say.

I pecked her on the cheek. "Honestly, you didn't have to leave work. A good afternoon pout is all I need to take the edge off." Well, it would be enough to let me feign being back to normal, anyway; I seriously doubted I'd ever be as optimistic as I once was. "I love you. Thank you for being here. And for the coffee." Shaking back my wet tresses, I set off in the direction of the living room and the bedrooms beyond.

"I love you, too," she said to my back, sounding both distant and amused for some reason. "But the coffee wasn't for you."

Some big sister Alice was. She could have given me more warning that a man was sitting in the living room, on the very sofa where he and I had been discovered only four nights before. Ethan sprang to his feet at the sight of me, then tried to sit again, before finally standing up and thrusting his hands deep into the pockets of his camel-colored sports coat. I wasn't prepared for the sight of him. I was even less prepared for him to see me in my bedraggled state. Only Alice's silent presence in the hallway near the front door kept me from running.

He seemed embarrassed as well. Was it because I looked so terrible? Or was it because he still couldn't bring himself to look at me? I blinked away the wetness in my eyes caused by my dripping hair and swallowed. "Hi," I said.

His hand jerked from his pocket to give me a wave. "Hi." Just as quickly, he thrust his fist back, burying it in corduroy. "Beckate."

The word made me laugh a little. I sniffed hard, afraid I might make an even bigger mess. "Ethward."

"I, uh—heard the show."

I still couldn't believe he was there. It was absolutely unthinkable that he could be back here once more. "I'm sorry." The two words sounded faint and choked. He'd never know how much effort it took to say them.

"About the show? No, it was good. Very good. You've got a voice that would be fantastic for . . . a bookstore." I narrowed my eyes at him, hoping he was making a joke. His face, however, remained deadpan. He nodded. "And a face like a peanut."

I wanted to hug him, right then.

I didn't. I was still sopping, and the mere notion of his being there was difficult for me to grasp. "Anyway . . ." Suddenly he was very businesslike and brisk. "That wasn't an insult. It's a good thing. Because I want to open a bookstore."

This was too much for me to take in, all at once. "Eighth Avenue Antiquarian?" I said faintly.

"No, no, no. Too old-fashioned. Not enough foot traffic. You do realize that the bulk of Sarah's sales were made online in the last year, don't you? I think my bookstore's going to be electronic. Completely on the Web. I can sell through eBay, through the store's virtual shopping cart, through affiliated book dealers—it's a much more profitable market." He spoke so authoritatively on the subject that I couldn't help but move forward into the room and perch on the edge of the sofa's arm. "Low overhead. Heck, a guy could work from home most of the time if he wanted to. Plus I think I know someone who'll sell me a lot of my initial start-up stock at a steal of a price."

"Have you talked to her about it?" I breathed, excited for him. He nodded. "It sounds . . ." How did it sound? "Like a wonderful opportunity."

"That's where I was this morning," he explained. I set my cup on the table, listening. "I got a little bit of a loan from my parents. I'm pretty sure I can sweet-talk a bank into giving me a small business loan. I've been studying the economics of it for months now, even before Sarah . . . but you know our former boss . . . well, change is kind of rough for some people." I was about to add a hearty *no kidding!* when he looked me squarely in the face and said, "How about for you?"

"What?" I wasn't sure what he meant. "No, I'm . . . yes," I admitted. "Change is rough for me." He wanted me to apologize. I had to say all the things I'd wanted to say earlier, but couldn't. "I overthink. Ethan . . ."

"Well, if you want to be my partner," he said, more quietly, "I hope you'll be willing to learn the ropes. A little new-fangled Web site maintenance, e-commerce . . .

but I hear you're a quick learner." When I looked at him, my heart thumping more loudly than the After Ten's sound system, he nodded. "I came to offer you an opportunity."

"A job?" I would have taken it, even if it led to nothing more, just so the two of us could have returned to our comfortable, comforting equilibrium.

He looked beyond me to the hallway. Alice had been standing in the doorway, listening, sipping her cup of coffee. "I'll be in the kitchen," she announced, realizing she'd been noticed.

Ethan waited until she'd gone before he stood up and stood in front of me. His hands reached out to take mine. "Not really a job," he said. "At least, I hope it won't feel like one." His eyes squinted in thought as he swung my arms with his. "More like . . . a seven-step method."

"Oh, really?" I said, amused.

"Step One: Target a business partner. Step Two: Approach her with my idea. Step Three: Convince her I'm a value-added businessman who knows his stuff."

I had to bite my lip to keep from grinning. "I see."

"Step Four: Convince her to join me." He stopped, crossing his arms.

"And the other steps?"

Not for the first time since I'd known him, he looked like a youthful kid, uncertain how to proceed. "I kind of thought we'd make them up as we went along. Unscripted. If that's okay with you. That'd be kind of the fun part of the partnership. An *unlimited* partnership, I mean. Sooo." He kicked at the rug with the tip of his Converse sneakers. "How about it?"

There's a certain type of woman who, when drenched, tousled, and unkempt, her wet clothes slowly deteriorating into paste on her skin, instinctively knows how to react to a business proposition with the proper degree of decorum and reserve. She has the unerring instinct for the exact right thing to say. I most definitely was not that woman. "Oh, hell to the yes," I said, pushing him into the sofa, not caring that I was going to mess up his pretty clothes, hair, or face, or that my sister was absolutely going to kill me for getting her leather wet yet again. "A thousand times yes! You've got yourself a partner."

"Deal," he breathed, reaching up to touch me as if he wasn't sure I was real. His thumb traced down the side of my cheek to my chin while we gazed at each other, uncontrollable smiles playing over our lips. With a mighty lunge, he sat up and separated himself and struggled to his feet. "Okay. Gotta go. See ya later."

"Not a chance, bucko," I growled, leaping up and running around the back of the couch, "I'm not letting you out of my sight again. Besides, I'm bigger than you!"

He feinted, then pretended he was going to dodge by. Laughter filled both our lungs as I tackled him and we wrestled our way toward the bedroom. Alice wasn't going to have to worry about that sofa, after all.

The door shut behind us. Between us, we had a few more steps to our method to make up.

I WENT TO
VASSAR
FOR THIS?
NAOMI NEALE

How exactly did a microwave mishap blast a hip and sassy modern-day Manhattanite back to 1959? Cathy Voorhees has no idea. But even without her trusty Palm Pilot, she's going to sort everything out:

Well, these clothes give me a killer figure...but the granny panties have to go! And I can change history...if only I knew any. Back here, I don't have to work for a short-sighted fuddy-duddy...but my boss thinks goosing is appropriate office behavior. Mmm, I wish our dreamy landlord would goose me...I can wow him with predictions of the future...and he'll have me committed...but padded walls could be fun....

THE MILE-HIGH HAIR CLUB

NAOMI NEALE

When worlds collide: My life in a nutshell

By Bailey Rhodes, talent producer, Expedition Network

NYC and Dixie have little in common. In New York, I have a fabulous career in cable television, incredible friends, and exciting culture. In Dixie, there's relatives who are, shall I say, two bubbles shy of plumb crazy. New York has the boyfriend who can't commit; Dixie has the agronomist with the heart of gold and biceps by the pound. Shrill, talentless anchorwomen try to claw their way into my programming in New York, while loud, talentless contestants try to claw their way into the sixty-fourth annual Miss Tidewater Butter Bean Pageant in Dixie.

But there's one thing New York and Dixie have in common: Big mouths, big heads, and even bigger hair in...

THE MILE-HIGH HAIR CLUB

- -

ATTENTION
BOOK LOVERS!

Can't get enough of your favorite **ROMANCE**?

Call **1-800-481-9191** to:

✳ order books,

✳ receive a **FREE** catalog,

✳ join our book clubs to **SAVE 30%**!

Open Mon.-Fri. 10 AM-9 PM EST

Visit **www.dorchesterpub.com**
for special offers and inside
information on the authors you love.

We accept Visa, MasterCard or Discover®.
LEISURE BOOKS ❤ LOVE SPELL